Books and Series
By
Carolyn Lampman

Meadowlark Trilogy

Meadowlark
Silver Springs
Wild Honey

The Cheyenne Trilogy

Murphy's Rainbow
Shadows in the Wind
Willow Creek*

The Time Tech Series

A Window in Time
Love Bytes*

The Pinkerton Trilogy

The Jinx and the Pinkerton
Winter Hawk

*Coming soon

Shadows in the Wind

Carolyn Lampman

RED CANYON PRESS

Shadows in the Wind

Printed in the United States of America

Formatting: Wild Seas Formatting
(http://www.WildSeasFormatting.com)

Editor: Gretchen Kent

Cover art: Kelly Martin

Photo by Louis Lampman

Proofreading: Emilee Bowling

Published by
RED CANYON PRESS
4530 W. Mountain View Dr. Riverton, WY 82501

Dedication

To my great-grandparents, Charles and Mary Lampman, whose real-life adventure of settling the West was far more exciting than any fiction, and to Irvin Kershner who gave them to me.

A special thanks to Kelly Martin and Louis Lampman for making my dream cover become a reality. Finally, four covers and twenty-six years later, the "W" graces the front of this book, just as it always should have!

Prologue

Stephanie fought to control the grief and rage that threatened to choke her as she stared out at the bleak landscape beyond the train window. It was barren except for an occasional antelope and mile after mile of grass bending to the wind. No escape there. The engine seemed to chuff *so close, so close, so close,* taunting her with her failure. Even with all her carefully laid plans, he'd managed to find her; she might as well never have left. She closed her eyes against the prickle of tears and a surge of desperation. *Think! There has to be a way out.*

Suddenly her eyes popped open. There was no town in sight, but the train was definitely slowing. *Perfect! An unscheduled stop.* Stephanie grabbed her cloak and threw it around her shoulders. The corridor outside her door was blessedly empty. Silently, she slipped from the private compartment and hurried to the end of the car, fastening the heavy cloak around her shoulders as she went. Taking a few seconds to pin her hat on more firmly, she took a deep breath and stepped out onto the platform at the rear of the car.

A shrill whistle rent the air as the locomotive screeched to a halt next to the water tower at a small station. Stephanie climbed down and sprinted toward the trees near the creek, careful to stay out of sight of the windows along the length of the train. Replenishing the engine's huge boilers seemed to take forever while she watched nervously, expecting her escape to be discovered at any moment. Finally, the train chugged off on its journey once more, and she was alone.

Stephanie smiled as she watched the train steam down the track and around a bend out of sight. *I almost wish I could be there to see Orson's face when he discovers I've given him the slip...again.*

Immensely pleased with herself, she set off for the tiny station. Once beyond the protection of the trees though, the wind struck her full force, and her entire concentration turned to keeping her feet clear of the cloak, which threatened to trip her. Buffeted by the gale, Stephanie fought her way to the platform, where she mounted the steps with a grateful sigh. Blinking the dirt from her eyes, she tried the door and found it locked. She peeked through the window next to the door and was shocked to see nothing but dust and cobwebs inside. It didn't look as though anyone had been there for quite a long time.

In her hurry to escape, she hadn't considered the possibility that the stop was used only for water. With a sinking feeling, she turned slowly and took in the utter desolation around her. Huge black clouds billowed over distant blue mountains to the west, and dust rose from the high, sparsely covered hills to the east. Between, tall grass undulated as far as the eye could see. The water tower, the tiny station, and a lonely road that skirted the buildings before disappearing between the hills were the only signs of human habitation.

"Oh, skunk whiskers!" she said aloud. Her impetuous flight had landed her in the middle of nowhere, with a storm fast approaching and not another soul or any shelter visible for miles.

Forcing herself to stay calm, she considered her options. Walking along the tracks was out of the question: that was the way Orson would come when he discovered she was gone. The road had to lead somewhere, though. All she needed to do was follow it. The question was, which way? And how far would she have to go before she found help?

Before she could decide, the wind snatched the hat off her head and blew it around the far side of the building. She ran after it, but as she rounded the corner of the station, her cloak tangled around her feet, and she fell to the ground.

Hearing a sharp noise, she looked up. A terrified scream

froze in her throat at the sight of hooves suspended in the air above her. There was a sharp pain on the side of her head, and then nothing.

CHAPTER 1

"Do you think we'll get home before it rains, Pa?" Josh Cantrell eyed the huge black thunderclouds. "I forgot my slicker."

Cole gave his son an annoyed look. "I thought you told Grandma Kate—"

His words were lost as the horse Josh was riding shied violently then reared into the air with a terrified whinny. Josh somehow managed to stay in the saddle, but instead of trying to bring the horse safely down onto all four feet again, he appeared to be trying to turn the animal while it was still rearing.

"Don't pull his head to the side, Josh," Cole Cantrell yelled. "You're throwing him off balance!" Cole watched in parental agony as his nine-year-old son fought for control of the huge stallion. The way Josh was twisting the animal's head could be disastrous. If Black should overbalance and fall—

A sudden scream rent the air as the horse finally came down, and Josh's shoulder twisted backwards at an impossible angle.

Cole was off his horse in a heartbeat. Seconds later, he was supporting Josh and holding Black, trying to quiet the frightened animal.

"Hang on, son. You did just fine."

Josh took a deep breath and swayed in the saddle. "Is...is she all right?"

"Who? Oh, hell!" For the first time, Cole saw the body lying in the dust on the road. With a feeling of dread, he saw blood welling from a gash above the woman's temple. "I don't know. I'll find out as soon as I get you off this horse. Can you hold on for a minute?"

"I think so." Josh gulped back a sob as he fought to stay upright.

Cole led the two horses to the hitching rack behind the station before looking at his son's injured arm. "Looks like a dislocated shoulder. That must hurt like the devil." As gently as he could, Cole pulled Josh from the saddle and laid him on the ground. "Rest now, I'm going to check on the woman."

At first, he thought she was dead. Her face was pale and strangely calm. Cole sighed with relief when he felt the weak pulse fluttering in her throat. He pulled out his handkerchief and dabbed futilely at the blood still welling from the cut on her head. She could bleed to death if he didn't find some way to stop it.

He did a quick mental inventory of the meager supplies he and Josh had with them. There was nothing he could use for a bandage.

"Sorry about this, ma'am," he said as he flipped up the edge of her skirt and tore a long strip of fabric from her petticoat. He ripped the cloth into pieces, folded them into a thick pad, and tied it to her head with the rest. It wasn't pretty, but the pressure did seem to slow the bleeding.

A roll of thunder reminded Cole of the approaching storm. It wouldn't be long before it hit. He returned to Josh. "I'm sorry," he said, as he gently smoothed back the hair from his son's forehead. "This is going to hurt."

Josh nodded, his tear-streaked faced white but determined.

Cole carefully probed the arm and shoulder with gentle fingers. Praying that he was doing the right thing, he pulled Josh's arm with a quick jerk.

Josh screamed in agony as the joint slipped back into place.

"It's all right to cry, son," Cole said as he gathered the boy in his arms and patted his back. "As I remember, your Uncle Levi yelled twice as loud when Charlie put his arm back, and he was older than you are." He ruffled the boy's hair then cast a worried glance at the sky. "Looks like we're in for a bad one. Do you think you could ride Black if I put a lead rope on him?"

"I guess so," Josh said. "Is he hurt?"

"No, he's a little skittish, but he'll do." Using Josh's

shirtsleeve, Cole fashioned a makeshift sling. "I know it won't be easy for you, but I'm going to have to take the girl on Midnight. He can't carry all three of us."

Josh twisted his head and peered over Cole's shoulder. "Is she—"

"She's hurt pretty bad, but she's still alive. We've got to get her inside, though. I don't think she can stand too much more."

By the time Cole had calmed the horses and looped his rope around Black's neck, Josh's color had returned. The boy struggled to sit up. "I'm ready, Pa."

"I knew I could count on you," Cole said. He lifted Josh onto the horse and tied him securely to the saddle. "This is what they do with wounded soldiers," he said when the boy started to protest. "You may be glad for the extra help by the time we get home."

Thankful for the blanket he always kept behind his saddle, Cole wrapped it around Josh and then turned his attention once more to the woman. He knelt next to her and checked her pulse again. It was no stronger, but the bleeding seemed to have stopped. *Now, what to do with you?*

The smartest thing would be to take her to Doc Addley's and let the physician take care of her. But lying there in the dust, she looked so incredibly vulnerable that he felt a sudden wave of protectiveness sweep over him.

It was almost as if his wife, Maggie, was peering over his shoulder at the injured girl. Before her death, Maggie had brought home any number of strays, human and otherwise. Cole knew what she would have done in this situation. "All right, Maggie. For you, I'll take her home."

The hour-long trip was a nightmare. Within minutes after they started out, torrents of rain poured from the sky. The wind drove it against horse and rider with stinging force. Every time lightning crackled and thunder rolled, Black jerked back on the lead rope.

Cole was a strong man and used to battling the elements, but it took everything he had to keep them all moving. By the time they reached the ranch house, he was glad he hadn't decided to make the longer trip to town.

As the two horses trudged into the yard, the door swung open, and Kate's comfortable bulk filled the doorway. "It's about time—Mercy sakes, Cole, what happened?"

At the sound of his stepmother's horrified voice, Cole suddenly became aware of the ache in his arms and the cold rain sluicing down his back. His discomfort was minimal compared to what Josh must be feeling.

"I'll explain later. The most important thing right now is to get these two inside."

Kate threw a shawl over her head and called back over her shoulder, "Charlie, Cole needs help." A tall, lean cowboy joined her almost immediately and strode out into the rain without a moment's hesitation.

Cole looked down at the grizzled old cowhand. "Am I ever glad to see you. I was afraid you'd still be out on the range."

Charlie shook his head. "Ain't like you youngsters. I got enough sense to come in outta the rain."

"I wish I did," Cole said, shifting the girl slightly to ease the agony in his arms.

Reaching up, Charlie relieved Cole of his burden as nonchalantly as if someone handed him an unconscious woman every day. Though the rain had washed away most of the blood, the sodden bandage and limp body told their own story.

"I'll go fetch Doc Addley."

Cole shook his head. "No sense in you going. I'm already wet."

"I expect you'll be needed here. 'Sides, I reckon I can be halfway to Horse Creek by the time Kate's done askin' all her questions."

Cole glanced at Kate, who was clucking over Josh like a mother hen. "I guess you're right," he said. "But I hate to send you out in this storm."

"Heck, I've weathered worse than this. It'll be a darn sight easier than watchin' Kate bustle around the way she does."

"Easier than following her orders, you mean." Cole smiled reluctantly. "All right, you win. Why is it you and Kate always seem to get your way around here?"

"I reckon it's 'cause your pa taught you to recognize good advice when you hear it!"

Three quarters of an hour later, Cole joined Kate in the master bedroom. He watched silently as she smoothed the bedclothes around the unmoving figure in the bed. "Any change?"

"No." Kate sighed and looked up at Cole. "She hasn't so much as wiggled a finger. How's Josh?"

"Asleep. He was still grumbling about having to stay in bed and miss all the excitement when he drifted off."

"He gets more like his father every day."

Cole smiled. "I'll take that as a compliment, though I don't think you meant it to be. I was mighty proud of him today." He looked down at the woman, shaking his head in amazement. "He saved her life, you know."

"Let's hope so, anyway." Kate paused, thinking. "Where do you suppose she came from? That train depot's been closed for over a year."

"I haven't the slightest idea. There was no sign of a carriage of any kind, and she wasn't dressed for riding. It's like she appeared out of thin air."

"Maybe she took a walk and got lost."

"That's a pretty long walk. It's a good ten miles from Horse Creek to the old crossroads. I'll ride into town tomorrow and see if anybody knows anything."

Kate looked down at the woman's pale face. "Her family should be told. If she dies..."

"Yes, I know," Cole sighed. "I guess we'd better go through her things. Maybe we can find out who she is."

"There wasn't much." Kate retrieved the heavy cloak from the back of a chair and pulled a plain cloth reticule out of the pocket. "Only this and the clothes on her back. Kind of odd to be wearing something this warm in the middle of the summer," she said, eyeing the cloak.

"I'm glad she was, though. It kept her dry." Cole took the bag from Kate's hand and hesitated for a moment before dumping the contents on the washstand. It seemed wrong, somehow, going through the stranger's possessions, but the pile was disappointingly small and impersonal. The contents could have belonged to anyone: a comb, several coins, a handkerchief, and a hatpin. Nothing that gave the slightest clue to the woman's identity.

"Cole, look at this." Kate held out an ornate gold ring. "I found it in the pocket of the cloak. It's a wedding band."

Cole took the ring from her. "I guess it could be," he said, studying the intricate design closely. "It's certainly unusual."

"How odd that she had it in her pocket. You'd think she'd want to wear— wait, what's this?" Kate pulled a small square of pink stationery out of the other pocket and unfolded it. "Look, a note of some sort."

Together they scanned the graceful script.

Dear Stephanie,

I beg you to reconsider the drastic step you are taking. Your mind is so befuddled by grief that you aren't thinking clearly. Surely your situation is not so intolerable that you must desert those who depend on you and turn your back on your responsibilities. This course of action is not only irresponsible, it is dishonest.

Nance

Kate was the first to break the silence. "She's running from her husband."

"Now, Kate, don't go jumping to conclusions," Cole said. "It may not be a wedding ring."

"But the dishonesty—"

"Might be no worse than dyeing the neighbor's horse blue."

"Don't be ridiculous. You and Levi were boys when you did that," Kate said. "I'm sure this is more serious."

Cole shrugged. "She could be a widow. People do stupid things when they're grieving. Maybe she threatened to sell the family heirlooms or something. If she survives, we'll have plenty of time to find out what it means."

"Just how do you plan to do that?" Kate demanded. "Ask her? You're far too trusting for your own good!"

"Maybe I am. I'm not even sure why I brought her home. My first notion was to take her straight to Doc Addley's, but then I thought of Maggie."

"What's Maggie got to do with it?"

"Remember when she brought Lame Deer home even though she knew his people wouldn't take kindly to us having him here?" He looked at the woman with a sad smile on his face. "Maggie wouldn't even have hesitated."

Kate stared at him for a long moment as though she couldn't quite believe what she'd heard then seemed to shake herself. "Land sakes, what am I thinking of, standing here talking to you when there's supper to fix? If you'll sit with the young lady, I'll go see to it."

Cole watched Kate's rapid exit with surprise and wondered what was going through her mind. It wasn't like her to give up so easily. No doubt she'd have plenty more to say later. She was probably right about him being too trusting, too. It was something only time would tell.

He studied the young woman lying so still on the bed. She was tall, he'd realized that as soon as he picked her up, but he'd paid scant attention to anything else about her. Now, with the opportunity to look at her closely, he noticed the hair pulled over her shoulder in a single thick braid that fell nearly to her waist. It glowed in the fading sunlight, the warm reddish-brown a stark contrast to her deathly pale skin.

With no animation in her face, it was difficult to say

whether she was pretty or not. The tiny cleft in her chin and her full, soft mouth were attractive, but it was the faint sprinkling of freckles across her long, straight nose that gave her an endearing quality.

Gazing at her long eyelashes, Cole found himself wondering what color her eyes were. Surely fate wouldn't be so cruel as to let her die without her ever opening them. He picked up a limp wrist and felt her pulse. It seemed a bit stronger than before, but she lay so still.

Suddenly, he had the oddest feeling Maggie was there beside him, watching the stranger as he did, willing her to live. He felt the fierce surge of protectiveness he'd experienced when he'd knelt beside her on the road again. Cole knew that it was nothing more than an illusion created in his overly tired mind, but no matter who this woman was or what she'd done, she had to survive!

CHAPTER 2

She was floating on a vast cushion of darkness. The tiny light shining above was very far away. It wasn't worth the struggle to get there. She'd rather stay in her warm, safe cocoon.

"No, Annie, you can't stay here." A familiar voice gave her a gentle push.

Lizzie? She strained toward the familiar presence. *Oh, Lizzie, I have to find you!*

"Shhh, it's all right, Annie." There was a more insistent push toward the light. "They're waiting for you."

As she drew closer to the light, the voice changed. "Stephanie...Stephanie...Steph..."

Opening her eyes, she saw a young boy bending over her. His was the voice that had pulled her up from the depths, but the gray eyes and freckled face were unfamiliar.

"Pa, Grandma Kate, she's awake!"

She heard footsteps hurrying closer. "Joshua Cantrell, what are you doing in this room? I thought I told you to leave her be!"

"But, Grandma Kate, I figured she might wake up if she knew somebody was here." He looked triumphant. "And I was right!"

A round, cheerful-looking woman appeared next to the boy. "Glory be! Cole, she's awake."

Stephanie turned toward the sound of boots on a hardwood floor and found herself looking up into a pair of incredibly blue eyes and yet another unfamiliar face. Who were these people?

Confusion swirled through her mind. Where on earth was she? "I...I don't understand. Do I know you?" Her hand seemed to weigh a hundred pounds as she raised it to her aching head and encountered a bandage. *What happened to me?* She searched the fog in her head, trying to remember, but there was nothing there, nothing at all. Not even a dim memory or hazy recollection. "I can't seem to remember anything," she whispered.

The woman picked up her hand and patted it. "Now, Stephanie, don't you fret. Just sleep, you'll feel better when you wake up."

Stephanie relaxed. They knew who she was and would explain everything when her head didn't hurt so badly. The fear subsided, and she drifted back into sleep.

Kate tucked the blanket around her patient and motioned Cole and Josh to follow her out of the room.

"Josh," she said, closing the door behind her, "would you run out to the spring house and bring me in some fresh water? I want to make some broth for her."

"What about my arm?" He touched his sling as though he were in great pain.

"You have another one," his father reminded him. "I don't think carrying a bucket of water will do you any harm."

"I always miss the good stuff," Josh grumbled as he shuffled out the door.

Kate looked at Cole. "Do you think she's really forgotten everything?"

"She's still groggy. Doc said she might be disoriented for a while."

"Let's hope that's it," Kate said. "She's so young. It would be a shame if she was addled."

"I suppose time will tell." Cole put on his hat. "Time I got back to work. Send Josh to the barn if you need me." He smiled to himself as he walked toward the barn. He wasn't even surprised at how easily Kate's compassionate nature had overcome her suspicions during the last three days. His stepmother was just as likely to take in strays as Maggie had been.

Figuring that the young woman would go back to wherever she came from once she regained consciousness, he hadn't worried about who she was or where she was from. A memory loss put things in a different light. Until they could find out where she belonged, she was his responsibility, and there was no way of knowing if his inclination to keep her here was a good one. Of course, she couldn't do much harm in her condition.

His curiosity had been satisfied on one point at least. Her eyes were green, the color of summer leaves. Cole felt an inexplicable urge to whistle.

When Stephanie awoke again, she felt much better. Her head throbbed, but she was at least able to think coherently. Telling herself not to panic, she probed the dark recesses of her memory but found only a blank wall. She forced herself to breathe slowly. *It will be all right. They know my name. They can help me remember.* She was still willing herself to be calm when the kind woman stuck her head in the door.

"Good, you're awake again. I'll be right back." The woman disappeared and returned a short time later with a tray of food. She set the tray on the dresser, then came to plump the pillows and help Stephanie sit up. "How are you feeling?"

"My head hurts," Stephanie admitted, "and my whole body feels like I fell down a staircase or something."

"I'm not surprised. You've got a nasty bump on your head. The doctor said you'd probably have a bad headache for a while."

"It is a little better now," Stephanie said. "I'm sorry, do I know you?"

"Oh heavens! Where are my manners? I'm Kate Cantrell. My son is the one who found you."

Stephanie frowned. "Found me?"

"It's a long story and best told by him. He'll be in from doing chores soon." She moved the tray closer and took a seat next to the bed. "I fixed you some broth."

"Then I'm not from here?"

Kate gave her an apologetic look as she dipped the spoon into the bowl. "Not as far as we know, anyway. There are new folks moving in all the time, though.

"Then what do you know about me?"

"Not much, I'm afraid. What do you remember?"

Stephanie shook her head then winced as pain shot through it. "Nothing, not even my name."

"The doctor said not to force it, that your memory will probably come back on its own and to focus on healing." Kate patted her hand comfortingly. "In the meantime, you're safe here with us. You'll feel much better after you eat."

Stephanie obediently opened her mouth and accepted the spoonful of broth Kate offered. Flavor exploded on her tongue, and she closed her eyes for a moment, savoring the taste. "This is amazing!"

Kate smiled. "Hot broth always tastes that way when you're hungry."

"What's in it?"

"Mostly boiled beef with some herbs and spices." Kate gave her another spoonful. "My husband would tell you it's because it's made from Hereford beef rather than Longhorn."

Stephanie swallowed. "What does that mean?"

Kate smiled. "My husband is something of a cattle snob. He has a herd of Hereford cattle that he insists are superior to the Texas Longhorns our neighbors all own. He says Hereford meat tastes better and therefore makes better broth. Personally, I think it has more to do with the recipe I got from my daughter-in-law. She was a remarkable cook."

"Was?"

Kate's lip trembled slightly. "We lost her to a fever last spring."

"Oh, I'm so sorry!" Stephanie felt a stab of remorse that

she'd inadvertently brought this woman pain.

"Thank you." Kate sighed then forced a smile. "My husband and his cattle have been a source of entertainment as long as I've known him. The first year I was here, he had a bull shipped all the way from England, and..."

The amusing story kept Stephanie's mind occupied as Kate fed her the rest of the broth. "Would you like some more?" Kate asked when Stephanie had swallowed the last mouthful.

"No, thank you. It's delicious, but I'm quite full."

"There's plenty more on the stove if you change your mind." Kate paused in the act of gathering the dishes when the sound of a door closing somewhere outside the room came to them. "That's probably Cole now. I'll send him in." She gave Stephanie one more bright smile and left, closing the door behind her.

Stephanie could hear the murmur of voices beyond the door but not what they said. After a few minutes, the door opened again, and the man with the beautiful eyes came in. His presence seemed to fill the room. Though his chiseled features and neatly trimmed mustache weren't youthful, his black hair fell in a boyish wave over his brow. He looked like a man guaranteed to set a young lady's heart aflutter, but Stephanie eyed him with misgiving.

"I'm Cole Cantrell," he said as he pulled up a chair and seated himself next to the bed. "Kate says you still don't remember anything?"

"Nothing. I don't even know where I am."

"That's easy enough. You're on the Triple C Bar ranch in Wyoming Territory, but I'm afraid I can't tell you much else. The first time I saw you was three days ago at the old crossroads. There's an abandoned train station there and not much else. My son Josh was riding a green colt and—"

"A green horse?"

Cole's smile made his face even more attractive. "A green horse, ma'am, is one that isn't completely broken—that is, trained."

"Oh."

"It was Black's first long ride, and Josh was having a tough time with the colt because of the storm coming. Then your hat flew into Black's face. One of his hooves apparently hit your head when he reared. We brought you here and sent for the doctor."

Stephanie wrinkled her brow. "Kate said you don't know me."

"No, we don't even know how you got there. The nearest ranch other than this one is a good fifteen miles away. Nobody in Horse Creek knows anything about you, and it's close to fifty miles to the next town."

"But Kate called me Stephanie. How did she know my name?"

"We aren't sure it is your name." Cole looked slightly embarrassed. "When we were afraid you might not make it, we took the liberty of looking through your reticule and cloak to see if we could find where you came from. All we found was a note and this ring." He picked them up from the small bedside table and handed them to her.

Stephanie looked at the ring for a moment before opening the note and reading it. "What does this mean?"

"Your guess is as good as mine."

"And there's no way to find out who I am or where I belong?"

"I don't think so. I'm sorry."

"What if I've done something horrible?"

Cole shifted in his chair. "Look, you were on your way somewhere. When you didn't show up, whoever was waiting for you probably started looking. If you just stay put, they'll find you."

"Stay here?"

"Where else would you go? Besides, I feel responsible. If I hadn't let Josh ride that colt with a storm coming, you wouldn't have been hurt."

"That's very kind, but—"

"Kindness has nothing to do with it," he interrupted. "Kate would have my hide if I let you go wandering off by yourself."

As if she'd heard her name, Kate bustled back into the room carrying a steaming cup in her hands. "It's time you left, Cole. Stephanie needs her rest." She gave him a pointed look. "Goodnight!"

"You see how it is around here," Cole said, rising and walking to the door. Then he turned and winked at Stephanie over the top of Kate's head. "I'm warning you, she's a tyrant."

"There are those that need to be tyrannized!" Kate said. "Now off with you while I give Miss Stephanie this tea and make her more comfortable."

Stephanie studied the ring Cole had handed her. It was a pretty thing with intertwining vines and tiny flowers carved into the gold. "It seems so strange that I can't remember this," she said, slipping it onto her right hand.

"It'll probably come back to you." Kate handed her the cup. "I made you some herbal tea."

Stephanie blew across the top and took a sip. "I think I recognize some of the things in this," she said thoughtfully. "It's meant to help me sleep, isn't it?"

"Good land. How did you know that?"

"I'm not sure. It just sort of popped into my head. How strange." She took another sip and sighed as her body began to relax.

By the time Kate had straightened the blankets and rearranged the pillows, Stephanie was drowsy. "Cole Cantrell," she murmured, settling down into the soft pillow. "What a nice name, and what nice eyes!" Letting her heavy eyelids closed, she heard Kate's snort as she drifted off to sleep.

Running was next to impossible, but she kept struggling anyway. Concentrating on making her legs move, Stephanie looked over her shoulder. The man chasing her was getting closer. His features were an indistinct blur, yet she had the feeling she knew him and that he meant her harm. Pushing harder on her unresponsive legs, she whimpered as they sank into the mists that swirled round her feet, slowing her down even more. Terrified, she looked back just as the faceless man grabbed her, his claw-like hand clutching her arm.

"No, no! Leave me alone!"

Stephanie awoke, sobbing in terror. As the dream faded away, she became aware of strong arms holding her and a deep voice whispering in her ear.

"Shh. It was only a dream. You're safe now. Shh."

She didn't even have to look to know that the big hand stroking the back of her head was Cole's. "There was a man chasing me." She shuddered against the solid protection of his body. "But he had no face, and I couldn't tell who he was."

"It was only a dream. It's all over now."

Suddenly aware that she was pressed against his naked chest, Stephanie pulled away abruptly. The moonlight bathed the room in soft white light, making the muscles of his powerful arms and chest clearly visible. Swallowing against a sudden constriction in her throat, she stammered an apology. "I...I'm sorry I woke you."

Cole smiled. "I wasn't asleep yet. I just came in from checking a mare that's getting ready to foal."

Remembering the feel of that soft mat of hair against her cheek, her eyes widened. "Without your shirt?"

His white teeth flashed in the darkness. "Actually, I was undressing for bed and didn't take time to put it back on." He stood up and smiled down at her. "If you're feeling better, I think I'll go back to bed before Josh starts his nightly snoring spree. It's hard to get to sleep once he gets going!"

"You share a room with your son?"

"Only when there's a beautiful stranger sleeping in mine," he said. "Good night." He walked to the door and closed it quietly behind him.

Wondering if he thought she was as foolish as she'd sounded, Stephanie lay staring at the heavy wooden panel until sleep once again overcame her.

CHAPTER 3

"Good morning." Kate set a tray of food on the small table next to the bed and pulled back the curtains. "How are you feeling?"

"Much better, thank you." Stephanie couldn't help thinking how Kate was like a ray of sunshine herself. Though her hair was closer to gray than brown and her figure matronly, she seemed filled with boundless energy. When she smiled, which she did frequently, her rather plain features became animated, and her hazel eyes sparkled with good humor. It would be almost impossible to be grumpy for long around Kate Cantrell.

"Cole said you had a nightmare last night," Kate said, turning from the window. "I suppose that's to be expected with the size of that bump on your head. Doc Addley said he'd stop by this morning. After that maybe you'd like a bath."

"I don't want to put you to any more trouble."

"Nonsense. A bath will do you a world of good." Kate set a basket of mending on the floor and settled herself in the chair next to the bed. "Besides, I already had Cole bring in the hip bath." She nodded toward Stephanie's plate. "Better eat before it gets cold."

"You've all been so kind, Mrs. Cantrell. I don't know how to thank you."

"By calling me Kate."

Watching Kate insert a darning ball into the heel of a sock, Stephanie felt like an imposter. These people were treating her like an honored guest instead of an uninvited stranger. "Mr. Cantrell told me I could stay until someone came looking for me or until my memory comes back." She moved the food around on her plate with her fork. "But that seems like an awful imposition."

"I told Cole I thought it was a good idea."

"But you know nothing about me."

"To tell you the truth, I'm not worried about who you are or what you're doing here. You're the answer to my prayers."

Stephanie was startled. "What?"

"Actually, my reasons are quite selfish. It's Cole, you see. I'm not sure why having you here has made such a difference, but it has."

"I don't understand."

"When his wife, Maggie, died last spring, a part of Cole went with her. He's been withdrawn and gloomy ever since."

"That's part of grieving."

"I know, but Cole can't let go. He was the same way after his brother disappeared."

"Disappeared?" Stephanie had visions of wild Indian attacks or gun-wielding outlaws spiriting Cole's brother away. "What happened?"

Kate frowned as she removed the darning ball from one sock and inserted it into another. It was obvious the memories were still painful. "Four years ago, my son Levi got tangled up with a woman. From the beginning, Cole told him she was no good, but even when she took off with another man, Levi didn't believe it. Several months later, he got a letter from her and went to San Francisco to find her. He never came home."

"Oh no."

"Cole went looking for him, of course; he even found Cynthia. It seems she'd only been trying to hoodwink Levi and wasn't best pleased when he showed up instead of sending the money she asked for. He'd left her in a towering rage, and Cole couldn't find another trace of him anywhere. My husband's hired detectives didn't have any better luck. It's like he just disappeared off the face of the earth."

"How awful," Stephanie murmured.

"Cole was in bad shape when he came home, but Maggie was there to put him back together again, just like she always did. Without Maggie, he's just kind of shriveled up inside. I haven't been able to help him through this."

"It's all so sad," Stephanie said, blinking against sudden moisture in her eyes. "But I still don't see how my staying here helps."

Kate met Stephanie's eyes squarely. "The first spark of life I've seen was the day he brought you in. Cole and Levi were just boys when I married their father. As far as I'm concerned, Cole is my son. If helping you gives him something else to think of besides what he's lost, then I'll keep you here if I have to tie you to the bed." She grinned suddenly. "Besides, having another woman around to talk to will be a joy."

"I hardly know what to say."

"Say you'll be glad to help me out, and no more talk of being an imposition. Your memory's bound to return soon. What can it hurt if you stay here until then?"

Stephanie smiled. "You're very persuasive."

"My husband says I'm a bully." Kate admitted with a chuckle as she dropped her mending into her basket and stood up. "But then, he's as obstinate as a pig, so we're a good match."

"I haven't met him yet."

"No, he's in England right now."

"England!"

Kate smiled. "It does seem a little odd, doesn't it? He and his cousin are there settling the estate of a great uncle of theirs." After giving Stephanie's bandage a cursory check, she picked up the tray. "Why don't you try to get some rest before Doc Addley gets here?"

"All right."

Kate left her, and Stephanie lay thinking for a long time. Only sheer willpower kept her panic at bay. It was as though her mind had built a wall, sealing her off from her past. Everything that had happened to her since she had awakened at the Triple C Bar was crystal clear, but she couldn't go beyond, back to whatever came before.

Remembering the story of Cole's brother, Levi, she closed her eyes. Were there people somewhere wondering about her the same way?

Sometime later she awoke to find a gray-haired man bending over her. "Well, hello. I'm Doc Addley." He smiled at her. "I was just getting ready to have a look at you." He made a thorough examination of her head and various other cuts and bruises. "Your wounds are healing nicely. I expect your head will hurt for a while, but I think we can dispense with the bandage." He sat back and folded his arms. "Kate says you don't recall anything before the accident?"

"Not a thing." Stephanie shook her head miserably. "What's wrong with me?"

"Well now, I've been doing some reading, and I think you have what's called amnesia."

"What in the world is that?"

"To put it simply, a loss of memory. It can be caused by any number of things—a high fever, bad shock, or in your case, a blow to the head. It's fairly rare, and nobody seems to know much." He shook his head. "It doesn't mean you're crazy, if that's what you're thinking."

"Is there a cure?"

"Nobody's found one yet. Still, in these cases the patient usually regains some memory, and often everything comes back. In the meantime, don't force it. You'll be more likely to remember things if you don't."

"But what if I never remember?"

The doctor uncrossed his arms. "I'd say that's a bridge you should cross when you come to it. For now, concentrate on getting your strength back." He flashed her an engaging grin. "Actually, you're doing Kate a favor. She loves to have somebody to fuss over, and I'm afraid my other patient doesn't take too kindly to it."

Stephanie looked at him in surprise. "Your other patient?"

"Ah, I see they haven't let the little rascal around you yet. Josh Cantrell. He dislocated his shoulder trying to hold that brute of a horse. That and some bad bruises have kept him tied to the house."

"Oh dear," Stephanie bit her lip. "I didn't realize he'd been hurt."

"Don't worry, he'll heal just fine," Kate said from the doorway. "Besides, he needs to learn there's more to life than horses. If you're finished, Doc, I've got Stephanie's bath water ready."

Soon, with Kate's help, she was soaking in a steaming tub of water. When Kate gently washed her hair, Stephanie could almost feel the aches and pains leave her body.

Clean, relaxed, and tucked into bed, Stephanie's mind drifted, half asleep. She could see a figure standing in a hallway. Something about him was familiar and very reassuring. "James?"

"No, it's Josh."

Stephanie jerked awake. "What?"

"You called me James."

Stephanie looked at the boy in confusion. "I said James?"

"Yeah, but my name is Josh."

"I think I must have been dreaming." She smiled at him. "I'm glad to finally meet you."

The dark-haired boy shifted uncomfortably. "I came to apologize. It's my fault you're hurt."

"That's not the way I heard it," Stephanie said. "If my hat hadn't blown into your horse's face, and I hadn't fallen in front of him, *you* wouldn't have gotten hurt." She looked pointedly at his splinted arm.

"But it's because of me you can't remember!"

"It's because of me you're stuck in the house." Stephanie held out her hand and smiled. "Can you find it in your heart to forgive me?"

His face crinkled in a grin that tugged at her heart. "Sure!" As he shook her hand, his eyes brightened. "Do you know how to play checkers?"

"To tell you the truth, I'm not sure. Can you?"

"You bet! Only nobody has time to play with me." He gave her a pleading look. "Do you think you could at least try?"

"I'd love to. Just between you and me, I'm beginning to get

a little bored."

As though afraid she'd change her mind, Josh quickly set up the checkerboard he'd brought with him. "Is it all right if Sam stays?" He pointed to a large gray and white, floppy-eared dog. "He likes to be near me."

"I don't see why not." Sam was lying in the sunlight, his eyes half closed, the epitome of canine relaxation. "He looks very comfortable there."

Josh pulled a chair up to the bed and looked at her expectantly. "Should I tell you how to play?"

Stephanie looked at the board with intense concentration. Somehow, it didn't look quite right. "Maybe you'd better."

Josh was a good teacher, and soon Stephanie was playing as though she had been doing it for years.

Two hours later, Kate came in to see what all the giggling was about and found a good-natured argument ensuing. She shook her head as Stephanie laughingly accused Josh of making up rules as they went along.

"I hope he isn't being a pest!"

Stephanie looked up. "Heavens no, other than I think he's taking advantage of a poor, defenseless woman." She reached over and ruffled his hair. "He's beaten me three games out of four, but now that I'm winning, he's changing the rules!"

Josh gave her a hurt look. "I am not. You tried to go backwards!"

"If you'd made it a king when you were supposed to—"

"I see Stephanie's caught on to your tricks already," Kate chuckled. "You've only got a couple of hours left until suppertime, and you promised your pa you'd clean tack this afternoon."

"Oh, gosh." Josh jumped to his feet. "I forgot!" Gathering up the checkers, he glanced at Stephanie. "Can we play again sometime?"

She laughed. "Only if you'll let me win occasionally!"

Josh looked shocked. "But if I let you win, you'll never learn to play any better!"

"Better get a move on or you'll miss supper," Kate said ominously.

Josh hurriedly returned the chair to its place by the window. "I'll be done in time, Grandma Kate. Don't worry."

Kate gave her a wink as she followed Josh out the door.

Stephanie lay for a few minutes looking at the window. The light streaming in looked so inviting. Surely she was strong enough to walk that far. She pulled back the covers and slowly climbed out of bed. Her head swam alarmingly at first, but after a few seconds the world righted itself.

Gritting her teeth, she walked slowly across the floor, her bruised body protesting every step of the way. After an eternity, she reached the high-backed oak chair and sank gratefully into it. Stephanie was instantly charmed by the vegetable and flower garden she saw directly beneath the window. The breeze blowing in through the open window felt so good on her face; she closed her eyes and relaxed.

An hour later, Cole stopped in the doorway and gazed at the sleeping woman. In the late afternoon sunlight, her pale skin appeared almost transparent. She looked totally vulnerable. It was impossible to see her as any kind of threat, but he couldn't forget the note and her dream of being chased by a faceless man. Were they connected? It certainly seemed possible.

Why on earth had he insisted she stay? He couldn't even be sure this amnesia thing was real, and yet he'd issued an open-ended invitation. Of course, there wasn't much she could do, except maybe steal a horse, and that was only if she could ride. Right now, she could barely walk.

Stephanie opened her eyes. She blushed when she saw him

leaning against the doorjamb watching her.

He straightened and walked toward her. "I thought Doc told you to take it easy."

"I was tired of lying in bed. Besides, walking to the window isn't exactly the same as running a foot race." She glanced toward the bed and sighed. "Although, by the time I got here I felt as though I had!"

Without warning, Cole scooped her up in his arms as easily as if she weighed no more than a child. Startled, she looked up into his face and encountered a heart-stopping smile. "Then allow me to escort you back to bed," he said.

Stephanie was fleetingly aware of a rock-hard chest and sapphire eyes so blue she could drown in them, as Cole carried her across the room. She was breathless and slightly light-headed when he placed her gently on the bed.

"Josh said you remembered someone named James?" he asked.

With an effort, she refocused her attention on what he was saying. "Not really. I didn't even realize I'd said it until he told me."

"Still, it must be someone you know." Cole rubbed his mustache pensively. "I think it's a good sign."

"I hope you're right, Mr. Cantrell."

"Please," he said, "my name is Cole. It's ridiculous for you to call me Mr. Cantrell when I can only call you by your given name."

"If it is my given name."

"Cole," Kate remarked from the doorway. "If you want anything to eat, you'd better get washed up for supper. Josh is hanging around the kitchen like a vulture."

He shook his head as he headed for the door. "On the verge of starvation, no doubt."

Kate set a tray down and felt Stephanie's forehead. "You seem to have more color in your face this evening."

"I sat by the window for a while. I guess the fresh air helped."

"Mother Nature has a way of healing. Let's get you fed and settled down for the night. You look all tuckered out."

"You don't have to stay. I'm perfectly capable of feeding myself." Stephanie raised an eyebrow. "Besides, who's going to tell Josh he has to wait?"

Kate laughed. "You're right. He thinks he'll starve if supper's a few minutes late. Are you sure you don't mind?"

"Not a bit."

Stephanie could hear Josh's excited chatter through the open door as she ate her supper. Smiling, she couldn't help wondering why she was so drawn to the boy. It was almost as if she already knew him.

It wasn't long before he appeared in the doorway. "I came to say good-night." He gave her an anxious look. "Grandma Kate says I'm not supposed to bother you, but you don't mind, do you?"

"Certainly not. Why, I'd have been bored to tears if not for you. I fully intend to beat you soundly the next time we play checkers."

"My son talked you into a game of checkers, did he?" Cole said as he walked into the room. He laid his hand on his son's shoulder. "He's always looking for competition. I hope he didn't bother you."

"Heavens, no. I enjoyed myself immensely, though I'm not sure I've been told all the rules of the game."

Josh looked affronted. "I have to keep you interested somehow, don't I?" He ran off to bed before she had a chance to answer.

Stephanie laughed and shook her head. "I'll bet he's a handful."

"At times, though Kate insists he's easier to handle than my brother and I because there is only one of him." Cole handed her a steaming cup. "She sent this in and said to tell you it's stronger than last night." He started to leave but turned at the door.

"Remember, I'm right next door if you need anything." He

smiled. "Good-night."

The thought of Cole Cantrell right next door wasn't Stephanie's idea of a sleep inducer, but it was rather comforting. Smiling to herself, she drank her tea.

CHAPTER 4

"**I** believe it's time I got out of bed," Stephanie announced the next day.

Kate eyed her skeptically. "Don't you think it's a mite too soon?"

"No. I'll go crazy if I have to stay in this bed much longer. Besides, maybe my clothes will trigger a memory."

"I hadn't thought of that," Kate said reluctantly. "All right, as long as you don't overdo."

The dress Kate brought in a few minutes later was an unattractive shade of gray and appeared to have little shape.

"I was wearing this?" Stephanie asked in dismay. "I'm not exactly a fashion plate, am I?"

The dress was just as unappealing when she put it on. Although it was the right length, it hung on her slender frame like a sack. Stephanie made a face as she looked over her shoulder at the back. There was nearly enough extra fabric for another dress. "Doesn't fit very well, does it?"

"It looks like you've lost a lot of weight," Kate observed. "Maybe you've been sick. You did have dark circles around your eyes when we found you, and the way you slept made me think you were exhausted, though Doc Addley did say it might be the head injury."

Stephanie peered into the mirror for the first time. Nothing about the pale face or the emerald green eyes was even remotely familiar. *It's like looking at a stranger's face,* she thought dispassionately.

Disappointed, Stephanie began the familiar task of taking down her hair. Unbraided, it fell in thick mahogany waves to her hips. She'd hardly noticed it when Kate had washed it the day before. Pulling Kate's brush through the silken mass, Stephanie had a sudden vision of a gray-haired man touching her hair lovingly.

"Your hair is exactly like your mother's."

The vision disappeared, and Stephanie gritted her teeth in irritation. Why couldn't she remember something useful? She rebraided her hair and wound it into a cornet on the back of her head. At least her wounds had healed enough that her hair no longer pulled uncomfortably against them.

She played checkers with Josh until mid-afternoon, when Kate shooed the boy and his dog out, saying Stephanie needed her rest. Though she didn't feel tired, she soon fell sound asleep.

She was seated at a small table set for two. The door opened, and she looked up as a shadowy figure entered the room. "Good morning, James. Would you mind handing me the morning paper?"

"Sorry, Horse Creek doesn't have a paper."

Stephanie's eyes popped open and found Cole looking at her quizzically. "Oh, I must have been dreaming."

"I wondered if you were. You just spoke to James again."

"I did?"

"You asked him for the paper." Cole crossed his arms and leaned against the dresser. "Remember who he is?"

"No, but I think I was about to have breakfast with him. At least, there were two places set at the table."

"He must be someone you know well, then. Not many people have breakfast with strangers."

She made a helpless gesture. "I wish I could remember."

"It's probably just a matter of time. Meanwhile, Kate wants to know if you feel up to joining us for supper tonight."

"I'd love to. These four walls are beginning to close in on me."

"That's easily taken care of," he said as he swept her up off the bed and carried her from the room.

"Just where do you think you're going, Cole?" Kate demanded as they walked through a large, airy kitchen.

"I'm taking her out for some air."

Kate frowned. "Are you sure you're feeling up to it,

Stephanie?"

"I think so. I know I'm ready for a change of scenery."

"All right, just don't tire her."

"Don't worry, Kate. I'll take good care of her," Cole said as they walked through the front door.

Stephanie felt the deep rumble in his chest and had an irrational desire to snuggle up to him. Being an invalid could become addictive with this man around.

Cole set her down on a bench that ran alongside the house, and she looked around with great interest. The ranch buildings nested at the northern end of a large valley, bounded on the east and west by high hills. A creek lined with huge cottonwood trees ran the full length of the valley, and to the south she could see waving grass stretching clear to the horizon. "This must be a very large farm."

Cole scowled. "It's a ranch. Farmers tear up the prairies to plant their crops. Ranchers use the prairie for grazing their herds. The only farming we do is to harvest wild grass for hay."

"I didn't mean it as an insult."

"Sorry," Cole's mouth curved into a slightly embarrassed smile. "I'm overly sensitive, I guess." He gazed out over the open prairie. "My father staked this valley out twenty-five years ago, long before the railroad came anywhere near this part of the country. My brother and I were just kids then, but I remember how sure he was that this was the ideal location for a ranch."

"And he was right?"

Cole chuckled. "My father is always right when it comes to business. Pa's passion is the cattle, but Levi and I convinced him to let us branch out into horses about fifteen years ago.

"Racehorses, clear out here?"

"Hardly." He smiled. "Although, my uncle raises racehorses just outside of Chicago. Levi and I wanted to try crossing Uncle Daniel's Thoroughbreds with quarter horses to see if we could get a faster horse that was agile and had endurance. Pa and Uncle Daniel found us some good breeding stock, and we started experimenting. We've improved them over the years until we have some of the finest horses in the country."

"But who do you sell them to?" Stephanie asked, glancing around. "You're so isolated here."

"In the beginning, the cavalry bought most of them. Now we only sell them our cull stock."

She gave him a blank look. "What are cull-stocks?"

"Cull-stocks?" He laughed and shook his head. "No, I meant our cull horses. Those that aren't good enough to keep. One Captain told me he'd rather ride a 'bad' Triple C Bar horse than someone else's best. We're finally starting to sell some of our breeding stock to markets back East. Someday, people from as far away as New York City will have heard of the Cantrell horses."

"You really love this place, don't you?"

"I never thought of it that way, but I suppose that's as good a description as any." He put his hands behind his head and leaned back against the house. "Frankly, I can't imagine living anywhere else. I tried once, but I soon came to realize this is where I belong."

This is where I belong. The words echoed through Stephanie's mind. *Is there some place I feel that way about?* She shivered.

"You're cold." He stood then bent to pick her up again.

She put out her hand to stop him. "I think I can walk."

He straightened. "Are you sure?"

"Only one way to find out."

"Give me your hand." He helped her to her feet then offered his arm as support.

Stephanie smiled up at him. "Thanks, I may need that."

With his help, Stephanie was able to walk to the kitchen and was soon seated at the table.

"It looks like fresh air was the best medicine after all," Kate said as Cole went back outside to wash up. "It's good to see you moving around so well."

"Feels good, too." Stephanie looked around the large, friendly room with interest. A huge cookstove where Kate was working, an oak hoosier cabinet, and several cupboards filled most of one wall. The two bedroom doors were in the opposite wall. She noticed a gun rack containing several rifles hanging between the doors and wondered uneasily what threat made it necessary to keep them so handy.

Her thoughts were interrupted by Josh, who came in talking a mile a minute to a tall, rangy cowboy. His hair was gray, and a lifetime of exposure to the elements had given him leathery skin, but it was impossible to judge the man's age. He could have been anywhere from fifty to seventy. Laugh lines around his mouth and eyes gave his face the aura of good humor.

A smile lit his pale blue eyes. "Howdy, ma'am. I'm Charlie Hobbs. Josh here has been singin' your praises since I got in off the range."

"Josh has told me all about you, too," Stephanie said, returning his smile. "I've been looking forward to meeting you."

"Charlie," Kate spoke from her place at the stove. "You best take Josh out and get washed up for supper."

"Glad to. I'm lookin' forward to one of your home-cooked meals. Get mighty tired of my own cooking out on the range."

Kate pointed her spoon at him. "If you think that's going to get you an extra piece of pie, you've got another think coming." She rolled her eyes at Stephanie. "I swear, the way those three eat, it's a wonder I'm not at this stove twenty-four hours a day."

Though Stephanie enjoyed eating supper with the family, most of the talk was about the ranch, and her mind drifted as the conversation flowed around her, until her attention was caught by something Charlie was telling Cole.

"I saw lots of bobcat signs. Ran into one 'bout a mile out. Wish I'd had ol' Sam along. He would'a treed that cat in nothin' flat. It took off like a shot when it seen me. Headed this way though, so we might see him again."

Stephanie stared at him wide-eyed. "What's a bobcat?"

Charlie looked up, surprised by her question. "Why, it's sorta like a small mountain lion. Meaner than he...er, heck. I've seen a cat tear up five or six dogs when he was cornered! Say, Cole, you remember that one that got into Widow Langton's chickens last winter?"

For the next fifteen minutes, Cole, Charlie, and even Josh filled Stephanie's ears with tales of the bobcats, coyotes, and wolves they'd had run-ins with over the years. Her unease grew as she listened.

"Do you think the bobcat you saw will come here?" she asked fearfully.

Charlie's face crinkled into a grin. "Nah, he's probably out chasing jackalopes this time of year."

"Jackalopes?"

"Why, sure. They're kinda like a big jackrabbit, only they got horns like an antelope. Easterners are always comin' around lookin' for 'em." He gave her a considering look. "I guess if you was to catch one, it'd be worth a lot of money."

"Really? Do you suppose I might get a chance to see one?" Stephanie asked.

Kate could contain herself no longer. "I don't see how, since they aren't real! Shame on you, Charlie Hobbs, trying to pull her in like you do all the greenhorns!"

Charlie only grinned and shrugged.

Realizing how gullible she'd been, Stephanie gave Charlie a wry look. "I guess that proves I'm a greenhorn, then. I believed every word!" To herself, she vowed Charlie wouldn't find her such an easy target in the future.

It wasn't until Stephanie was undressing for bed that she remembered Charlie had neatly evaded her question of whether the bobcat was headed toward the ranch house. It wasn't clear from Charlie's description what one looked like, but she did know what a lion was. She was sure she'd seen pictures of them somewhere, great fearsome beasts with bushy manes and sharp teeth. The idea of a slightly smaller version of the same animal made her blood run cold. All at once, the story of the jackalopes took on a sinister significance. Charlie hadn't wanted to scare her by admitting the bobcat might be close by!

Nervously, she climbed into bed. Surely she was safe enough inside the thick log walls. Her exhaustion caught up with her, and she was asleep within minutes.

A huge lion loped toward her, his fangs bared and his mane blowing in the wind. There were dogs snapping at his heels; she could hear their excited yips as the beast drew closer.

Stephanie awoke with a start to find the yips were real. Sam was chasing something, and it was coming directly toward her open window. Paralyzed, she stared at the curtains billowing in the night breeze. Suddenly, an animal leaped to the sill and stared at her with great feline eyes.

CHAPTER 5

At first Cole thought Stephanie was having another nightmare, but as he pulled on his pants, he realized it was his name she was screaming. He grabbed his rifle as he ran past the gun rack and stopped just inside the bedroom door to stare at the bizarre scene. Stephanie was standing on the bed jumping from one foot to the other, as though trying to raise both feet off the bed at once. She kept looking at the side of the bed, her eyes wide with terror as she screamed for Cole.

"What—" he began.

The moment she saw him, Stephanie yanked her nightgown up past her knees, leapt off the bed, and dashed behind him. He only had a glimpse of shapely legs before he felt her molding herself to his back, sobbing in fear. "Under the bed! It's under the bed!"

Cole tried to look, but Stephanie was hugging him so tightly that bending over was next to impossible. "What's under the bed?"

"B-b-bobcat," she sobbed, pressing her face against his back.

Josh, who had followed his father, stooped down and peeked under the bed. When he looked up, his eyes were sparkling. "Pa, it's Thomas!"

Cole burst out laughing. "A bobcat!" Still laughing, he leaned his rifle up against the wall and tried to peel Stephanie off his back. Since she wouldn't let go, he wound up with her plastered to his chest instead.

By then, Josh was standing next to them, a large yellow tiger cat nestled in his arms. "Stephanie, look, it's only Thomas." But she was too terrified to hear him. Her eyes shut tightly, she kept her face buried against Cole's chest, her body shaking with fear.

Cole put his arms around her. "Stephanie!" The ring of authority in his voice broke through to her, and she peeped up at him.

"It's not a bobcat. Look."

The humor Stephanie saw in Cole's eyes convinced her as much as what he said. Slowly turning her head, she found herself face to face with a large, disgruntled tomcat.

Josh looked at her with concern. "Don't be scared, Stephanie, it's just Thomas. He won't hurt you."

"A-a cat?"

Josh nodded.

"Oh." But she continued to stare at the animal with loathing.

"Son, why don't you take Thomas back to the barn," Cole said. "Put him where Sam can't get him, or he'll be right back."

Josh nodded again and looked at Stephanie. "You'll like him once you get to know him." He left, shaking his head.

"I'm afraid you'll have to beat him at checkers to win his confidence back now," Cole chuckled. "Scared of a cat! You'll never live that down."

"I thought it was a bobcat!"

Cole was beginning to enjoy himself. Since Stephanie was somewhat taller than the average woman, the top of her head brushed his chin as her breath whispered across his naked chest in a feather-light touch. She was hugging him so tightly he could feel the pounding of her heart. "You don't need to worry. No bobcat in his right mind would come inside a house. Believe me, it would be more afraid of you than you would be of it."

"It couldn't be!"

Cole chuckled again and began to stroke the back of her head. "I think we can safely say you aren't used to being around bobcats."

Stephanie's mind still held visions of being ripped apart by a wild animal, but she felt safe in Cole's strong arms. With no warning, she began to cry.

Startled, Cole stared down at her. "What did I say?"

"Nothing. Everything." She sniffed. "I'm afraid."

Gently, he raised her chin with his forefinger. "The cat's gone."

"It's not that."

"Then what is it?"

She hugged him tighter. "What if I never remember?"

"You will." Cole drew her to the chair by the window and sat down with her on his lap. With his hand stroking the back of her head, he murmured soothing words to her until the tension gradually eased from her slender body, and she slipped into sweet slumber.

Shifting her slightly, he looked down at her. The lantern bathed her face in an appealing combination of light and shadow. Cole gently traced the curve of her cheek with his hand. It was soft and warm, her skin like a silken caress against his fingers.

Stephanie smiled and cuddled into his shoulder. Cole jerked his hand away as though it had been burned. What the hell was he doing? It wasn't the first time he'd allowed himself to get attached. An image of Old Blue rose in his mind. The stray had been nothing but a scruffy mongrel, but as a twelve-year-old, Cole had become very fond of him. He'd been so devastated when the owner showed up to claim his dog, he sworn he'd never go through that kind of pain again.

Cole rubbed his thumb along the gold band on Stephanie's finger. He already felt the tug of a physical attraction that was hard to resist. It was dangerous to let her affect him this way. It was only a matter of time before she left.

Determined to combat the unwelcome feelings stirring inside, he placed Stephanie on the bed and pulled the blankets over her.

Snuggling into the pillow, she sighed. "You haven't put me to bed for a long time, James."

Cole straightened. James ate breakfast with her and put her to bed at night? Only marriage allowed such intimacy. Maybe Kate was right. Maybe Stephanie was running from her husband. The thought caused an odd ripple of dismay. She wasn't a stray dog, but she'd rip his heart out if he let her.

Embarrassed by her cowardice, Stephanie took a long time getting dressed the next morning. How on earth was she going to face Cole? With a grimace, she twisted her hair into the usual coil. Terrified of a cat, for goodness sake, and clinging to the poor man like a vine. He must think her the biggest fool in the world.

With one last look in the mirror, she left the relative safety of the bedroom. Kate was setting Josh's breakfast on the table in front him, and Cole was nowhere in sight. "Good morning."

"Good morning, Stephanie," Kate said pleasantly. "How are you feeling this morning?"

"Much better. I'm feeling quite myself this morning." She made a rueful face. "At least I think I am. No dizziness, anyway."

"You're just in time for breakfast."

If Josh's welcome was less enthusiastic than usual, Stephanie pretended not to notice as she sat down at the table. "Josh, I think you'd better tell me about bobcats."

"Why?" It was obvious she had dropped a long way in his esteem.

"When Charlie described them, I thought they were about this tall." She held her hand out to the side. "I get the feeling I misjudged them."

"Heck yes. They're smaller than Sam. No wonder you were so jumpy. You were thinking of a mountain lion."

"Oh. Are there any of those around here?"

"Only in the mountains."

"Well, thank heaven for that. No wonder you and your father laughed at me last night." She shook her head. "How embarrassing."

"Aw, that's all right," Josh assured her. "Hey, do you want

me to show you around later?"

"Why, yes. I'd like that very much." Answering Kate's grin with a conspiratorial wink, Stephanie calmly finished her breakfast.

At precisely eleven o'clock, the two set out. Predictably, Josh headed straight for the corrals. "There are only a few brood mares and the saddle horses around this time of year. Most of the herd is up on the mountain," he explained. "I was supposed to go on the roundup this year." He gazed longingly at the blue mountains to the north. "But Pa says my arm won't be healed in time."

Stephanie felt a pang of sympathy. "Actually, I'm glad there are only a few horses around. It will be easier to remember their names."

Josh's face brightened immediately. "That's right." He clambered up the fence and began eagerly pointing out the individual horses. A big black horse trotted over and playfully nudged the boy's leg.

"This is my horse, Black," he said proudly.

"My, aren't you a beauty?" Stephanie reached out to rub the young stallion's nose. "He's huge, Josh! How did you ever manage to hold him when I fell in front of you? You must be an incredible horseman."

"Black does what I want him to, even when he's scared," Josh boasted. "He's big, but he's gentle as a kitten. You must have been around horses before," he observed as Black lowered his head for Stephanie to scratch him between the ears. "Black's usually leery around strangers, but you know exactly how to handle him."

Stephanie smiled. "I have to say, I feel a lot more comfortable around horses than bobcats."

Josh's answering grin struck an odd chord in her mind, almost like a memory, but the fleeting impression was gone in an instant. "Want to see the new filly?" he asked, climbing down from the fence.

"Certainly."

He led her around the side of the corral and into the barn. The nostalgic odor of sweet- smelling hay drifted down from the haymow. Glancing around the huge structure, she saw a number of stalls and several large pens. The Cantrell operation was obviously a big one.

Josh stopped next to one of the pens where a tiny, long-legged foal stood next to its mother. The mare drew Stephanie's admiration right away. The color of a dark buckskin, her mane and tail were deep reddish brown rather than black. "Oh, she's beautiful!" she said.

Charlie sauntered out from the back of the barn and leaned his elbows on the top of the stall's gate. "Yup, she's a beauty, all right. Don't usually keep them in this long, but this is Sunrise's first foal, and Cole don't want to take any chances with her."

"Most of the mares have colts in the spring, but Pa decided not to wait." Josh reached out to pet the tiny foal. "He named her Dreamer."

At the feel of something brushing against her leg, Stephanie looked down and found herself being regarded by a large yellow tomcat. "And this must be Thomas." Mindful of Josh's watching eyes, she picked the cat up and began to scratch him under the chin. "I wasn't at my best when we met last night."

Charlie cleared his throat. "Cole said somethin' about that this morning." He tried to look serious. "I'm real sorry 'bout scarin' you like that."

"It was *horrible*." She closed her eyes and buried her face in Thomas's fur dramatically.

"I didn't mean nuthing by it." Charlie shifted uncomfortably. "Didn't think 'bout Thomas payin' you a visit, neither. Truth is, I was only havin' a little fun, and it sorta backfired. I promise not to do it again."

Stephanie raised eyes brimming with laughter. "Until the next time. I'm warning you though, Mr. Hobbs, I won't be taken in quite so easily again."

Charlie blinked in surprise. Then, realizing he'd been completely fooled, he chuckled. "I reckon I just got paid back."

Stephanie grinned as she set Thomas on the floor. "I certainly hope so."

"I'm real sorry it happened."

"I'm sure you are." Stephanie smiled sweetly. "Just as I'm sure you and Mr. Cantrell spent an enjoyable fifteen minutes laughing and feeling sorry for me this morning. Well, Josh, if you have any more to show me, we'd better get going or we'll be late for lunch."

At Stephanie's reminder of lunch, Josh must have begun to worry that his grandmother might not save any food for him if they were late, because the rest of the tour went much faster.

Stephanie was hard pressed not to laugh when she peeked through the door on the 'cow' side of the barn, and then dashed by the chicken coop so fast the chickens sent up a squawking as they moved through them. Josh slowed a little when they came to a long, low building he called the bunkhouse.

"It's where the men stay during round-up or haying, or whenever Pa has to hire extra hands." Josh pointed out two rooms at either end of the building. "That's Charlie's, and the other one used to be my Uncle Levi's." He glanced at the sun, which was approaching its zenith. "I'll show you the inside some other time."

Rounding the side of the house, Stephanie stopped in stunned amazement. The beautiful little cabin she saw was the last thing she'd expected. It had green shutters, flower-filled window boxes, and frilly white curtains, a piece of whimsy among the otherwise utilitarian ranch buildings.

"That's where Grandma Kate and Grandpa live," Josh explained.

"How pretty!"

Josh nodded. "My Grandpa said it was hard for Grandma Kate to give up her homestead when she married him. So, when she went to Denver to visit her brother, we had a house raising to surprise her. Us men built the house, and Ma and the other ladies made quilts and curtains and stuff." He shook his head. "Grandma Kate cried when she saw it and called Grandpa a romantic fool. I thought she hated it, but Pa says that sometimes a woman's heart gets so full of happiness it turns into tears." He looked at Stephanie curiously. "Do all women do that?"

"I guess most of them do."

Josh wrinkled his nose in disgust as he led her around to the front of the house. "It's a dumb way to show you're happy, if you ask me."

"Well, I expect some day you'll understand."

"Good morning!" Cole said as he strode up the path toward them. "Braving the great outdoors?"

"Your son and I have just finished patrolling the area," she assured him. "There doesn't appear to be a single bobcat on the premises."

He chuckled. "I can't tell you how that relieves my mind."

"I thought it might." Stephanie glanced around. "Your son seems to have deserted us."

"Kate must have lunch on the table, then. He's never wrong about mealtime." Cole gestured toward the door. "After you."

That evening, Cole offered to teach Stephanie his favorite game, chess. When the board was set up, she studied the pieces intently. Finally, she glanced up. "You know, I think I've played this before. Shall we try a game?"

Two hours later, Cole looked at her with new respect. "My father's the only one who ever pushed me as hard as you just did."

But Stephanie was lost in thought as a picture came into her mind. *"Concentrate, Stephanie, I just took your queen!"*

"What's wrong, Stephanie?" The picture faded with the sound of Cole's voice. "You look like you've seen a ghost."

"Maybe I have. I just had an image of the man who taught me how to play chess." She leaned her chin on her hand dejectedly. "And I have no idea who he is. This is so frustrating. All I get are bits and pieces. Nothing fits together."

"At least things are coming back."

Stephanie sighed. "I know."

"You mentioned James again in your sleep last night."

"I did?"

"You said it had been a long time since he put you to bed."

"Put me to bed!" Stephanie was shocked. "Who is he, my uncle?"

"Or your husband," Cole put in gently.

"My husband! That's ridiculous."

"I'm not so sure. When Kate first saw your ring, she was sure it was a wedding band."

Stephanie looked down at her hand with new eyes. *A wedding ring?* It was a possibility she hadn't even considered.

CHAPTER 6

"Sure wish your pa had time to give me a hand with that pen full of mares," Charlie remarked as he finished his breakfast.

Josh jumped up. "I can help."

"You think so?" Charlie gave the boy a speculative look. "I figured you'd be too busy layin' around the house."

"Doc said I could start doing a little bit if I'm careful," Josh said hopefully.

"Well, I expect it'll be all right, then." Charlie put on his hat, and Josh dashed out the door. "Figured it was about time I got that young varmint out from under your feet for a while."

"Thank you," Kate said with feeling. "I swear, you'd think he'd been cooped up for two months instead of two weeks. I hope you don't regret it, Charlie."

"He ain't any worse than his pa was," Charlie said as he followed Josh out the door. "Course I was a mite younger then."

"Well," Kate remarked as she and Stephanie cleared the table, "that's the last we'll see of Josh until lunch."

Stephanie chuckled. "Horses do seem to be his passion in life."

"More like an obsession. Just like his pa. From the time Cole and Levi caught their first wild horse, that's all those boys could think of. Of course, it did help keep them out of mischief, and I was grateful for that." She shook her head. "I could write a book about the shenanigans those two pulled."

"And now there's Josh."

Kate's mouth curved in a fond smile. "Yes, now there's Josh. Thank heaven he's not as full of the devil as his pa and his uncle were, though he's plenty bad enough."

Stephanie smiled and glanced longingly toward the door. With her bruises mostly healed, she was as anxious as Josh for a little physical activity. "Are there some chores I could help you with?"

"Let me think." Kate pursed her lips. "I haven't gathered the eggs yet. It's usually Josh's job, but I've been doing it while he's been laid up. Neither of us would mind if you took over."

"Perfect!" Stephanie jumped to her feet enthusiastically then frowned. "I'm not exactly sure I know how to gather eggs."

Kate laughed and picked up the small basket by the door. "Come on, I'll show you."

The chicken coop was mostly deserted when the two women entered. Gathering the eggs from unoccupied nests was a simple enough task, and Kate showed her how to get the eggs out from under the two hens that were sitting on nests After they scattered corn in the barnyard for the rest of the flock and returned to the house, Stephanie was pleased to find she still had plenty of energy. "Would you mind if I worked in the garden this morning?"

"Heavens, no. I wouldn't mind at all. I never seem to find the time." Kate made a face. "It's not my favorite chore anyway."

The morning passed pleasantly for Stephanie. A serene peace stole over her as she dug in the soft, rich soil. The garden had beckoned to her from the first, and this was obviously a much-loved task. Perhaps it was another small piece of her former life. Why did none of the things she knew seem to fit together? Her instant kinship with Josh seemed to point to a close relationship with someone, a son, a younger brother, maybe even the James she spoke to in her sleep.

"Do you know what that is?" Cole's deep voice broke her concentration.

"Of course I do. It's basil, and it's at exactly the right stage to dry, so I'm..." Stephanie's voice trailed off as she looked down at the plants in her hand. "How strange, I didn't even think about it."

"Well, you seem to know what you're doing," Cole said

with a hint of a smile. "I think I just saw my son streak by, and that can only mean one thing: lunch is ready. We'd better go in while there's still something left to eat."

"If he's already inside, we may be too late," she said as he helped her to her feet.

Lunch turned out to be quite enjoyable for Stephanie. Charlie entertained everyone with a humorous tale of his morning spent schooling the new colts, while Cole added teasing commentary.

Kate was delighted. She later told Stephanie she hadn't seen her stepson in such a good mood since Maggie's death.

Stephanie returned to the garden after lunch. It wasn't long before her mind again wandered from her work, this time to dwell upon a certain blue-eyed rancher who made her stomach react in the oddest way. She was in a decidedly buoyant mood as she walked into the house with a basket full of squash and a feeling of deep satisfaction.

"Goodness, you've been busy—Oh my." Kate eyed the stains on the front of Stephanie's skirt where the younger woman had knelt in the dirt. "I don't think anything short of a scrub-board will take that out."

Stephanie glanced down and made a face. "Oh dear. I didn't even think about it."

"No matter. You can wear something of Maggie's." Kate went into the bedroom and pulled a work dress from the closet. "It'll likely be loose and a bit too short, but it will come closer to fitting than any of mine."

Gratefully, Stephanie changed clothes. Maggie's dress fit just as poorly as Kate had thought it would, but it was still an improvement over the gray monstrosity. Using the washboard proved to be a bit of a challenge, but once Kate showed her the proper way of it, Stephanie soon had the dress washed and hung on the line outside to dry.

She rejoined Kate in the kitchen and sat down to watch her work. "You know," she said after a few minutes, "the washboard didn't seem at all familiar to me, but what you're doing does. Do you suppose I know how to cook?"

Kate looked up. "Could be. You wouldn't be the first who would rather cook than wash clothes. I was going to set some bread this afternoon. Want to try that?"

It wasn't long before Stephanie was tossing ingredients into a bowl and feeling quite at home with the task.

Whistling, Cole unsaddled Midnight. As he gave the stallion a vigorous rubdown, he found himself looking forward to a quiet evening and a good game of chess with Stephanie. He smiled when he thought how much that would please Kate. Usually when he finished up early, he went to visit Sally Langton, a vivacious young widow who lived on a neighboring ranch.

Kate and the much younger Sally had disliked each other from the first moment they'd met, but when Sally married Clay Langton, an old beau of Kate's, the women's animosity intensified until social contact between the two families had nearly ceased. Cole knew Kate would have something to say if she had any idea how far his relationship with Sally had gone. He had no doubt she'd give him a lecture about playing with fire, being blinded by lust, and using something other than his brain to think with.

The truth was, he was in no danger of succumbing to the beautiful widow's considerable charms. He was a man, and Sally was a most willing partner. Almost too willing. Cole had occasionally wondered if the elderly Mr. Langton had died of exhaustion. The woman was insatiable. But tonight, he was more in the mood for a stimulating conversation with Stephanie than a sexual marathon with Sally.

A cheerful greeting froze on his lips as he entered the house. *MAGGIE!* His heart lurched in glad recognition then plummeted an instant later. It wasn't Maggie working at the kitchen table in her favorite dress. It was Stephanie. There was a spot of flour on her nose and a soft half-smile on her face as she kneaded the bread dough with the same loose-jointed rhythm Maggie had always used.

Maggie was dead, her gentle heart and warm laughter stilled forever. A stranger worked in her kitchen, wearing her dress, baking bread for her family. It was so damned unfair!

Stephanie looked up and smiled when she saw him. "Guess what! I've discovered I can cook..." Her voice trailed off uncertainly when she saw the look in his eyes.

"What the hell do you think you're doing? Sleeping in her bed doesn't give you the right wear her clothes." His voice was as cold as a shard of ice, and his eyes narrowed suspiciously. "Or are you finally starting to show your true colors? Maybe your strange memory loss is nothing more than a pitiful effort to get close to the Cantrell money."

Speechless, Stephanie stared at him, her eyes wide with shock, looking for all the world like a frightened fawn.

"Oh, hell..." With a muttered curse, Cole turned on his heel and left.

"Cole Cantrell, you get back here this instant!" Kate called after him. Her lips thinned in irritation as his long-legged stride continued on without a pause. "Of all the pig-headed—" She snapped her mouth shut as she saw Stephanie's face crumple.

"Oh, Lord," Stephanie buried her face in her hands. "I didn't mean... I don't want..."

"Here now, don't take on so. It was just the shock of seeing you in Maggie's clothes. Cole will feel like a fool once he cools down, and he'll know good and well it was my fault." Kate put her arms around Stephanie and patted her back comfortingly. She shook her head. "He's just like his father. They both have a bad habit of reacting then regretting it later."

"And right now he's regretting his decision to let me stay here." Stephanie wiped her eyes with her apron and sighed. "It's probably time for me to leave. Will you drive me to town?"

"I will not!" Kate said indignantly. "Running away never solved anything. Besides, you're still not completely well. Look how weak you are."

"Oh, Kate, you heard what he said. He thinks I'm some kind of fortune hunter."

"Huh! If you were a fortune hunter, you'd aim a whole lot higher than Cole Cantrell. Every penny we have is tied up in this place, just like it always has been and likely always will be. If he had a million dollars, he'd just buy fancier horses."

"But I can't stay here. I could never sleep in that bed again knowing how he feels."

"Then you can move to my cabin. I have an extra bed that Josh uses when his father is visiting that yellow-haired—" Kate cleared her throat. "Anyway, it's kind of lonely with Jonathan gone, and I'll be glad of the company." She took a clean hanky out of her pocket and handed it to Stephanie. "Now, pull yourself together while I fix us a cup of tea. It won't do for Josh to come in and find us sogging up the bread dough."

Stephanie wiped her eyes again and blew her nose. "I still think I've imposed on the hospitality of this house long enough."

Kate put her hands on her hips. "Horsefeathers! You've brought this house back to life. Cole has smiled and laughed more since you've been here than he has for months. It's us that owe you a debt of gratitude, not the other way around." She turned back to the stove. "I told you once before, I'm a selfish woman where my family is concerned, and you're the best thing that's happened to us in a good long time. You're staying!"

Cole was still angry when he tied his horse to the rail in front of Sally Langton's house. He stomped through the door without bothering to knock and went down the hall to her office, where she was working on her accounts. "Hello, Sally."

"Why, Cole." Ignoring his rude entrance, Sally smiled up at him with luminous eyes. "How nice of you to drop by. Shall

I ring for refreshments?"

"You know why I'm here," Cole said. He hated her grand-dame-of-the-manor act.

Immune to his barbs, she gave him a coy smile. "I'll bet I can hazard a guess. Would you like to retire to a more private room to discuss it?" She rose, took his hand, and started toward the stairs. "There's something deliciously wicked about making love in broad daylight, isn't there?"

"I never thought about it."

Sally closed the bedroom door and turned to find him already undressing. She raised her eyebrows in surprise. "My, you *are* impatient today." She smiled as she turned to let him unbutton her dress. "How nice. I won't have to coax you into my bed for a change."

"I'm not in the mood for games, Sally."

She heard the bed ropes squeak as she dropped her dress to the floor. Turning, she found him lying on the bed, watching her with hooded eyes. "Then by all means, let's be serious," she murmured in a silky voice. Shedding the rest of her clothing with slow, provocative moves, she walked over to the bed, hips swaying enticingly. Settling herself next to Cole, she ran a fingernail down the middle of his chest to the line of hair that grew down his belly; she wet her lips seductively. "Now, what was it you wanted to discuss?"

"How about why we waste so much time talking?" he said with a growl, pulling her into his arms and capturing her mouth in a hot, searing kiss.

Sally gasped with surprised delight as he drove into her willing body with no preliminaries. Far from being offended by such fierceness, she encouraged it, moaning her pleasure and responding with a wildness of her own. Cole was usually the gentlest of lovers, but today their mating was a carnal thing, all heavy breathing and sweat-slickened bodies writhing together as late afternoon shadows filled the room.

Afterwards, Cole rolled to his back and threw an arm over his eyes, his heart slamming against his ribs and his breathing ragged. "Damn!" he said. "I'm sorry, Sally. You didn't deserve that."

Sally raised herself on one elbow and looked down into his face. "What are you talking about? That was unbelievable!"

He lifted his arm off his eyes and blinked at her. "Are you serious?"

"Absolutely! I don't know what got you all worked up, but I loved it. Shall we try it again and see if we get the same results?"

He stared at her for a long moment, then shook his head. "Sometimes, I think you have the instincts of a courtesan."

Sally smiled and lowered her head to nibble on his ear. "I prefer *seductress*." She kissed him deeply, her tongue mating with his as her hand wandered along his body, arousing him in ways she knew he couldn't resist.

Finally, he groaned and rolled over, pinning her beneath him. "God, Sally, you're an insatiable witch."

"Does that mean I've bewitched you?" She wriggled her hips sensuously.

He laughed deep in his throat. "Is that what it is? And here I thought it was just your way of getting what you want."

Sally gave him her most adorable pout. "But I'm not getting what I want now."

He didn't answer her with words.

Hours later, Cole emerged from the house and sighed as he climbed into the saddle. He'd left Sally purring like a kitten, but he felt only exhaustion. For the first time, his affair with Sally seemed sordid, her creative lovemaking practiced rather than exciting. He should have stayed home and played chess with Stephanie.

Damn his temper anyway. He felt a sting of remorse as he remembered the things he'd said and thought how his words must have devastated Stephanie. She only had the one ugly gray dress, and Kate was perfectly right to loan her one of Maggie's.

Kate had surely smoothed things over, explaining he

hadn't meant the awful things he'd said. She was used to his temper and had probably spent the afternoon shredding his character. At least Stephanie would know it wasn't the first time he'd done something stupid.

By the time Cole reached home, he'd decided to apologize to Stephanie right away. He'd have to wake her up to do it, of course, but this was something that couldn't wait until morning. Swinging out of the saddle as soon as he reached the barn, Cole gave Midnight a quick rubdown and turned him out into the corral almost before he was dry.

He entered the silent house and crossed the kitchen to his bedroom. Quietly, he opened the door and stopped on the threshold. The bed was empty, and Stephanie's few possessions were missing. With an increasing sense of foreboding, he searched the house. It, too, was empty.

She was gone. Where? How? It was a frightening prospect. Had she left before or after Josh had gone to his grandmother's cabin? Stephanie's chances of surviving in the wilderness alone were nonexistent.

With a terrifying sense of urgency, he traversed the short distance to his parents' cabin. First he'd wake Kate, then Charlie. Between the three of them, they ought to be able to locate Stephanie. He hardly even glanced at Josh asleep in the extra bed in the sitting room as he strode into the bedroom.

"Kate!" Cole whispered, bending over his stepmother's sleeping form. "Kate, wake up. Stephanie's gone." He shook her shoulder. "We've got to find her before..." He halted in surprise. The blanket-draped body in the huge cherry wood bed wasn't shaped right for Kate. He jerked the blankets back. "What the hell?"

Stephanie awoke with a start and sat up, blinking at Cole in confusion.

"What are you doing here?" he asked, his voice still raw with his worry.

She pulled her knees to her chest and cowered away from him. "K-Kate said I could." Stephanie dropped her face miserably to her knees. "I'll leave first thing in the morning."

"Like hell you will!" He dropped the blankets and scooped her up in his arms. "You're going back to the main house where you belong."

He turned and came face to face with Kate, who was glowering up at him, her braid askew and her robe clutched around her.

"Put her down this instant. I leave for five minutes to go to the outhouse, and you come charging in here, scaring the wits out of everybody. What's the matter with you anyway?"

"Stephanie belongs in the main house," he repeated stubbornly.

"She'd rather stay with me."

"Where she has to share a bed?"

"When Josh goes back to the house, she'll have her own bed. In the meantime, mine is plenty big enough for both of us. Now, put her down before you do something even more stupid than you have already."

Cole looked down into Stephanie's frightened green eyes. "Is that true? Would you rather stay here?"

She nodded, her lower lip quivering.

Without another word, Cole gently laid her back on the bed and pulled the covers over her again. When he turned around, he found Josh standing beside Kate, his eyes wide.

Cole sighed. "Come on, Josh, let's go to bed."

Walking back to the main house, Josh glanced up at his father's stern profile. "Pa, are you mad at Stephanie?"

"No." Cole looked at his son. "You really like her, don't you?"

Josh nodded. "You won't make her go away, will you?"

Cole sighed as he put his arm around Josh's shoulder. "No, I won't send Stephanie away. I just hope I can convince her I didn't mean all the things I said."

Cole lay awake long into the night. Stephanie was afraid of him, and with good reason. He'd acted like an idiot from the moment he'd walked into the house that afternoon until his final performance in Kate's bedroom. There had to be some way he could smooth things over, to convince Stephanie he wasn't a total jackass. He finally hit upon a scheme just as the sun began to brighten the eastern horizon and went to sleep with a smile on his face.

Kate was alone in the kitchen when Cole came in from doing his chores later that morning. She slapped a plate of ham and eggs on the table in front of him and turned back to her work. Cole knew she was dying to give him a piece of her mind.

"Where's Stephanie?" he asked nonchalantly.

Kate whirled around, a wooden spoon clutched in her hand. "She's still in bed. I don't think she slept too well after you barged in. And I'll tell you another thing..."

Cole meekly ate his breakfast as the tirade broke over his head. Kate never forgot a mistake, and she threw several of his worst in his face. He marveled at the length and depth of his transgressions.

"And I'm not sure how I'll ever convince her to stay after the way you handled things," she finished at last and stood glaring at him with her hands on her hips.

Cole slid his chair back and stood up. "Neither am I, but I have faith in you, Kate. You'll figure out a way." He put his hat on. "Just keep her here until I get back from town."

"What are you planning to do, Cole?"

He winked at her and walked out the door.

"Cole Cantrell, don't you dare leave until you tell me what—"

CHAPTER 7

"Good morning, Frank," Cole greeted the storekeeper cheerfully as he entered the Horse Creek Mercantile. "I need some cloth."

"Sure thing, Cole, I'll show you what I've got." He peered over his glasses. "Still got that young lady out there?" Cole nodded, and Frank raised his eyebrows questioningly. "Her memory come back yet?"

Cole shrugged. "Bits and pieces. Heard anything?"

"Nope, and I've asked everybody who's come in. Nobody missing as far as anyone knows. A stranger came in looking for somebody named Elizabeth Scott, but he seemed to think she'd lived here a long time."

"Well, keep asking. Something may turn up yet."

"Glad to." Frank laid the bolts of fabric out on the counter for Cole to examine. He chose four, then scanned the shelves behind the counter. "I'll need a dress length of each of these and about ten yards of that white cotton, I guess."

Frank nodded and began to measure the cloth.

The bell over the door sounded, and Sally Langton strolled in. "Why, Cole, what a surprise. You're certainly in town early this morning."

Cole glanced at Midnight, conspicuously tied to the hitching rack outside. Some surprise; his horse was as well known as he was. "Good morning, Sally. You're out pretty early yourself."

"I had a few things to attend to." She looked at him from under long, sooty lashes. "You look kind of tired. Been working hard?"

"You could say that. I went for a long, hard ride yesterday afternoon, and it wore me out."

"I've always found riding to be rather invigorating," she

said with a sly smile.

"True, but you have to give your horse a rest now and then." For some reason, Cole found her coy banter irritating this morning and turned his attention back to the storekeeper. "Can you wrap that up tight, Frank? I didn't bring the wagon."

Frank grinned to himself as he finished tying the bulky package. It was no secret the attractive young widow had set her cap at Cole, and the bets were running about even as to whether she'd succeed or not. Frank would have given a healthy share of his weekly proceeds to know what Cole had said to make Sally blush that way. If he hadn't known better, he'd have thought she was embarrassed.

With a nod to Frank, Cole picked up the package, tipped his hat to Sally, and walked out the door.

"Is Mrs. Cantrell ill?" Sally asked Frank.

The storekeeper looked surprised. "Not that I know of, why?"

Sally fingered the brown wool with seeming nonchalance. "I find it odd that Cole would take the time to come to town to pick up her dress goods, that's all."

Frank was not particularly fond of Sally Langton and was one who hoped Cole would escape her clutches. Now he saw a perfect opportunity to thrust a spoke in her wheel. "I figured it was for the young lady."

Sally gave him a sharp look. "What young lady?"

"You haven't heard? There was an accident a couple of weeks back. Josh's horse got spooked somehow and hit the young lady in the head. Cole managed to save her life, but when she finally woke up, she couldn't remember a thing. He feels kind of responsible for her, so she's stayin' at the ranch till they find out who she is." He gave Sally a bland look. "Guess Kate's taken her under her wing. Seems real fond of her already. Doc Addley says she's quite a looker."

"How interesting," Sally murmured, her eyes narrowing in speculation. "Maybe I should do the neighborly thing and drop by for a visit."

Frank swallowed a chuckle. It would be interesting to see what Sally Langton would do with a little competition.

Stephanie was sitting at the table peeling potatoes when Cole came in and unceremoniously dropped the heavy package in her lap. "I figured you'd know how to make use of this," he said.

She looked up at him in surprise. He reminded her of a little boy as he stood there, hat in hand, watching her expectantly.

"Well, open it!"

Untying the string, Stephanie uncovered a pile of white cotton fabric. She stared at it for a moment then peeped up at Cole questioningly.

"Uh...I thought you could use that for nightgowns and...other things." There was a suspicion of a blush under his tan as he pushed it aside to reveal a calico print. "There's enough of each of these others to make several dresses."

"Oh." Stephanie looked down at the material with new interest. Inspecting each piece of yard goods, she exclaimed with delight over each of the two calicos and the brown wool. At the bottom of the pile she came across a length of soft green wool. "It's beautiful!" she cried, holding it against her cheek.

When she raised shining eyes to Cole, he caught his breath in surprise. Color glowed in her cheeks, and the deep green reflected in eyes exactly the same shade. He blinked and took a deep breath.

"Thank you, Cole, they're wonderful. I can't wait until they're made up." Stephanie stood and began to gather her gifts.

"Wait," he said as she started to fold the paper back over the fabric. "I...I'm sorry for the way I acted yesterday. I had no call to yell at you that way. It was Maggie's dress. It caught me by surprise, and I—"

"No, it's all right." Stephanie placed her hand on his arm. "Kate explained all that to me, and I understand. I'm sorry it caused you pain."

Cole ran the crease in the crown of his hat between his thumb and fingers. "Can you forgive me?" he asked hopefully.

"If you'll forgive me for blundering so badly. Kate and I didn't mean to…"

He swallowed hard then nodded. "I know."

Stephanie picked up the parcel and hugged it to her chest. "I'll go put these away before I get them dirty," she said, and swept out the door.

Left alone with her stepson, Kate tapped her foot. "I'd say she's forgiven you, though I'm not at all sure you deserve it!"

Cole walked to the door. "But *you're* not about to forgive and forget, are you?" He sighed dramatically. "Ah well, Stephanie seems pleased. I guess I'll have to be satisfied with that."

He stared silently out the door for several minutes, his smile gone. When he spoke, it was with deep sadness. "I guess it's time to put Maggie's things away." His hand clenched on the brim of his hat. "I don't know if I can do it."

Kate closed her eyes. "I'll take care of it this afternoon."

"Might as well take the music box to your place." He sighed again. "And I suppose Stephanie can make use of the comb and brush." His voice cracked on the last word as he jammed his hat on his head and strode down the walk.

Helping Kate with her sad chore that afternoon, Stephanie found herself developing an odd feeling of kinship with the dead woman as she handled the things that had been part of Maggie Cantrell's life. She was especially drawn to a beautiful little music box. When she lifted the lid, the lilting tune tumbled through her mind like the wisps of a near-memory.

Kate's eyes brightened. "Maggie loved that. She used to listen to it all the time."

Stephanie rubbed her fingers reverently over the polished wood. "It's lovely."

"Oh," Kate said, reaching into a drawer, "I nearly forgot. Cole said you could use these."

Stephanie stared at the silver comb and brush Kate put in her hands. "He said I could use these? Why?"

"I guess he figured you'd need something for your hair. It might be best if he doesn't see you use them, though. He used to love to watch Maggie brush her hair."

They had just begun to pack the clothes into a trunk when they heard the sound of a carriage outside. "That'll likely be Doc Addley," Kate said. "Why don't you show him in while I finish up here?"

But when Stephanie reached the front door, it was not the doctor but a beautiful blonde who alighted from a very expensive buggy and walked toward the house. She was dressed in the height of fashion, her exquisitely tailored dress hugging a voluptuous figure enticingly. When she reached the bottom step, she raised her perfectly arched eyebrow in feigned surprise. "Good heavens, you must be the young lady Cole rescued."

"I'm Stephanie," she said cautiously as she surveyed the visitor. Beneath the perfectly coiffed hair, the woman's luminous brown eyes had an assessing look. It appeared she had already judged Stephanie and found her lacking somehow. *Not somebody I'd trust to cover my back.* "I'm sorry, I didn't catch your name."

The woman inclined her head in a condescending manner. "I'm Sally Langton, of course. The Langtons and the Cantrells have been neighbors simply forever."

Stephanie smiled uncertainly. "I see. How nice to have you drop by."

Without waiting for an invitation, the diminutive blonde

swept past her into the house. Stephanie lifted her brows in surprise. "Won't you come in and have a cup of tea?"

"Why, yes, thank you." Though the perfectly formed mouth smiled, it didn't reach her eyes.

Busying herself fixing the tea, Stephanie could feel Sally's eyes upon her. She was puzzled. There had been a hint of superiority and something else that could have been dislike. It was very odd coming from a stranger.

When she set the cups on the table and sat down, Sally smiled pleasantly. "I hope you don't mind my dropping by without an invitation, but Cole and I are such old friends..." She let her voice trail off significantly as she took a sip of tea.

"Cole's out on the range this afternoon," Stephanie said. "We're not expecting him back until supper time."

"Oh, that's too bad. I had hoped to catch him," Sally said.

Though she wasn't sure why, Stephanie had the distinct feeling that Sally was lying and that running into Cole was the last thing she'd wanted. This visit was becoming more peculiar by the minute. "Perhaps Kate could help you if it's a business matter."

"I think not." Sally's eyes darted around the kitchen almost nervously. "I've never really gotten to know Kate very well. She's quite a bit older than I am, and we really have nothing in common. You understand how it is, I'm sure."

"How uncomfortable for you both," Stephanie murmured. *So, Kate doesn't like you either. Well, that makes you fair game, Sally, m'dear.*

"You know, I didn't even realize you were here until this morning." Sally nonchalantly circled the rim of her cup with the tip of her finger. "Cole didn't mention you at all when he stopped by yesterday, though he was there the longest time."

With a flash of surprise, Stephanie realized Sally Langton was jealous of her. How ridiculous. This beautiful little package of sensual femininity was obviously Cole's mistress, the one Kate had spoken of so disparagingly the day before.

Trying to ignore the talons of green-eyed envy herself,

Stephanie smiled. "I'm sure it slipped his mind. Being such good friends, you probably had much more interesting things to discuss than a stranger."

Sally gave a brittle laugh. "Men can be such beasts. I don't suppose Cole told you about me, either."

"Why, no, I don't think he ever did, but Kate was talking about you just yesterday." Stephanie smiled pleasantly as she sipped her tea. "She specifically mentioned your hair, I believe."

Sally self-consciously touched her perfect coiffure. "I was sorry to hear about your accident." Sally didn't quite manage to disguise her malicious tone as she raised her cup to her mouth. "I can't say I'm surprised, though. Dear little Josh is a delightful child, of course, but he needs more discipline. I've been telling Cole something like this would happen, but he's such a doting father he never listens."

"You were obviously misinformed. It was Josh's quick thinking that saved my life," Stephanie snapped. To hear Josh maligned made her angry enough to take the gloves off and flex her claws a bit. "I'm not in the least offended by Josh's high spirits. He's rather like his father, and I find them both very stimulating."

Sally gave her a scornful glance. "What in the world could you possibly find to talk about with Cole?"

"You'd be amazed how many interests he and I share. We spend a lot of time playing chess. Cole is an avid player, you know." As an afterthought, Stephanie inquired politely, "Do you play?"

"No, I don't," Sally gritted out.

"Oh." Stephanie gave her a pitying look. "That is too bad, but I'm sure you and Cole must have something in common. I can't think he'd spend much time with someone who bored him."

Sally looked momentarily disconcerted, then apparently decided it might be prudent to change tactics. "How very disconcerting it must be to remember nothing of the past. Why, you might have been *anything* before." She made it sound as if Stephanie had spent her life in a brothel, or worse.

Stephanie smiled pleasantly. "Yes, I might've been, mightn't I? Anything at all."

"What happens when someone shows up who knows all about you and your past?"

Stephanie blinked in apparent surprise. "Why, then I won't have to wonder anymore." Indicating Sally's empty cup, she asked politely. "Would you care for some more tea?"

Sally stood up. "No, I really must be going. You must be dying to start sewing on the cloth Cole bought this morning at the store." She looked pointedly at Stephanie's dress. "I thought it odd he bought so much, but I can see it was a dire emergency."

"Wasn't it sweet of him?" Stephanie smiled softly as she rose to her feet. "I had no idea he'd even noticed."

Sally gritted her teeth in vexation. Sweeping toward the door, she couldn't resist a parting shot. Eyeing the slender woman towering over her by a good six inches, she remarked. "My goodness, it must be difficult to be so tall!" She smiled condescendingly. "Men do seem to like small women."

"Do they? I don't really remember." Stephanie shrugged. "But then, I only come to Cole's shoulder, so I hadn't thought about it." Smiling brightly, she walked Sally to the door. "I'm so glad you stopped by. I've enjoyed our little visit. I do hope you'll come back!" She watched Sally climb into her buggy and waved cheerfully when the other woman cast one last angry glance at the house before driving away.

Kate came and stood next to her. "I don't think we'll see her around here for a while!"

Stephanie glanced down at her, shame-faced. "You heard?"

"I did indeed," Kate said with satisfaction. "I was about to bounce the little tart out of here when I realized you were more than a match for her." She glanced up at Stephanie. "I wonder where you learned to deal with the likes of her."

Stephanie sighed. "Who knows. It's certainly not a skill I'm proud of. I was worse than she was."

Kate bristled. "She deserved everything you gave her and more. That woman has some nerve, coming to look you over as if she had a right to."

Stephanie gazed after the departed carriage. "I'm not so sure. She must have some claim on Cole, after all. I assume there's been bad blood between the two of you in the past?"

"You could say that. I didn't take kindly to her trying to get her claws into my husband. I might have forgiven her if she'd taken no for an answer, but she wouldn't leave him alone. Didn't bother her at all that he was old enough to be her father and married to boot."

"What happened?"

"Jonathan ignored her, but she persisted until I was forced to take matters into my own hands," she said. "When she couldn't get the best-looking man in the valley, she went after the richest. Poor Clay didn't have a chance. Even then, she couldn't keep her eyes off Jonathan." Kate paused. "Well, I guess I can't really blame her for that, and I do think she made Clay happy," she admitted grudgingly. "But I've never trusted her around my husband, and I don't trust her around my son!"

"Why didn't she go after Cole in the first place?" Stephanie asked. "I mean, he's closer to her age."

"She came when he was off at college, and Levi was in Chicago working with his uncle. I'm not sure it would have made any difference anyway. Once she saw Jonathan, she was like a bitch in heat."

Stephanie grinned. "Tell me, does Cole look like his father by any chance?"

"Quite a bit. Sally does have an eye for a handsome man."

Stephanie was silent for a moment. "Maybe it would be best if we forget to tell Cole Sally was here," she said, turning away from the door. "He might not appreciate the way I treated her. I'm a little ashamed of myself." She gave Kate a sideways glance, her eyes twinkling. "But only a little."

CHAPTER 8

"Don't peek," Stephanie called over her shoulder. "And remember, all the way to one hundred this time."

Josh laughed. "It won't matter if I count to a thousand, Sam and I will still find you."

"Not this time you won't," she muttered to herself as she changed direction and headed for the barn. Her eyes sparkling with merriment, she climbed into the haymow and pulled up the ladder. Checking to make sure she was out of sight, Stephanie sat down to wait.

Josh hadn't been able to go to round up the cattle on the mountain with his father, Charlie, and half a dozen other men. He'd been so woebegone that Stephanie agreed to help him train his dog. Though it turned out to be nothing more than a glorified game of hide and seek, it had been just the excuse she needed. Her new clothes were all ready to sew, but for some reason she was strangely reluctant to begin.

"Find Stephanie!" She heard Josh give the command and bit her lip to keep from giggling. They'd never locate her this time.

Soon, Sam was snuffling below. He spent several minutes pacing back and forth directly beneath her and then dashed out of the barn. Stephanie grinned. She'd outwitted them at last. Stephanie had barely begun wondering how long she'd have to wait before Josh gave up when he came running into the barn behind Sam. The dog barked excitedly toward the rafters.

Josh laughed. "You may as well come down, Stephanie. We found you."

Crawling over to the edge of the haymow, she looked down. "Sam, you traitor! Is this how you repay me for slipping you that extra bone last night?"

The dog's tongue lolled out in a canine grin as Josh danced

around in delight. "He'll find you no matter where you hide. Face it, Stephanie, he's a great tracker." At that moment, Sam scurried to the wall of the barn, barking furiously.

"And a great hunter. Why couldn't he have been distracted by that mouse five minutes ago?" Stephanie grumbled with mock annoyance. "Stay there, Josh. I need you to steady the ladder for me." She disappeared back into the loft. The ladder was difficult to maneuver among the piles of hay, and Stephanie struggled with it for several minutes before it was in place. "Are you holding it?"

"Yes," came the muffled answer from below.

"All right. Here I come." Swinging her legs over the edge, Stephanie started down. She was still several steps from the bottom rung when the ladder began to shake. "Stop it, Josh. I'll fall."

All at once she was grasped around the waist by a large pair of hands. "Don't worry, I'll catch you."

Startled, Stephanie looked over her shoulder, right down into the smiling blue eyes of Cole Cantrell. With one arm around her waist and the other around her knees, he plucked her from the ladder and twisted her around to face him. She put her hands on his shoulders to brace herself.

"Where's Josh?"

"He ran off to find Charlie and left me to finish up here." Cole continued to hold her suspended above the ground, his expression teasing.

"Well?" she asked.

"Well what?"

"Well, aren't you going to put me down?"

He appeared to consider this. "Hmm, that's a good question. Tell me why I should."

"Because I'm heavy?"

"Strange, you don't feel heavy. There must be a better reason."

"How about that great heights make me dizzy?" In truth, she did feel a little lightheaded, but it didn't have anything to do with height.

Cole raised an eyebrow. "So?"

"So, my stomach gets dizzy too."

"That does put a different light on things."

Stephanie gave him an arch look. "Yes, I thought it might."

He slowly let her body slide down his until her feet touched the floor. Still holding her lightly, he raised one hand to pluck the hay from her hair. "You're a bit untidy. If I let you go back to the house looking like this, Kate will accuse me of all kinds of indiscretions. What were you doing in the loft, anyway?"

"Hiding from Josh," she said in a dazed voice. During the week he'd been gone, she'd somehow forgotten how handsome he was.

Cole nodded. "That explains it. A logical place for a grown woman to hide when threatened by a nine-year-old boy."

"We were playing a game. He sends Sam after me and...."

Her voice trailed off when she realized how inane it all sounded.

He smiled tenderly as he pushed back several strands of hair that had fallen across her forehead. "That's a new one on me."

"Josh thought it was a good way to teach Sam to track people," she whispered. "You never know when someone might get lost."

"And has this training been successful?" he asked softly.

Shocks of sensation began to run through her as Cole gently traced the line of her face. "He always seems to find me."

The blue of his eyes deepened as his fingers strayed to the back of her neck, where he lightly stroked the tender skin that lay beneath the soft hairs.

"I hope I'm not interrupting anything," came a silky voice from the doorway.

With seeming indifference, Cole turned toward the voice. Stephanie wasn't quite sure how, but by the time she saw Sally standing impatiently in the open barn door, Cole had put enough distance between them that their positions appeared innocent. That he continued to pick hay leaves from her hair added to the illusion.

"Hello, Sally. What brings you out this way?"

Eyes sparkling with anger, Sally lifted her skirts and delicately picked her way across the barn. "I came to find out how many of my cattle came down with yours."

Cole leaned negligently against a timber that supported the roof. "Somewhere around twenty head. Charlie left several men to bring them on in. I was planning on leaving in about ten minutes if you'd like to ride out and meet the herd."

"Yes, I think I will, if you'll lend me a horse. I came over in my buggy." Glancing at Stephanie, Sally looked questioningly at Cole.

"I don't believe you've met Stephanie," he said pleasantly.

As Cole made the introductions, Stephanie wished she could sink through the floor. Any minute, Sally would tell her lover how rudely she'd been treated.

"So nice to meet you."

Stephanie blinked in surprise. "You, too," she murmured. She couldn't fathom why Sally chose to act as though they'd never met, but she wasn't about to rock the boat.

Cole gave Stephanie a brotherly pat on the shoulder. "Run along now, and tell Kate we'll be in for supper in about four hours. There'll be six extra hands to feed."

Stephanie stiffened. Dismiss her like a schoolgirl, would he? "I'll give her your message." She turned on her heel and stomped out of the barn. Ten minutes ago she'd been ready to melt in his arms, and now she was fighting the urge to slap his face.

Cole was almost thankful for Sally's interruption. Though seduction had not been his intention when he agreed to hold the ladder for Josh, if Sally had arrived five minutes later, she might have walked in on a far more embarrassing scene.

Smoothing out her irritated frown, Sally turned to Cole. "It's so kind of you to take in the poor girl like you have." She paused slightly. "But aren't you afraid her memory loss might be a bit too convenient?"

He raised his eyebrows. "Convenient?"

"I mean, to be at just the right spot when you came riding by and then to have no recollection of anything. It seems a little too coincidental." She patted his arm in a proprietary manner. "You're far too trusting, Cole. I don't think you realize the lengths some women would go to catch someone like you."

And you know better than most, Cole thought cynically. He gave her a slow lazy smile. "Jealous, Sally?"

Her eyes widened in amazement. "Jealous of her? Don't be absurd." She looked pityingly toward the door. "But I can understand why she might go to extraordinary lengths to get a man."

"Oh? What exactly do you mean by that?" It was well for Sally's peace of mind that she missed the anger that flashed across Cole's face.

"Men never give a woman that tall and plain a second glance. As for the way she wears her hair...!" Sally shuddered delicately. "Why didn't you tell me she was here? I was hurt to have to hear it from Frank Collins."

Cole shrugged. "I never thought about it. You told me a long time ago that family business didn't interest you."

"This is different."

"Oh, how do you figure that?"

"She's not family."

"So?"

Sally lay her hand on his arm in a proprietary manner. "So maybe if I'd known she was here, I could have helped."

Cole snorted. "Somehow I don't see you volunteering to help nurse a stranger."

"No, of course not." An expression of revulsion crossed her face. "Kate wouldn't have let me anyway. I merely meant I could be of assistance showing her how to dress and fix her hair." She flicked an imaginary speck from the sleeve of her expensive riding habit. "She must feel terribly unattractive, poor dear. I could help her become...well... not beautiful, of course, but less homely."

It was all Cole could do not to give a derisive snort. Stephanie, homely? Didn't the woman have eyes in her head? Still, maybe it was for the best. The last thing he wanted was for Sally to see Stephanie as a threat. She'd destroy someone so young and naive with a few words and continue slicing until she drew blood. Cole sighed inwardly. Time for a distraction, and with Sally, that meant one thing.

"Do you want to stand here talking all day, or shall we get moving?" He gave her a suggestive look. "There's a nice private grove of trees between here and the herd. My bedroll is still on my saddle, and if we hurry, we can probably stop for a little...rest before we meet the herd."

Cole almost laughed at the way her eyes lit up in anticipation.

"That sounds absolutely lovely!" Sally replied, all thought of Stephanie quite effectively wiped from her mind.

"Then, let's go." He gave her a slap on the behind and walked away.

Kate looked up as Stephanie stomped into the house. "I saw Sally go by. What's that vixen done now?"

"Nothing really. In fact, she acted as though we'd never met."

Kate gave her a disbelieving look. "If she didn't do anything, I'd like to know why you're so upset."

"Oh, I made a fool of myself, that's all." She shrugged. "But they were both so anxious for me to leave, I don't think they even noticed." Trying to ignore an intense wave of jealousy, she gritted her teeth and rolled up her sleeves. "At any rate, we've got our work cut out for us. Cole says they'll be in with the herd in about four hours."

She did some quick mental calculations. "Let's see, dinner for ten. I think I know just the thing. I wonder if we have everything we need...."

Kate looked on in amazement as Stephanie began digging through the cupboard. It was almost as though her irritation with Sally and Cole had opened a door in her mind somewhere. Kate didn't say a word as a Stephanie she'd never seen before suddenly emerged.

The two women had often worked together, but today Kate was aware of a subtle change. As Stephanie planned and executed each phase of the cooking, she unconsciously assumed command for the first time.

Both ladies were engrossed in supper preparations when Josh wandered in. "Charlie and Pa left, and I don't have nothing to do," he said plaintively.

Stephanie looked up. "Josh, just the person we need. Would you mind making the butter?"

He made a disgusted noise. "Women's work! I want something fun to do."

"Don't pull that long face with me, young man," Kate said. "If you really want something to do, that cream needs to be churned!" She pointed to a small, round, half-gallon churn sitting on the table, and Josh looked at it unhappily.

Stephanie laid her hand gently on his shoulder. "We really do need your help, Josh. Neither your grandmother or I have time to do it."

Picking up the churn, Josh sat down and gave the handle a few desultory turns. All at once his face brightened. "Can I take it outside?"

Kate shrugged. "I don't see why not. Cream doesn't care much one way or the other. Run along, but mind you churn it up good. Your pa will be very unhappy if there isn't any butter for his rolls."

Josh tucked the churn under his arm. "Don't worry, Grandma Kate, it'll be the best butter you ever tasted!"

"Now, what do you suppose got into him?" Kate asked suspiciously as Josh practically ran out the door. "That boy hates to churn butter."

When Stephanie pulled an angel food cake out of the oven and replaced it with a pan full of rolls nearly two hours later, Kate shook her head in amazement. "I don't know what you did before, but you sure can cook! This'll be the best feed those cowhands have had in a good long time."

Stephanie blushed with pleasure. "I enjoy it, too. It's strange how things keep coming back." She sighed as she closed the oven door. "Everything but my memory."

Stephanie was stirring a sauce when Josh slipped into the kitchen and put the churn on the table. "Here's your butter." His freckled face looked sublimely innocent.

"What are you up to?" Kate asked sharply.

Josh gazed at her with a look of such injured surprise that Stephanie was hard pressed to keep from laughing.

"Nothing! I just made the butter like you asked."

"I've seen that look more times than I can count, and it usually means you're hiding something." Kate picked up the churn and poured off the buttermilk. "Your pa and Uncle Levi used to wear that cat-who-ate-the-canary look, too. It always means trouble."

Behind his grandmother's back, Josh flashed Stephanie a look of pure mischief.

CHAPTER 9

Supper was ready by the time the men arrived fifteen minutes later. Cole came in while the others were washing up and frowned at his son. "Josh, what did you do this afternoon?"

"I churned butter for supper. Just ask Grandma Kate."

"Then who did I see riding Tater?"

Josh squirmed. "T-Tater? I don't know."

"I want the truth."

Josh stared at his father for a minute before hanging his head and blushing scarlet. "It was me, Pa, but I had a good reason."

"You'd better have. Doc Addley said no horseback riding until your arm's healed and he says you can."

"Charlie said Tater need to be exercised cause she's getting so fat. When Stephanie told me to churn the butter, I remembered how Tater's trot is rough enough to jiggle your teeth loose and I...I..." his voice trailed off.

"You what?" Cole's voice held a dangerous note.

Josh stared at his hands miserably. "I saddled Tater, tied the churn to the pommel, and trotted her around the corral until it turned into butter."

There was complete silence in the kitchen. At last Josh looked up in trepidation. His father had the strangest expression on his face.

"You deserve that boy, Cole." Kate's said as she crossed her arms beneath her ample bosom. "And I've been waiting for this day for twenty years."

Cole glanced at Kate, who raised her eyebrows expectantly, then back at his son. "Josh," he began sternly. There was a moment of strained silence. "Oh hell." With a shake of his head, Cole dissolved into laughter. "Churning butter on a horse! Lord, I wish I'd thought of that."

Kate rolled her eyes. "I'm surprised you didn't," she said. "And I might have known you'd encourage him."

"Oh, Josh." Stephanie knelt down and gave him a quick hug. "You're very clever, but what if you'd damaged your arm? You could have crippled yourself for life."

"Tater's the horse I rode when I was a little kid," he said scornfully. "I can ride her with one hand tied behind my back, and that's what I did...sort of. Anyway, I didn't use my bad arm."

"The fact remains you disobeyed your father." Everyone turned to stare at Sally, who had come in unnoticed. "If you were my son, you'd be sent to bed without any supper after you received the whipping you deserve!"

Josh jumped up, his eyes blazing. "But I'm not your son, you old witch! If my pa decides to whup me, I'll take it because I deserve it, but it's none of your damn business!" He rudely brushed past her and ran out the door.

With a stricken look at Cole, Stephanie made an inarticulate sound and hurried after Josh.

"Cole, are you going to let your son speak to me that way?" Sally demanded.

Cole's eyes flashed. "I'd say you asked for it."

Sally's eyes momentarily widened with surprise then filled with tears. "I'm sorry, Cole," she murmured, her brown eyes swimming. "I only want Josh to grow up right. The way she was talking to him would only encourage him in his wildness. You can tell she knows nothing about raising children."

"And you do? This is the second time today you've maligned Stephanie for no reason, and she's never been anything but nice to you."

He gave Kate an odd look as she went into a sudden fit of coughing.

Stephanie found Josh leaning against the corral, his head

on his arms as he struggled against his anger.

"Oh, Josh."

With a strangled sob, he turned and buried his face against her shoulder. She held him in her arms, rocking gently back and forth until the last hiccuping sob died away. "Are you all right?"

He nodded. "I shouldn't have said those things to her, but she wants to marry my pa, and I hate her!"

"Sally isn't worth your tears. She makes you want to say mean things, but in the end, you wind up being the one who feels bad."

"You don't like her either, do you?"

"Not particularly."

"Good," Josh said with satisfaction.

There were several moments of silence, then Stephanie chuckled. "I can't believe you used Tater to churn butter!"

"It took an awful long time," he admitted. "What did Grandma Kate mean Pa deserved me?"

"I suspect that was just the sort of thing he used to pull."

"Really? No wonder he thought it was funny." Josh reached out and rubbed his hand along the fence pensively. "What do you think he'll do to me?"

"I don't have any idea, but probably nothing before supper. So there's no reason for us to stand out here starving when Kate and I have fixed a mouth-watering feast. Let's go in."

Josh held back. "What if she's still there?"

"We'll just ignore her, and she'll look pretty silly if she says anything to either of us. Besides, if we stay out here, we'll miss our supper, and she'll have gotten rid of both of us. Frankly, I can't stand the thought of her winning."

"Me, either!" Josh said. "Let's go."

Sally was gone when they returned, and no one mentioned her. The cowhands were as pleased with Stephanie as they were with her food and were full of compliments for both. Cole was relieved to see Stephanie keep her distance without offending anyone. Though they treated her with the utmost respect, some of them were pretty rough characters.

After the men had gone to the bunkhouse for the night, Cole had a long talk with his son. As punishment, Josh was to churn all the butter until his arm healed.

"You know, Pa," Josh said climbing into bed, "Stephanie's right about Sally."

"Oh?"

"She makes you say mean things, but you wind up feeling worse than she does. I think I'll be nice to her from now on." He yawned. "It'll make her mad, cause then she'll have to be nice to me, too." Pulling the blankets up, Josh snuggled down into the bed and closed his eyes. "Good-night, Pa."

"Good-night, Josh." Cole reached down and touched his hair fondly. "I'm glad I have you for a son."

Josh smiled sleepily. "Me too, Pa."

Kate was washing the supper dishes when Cole walked back into the kitchen.

"Where's Stephanie?"

"My cabin. She's only been gone about five minutes, so she'll still be up if you want to talk to her."

Traversing the short distance between the two houses, Cole suddenly realized the last of his reservations about Stephanie had disappeared. She had Kate and Charlie practically eating out of her hand, and the way she handled Josh was nothing short of miraculous. The only one who didn't like her was Sally, and that was probably a vote in Stephanie's favor.

The thought of Sally was like a bad taste in his mouth. They'd come across the herd earlier than expected, so at least he'd avoided making love to her this afternoon. He really hadn't wanted to.

Puzzling over that surprising thought, he opened Kate's door and stood transfixed on the threshold. Dressed in her nightgown, Stephanie sat in front of the mirror, stilled in the process of brushing her hair, staring up at him like a frightened doe.

Cole was thunderstruck. Never had he seen such hair. Falling to her hips in silken waves, it glowed like polished mahogany in the soft candlelight. Red highlights shimmered among the strands of brown enveloping her body in a cloud. Who would have thought so much hair could be restrained in a single braid? It was extraordinarily beautiful, and suddenly so was Stephanie.

Cole's chest tightened as she relaxed and smiled at him in relief. "You startled me."

As if in a dream, he crossed the room and picked up a shining lock, watching it curl enticingly around his hand. It felt just as soft and silky as it looked, and he couldn't help wondering what it would be like to make love to her with the glorious mass curling around him. With the thought, he became aware of her innocent, trusting look and dropped the lock as if he'd been burned. "Why do you hide your hair?"

Stephanie blinked. "Do I?"

"Something that pretty should be flaunted, not bound up in a braid where nobody can see it." Cole turned abruptly and walked to the window.

"I came to thank you for all your help with Josh. I don't know what I'd have done without you. It's damn hard to be mad over something like that. I tried but..." He shrugged helplessly. "Kate wasn't about to help me, either."

"I know." She chuckled. "Josh confessed it took longer than he expected. I take it Tater doesn't have the smoothest trot?"

"Lord, no! I imagine Josh felt like he'd been beaten by the time he was done, and it serves him right." Cole crossed his arms and leaned against the wall. "You've been very good to him. I meant to thank you this afternoon in the barn for taking the time to play games with him. I appreciate it."

Stephanie dismissed his thanks with a wave of her hand. "I enjoy being with him. He really is a delight. Sometimes I feel like I've known him all my life."

"Maybe you have a son of your own."

"Or a younger brother."

Either way, there is someone somewhere who has a prior claim to her, Cole reminded himself. "I'm sorry about Sally. She gets carried away sometimes."

Stephanie's heart sank. If he felt the need to make excuses for Sally, maybe Josh's fears weren't so far off. It was none of her business who Cole chose to marry, of course, but he really should know how his son felt about his intended bride. "I don't think Josh is very fond of Sally," she ventured.

To her surprise, Cole grinned. "Do you know what he plans to do in retaliation for the way she treated him? He's going to be nice to her! He figures she'll have to be nice in return, and she won't like that."

Glancing down, he noticed the pile of cut cloth stacked neatly on the small table next to Stephanie's bed and frowned. "You haven't been making your new clothes. Didn't I choose the right colors?"

She squirmed on her stool. "No, no, the cloth is perfect. I've just been so busy I haven't found the time..." Her voice trailed off when she saw the look of hurt disbelief on his face. "Here, let me show you. She picked up the sketches she'd made and walked over to him. "See, this is the green wool, here's the brown, and these are the two calicos. To tell you the truth, I don't know why I haven't started. I can't wait to wear the dresses, but I keep finding other things to do."

But Cole had lost all interest in the clothes. He was distracted by her hair swirling around her when she walked. As she flipped it over her shoulder, the light of the candle shone through the material of the voluminous nightgown, giving a tantalizing glimpse of the body beneath. His breath
caught in his throat.

The door opened, and Cole silently thanked Kate for her timely intervention. For the second time that day, he'd come close to losing his self-control. Somehow, he needed to find a way to keep reminding himself she'd be going back to her husband eventually.

"Kate, would you make sure Stephanie has time to sew?" he said curtly. "She says she's been too busy. Good-night, ladies." With that, he was gone, leaving both women to stare after him in surprise.

CHAPTER 10

It didn't take Stephanie long to figure out why she hadn't started sewing. She hated it! No matter how hard she tried, her stitches were crooked and uneven. After struggling for nearly an hour finishing a seam, she discovered she'd sewn the wrong sides together.

Cole was so obviously pleased when he came in for the noon meal that she heroically continued for most of the afternoon. By four o'clock, she was sure she'd torn out more than she'd sewn. Kate tried to help, and Stephanie's work did improve with guidance. Unfortunately, it was still mediocre at best.

Finally, frustrated beyond bearing, she wadded up the piece she'd been working on and threw it clear across the room into the corner. "There, you stupid, rotten thing. You can stay there for all I care!"

She hadn't seen Cole walk in, but she whirled around to glare at him when she heard his poorly contained mirth. "Oh, so you think it's funny, do you? It'll serve you right if I die of blood poisoning from sticking the needle in my finger so many times. I'll come back and haunt you until your dying day!" She marched to the door. "After due consideration, I've decided my gray dress isn't so bad after all. In fact, I love it, and I intend to wear it until it falls off!" She flounced out, ignoring the laughter in her wake.

Half an hour later Stephanie returned, looking no less belligerent. Picking up the offending garment, she shook it out and then looked at it closely.

Kate's eyes twinkled. "Ready to do battle again?"

"No, I'm looking for your needle. As soon as I find it, I'm taking this out and burying it! I don't think sewing is one of my favorite pastimes," Stephanie said, glaring at the material in her hand. "In fact, it was probably used as discipline, if not torture, when I was very young."

A snort brought Stephanie's head up with a jerk. Her eyes narrowed as she looked at Kate, who was trying very hard to maintain a straight face. They stared at each other for a long moment, then Stephanie's lips twitched slightly, and a giggle escaped. Suddenly they were both laughing helplessly.

At last, Kate wiped her eyes on her apron and gestured toward the pieces of cloth Stephanie still held in her hand. "Here, let me take a look." She examined them carefully. "Put your shovel away, it's not hopeless quite yet."

Stephanie shook her head sadly. "No, it's useless. Even if I could sew, I'd never have the patience to finish even one dress." She touched the cotton regretfully. "They'd have been beautiful, too."

"I love to sew," Kate said. "I could have these finished in a couple of weeks."

Stephanie was shocked. "Oh, no. You'd never have time with all the men to cook for."

"Why couldn't you do the cooking?"

"I'm not completely sure I could handle it. Cole might object if he started losing men because of the meals."

"Nonsense! You're a wonderful cook. If I can get him to agree, would you trade?"

Stephanie shrugged. "I suppose so."

"Good, then it's settled. The whole thing was Cole's idea in the first place."

"Well, of all the high-handed—" Stephanie paused, then gave Kate a wry look. "Perhaps this is one of those times I should give in gracefully. I really would like something different to wear."

"Good idea," Kate said.

In the end, both women were well satisfied with their bargain. Within three days, Kate had finished the first dress, and Stephanie had rediscovered culinary talents she hadn't known she possessed. The men seemed to enjoy her experimentation and were full of compliments for every new recipe she tried.

One afternoon, Cole came in just as she was removing a pie from the oven. Her face was flushed from the heat as she straightened and placed the pan on the table. Unaware she wasn't alone, she put her hands on the small of her back and stretched.

"Tired?"

"Oh!" She jumped slightly when he spoke, then gave him a sunny smile. "A little, but it's a very pleasant tired."

Cole hung his hat on the peg by the door and sat down at the table just as Charlie came in and sniffed the air.

"Somethin' smells mighty good!" He gave Stephanie a hopeful look.

She put her hands on her hips. "That pie is for supper!" Charlie gazed at her with such a woebegone expression she was hard put not to giggle. "Oh, all right. I made three more, so I guess it wouldn't hurt if you two had a piece now."

Stephanie cut two thick slabs of the hot apple pie and poured three cups of coffee. Sipping hers, she watched the two men eat. "How's the work going?"

"Pretty well," Cole told her between bites. "Most of the cattle are gathered off the range. I figure we'll be able to cut and brand tomorrow."

She gave him a blank look. "You'll be able to what?"

Cole laughed. "I don't know where you come from, but it sure wasn't anywhere in the West!"

"Two other ranches run their cows on the same range we do," Charlie explained. "Them critters don't give a hoot who they belong to, so they just all kinda mix together. When we round them up in the fall, we have to cut our cattle out from everybody else's." He paused. "That means to separate them."

"How in the world do you know which cows are yours?" Stephanie wanted to know.

One corner of Cole's mouth curved upward. "You really are a greenhorn, aren't you?"

"Everybody has their own mark, a brand, that we put on our animals," Charlie said, ignoring Cole's comment. "All you have to do is look at the brand and you know whose critter it is. Our brand is the Triple C Bar, Langton's is the Rockin' L, and Simpson's is the Flyin' J." Seeing her confused expression, Charlie began to trace the brands out with his finger. "Look, three C's over a line is the Triple C Bar. Widda Langton's is an L over a curved line, the Rocking L, and these two little lines at the top of the J make John's a Flyin' J." He took a sip of coffee. "Most of the calves got branded 'fore they went up the mountain last spring, but we missed a few. We need to get brands on them while they're still with their mothers so we can tell who they belong to."

"That makes sense," Stephanie said. "But how do you brand them?"

"I don't reckon you really want to know."

"Of course I do, or I wouldn't have asked."

"It ain't a question of interest," Charlie said, scratching his cheek. "I'm thinkin' it could make you a might squeamish."

"What do you mean?"

Cole sighed. "We set our metal branding irons into the fire until they're red-hot, and then we burn a brand into the calf's side. It heals into a scar that looks just like the branding iron."

Stephanie looked a little ill. "Doesn't that hurt?"

"Yeah, it hurts." Cole appeared to decide it was time to change the subject. "Where's Kate?"

Stephanie's expression brightened immediately. "She's putting the finishing touches on my new dress so I can wear it tonight. I'll be so glad." She made a face as she looked down at her gray dress. "I really do hate this thing."

Charlie chuckled. "I thought you figured on wearin' it a mite longer. In fact, seems to me I heard something about wearin' it till it fell off!"

She grinned. "That was before Kate saved me." She looked at Cole. "I never thanked you for suggesting it."

"It was pure selfishness on my part. I could clearly see I'd have no peace around here if you continued to do it on your own. Besides, having my own personal ghost, no matter how charming, doesn't appeal to me."

"Aha, that got to you did it? I'll have to remember that. Never know when I might need to shake you up."

Charlie grinned. "Don't recall needin' ghosts for a man to be shook up by a pretty girl!"

The expression on Cole's face was unreadable, but for some reason it made Stephanie feel like smiling.

Stephanie gazed in admiration at her reflection in the mirror. "Kate, when you said you could sew, you grossly understated the matter. This is wonderful!"

"I don't think it's just my ability with a needle," Kate said, shaking her head. "You don't even look like the same person. Who would have thought a dress could make that much difference?"

Stephanie looked at herself critically and realized Kate spoke the truth. Her sallow complexion had departed with the gray dress. The apple-green print made her skin glow and her eyes an even more vivid green. A high, tight collar and leg-of-mutton sleeves should have made the dress demure, but somehow had the opposite effect. The tight bodice emphasized the firm breasts and tiny waist, while the skirt hugged the smooth line of her hip as it fell gracefully to the floor. Gone was the skinny child Sally so casually dismissed, replaced by a tall, elegantly slender woman.

While Stephanie admired her new dress, she suddenly remembered Cole's words. *Something that pretty should be flaunted, not hidden.*

"Hmmm. I think this calls for a new hair style." Pulling out the pins that held her braid in place, she began to unplait it with deft fingers. "We may as well make a complete change-over while we're at it."

It soon became apparent that Stephanie was used to wearing her hair in a variety of styles as she tried one after another in rapid succession. At last she was satisfied. With soft waves pulled up into a loose bun at the top of her head, and a few stray ringlets allowed to escape framing her face, Stephanie became utterly feminine. That the deceptively simple coiffure looked as though it might come tumbling down at any minute only added to the charm.

"If I hadn't seen it with my own eyes, I wouldn't believe it," Kate said.

"It is quite an improvement, isn't it?" Stephanie turned and looked over her shoulder at the mirror image of her back. "It's certainly better than that ugly gray thing."

Josh was the first to see the transformation, but his reaction was a little disappointing. He came tearing into the kitchen and stopped in his tracks when he saw her. "What did you do to your hair?"

"I changed it. Do you like it?"

"Won't it get in the way like that?"

"I suppose it might, but I can always wear it the old way when I want to," she assured him.

"Oh, well I guess it's all right, then," he said, and went to wash his hands.

Stephanie smiled wryly. "With Josh around, I certainly don't need to worry about getting swell-headed, do I?"

"Not likely," Kate muttered in disgust. "I haven't met a Cantrell yet that was any good with compliments."

Charlie more than made up for Josh's tepid response a few minutes later. He took one look, swept his hat off his head, and stepped back in surprised approval. "If that don't beat all! Miss Stephanie, you make me wish I was thirty years younger."

His tone was so admiring that Stephanie blushed. "I think, Mr. Hobbs, that you are a flatterer, but I thank you. You make me wish I were thirty years older."

When Cole came in with the rest of the men, his eyes widened in stunned surprise. Speechless with amazement, all he could do for several minutes was stare at her. The cowhands were not so reticent, and before long Stephanie was hard put not to laugh out of sheer, heady pleasure.

After one cowboy paid her a particularly fulsome compliment, Stephanie happened to glance in Cole's direction. His scowl was so forbidding that she looked away in confusion. Several minutes later she peeked at him from the corner of her eye to find his expression even darker than before. *What on earth did I do this time?* she wondered.

He glowered all through the meal, only speaking when someone addressed him directly. Stephanie's discomfort increased until she finally stopped looking at him all together.

The men were discussing the branding that was to take place the next day, and Stephanie listened with interest. Somehow, it sounded more appealing than what Cole had described to her. "Could I come watch for a little while if I stay out of everybody's way?" she asked.

There was a chorus of affirmative answers until Cole's explosive "NO!" brought all conversation to a halt.

Everyone looked at him, but he just continued eating, ignoring the stares.

Charlie finally broke the long silence that filled the room. "T'ain't near as excitin' as these cowpokes make it sound. Truth is, it's hard, smelly work, and it ain't likely you'd enjoy yourself much."

Gradually, the conversation resumed, but Stephanie finished her supper in silence.

Needing time alone to think, Stephanie sent Kate to bed soon after supper and finished cleaning up by herself. Her disappointment was nearly tangible. Not only had Cole not mentioned her changed appearance, he was angry with her for some reason she couldn't fathom. She still hadn't figured it out by the time she set out for Kate's cabin.

"Just a minute." Cole's deep voice came out of the darkness. "I want to talk to you."

Stephanie gave him an uncertain smile. "Oh?"

"I was appalled by your behavior at dinner."

Stephanie blinked. "My behavior?"

I'm talking about the way you were flirting with my men."

"Flirting!" Stephanie's eyes flashed dangerously. "They paid me a few compliments, and I thanked them. I certainly wouldn't call it flirting."

"They've never acted that way before."

"And you don't like it?" Stephanie's anger erupted in a white-hot geyser. "Well, too bad! If you'd left well enough alone, no one would have given me a second glance. I didn't ask for new clothes, and I didn't ask Kate to sew them for me. It was even your suggestion I wear my hair differently. And now, when I get a reaction, it's my fault?"

Perversely, the fact that Stephanie was right made Cole even angrier. "You don't have any idea how dangerous the game you're playing is. These men aren't used to being around women like you."

"Not one of them has ever been anything but a complete gentleman."

He grabbed her upper arms and hauled her up tight against his chest. "Damn it, Steph, don't you realize..." his voice trailed off. The anger faded from her eyes to be replaced by a luminescent glow as they gazed up into his. Never had a woman looked more kissable.

Cole nearly groaned aloud as her lips parted slightly, and his heart began pounding in response. Damn, the temptation she represented. A temptation he had to resist at all costs, he reminded himself sternly. The lady was married. If someone had taken advantage of Maggie in the same situation, he'd have probably killed them. The thought of his dead wife knifed through him like a shard of ice, and he thrust Stephanie violently away.

"If that's the way you react every time a man gets close to you, I hope to hell none of my men ever try. I doubt they'd ignore an invitation like that."

Stephanie's shocked gasp, closely followed by a stinging

slap that made his ears ring, brought Cole to his senses. Suddenly, he realized he was acting like a complete idiot. "Steph, I—"

"Don't even speak to me, you... despicable...Ooo!" Stephanie turned and stalked into the cabin, slamming the door behind her.

Cole stared at the door for a long moment, wondering what madness had possessed him. With a deep sigh, he turned away. Maybe it was better this way. At least he wouldn't have to worry about giving in to temptation. He'd be damn lucky if she ever spoke to him again.

Throwing herself on the bed, Stephanie buried her face in the pillow, her anger still seething within her. How dare he accuse her of flirting? It wasn't like she'd purposely drawn the cowboys' attention or asked for their compliments. How was she supposed to know they'd react that way?

Stephanie jumped to her feet and paced to the mirror. What did she care what Cole Cantrell thought of her, anyway? She tugged her hair loose with shaking fingers and began brushing it with angry strokes. The familiar pull of the brush through her hair calmed her as nothing else could. It wasn't long before her anger melted away, and she found herself fighting tears.

Calling herself a complete and utter fool for letting Cole's attitude affect her so, Stephanie opened the top of Maggie's music box and let the tinkling melody flow around her while her tears fell on the polished wood.

CHAPTER 11

"**G**ood morning," Stephanie murmured to Kate as she slipped into the house to help prepare breakfast. Garbed in her old gray dress, her hair in the familiar braided cornet, she looked the same as she did every morning, except there was no smile on her face.

Cole's guilt was intense, but to see her back in the hated dress was almost more than he could stand. "Why are you wearing that damn thing again?"

She lifted her chin and turned her shoulder toward him in a dismissive gesture. "I don't want to get my new dress dirty after Kate worked so hard on it," she said, joining the other woman at the stove. "Besides, this is more comfortable."

Cole had spent a sleepless night berating himself. Stephanie had been so beautiful in her new dress, with her hair all soft around her, he hadn't been able to take his eyes away. Jealousy had inflamed his temper, but he'd been serious about the warning he tried to give her. She didn't realize how her friendly banter and delicious smiles might be misconstrued by cowboys who were seldom around decent women. But the way he'd done it was unforgivable, and he knew it.

Stephanie avoided contact with anyone but Josh and Kate all during breakfast. One of the cowhands tried to strike up a conversation with her, but she ignored him. After two attempts, he shrugged and turned his attention to his breakfast.

Finally, Cole could take no more. Scowling darkly, he rose from the table and stalked over to the stove, where Kate was cooking thick slabs of ham. "John Simpson said they'd be here early, so you can expect Prudy any time, and stop glowering at me that way. I know what you're thinking, and you're probably right." He slammed his hat on his head. "Just do me a favor, will you? Next time she takes that damn dress off, burn it!"

Prudy Simpson proved to be a jolly, good-natured soul who arrived a short time later amid baskets overflowing with food. She was about Kate's age, and it was obvious the two were close friends. Stephanie found herself surrounded by friendly chatter the minute Prudy walked through the door. It wasn't long before Stephanie knew the Simpson family had four boys, the oldest and youngest of whom had been left at home.

"Billy Ray was plumb disgusted with Tommy falling into that cactus yesterday. He figured it was bad enough he had to stay home to look after things and miss the branding, but now he has to take care of his little brother, too." Prudy chuckled. "Don't know which was the most put out. I just hope they don't kill each other before we get back!"

Good humor filled the kitchen like sunshine as the three women prepared the huge quantity of food needed to feed the branding crew. Stephanie soon felt her bruised feelings begin to heal. It was difficult to stay morose around Prudence Simpson. The woman only uttered one unkind thing all morning.

"*Humph*, seems to me if Sally Langton can send her men over to brand her cattle, she should be here to help feed them." She shrugged her plump shoulders. "I reckon if the men would let her stand around out there, she'd be here right enough!" She glanced at Stephanie questioningly. "You meet our merry widow yet?"

"Unfortunately. She stopped by for tea several weeks ago."

Prudy nodded knowingly. "Couldn't wait to get a look at you. Once she gets her mind set on something she wants, she's not about to take a chance on anything getting in her way." Prudy gave Stephanie a level look. "Sally's set her sights on Cole Cantrell and this ranch. You'd best watch your step around her. She's got a vicious tongue and likes to use it!"

"You don't need to worry about Stephanie," Kate said,

grinning from ear to ear. "Sally already tried her wicked tongue on her. I wish you could have heard it, Prudy. Stephanie had Sally tied in knots, without saying a thing that could even be considered rude."

Stephanie smiled slightly. "No, but the intent was there, and Sally knew it."

"Sally didn't have a chance." Kate chuckled. "I almost choked when she said..."

By the time Stephanie's confrontation with Sally had been thoroughly discussed, it was time to set up long tables and benches outside. With twenty people sitting down to eat, the meal took on a festive air.

After lunch, Josh introduced Stephanie to his friends Ben and Clint Simpson. "You'd hardly know she's a girl."

As a compliment, it was a bit left-handed, but Stephanie smiled and asked if the boys had enjoyed their morning.

"We've been helping," Josh told her proudly. "Pa says we're as good a crew as he could ask for."

"They've been a big help running the irons back and forth to the fires," a deep voice broke in. "I don't know what we'd have done without them." Cole smiled, and all three boys glowed with the praise. "If you hurry, you'll have time to show Ben and Clint the new foal, Josh."

The boys were off like a shot, and Stephanie was left alone with Cole. Her face was flushed, but her voice was cool. "If you'll excuse me, Mr. Cantrell, I have work to do." Lifting her skirts, she started to walk away, but a large firm hand on her elbow stopped her.

"Take a walk with me, Steph." Cole's voice was soft but insistent.

"I don't want to go anywhere with you."

"You don't have to be afraid of me."

"I'm not. I just thought it would be impolite to hit you again after you've shown me so many kindnesses in the past."

He gave her a crooked grin. "Is that what you'd like to do?"

"It was rather satisfying," she said primly, then gave him a side long glance. "Do I need to do it again?"

"No," Cole said with a chuckle. "Once was enough. It got your point across."

She tossed her head. "Good. It stung my hand."

Cole laughed outright at that. While they'd been talking, he had guided her around the edge of the house and headed toward the barn, the only relatively private spot around. "My temper got away from me last night, and you have every right to be angry." His mouth twisted ruefully. "I'm no good at apologies, but I am sorry."

She fought hard to hang on to her anger. After all he'd said... But he seemed so genuinely contrite, embarrassed even, that Stephanie's sense of umbrage began to fade. He'd had a point, after all, even though he'd probably overstated the danger and been an ass about it, to boot. What did she know about men like his cowhands, or any man for that matter? Lesson learned.

"I didn't realize how it looked," she admitted, "and I hadn't even considered the possibility of anyone misunderstanding. It won't happen again." They had reached the corral, and she leaned her arms against the top rail to better gaze at the horses.

"Steph, you didn't do anything wrong," he said softly. He grasped her shoulders and turned her to face him. "Don't let your pride and my stupidity go too far. Think how hard Kate worked on that dress." He raised his hand to finger the thick braid. "And I was right about your hair. It was beautiful."

In spite of her wounded pride, Stephanie felt herself responding to his soft words and gentle touch. Staring into his blue, blue eyes was having the strangest effect on her breathing, and her heart pounded uncomfortably in her chest. Suddenly, something struck her between the shoulder blades, and she was thrown forward, right into Cole's arms.

A deep, rumbling laugh rose in his chest as he set her back on her feet. "I'm afraid Midnight isn't much of a gentleman."

Stephanie swung around and found herself being regarded by a huge black horse she recognized as Cole's usual mount.

Though she'd occasionally seen him from a distance, she'd never been this close before. Josh's Black was big, but Midnight was enormous. He was the image of pure brute strength, with heavy muscles rippling under the shiny black coat.

"Oh, Cole, he's gorgeous! I had no idea," she said, stepping closer to get a better look. Where have you been hiding him?" she exclaimed.

Cole nodded toward the other horses in the corral. "He's been here in the breeding pen with some of the mares when I'm not riding him."

"I can see why. He's absolutely magnificent!" she said, reaching out to stroke the stallion's nose.

"Careful," Cole warned. "He tends to be bad tempered with strangers."

"How can you malign him so?" Stephanie patted the massive neck. "He's a sweetheart." Midnight lowered his head and nudged Stephanie's shoulder as if to prove her point. Instead of backing up, she chuckled and rubbed the space between his ears.

Cole was incredulous as he watched the massive stallion acting for all the world like a pet dog.

"If this is an example of the horses you raise, the world will be flocking to you in droves," Stephanie said with awe. "He's glorious!"

"Actually, he's the product of many years of intensive breeding. So far his foals have proven to be well worth the effort."

Stephanie looked up with her eyes shining. "The mare Sunrise, is her foal by him?"

"No, I wanted to see if she had any trouble foaling first. Midnight's colts tend to be big, and she's too valuable to risk. She did well though, and her next one will be his." Cole smiled. "I hope to start a new line with those two."

"And what a line that will be!"

"You seem to know a lot about horses. Shall we find out if you can ride one?"

"Oh, yes."

"All right, tomorrow morning then." He glanced up at the sun. "The crew should be ready to go out again. Guess we'd better be getting back."

Their return signaled the end of the midday break. The men went back to work, and the three women began the hour-long cleanup.

"Many hands make light work," Prudy said when they had finished. "We've got almost an hour before we have to start supper for that bunch."

When Kate and Prudy sat down with their sewing, Stephanie decided it was time to find other diversion. Surely it wouldn't hurt if she were to watch the branding from a distance.

It wasn't difficult to find; the noise was deafening. Cows and calves bawled to each other as cowboys worked to cut individual calves away from the rest of the herd and then catch them with expertly thrown lariats. Off to one side Stephanie could see men grabbing the calves the riders dragged in and throwing them to the ground.

Determined to get a closer look, she moved forward until she could see the fires and smell the acrid odor of burning hair. A calf stood panting a short distance away. Its head was hanging as blood dripped from a slashed ear, and its sides heaved under the blackened brand.

Suddenly, Stephanie decided she didn't want to see any more and turned toward the now empty corrals. Climbing up on the fence, she gazed north toward the Big Horn Mountains, which rose majestically to the sky.

Her mind wandered lazily as her eyes traced the twin canyons that cut a gigantic 'W' into the mountain. She smiled wryly as she remembered Josh's assurance that the peculiar landform stood for Wyoming Territory.

"Well, if it isn't dear little Stephanie," a sarcastic voice cut into her thoughts.

Glancing over her shoulder, Stephanie saw Sally Langton

mounted on a pretty gray mare. Even dressed in a shirt and denim trousers, with her hair tucked up under a cowboy hat, she was gorgeous. Stephanie felt at a distinct disadvantage, but she hid it well as she favored Sally with a cool smile.

"Why, thank you, Sally. It's been a long time since anyone called me little." Climbing down from the fence, she raised her eyebrows. "I can see you didn't come by to help cook for the crew."

"I don't cook."

"Somehow that doesn't surp—Oh Sally, your horse!" Stephanie cried when she saw bloody foam dripping from the mare's mouth.

"It's her own fault. She fought her head all the way over here," Sally muttered crossly.

"No wonder, the bridle's too tight," Stephanie observed, rubbing the mare's neck to calm her. "The bit must be cutting into her mouth every time you pull on the reins. Here, let me loosen it for you."

As Stephanie reached up to unbuckle the leather strap, Sally jerked the reins, and the horse jumped away. "Don't tell me how to handle a horse! I'm sick to death of your little-miss-perfect attitude. I can't wait for the day when Cole finds out what you really are. And he will, never doubt it!"

"I wouldn't waste my time worrying about someone else if I were you," Stephanie snapped. "When Cole sees what you've done to that horse, he's going to be furious! She turned on her heel and marched off to the house.

Kate and Prudy glanced up in surprise when Stephanie stormed in, eyes blazing and fists clenched. Her curt, "Sally's here," was explanation enough.

Shortly before dinner, Stephanie changed into her new dress. Her long curls fell gracefully over her shoulder from a Grecian knot high on her head. "All right, Sally," she muttered. "If you want to play dirty, I'm ready for you!"

CHAPTER 12

Stephanie was just putting the first bowl of potatoes on the table when she heard Sally's petulant voice.

"Poor Princess, her mouth must have been torn by the bit when she bolted." Sally was clinging to Cole's arm as they came around the side of the house. "I hate to see her in such pain. Can't you do something?"

"Charlie's already taken care of it. If you had paid more attention to the way the bridle fit, it wouldn't have happened." Cole sounded disgusted, and Stephanie fought the urge to smirk.

A moment later she heard Sally suck in her breath in startled surprise when she caught sight of her nemesis. Stephanie raised an eyebrow and smiled blandly. She turned back to her work but not before she saw Sally's eyes narrow with malice and her lips thin. *Tch, tch, tch, shouldn't grind your teeth that way, Sally. You'll wind up a toothless old crone,* Stephanie thought with another small smile. She was aware of a prick from her conscience, but it was only a very tiny prick, and Sally's reaction had been completely worth it.

Her small victory felt hollow to Stephanie, but it helped get her through dinner as she watched Sally fawning over Cole. The attention he gave the beautiful widow lacked sincerity, and his flattery seemed forced. She was all too aware of Sally's victorious smile, but she was able to tell herself that the other woman was having to work a little harder than usual. Though the meal was interminable, the food ashes in her mouth, none of Stephanie's feelings showed on her face as she joined the mealtime conversation.

At last it was over. Sally cast Cole a melting look. "I'm worried about riding Princess with her mouth so sore. Do you think you could ride at least part way with me to make sure it's safe?"

"With Tom and your other men along, I hardly think you need me, too," he said. "Besides, Prudy and John are staying tonight, and I'm looking forward to a long visit."

Thus dismissed, Sally had no choice but to say her regretful goodbyes. Stephanie found it very difficult not to show her satisfaction as her rival disappeared through the door.

John Simpson proved to be as jovial as his wife, and with all the friendly banter, Stephanie's mood lightened. As long as Sally left her alone, she didn't care what went on between Cole and his mistress.

Oh no? said a small voice inside her. *Then why were you so glad he sent her home by herself?* Stephanie chose to ignore the thought.

Once the boys were packed off to bed, Prudy reminded Cole he'd promised to teach her to play chess. There ensued an hour of hilarity as Cole and Stephanie gave instructions.

Finally, Prudy threw her hands up in defeat. "How's a body supposed to remember all these confounded moves? I'm not so sure you aren't making half of them up."

"I swear I'm not," Cole said. "The knight really does move that way. Besides, look at this. You could have my queen in three moves."

"As if you'd let me," she favored Cole with a mock frown. "I don't even feel guilty about putting you out of your bed tonight. You deserve to sleep in the bunkhouse."

"I guess there's no pleasing some people," he said, giving Stephanie a helpless look. "We may as well leave."

With a great deal of teasing, good-nights were said, and Cole escorted Stephanie outside. He took a deep breath of the night air. "There's a touch of fall in the breeze tonight," he said. "It won't be long before the snow flies. We'd better get the horses out of the high country soon."

"It is a bit chilly," Stephanie admitted, rubbing her arms.

He glanced down at her. "You still want to ride tomorrow?"

"If you're hoping I'll change my mind, you're out of luck. I can't wait."

"Somehow, I thought you'd feel that way." Unable to resist the temptation, he traced the soft line of her cheek with his thumb. "I like your hair that way. It's much nicer than the braid."

"Thank you," she said a bit breathlessly. Something warm and wonderful uncurled in the pit of her stomach.

With a reluctant sigh, he dropped his hand. "I guess I'd better get to the bunkhouse. Good-night, Steph. Sleep well."

She stood watching him until he disappeared in the darkness.

The Simpsons left soon after breakfast the next morning. Prudy hugged Kate and turned to Stephanie. "I hope you'll be here for a good long time." As she gave her a quick hug too, she whispered, "Don't give Sally a second thought. She'll never be more to Cole than a bed warmer." Amid the flurry of goodbyes, no one noticed Stephanie's blush.

"Well," Kate said as they disappeared down the road, "if you're going riding, we'd best hurry, or you won't be ready when the men get done with chores."

When they returned to her cabin, Kate pulled a riding habit from the armoire. "Jonathan gave me this when he decided it was time I learned to ride." She smiled ruefully. "It's one of the few times he didn't accomplish his goal. Even if I did ride, I'd never be small enough to fit into this

again. It might be a little short, but with boots it won't matter."

The habit fit surprisingly well, and it wasn't long before Josh arrived and led Stephanie to the corral. Cole and Charlie were leaning on the fence near a small black and white pinto who carried a side-saddle on her back.

"This is Tater," Josh said affectionately. "She's a mountain horse, and Pa says she's one of the best."

"How do you do, Tater." Stephanie stuck out her hand and laughed delightedly as the mare rubbed her head against it. "I think we're going to be great friends."

"Reckon you're ready to give it a try?" Charlie asked.

"As ready as I'll ever be." Placing her foot in his cupped hands, Stephanie sprang into the saddle.

A pair of gnarled hands patted her leg. "Remember, Miss Stephanie, you're in control, but you have to work with your horse, not against it." Fear and anticipation mixed as she looked at the straw-covered floor so far below.

"Steph?" Cole's voice sent the memory skittering back into oblivion. "Have you remembered something?"

She shook her head regretfully. "Only the first time I rode." She sighed. "Just once I wish I'd get more than a glimpse. At least I know I've been on a horse before."

Setting Tater through her paces inside the corral, Stephanie could well understand why Josh had thought of using the mare to churn butter. Her gait was bone-jarring. It didn't matter though. Just being in the saddle was wonderful.

"Please, Cole, can we leave the corral? Tater and I are both in need of a good run."

Cole chuckled. "If that isn't just like a woman, give her an inch, and she wants a mile. All right, I'll get Midnight, and we'll take you ladies for a ride."

Stephanie could barely wait for Charlie to open the gate. She obediently followed Cole and Midnight down past the house to the grassy prairie. He slowed his horse so she could ride up beside him.

"Just head me in the right direction, and we're off," she said.

Cole pointed toward a stand of cottonwoods about half a mile away. "The ground is pretty safe between here and those trees over there."

Stephanie nodded and kicked her horse gently. "Come on, Tater. Let's show these two men how it's done." One thing for sure, she'd definitely ridden before. Even with Tater's impossible gait, it felt as natural as walking.

Cole rode slightly behind, probably to see if she knew what

she was doing. Stephanie and Tater stopped under a large cottonwood and waited for Midnight to catch up.

"That was wonderful! Much more fun than sewing," Stephanie said, her eyes shining with pleasure.

"You do it a whole lot better, too."

She gave him a saucy look. "It's a good thing, or you'd never let me anywhere near your horses."

"Would you blame me? Come on, I'll show you some of the ranch."

They spent a pleasant morning with Cole pointing out landmarks and reminiscing about things he and his brother had done in their youth. The only dark moment came when Stephanie asked about a burned-out shell of a cabin next to the creek.

"It was Charlie's place." Cole said, a shadow crossing his face as he stared at the blackened ruins. "He walked away the day his wife died, and he's never been back."

"He was married?" Somehow, Stephanie had never thought of Charlie having a family.

Cole nodded. "To an Indian woman named Moonflower."

"What happened?"

"They'd been married seven or eight years." He shifted uncomfortably in the saddle. "One day, while we were all out on the range, a gang of rustlers found her alone in the cabin and...abused her. She was still alive when Charlie found her, but there was nothing anyone could do. When she died, he torched the cabin, then he and Pa disappeared for six long days. Both came back looking like they'd seen the fires of hell." Cole shook his head. "Kate said, 'It's done, then?', and Charlie just nodded. None of them ever mentioned it again, but I'll never forget it."

Stephanie shivered in the warm sunshine. It was hard to picture the taciturn Charlie doing such a thing. "He must have really loved her."

"Yeah." Cole turned Midnight away. "But that was a long time ago. What do you say we ride on down the creek a ways and rest the horses before we start back?"

Topping a small rise, Stephanie spied a grassy meadow. "Is it safe for a run?" she asked Cole.

"Yes."

"Good!" Kicking Tater, she called back over her shoulder. "We'll race you." Even with her head start, Midnight outdistanced them so far that Cole was already dismounting when Stephanie and Tater came loping up.

"It was worth losing just to see him run. He must be wonderful to ride!"

"Don't get any ideas. He's way too much horse for any woman to handle." The teasing light in his eye took the sting from his words. Reaching up, Cole grasped her around the waist, lifted her effortlessly out of the saddle, and set her feet firmly on the ground.

Breathlessly, she stepped back and looked around as Cole tied both horses to a log. The trees along the creek were bright with autumn colors under the bluest of skies. "It's beautiful here."

"Mm. Thirsty?"

"Yes." She eyed the clear water of the stream. "I don't suppose you thought to bring a cup?"

Cole laughed. "Definitely a greenhorn. You use your hands like this." He showed her how to cup her hands and drink from them.

Stephanie had trouble getting the hang of it, spilling far more of the cold water than she managed to get in her mouth. Hearing something that sounded suspiciously like a snort, she looked up and found Cole struggling to keep a straight face. "Think it's funny, do you?" she said. With a sweet smile on her face, she rose to her feet, flipped the water from her hands into his face, and darted away.

"Why, you little..." Cole reached out to grab her, but she was too quick. He chased her around the meadow, but each time he nearly had her, she jumped nimbly out of the way.

After several near misses, they stood facing each other,

coiled to spring one way or the other. Feinting to the right, Cole lunged straight at her as she dodged to the left. Wrapping his arms around her, he pulled her off her feet, and they both fell to the ground laughing.

"Throw water on me, will you!"

She giggled. "I didn't see any reason why I should be the only one wet."

"You'll have to pay the price of your folly." Cole glanced at the nearby creek.

Her mouth dropped open. "You wouldn't dare."

"Oh yes, I would." He sighed regretfully. "But you'd probably freeze to death before we got home." With lightning speed, he rolled over, pinning her beneath him. "This will work just as well!

She squealed as he rubbed his wet face against hers. "There, now I'm dry."

She touched his mustache. "Not quite. You forgot this little item."

"That's easily taken care of," he growled, rubbing the wet hair against her upper lip. The touch became a kiss, soft and unbelievably sweet. Stephanie's arms slid around his neck as his tightened. Together they spiraled into a sea of sensation. Cole gently pulled the pins from her hair.

When one became tangled, the momentary pain jerked Stephanie back to her reality, and she tried to pull away.

At first Cole resisted. She felt so good in his arms, he wanted to keep her there forever. It would be pleasant and probably easy to kiss her into submission again. Then, with a sudden guilty lurch, he realized what he was thinking. Theirs was a simple, uncomplicated friendship, one that wouldn't hurt either of them when the time came for Stephanie to go. Kisses in a grassy meadow had no place in it. He released her abruptly.

Stephanie sat up, drew her legs up to her chest and dropped her head to her knees.

"Steph?"

Her only response was a shake of her head.

He moved to her side and raised her face with a finger. Her tears surprised him. "What's wrong?"

"I shouldn't have acted like that."

"Like what?"

"Like a...a whore!"

He stared at her. "Steph, it was only a kiss!"

"But I liked it!"

"So did I."

"But women aren't supposed to. Sally thinks I have something to hide. If I'd been...well, one of those women...maybe I can't remember because I don't want to."

"That's ridiculous. Women like kissing as much as men. And you weren't a prostitute."

"How do you know?"

"Your response was too natural. It wasn't practiced." He stared off toward the mountains. "Steph, don't be ashamed of responding to a man's kiss. It's a reflex, kind of like breathing. These things happen between men and women, especially if they like each other."

"Just a kiss between good friends?"

"Yes."

She smiled slightly. "Do you kiss all your friends?"

"Only the women."

"Did you ever kiss Mrs. Simpson?" she asked in a teasing voice.

"No, but then Prudy never threw water on me, either."

"That's probably because you never tried to drown her."

"You did that yourself. It's not my fault your hands leak." He rose to his feet and extended his hand. "Come on. It's time we went home." He pulled Stephanie to her feet and handed her three hairpins. "Here, you'll need these." Without another word, he walked off to catch the horses.

CHAPTER 13

"**Y**ou know, Cole, I've been riding Tater over a week now," Stephanie said one morning at breakfast. "And I haven't had a single problem with her."

Cole looked up from his breakfast. "So?"

"So when can I ride a different horse?"

"When I'm convinced you can handle one. We don't have any other horses gentle enough for a woman."

Stephanie was indignant. "I can handle any horse on the place!"

The look Cole gave her said more clearly than words what he thought of that claim. "I'll say when you ready. Until then, Tater will just have to do."

Though it wasn't easy to do, Stephanie wisely held her tongue. A devious plan was already beginning to form in her mind, and she didn't want Cole to be suspicious.

When Josh finally got Doc Addley's permission to ride, he immediately started working Black again and didn't seem to mind when Cole and Charlie took the crew back to the mountain to round up the horses. In fact, he barely even took time to talk to John Simpson, who stopped by the house before joining the other men.

John didn't appear to notice. He was almost apologetic as he handed Stephanie a package. "Prudy said you'd be needin' these, but what you want with Billy Ray's outgrown clothes is beyond me."

Mystified, Stephanie thanked him, and he walked away shaking his head. Inside the brown paper, she found a cryptic note lying on top of a shirt and denim trousers.

Sally's not the only one who can ride with the men.

Stephanie smiled at the less-than-subtle hint. So, Prudy thought she should learn to ride astride. Maybe that wasn't a bad idea.

She took the clothes to the cabin and changed. With Josh's help, it wasn't long before Tater was saddled, and Stephanie was mounted up. To her surprise, it felt as natural as the side-saddle. Obviously not all of her riding had been lady-like.

Josh and Stephanie spent most of the next three days riding together. When Cole returned, it was to find Stephanie apparently quite content to ride Tater.

She hadn't mentioned the possibility of riding a different horse, but she was far from complacent. One morning while she was down at the barn watching Charlie mend a bridle, she broached the subject with him. "Charlie, you've seen me ride. Would you say I'm competent?"

"I reckon you're a durn sight more'n that. I ain't never seen a woman could ride as good as you, ceptin' Miss Maggie, and she wasn't any better."

"Then why won't Cole let me on anything but Tater?"

"You gotta understand Cole." Charlie removed his hat and ran his fingers through his hair. "He don't always use good sense, but he's got a protective streak in him a mile wide. He's afraid you'll get hurt, and this is his way of protectin' you. I reckon he'll change his mind soon enough."

Charlie's insight strengthened Stephanie's resolve to prove to Cole that she was a capable rider. If Charlie suspected anything was afoot when she started paying visits to the barn at odd hours, he never said a word.

One evening, while feeding Midnight a carrot and talking quietly to him, Cole's voice made her start guiltily.

"Are you trying to spoil my horse?"

Stephanie knew a moment of panic until she looked up into his smiling face. When there was no accusation, only gentle, teasing humor, she decided to brazen it out. "No. I just decided he deserved something special. Carrying you around all day can't be easy."

"That's true. It takes a big horse to pack my weight, and he does a good job of it. Still, if you keep feeding him all these carrots and apples, he'll get so fat I won't be able to get my saddle on him."

"Apples?" Stephanie asked innocently.

Cole's mouth twisted sardonically. "Yes, apples. I found pieces of them in his stall."

"Well, he appreciates it even if you don't. Isn't that right, Midnight?" As if in answer, the huge horse blew gustily through his nose.

"I see how it is. You're not satisfied with having my family wrapped around your little finger. You have to win my horse's affection too."

It was so close to the truth that Stephanie avoided his eyes. "Did you want me for something?"

"As a matter of fact, I came to challenge you to a game of chess."

"Oh?" she asked sweetly. "Are you in the mood to lose?"

"Ha, I have no intention of losing. I plan to show no mercy."

"And that's supposed to scare me?" Giving Midnight one last pat, she left the barn with Cole still completely unsuspicious.

The next morning, Stephanie rose silently and dressed in her britches just as the sun was beginning to lighten the eastern sky. With a bridle in one hand and an apple in the other, she crept stealthily into the barn. Midnight whickered a greeting and accepted the apple without hesitation. Munching happily on his apple, he didn't even react as she slipped the bridle over his head. Nor did he pay any attention as she lugged the saddle over. The horse was so tall she had to balance the heavy saddle against her chest and heave it up with her arms. Panting from the exertion, she tightened the cinch under his belly. Once outside, she opened the corral gate and handed him the carrot she'd stowed in her pocket. "Well, boy, are you ready for this?"

Stephanie had difficulty getting her left foot high enough to place it firmly in the stirrup. When she did, she had to bounce a couple of times on her right foot, to gain enough momentum to pull herself up and swing her leg over the saddle. Midnight pranced around a bit, unaccustomed to the much lighter weight on his back. Tossing his head, he tested her hold on the reins and found it firm. Stephanie sighed in relief when he settled, apparently satisfied that his rider was in control.

She rode him away from the barn and headed north. She didn't want to go by the house and risk discovery before she'd had her ride. In her explorations with Josh, she'd learned the lay of the land and now set out for a huge grassy area about a mile from the house. Gradually increasing their speed until they were cantering, Stephanie was amazed at how smooth his gait was and marveled again at the magnificence of the animal. By the time they reached the meadow, Midnight was pulling at the bit, and Stephanie could tell he was as anxious for a run as she was.

Taking a deep breath, she gave him a gentle kick and felt his muscles bunch beneath her. In an explosion of power, he took off at a high lope. It was just like riding a smoothly rolling river as Midnight lengthened his stride. The stallion's amazing power and speed coupled with his easy flowing gait was even more incredible than she had expected.

Everything ceased to exist except the wind whipping past her face and the stallion beneath her. Stephanie laughed in sheer exuberance as they thundered across the prairie. When they reached the hills, she reined in and patted the horse's neck. "Oh, Midnight, you are a love!"

Turning toward home, she sighed in regret. They'd been gone long enough for her absence to have been noted, and it was no part of her plan to cause anyone to worry. At least when all hell broke loose—and she was sure it would—she'd have this glorious ride to remember.

They returned at a more sedate pace and had almost reached the house when Stephanie caught sight of Cole standing outside. She felt a surge of defiance. "Might as well be hung for a sheep as a lamb," she muttered. Kicking Midnight to a gallop, they thundered into the yard and slid to a stop just inches from Cole.

"What the hell do you think you're doing?" His voice was very quiet, but a muscle jumped in his cheek and his eyes glittered dangerously.

"Oh, just going for a ride," she answered with a nonchalance she didn't feel.

"Damn it, woman," he roared. "What are you using for brains?"

Midnight danced nervously, and Stephanie leaned down to rub his neck soothingly. "Cole, you're upsetting him!"

He lowered his voice. "You little fool, you could have both been hurt. I told you before, he's too much horse for you to handle."

"On the contrary, I had no problems with him at all. We've had the most delightful run, and as you can see, we both came through it just fine. And for your information, my brains are working perfectly. I believe I just proved I'm ready to move up from Tater."

"That's not the point," he ground out. "You went against direct orders, endangering yourself and a very valuable horse in the process."

"There was never the least danger for either of us. I've ridden that ground a dozen times with Josh this past week, so I knew it was safe. I also made very sure I could handle Midnight before we ever left the yard. Anyway, you never forbid me to ride Midnight or any other horse for that matter."

Cole gritted his teeth. "Are you coming down off that horse, or do I have to pull you off?"

"Not just now, I think. Midnight needs a rub-down, and I intend to give it to him. I don't think he'll let you pull me off his back, either. He doesn't take kindly to rough handling."

Hearing a smothered laugh, Stephanie glanced over Cole's head. Kate and Charlie were standing at the door, both grinning. She looked back at Cole's glowering countenance. "If you'll excuse me, I think Midnight's been standing long enough. I don't want him to take a chill."

Cole's expression was decidedly odd as it gradually changed from a glare to something else. Then, unexpectedly, he began to laugh.

"Cole?" Stephanie stared at him. Had he lost his mind?

But Cole only laughed harder. The loud noise made Midnight nervous, and Stephanie had her hands full trying to control his prancing.

At last Cole subsided. "All right, you win! Damned if Maggie didn't do the same thing. Go ahead, give him his rub-down. It'll serve you right if you have trouble getting the saddle off. I can't imagine how you got it on him in the first place." Giving Midnight a slap on the hind quarter, he chuckled to himself as he watched them trot off to the barn.

By the time Stephanie was through with Midnight, the others had almost finished breakfast. She slid into her place and calmly picked up her fork. "Pass the eggs, please."

With a sardonic grunt, Cole threw down his napkin and stood up. "Have you had enough, or would you like another ride this afternoon?"

She looked up at him. "On Tater?"

"No, you proved your point. I think I have just the horse for you." He put on his hat and strode to the door. "I'll see you at noon." He paused and gave her a warning look. "And stay off my horse!"

Stephanie sighed in relief the minute he walked out the door.

Josh bubbled with curiosity. "Did you really take Midnight for a run?"

Stephanie nodded. "Yes, and it would have been worth it even if your father had given me the beating I deserve."

"How did you do it? Nobody but Pa has ever ridden him before. He won't even let Charlie on his back."

Startled, Stephanie looked at Charlie, who grinned back at her. "That's so. I can't even get a foot in the stirrup 'fore he blows higher'n a kite."

"Oh, Lord!" Swallowing hard, Stephanie laid her fork

down on her plate. "Thank goodness that horse is a fool for apples."

Josh and the two men were so obnoxiously mysterious during lunch that Kate was finally driven to retort, "Land sakes, if you three aren't a sore trial! Settle down, or I'll box all your ears!"

The minute the meal was over, Josh jumped to his feet and grabbed Stephanie's hands. "Come on. We've got a surprise for you."

"As soon as the dishes are done," she said. "It wouldn't be fair to leave Kate with all the clean-up."

"No, no, you'd best go with them," Kate said. "We can't get much done with all these men underfoot anyway. Besides, I want to see what they're up to myself."

"Best git yer ridin' togs on." Charlie's leathery features looked almost as excited as Josh's. "I got a feelin' you ain't gonna want to take time to change later."

Cole smiled. "I'll be at the barn. You bring her down when she's ready, Josh."

Infected with the men's excitement, Stephanie donned her riding habit in record time. Josh grabbed her hand as soon as she appeared and made her close her eyes. With Josh and Kate leading her, it was only with supreme effort that she was able to resist peeking, especially when she heard

Kate's murmured, "Glory be!"

After what seemed like an eternity, Josh said, "You can open your eyes now!"

There, standing patiently at the hitching rack, the side-saddle on her back, was Sunrise. Stephanie's eyes flew to Cole and Charlie, who were grinning like two schoolboys.

"Oh, Cole," she breathed. "Sunrise?"

"If you can ride Midnight, you can handle her with no trouble at all. Neither Charlie or I have the time to give her the exercise she needs, and Josh is too busy with Black."

"Besides," Josh put in, "you belong together. Her mane and tail are the same color as your hair."

It took about thirty seconds in the saddle for Stephanie to fall madly in love with the mare. Sunrise proved to be as smooth a goer as Midnight and much easier to handle. This time when Stephanie challenged Cole, he and Midnight were hard pressed to keep up with the lighter pair. They finished neck and neck, with Stephanie's laughter ringing on the wind.

When Cole lifted Stephanie down, she was bubbling with enthusiasm. "Thank you, thank you, a thousand times thank you! She's wonderful, marvelous, fantastic! Oh, how can I tell you?"

"I take it you're satisfied with my choice?"

"She's perfect." She threw him a mischievous look. "Besides, if I ever want variety, I can just borrow Midnight."

"If I ever catch you on him again, I'll put you on bread and water for a month!" Cole warned.

Suddenly, she sobered. "No, I won't, Cole. I had no idea he was a one-man horse. If I had, I'd have never attempted such a foolish stunt."

"I still can't believe he let you do it. He half killed a man who tried to steal him two years ago. Must be a sucker for a pretty face."

Stephanie giggled. "More like a sucker for apples. I never saw such a pig. I swear he ate a barrel full. I finally had to start giving him carrots. The only time I was afraid I'd made a mistake was when you started laughing like an idiot. I almost lost him, you know."

Cole shook his head. "He was only playing around. I don't know how, but you charmed him."

"I couldn't think of any other way to convince you I could ride. What was so funny anyway?"

"You. Your expression looked just like Josh's when he churned the butter, sheepish and defiant at the same time."

"At least I finally got through to you."

"Actually, this is the second time I had been taught that lesson. Maggie did the same thing."

"She rode Midnight?"

'No, this was long before I had Midnight. Josh was just a baby at the time." He smiled softly, remembering. "When I came in for lunch one day, she put a squalling Josh in my arms, then calmly walked out, got on my horse, and rode away. Jupiter wasn't a brute like Midnight, but he was plenty big. It seemed like she was gone forever, and I was scared half to death."

"When she finally came back, she swung down, handed me the reins, took Josh, and walked into the house without saying a word. I raged at her for a good half hour, but she just sat there feeding the baby. After I finally ran down, she looked up and said, 'So when do I get a decent horse to ride?'"

"After that she always got the best." He sighed. "We spent two years looking for just the right mare for Midnight and picked Sunrise out together... She never even got to ride her." His voice broke, and he looked away.

A lump formed in Stephanie's throat as she watched him. Maggie must have been very special for him to have loved her so much. She touched his arm regretfully. "I'm sorry, Cole."

He looked down at her and smiled sadly. "Maggie would have loved the way you came in looking for all the world like you'd just taken Midnight for a casual morning jaunt. If she'd been here, she'd have probably demanded I put you on Sunrise herself."

"I wish I could have known her."

"Me too. You'd have liked each other, I think." Suddenly, he gave Stephanie a wry smile. "I never thought I'd meet another woman as headstrong and uncontrollable as Maggie, but I do believe you might be worse. Not even she ever dared to ride Midnight."

CHAPTER 14

"Queeny went back up the mountain?" Cole looked concerned as he joined Charlie at the table for lunch. "Are you sure?"

"'Fraid so. I was keepin' a look out for her cause she's been acting sorta strange since she lost her colt. I ain't seen hide nor hair of her or that bunch of two-year-olds that hang around her for almost a week. This morning I found their tracks headin' back up the mountain."

"Damn, if it were any mare but Queeny..." He glanced out the window. "We're due for snow in the high country any day now. I don't know why it's held off this long."

"Can't help wonderin' why they went back up. Animals ain't usually so stupid." Charlie was as stoic as always, but Stephanie detected a thread of worry in his voice.

Cole sighed. "We'll have to go after them. We can't afford to lose Queeny. She's one of our best mares."

"I sorta figured you'd feel that way." Charlie took a sip of coffee. "We ought to go tomorrow, but that mountain's too big fer just you and me. We need at least two more men.

Can't take a chance on bein' alone up there."

"I'll go!" both Josh and Stephanie chimed in at the same time.

"No!" Cole was adamant. "That's rough country, and it'll be a hard ride."

"I did all right when I went up before," Josh pointed out. "And Stephanie can ride better than most men. You said so yourself."

"Don't see as how we got much choice, Cole," Charlie said, ignoring Cole's stubborn expression. "They both got the stuff it takes, and we know we can trust these two. Never know what you're gettin' for sure when you go to town and hire a couple of out-of-work cowboys."

"We can't take Dreamer away from Sunrise for that long, and I don't want to take Stephanie up the Mesa Trail on a horse she isn't used to."

"Dreamer's a good strong colt. I reckon she'll do just fine."

Cole looked at Stephanie. "Are you sure you want to go? It's considerably rougher than any riding you've done around here," he warned.

"I'm not afraid of a little hard riding. I rode Midnight, didn't I?"

Cole rolled his eyes. "It's not the same thing, believe me."

They rose before the sun and were already finishing breakfast when the eastern horizon turned pink. In spite of her bravado, Stephanie felt a tremor of dread as they rode toward the Big Horns. She didn't think she knew much about mountains, but these seemed very different from what her limited experience told her was common. They didn't form peaks at the top but rather rose straight up from the foothills to a gigantic, flat-topped rimrock. The barren, rocky face had been cut and gouged over the eons by myriad streams that had long since disappeared. They looked impossible to climb.

She was relieved when they headed away from the twin canyons that formed the *W*, toward a portion of the mountain that appeared much gentler. As Sunrise followed the well-defined trail through the sagebrush, Stephanie wondered again why Cole had been so insistent about leaving the side-saddle home. Even stranger was Josh's calm acceptance of his father's decree that he'd be riding Tater instead of Black. In less than half an hour, Stephanie found out why.

Cole called a stop to rest the horses before beginning the ascent. He pointed to a narrow trail snaking its way up through a pile of tumbled rock perhaps one hundred fifty feet high. "Well, Steph, that's the Mesa Trail." He gave her a challenging look. "You can still change your mind and go home. Nobody will say a word."

Stephanie was tempted to do just that as she stared in disbelief at the rugged trail. Charlie's face was carefully blank, but she could tell Cole expected her to turn tail and run. She stiffened her spine. She wouldn't show a crumb of anxiety, even if it killed her. "Don't be silly."

Charlie looked up at the mountain. "It ain't so bad once you get past the hogback." He pointed to the top of the huge pile of rocks. "From there on, you just go up the face." Since the mountain looked like it rose nearly straight up from the top of the hogback, Stephanie wasn't exactly soothed by the information.

All too soon, they were ready to go. Cole led the way, instructing Stephanie to stay a fair distance in back of him and to let Sunrise find her own footing. Dreamer trailed behind her mother, and Josh and his dog, Sam, fell in behind her, with Charlie bringing up the rear. It was far worse than Stephanie had imagined. The trail was impossibly narrow as it wound in and out among the huge rocks. When they finally reached the top of the hogback, the barren face of the mountain stretched above them ominously. The trail zig-zagged up, skirting boulders and sagebrush as it climbed. Nervously, she clutched the horn of her saddle, and a somehow familiar voice rang in her head: *A good horseman has no need to hang on with their hands. The horn wasn't put there for that purpose.*

Oh, shut up! Stephanie thought irritably. Whoever told her that had obviously never been asked to ride up the Mesa Trail. The climb was so steep Stephanie felt as if she were going to slip off the back of the saddle as Sunrise labored up the slope. Once, when Cole was above her on the zigzag trail, Midnight's hooves sent a small avalanche of rocks tumbling toward her, and Stephanie nearly choked on the knot of fear that rose in her. Moments later, Sunshine stumbled, and Stephanie's heart jumped to her throat once again.

The others seemed totally unaffected, laughing and joking back and forth during the frequent stops to rest the horses. Otherwise they rode single-file, making conversation impossible. Stephanie was glad. She didn't want anything to interrupt her concentration as she repeated to herself, over and over, *I will not scream. I will not cry. I will not scream. I will not...*

After what seemed like an eternity, they rounded a huge granite cliff. They had reached the rimrock at last. Though the trail still continued upward between two rock walls, it was wider and not as steep. Cole pulled Midnight to the side. "Wait a minute, Steph, I want to show you something."

Stephanie couldn't resist a sigh of relief as she reined in behind Midnight to allow Charlie and Josh to pass. She was still saying silent prayers of thanks when Cole pointed back over her shoulder.

"Look."

She looked back and gasped at the sight that met her eyes. From the high vantage point, the whole world seemed to lie at their feet. She felt as though she could see forever in three directions, and it was an awe-inspiring sight. Most of the land undulated in high rolling hills, covered with bluish-gray sagebrush, with an occasional bright splash of fall colors along a creek. Cole pointed out the blue mountains to the west, hazy in the distance. "That's the Owl Creek range. Those mountains are almost a hundred miles from here." He raised his eyebrows questioningly. "So, was it worth the ride?"

"Oh, yes, it's beautiful!" She gave him an innocent look. "What makes you think the ride bothered me?"

"I heard you muttering under your breath all the way up here."

Stephanie blushed, unable to think of a suitable reply.

"Maggie cursed nonstop the first time she came up, and she didn't do it under her breath, either," Cole said as he pulled Midnight's head around and started back up the trail. "Guess we'd better get moving, or Charlie and Josh will be wondering what happened to us."

Within a few minutes, they stood on the edge of a huge grassy mesa. After the brutal climb, Stephanie was amazed at the gently rolling mountain top. It appeared almost flat, and she blinked her eyes several times to make sure she wasn't seeing things.

"We'll rest awhile and let Dreamer nurse," Cole said, swinging down from the saddle. "You may as well get down and stretch your legs."

She dismounted, grateful for the chance to exercise her cramped muscles. Cole stood watching Stephanie and Josh gamboling through the yellowed grass with Sam. "You'd never guess she was scared spitless such a short time ago," he remarked.

"Reckon she's one who bounces back pretty fast." Charlie lifted his hat and scratched his head. "If Josh and me go around by Red Canyon and you ride over by Packsaddle Springs, we'd pretty much cover the range."

Cole nodded. "Sounds good. We'll meet over by the Quakers and noon up." He glanced at the sun. "If we haven't found the horses by then, we'll at least have a pretty good idea where to look."

Stephanie was enthralled by the beauty of the landscape as they rode across the mountaintop. Most of it was open range, but there were some stands of pine and a few aspens whose bright autumn orange lent a splash of color. They rode for over two hours, crossing small streams, skirting granite boulders, and finally going through a small but rugged canyon.

"There's the Quakers," Cole told her, nodding toward a large stand of quaking aspens. "We'll meet Charlie on the other side."

They came out onto a huge grassy meadow surrounded on three sides by quaking aspens. The fourth side fell off into a blue-green haze where the meadow met the edge of the mountain. "How beautiful," Stephanie murmured, taking a deep breath of the pungent mountain air. "Does this place have a name?"

Cole shrugged and nodded toward a small spring that burbled up through some nearby rocks. "The same as that, I guess. They call it Rat Springs."

"Rat Springs! How could they name such a wonderful place something like that?" Stephanie asked indignantly.

"Cowboys don't have much imagination when it comes to naming things, I guess."

"Well, I think whoever thought it up should be shot," Stephanie told him indignantly.

"He was," Cole said as he pulled the saddle from Midnight's back. "When the ladies of Horse Creek found out who was responsible, they were so mad they formed a vigilante committee. He was an old man by then and didn't put up much of a fight when they sent him before a firing squad, demanding justice." Cole shook his head. "The men folk were a little embarrassed by the whole thing, so they buried him over there by the spring."

Stephanie glanced at the nearby stream. When she turned back and found Cole grinning at her, she knew she'd been duped. "You weasel!" She swept her hat from her head and threw it at him. Cole ducked, his eyes dancing with merriment as he pulled the hobbles from the saddle bag.

While Cole unsaddled Sunrise, Stephanie unpacked the lunch they'd brought and spread a blanket on the ground to sit on. After hobbling both horses, Cole stretched out next to her on the blanket with a sigh and put his hat over his face.

A glimmer of mischief entered Stephanie's eyes. Plucking a long stem of grass, she began to tickle his ear. He brushed what he thought was an annoying insect away, only to have it return again and again. Without warning, he reached up and grasped Stephanie's wrist in a crushing grip.

"People have died for less than that," he growled.

"I know," She giggled. "Why, the poor soul who named this place met his maker in front of a firing squad!"

"You're asking for trouble, young lady." He removed the grass stem from her grasp. "Punishment in the West is swift and merciless."

"Oh, I'm scared!"

"You'd better be." Releasing her arm, Cole settled himself again.

Stephanie felt a warm glow of contentment and realized suddenly that she was happy here.

But even today the dark shadow of uncertainty rose to destroy her pleasant thoughts. She had begun to dread the day when someone showed up to claim her. What if her past was something she didn't want to return to?

Not knowing who she was or how she came to be stranded in the middle of nowhere haunted her. The nightmare didn't come so often now, but it always made her think she must have left someone behind, someone she was terrified of. Suddenly she didn't want to be alone with her thoughts anymore.

"Cole?"

"Mmm?"

"Have you ever wanted to live anywhere else?"

"Nope."

"Even when you were away at college?"

Cole lifted his hat and looked at her. "Especially not then. It was the worst four years of my life."

"Then why did you go?"

"I didn't go. I was sent."

"Sent! By who?"

"My father." He put the grass stem in his mouth. "It was part of the deal when Levi and I convinced him to let us raise horses. He said he'd back us financially and help us get started if we'd agree to get the proper training."

"They teach that in college?"

A brief smile crossed his face. "My father figured we'd need eastern connections if we were going to sell to men rich enough to spend a fortune on a good horse. He decided one of us should go to his alma mater and mingle with the sons of the elite while the other spent three years working with my Uncle Daniel."

"Your uncle?"

"He raises Thoroughbreds in Illinois. Pa left it up to us to decide which of us would go where. We fought about it for several days and finally wound up drawing straws."

"And?"

"I lost." He put his hands behind his head as he watched a few fluffy clouds overhead. "Levi went to Chicago, and I went to the College of New Jersey in Princeton."

"New Jersey? Surely you could have gone someplace closer."

"Probably, but my father had been a professor there before the War between the States, and he had connections. Still does, for that matter."

"Your father was a professor at Princeton?" she said in surprise.

Cole nodded. "He taught mathematics, but he knew enough about everything else to give my brother and I a well-rounded education." He sighed. "I think Pa had always figured on at least one of us attending a university, because I wasn't behind in my studies when I got there."

"So you fit right in."

Cole gave a humorless laugh. "Hardly. I was too big, too loud, and too different. It didn't take long to discover the people I was supposed to meet were not the kind I'd willingly choose for friends."

"Why not?"

"We had nothing in common. Since I came from the West, they considered me completely uncivilized. The men were constantly trying to show me how ignorant I was and unskilled at their pursuits. It sort of became a hobby with me to beat them at their own games. I even took up fencing."

"Fencing! You don't seem like a swordsman to me."

"Actually, I wasn't half bad, not that I've had much chance to use it since," Cole said. "My best skill was boxing, probably because of all those fights with my brother. A few knockouts, and I had most of the men won over."

"And things got better?

He shrugged. "A little, I guess, but I still didn't have the faintest idea of how to get along in society. Besides, they disgusted me as much as I disgusted them. Not one of them had ever done a day's worth of work in his life. Money was a god to them, but they had never earned a penny of it for themselves."

"Surely they weren't all that bad."

"No, not all," he admitted. "And once I kind of got the hang of how to act at fancy dinner parties and balls, I was more acceptable."

"Somehow I can't picture you on a dance floor."

Cole shrugged. "To be honest, that's about the only thing I enjoyed."

"Ah." Stephanie nodded wisely. "I might have known you were a ladies' man."

"No, it was the dancing I liked, not the women. They were worse than the men. I never met one I could stand or that was interested in anything but money and social standing. Every last one of them was vindictive, spiteful, and mean."

"I find it hard to believe that all the women behaved so shabbily toward you," Stephanie protested.

"Oh, there were a few that were willing to overlook my unfortunate background. I even fell for one named Penelope Van Horn. She was the most beautiful girl I'd ever seen, and I thought she cared for me, too."

"Are you sure she didn't?"

He gave her a sardonic smile. "Positive. I overheard her telling her friends how amusing it was to be courted by such a man, because you just never knew when the trappings of civilization were going to fall away and expose the barbarian beneath. Then she shared some of our more private moments. They were all highly entertained by my ineptitude."

Privately, Stephanie couldn't help thinking he had misread the situation. There was no way all the young women would scorn a man as handsome as Cole, even if he weren't quite socially acceptable. More likely they were titillated by the stories Penelope told and giggled because they were all aflutter with lustful yearnings. It was not something a man like Cole would comprehend. "Perhaps you misunderstood."

Cole shook his head. "Ah, no...I don't think so. The parties were like battle zones, with all of them trying to outdo each other. After the first few I stayed away."

"You must have been horribly lonely," Stephanie murmured.

"I was until I looked up an old friend of Kate's." Rolling onto his side, he braced himself on one elbow and took the grass out of his mouth. "If Kate had known, she'd have skinned me alive."

"Why?"

"Rosie owns a....well...a brothel."

Stephanie drew in a shocked breath. "And she was a friend of Kate's?"

"Still is, though they haven't seen each other in years. She was one of the few women here when Kate came to Wyoming. Kate says she owes Rosie a debt she can never repay." He gave Stephanie a roguish smile. "So do I. You'd be surprised how many friends I made by taking them to Rosie's place. I brought in so much business, Rosie jokingly offered to make me a partner."

Stephanie smiled. "Somehow I have a feeling you never told Kate about that, either."

"Not hardly! She'd have blistered my ears if I had. Anyway, Rosie didn't mind if I took her girls out for drives, on picnics, or just sat there and talk to them if I wanted to. It kept me from dying of loneliness."

"And you accomplished what your father sent you to do?"

"Sure did. Over the years, we've sold a lot of horses through the contacts I made. I got a pretty good education out of it, too," he admitted ruefully. "It also convinced me I have no desire to rub elbows with the wealthy except to sell them horses. I'd rather deal with an irritated grizzly than a rich woman."

Looking down at the piece of grass in his hand, Cole's

brows came together. "Hmm, seems to me there's a small matter of revenge to be taken care of."

Stephanie suddenly found herself pinned to the blanket. "Western justice is merciless," Cole said, tickling her face with the piece of grass.

She squealed in protest as the grass traced the sensitive skin between her lips and her nose in light, feathery strokes. It was pure torture, and he knew it.

Cole grinned as she twitched her nose helplessly. "When will you learn I always get even?"

"Let me scratch my nose before I go crazy!" she shrieked at him.

"Do you have an itch? Where?" He kissed the bridge of her nose. "Here?" His lips touched her eyebrow. "Or maybe here? No...I think here." His mustache brushed the corner of her mouth, and she was lost as his lips caressed hers with gentle persuasion.

Cole pulled the pins from her hair. The silky mass fell about them in glorious abandon, shining in the sun-kissed mountain air. Just as his hand brushed her breast in a tingling caress, Midnight nickered a greeting to another horse.

Cole rolled to his feet in a single fluid motion. "That'll be Charlie and Josh."

Startled, Stephanie blinked up at him.

Sheepishly, he opened his hand and let the hairpins he held fall into her lap. "I can't seem to leave these things alone." Gazing at her face, he almost groaned aloud. Tousled hair framed her flushed face, and the emerald eyes were luminous with desire. It was all he could do not to pull her into his arms and finish what he'd started. Watching her efficiently braid her hair and wind it around her head didn't slow his pulse at all. Neither did the thought that he had no right to touch her in the first place.

All at once, her eyes widened in surprise. "Cole, I saw something move in those trees. Look—there it is again."

Cole turned and squinted at the stand of aspens. Sunrise

whinnied and was answered from the trees. "Son of a gun, they came to us!" He picked up his hat and strode toward the grove.

Midnight must have been calling to the other horses. "Skunk whiskers!" she grumbled as she scrambled to her feet. "Dratted horses could have waited five minutes!"

"What is it, Cole?" Stephanie peered around his broad back as she stepped into the grove. At first, all she saw were five horses standing under the trees, switching their tails as they stared back at the two intruders. Then, as her eyes began to adjust to the dim light, she realized the large bay mare was protectively guarding a colt. The foal had stepped on a discarded deer antler, and its leg was now tightly wedged among the branches of the hard, bony structure. The foal was larger than Dreamer, but its ribs stuck out pathetically.

"Oh, the poor thing." Stephanie started toward the youngster.

"No, don't go near it!" Cole grabbed her shoulder. "She won't let you touch it. Go get my rope."

Stephanie ran back to the meadow, grabbed the rope from Cole's saddle, and returned as fast as she could.

Cole was talking to the mare as he rubbed her neck. "Good old Queeny, we won't hurt you or Starlight. We'll get him home, don't worry."

"It's almost like she understands what you're saying," Stephanie whispered in surprise.

"No, she's reacting to the tone of my voice, not the words. It doesn't matter what you say as long as you use a soothing tone." Cole's voice never changed as he gently looped the rope around the mare's neck and across her nose. He led the mare out of the trees with the hastily
contrived halter.

The other animals followed, and Stephanie watched the colt with concern. He could put some weight on his diminutive hoof, but the antler caused him to move with a slow stumbling gait.

Charlie and Josh rode up just as the procession reached the

meadow. "Son of a bi—uh..." With a glance at Stephanie, Charlie hastily cleared his throat. "No wonder he got left behind. Poor critter couldn't follow his mama off this mountain."

"Good old Queeny. She came back after him the first chance she got." Josh's voice was filled with pride and admiration.

"Stephanie," Cole said, "I need you to hold Queeny while we work on Starlight. Josh, you stay on Tater and keep the other horses away." He frowned. "You ready, Charlie?"

Stephanie kept the mare turned away from the men as they threw the colt to the ground. With an occasional muttered curse, Cole managed to dislodge the antler and toss it aside. Running his fingers along the fragile foreleg, he sighed in relief. "The leg's all right!"

Charlie and Cole both stepped away, but the colt just lay on the ground, apparently overcome with exhaustion.

When Stephanie released Queeny, the bay joined her baby and nudged him with her nose. Weakly, Starlight struggled to his feet and turned toward his mother's flank.

Charlie watched the pair regretfully. "She's been away from him too long. Her milk's done dried up. Dang it, he's almost old enough to make it on grass. If we could just git a mite'a milk into him."

"Sunrise has milk." Stephanie turned hopeful eyes to the two men. "Do you suppose she'd..."

Charlie lifted his hat and ran his fingers through his hair. "I dunno, she might, but it'll take some pretty strong convincin'. Let's have lunch and let him graze a bit first. We'll see how he does."

By the time they had finished eating, the colt appeared a bit stronger, but Cole and Charlie decided to try the surrogate nursing anyway. It didn't take long for Stephanie to see why they'd been skeptical. Sunrise wasn't the least bit amenable to having a strange colt nurse and let them know in no uncertain terms. Even hobbled and tied to a tree, she objected strenuously when Charlie tried to wrangle the colt into place.

In an attempt to hold her stationary, Cole threw one arm around her neck and pressed her throat with his bicep, his other hand low on her neck. Snorting, Sunrise tried to prance, her eyes rolling as Cole applied more pressure to her throat. Obviously displeased by such rough treatment, she jerked her head around and bit Cole in the middle of his back.

With Cole's loud curses ringing in her hears, Stephanie motioned for Josh to take her place with Queeny and calmly approached. "Maybe she'll stand for me," she said, placing her hand gently on Sunrise's heaving side.

"Damn it, Stephanie. This is no place for you. Get out of here!"

"But she trusts me. Maybe she—"

"No!" he exploded. "You don't know what the hell you're talking about!"

It was like throwing kerosene on a fire. Stephanie's temper flared to match his. "Of all the idiotic, stupid men in the world, you must be one of the worst. The more you manhandle her, the more she'll fight you. Can't you see you're scaring her half to death?" She gave his arm a push. "Get out of my way, you pig-headed fool."

Cole's eyes blazed, and the muscles in his jaw bunched.

"You know, Cole," Charlie's voice broke in. "It might be worth a try. We'll never get nowhere this way. We can always throw the mare if Stephanie's idea don't work."

His lips thinning, Cole stepped away. "All right, go ahead. Try your damnedest, but don't expect me to feel sorry for you when you get hurt."

Ignoring him, Stephanie began talking softly to Sunrise as she grasped the strap of the bridle in one hand and gently rubbed the side of the mare's face with the other.

"There, there, Sunrise, he won't hurt you anymore. I'm here now. Everything's going to be fine." Remembering Cole's comment that a gentle tone was more important than the words, Stephanie kept her voice gentle and steady. "Don't be frightened, precious love. I won't let anything hurt you."

The sound of her voice seemed to have a soothing effect on Sunrise, and in a very short time, Charlie was able to gently slip Starlight's head into place. He stepped back as the colt began to nurse greedily. Stephanie never stopped talking, the inanities falling from her lips without thought. She stood there a good ten minutes talking, soothing, stroking the mare's neck, totally ignoring the men.

When Starlight had finally eaten his fill, Stephanie patted Sunrise on the neck. "Thank you, love. You were wonderful." She gave Cole a scornful look. "You obviously don't have the least idea how to treat a lady!" Without another word, she turned on her heel and walked away.

Cole glared after her as Charlie chuckled. "I reckon this time you ain't got a leg to stand on, Cole." He slapped the younger man on the shoulder. "I expect we'd best get movin' if we're gonna make it home before dark."

The trip home was accomplished without incident. Cole pointedly ignored Stephanie, and she pretended not to notice. When she discovered she was to walk down the mountain instead of ride, because it was easier on the horses, she didn't even try to hide her heartfelt sigh of relief.

The sun had set by the time they reached the barn, but even in the near darkness Stephanie saw Cole wince as he dismounted. "What's wrong, Cole?"

"Your 'precious love' bit me, remember?"

Stephanie caught her lower lip in her teeth. "Let me look at it. Maybe I can help."

Charlie saw the stubborn look on Cole's face and shook his head. "You'd best let her look, son. She ain't likely to give up till you do."

Cole favored Stephanie with an icy glance. "All right, look if you must, but don't take all night."

Stephanie lifted up the back of his shirt and gasped in dismay. There was a huge purple lump the size of her fist. She pulled the handkerchief from Cole's back pocket. "Go dip this in the trough, will you, Josh?" Gently, she felt around the bruise in the fading light. "I don't think the skin's broken, but it must be very painful."

"It hurts like hell, if you want to know the truth." He gritted his teeth as she lay the cold, wet handkerchief on his back, then he sighed. "That does feel better."

Stephanie pursed her lips. "It needs to have cold compresses kept on it to take the swelling down. Charlie, can you and Josh handle everything here if I take Cole to the house?"

"Reckon so."

When Cole followed her into the house without a murmur of protest, Stephanie realized just how much his back must have been hurting all the way home.

Kate looked at the wound with concern. "You'd best take that shirt off while I get a bowl of cold water and some rags."

It wasn't long before Charlie and Josh came in. While Josh poured the tale of the day's adventures into Kate's ears, Stephanie tenderly applied cold compresses to Cole's back.

Her mind drifted back to the idyllic interlude on the mountain top. Thinking of the soft kisses they'd shared, the very masculine back beneath her fingers suddenly came into sharp focus. How would it feel to let her hands wander where they would, she wondered? She was tempted to go exploring, to run her fingers over the corded muscles, caress his broad shoulders and slide her hands down the length of the powerful back.

"Steph." Cole's deep voice brought her to her senses. "Kate said it's time to eat. Didn't you hear her?"

Stephanie gave a guilty start. Deep embarrassment flooded her as she realized how totally improper her thoughts had been. "Oh, I...I guess I was daydreaming." Resolutely pushing the tantalizing thoughts away, she vowed to get hold of herself.

That night, she didn't have the nightmare of being chased. She dreamed instead of a black-haired, blue-eyed cowboy making delicious love to her in a high mountain meadow.

CHAPTER 15

October drew to a close, and with it went the days of Indian summer. No snow had fallen, but the November winds were harsh and cold. Stephanie retrieved the cloak she'd been wearing when Cole found her. Though she'd always thought it strange she'd been wearing such a heavy wrap in the middle of summer, she was now grateful for its warmth.

The heavy russet wool set off the highlights in her hair, and she loved the feel of the satin lining. The color and fit were perfect for her, even if she did have a tendency to trip over the stiff hem.

Though it was rather worn, it was of good quality. Perhaps it had been a castoff from a former employer, and she'd brought it along because it was her one decent piece of clothing. Strangely enough, it seemed cut for riding, and Stephanie spent many hours on Sunrise, the warm hood covering her head while the folds fell gracefully around her.

Using cow's milk laced with molasses, Stephanie helped Charlie nurse Starlight back to health. The colt made an amazingly fast recovery, a fact Charlie attributed to his breeding.

"His sire is an old stud Maggie's father has. Conner O'Reilly laughed himself near silly when Cole wanted to breed Queeny to ole Slewfoot. Don't look like much, but the way that horse paces himself, even Cole couldn't ride him into the ground." Charlie gazed at the colt with a pleased smile on his face. "Any other colt would've starved to death. That's one Cole would've been real sorry to lose. We're plannin' on usin' him for breedin' when he's old enough."

"You're going to keep him, then?"

Charlie nodded. "Most of the colts, we geld and sell as ridin' stock. This little fella and Black are different. It ain't gonna be easy havin' three stallions around, but Cole figures we'll need them to — uh, well, we're gittin' quite a herd of brood mares," he finished lamely.

Stephanie smiled to herself. They'd become such good friends, sometimes Charlie forgot she was female. Now, judging from his sudden discomfort, it was obvious he didn't consider horse breeding a fit topic for her ears.

"You've certainly been keeping Josh busy. I hardly see him anymore."

"Yup," Charlie said. "I set him to cleaning tack. It ain't a job he's particularly fond of. Likes it 'bout as much as milkin' the cow, but I ain't heard a squawk out of him." Charlie chuckled. "I reckon he figures if he complains, his pa'll set his mind to roundin' up a new teacher. The last one only lasted four weeks."

"Four weeks?" Stephanie was appalled. "Surely the students weren't that bad!"

Charlie shook his head. "Not this time anyway. She married a handsome young fella by the name of Willowbe who owns a nice spread over on Bear Creek. Kate and Prudy figure she came out here lookin' for a husband and never had no intention of teaching."

"Why didn't they advertise for another teacher?"

"I reckon they did, but nobody wants to come to the middle of nowhere." Charlie gave her a speculative look. "Don't suppose you'd be interested in the job?"

"Me?" Stephanie was aghast. "Good heavens, no! I can't even imagine taking something like that on. Josh and his friends are just going to have to get by without school."

"Don't reckon that will bother them a whole lot."

"No, but I think all this good behavior is starting to wear on Josh," Stephanie commented, still smiling. "Got any ideas how I can distract him before he explodes?"

"Well," Charlie said considering the matter, "it might be a good idea to make a round of the range to make sure all the cattle got water. Some of the ponds'll be frozen over, and the younguns don't always know to move down to the creek."

"Sounds perfect."

Josh was delighted with the idea and challenged her to a contest to see who could find the most cattle by noon.

"I know you, you'll claim every cow I find," Stephanie teased.

"I wouldn't cheat! You can ride the west side of the range, and I'll ride the east. We'll bring all the cattle we find to the crossing down by that big patch of skunkbrush." His eyes sparkled as he warmed to his theme. "Whoever comes in with the most cattle will be the winner."

"And what's the prize going to be? I have to know if this is going to be worth my time."

Josh considered this for several seconds, then brightened. "If I win, you have to play checkers with me every night for a week."

"What if I win?"

"Well," Josh said, wrinkling his brow, "how about if you win, I'll do the dishes for the same length of time?"

"Good heavens. I can't believe you'd willingly do women's work."

"I won't have to. I'm not going to lose."

"Oh, is that so?" Stephanie turned Sunrise to the west. "You can start with the supper dishes tonight," she called over her shoulder.

"Sorry, I'll be too busy beating you at checkers for that."

Just like his father. Stephanie gave a rueful sigh at the thought of Cole. The fiasco with Sunrise and the lame colt had made the breech between them even wider. Surely there was some way she could prove herself to him.

She was so wrapped up in her thoughts, she almost missed the movement in the brush growing along the shores of a small, frozen pond. It was only when Sunrise shied that she realized something was there.

Moving closer, she cautiously peered into the willows and then chortled with glee. A dozen cows and calves stood there contentedly swishing their tails. Josh was going to have a hard time beating this even with Sam along to help him.

Because the brush was too thick to ride a horse into, Stephanie tied Sunrise to a clump of skunkbrush and began to slowly circle around the animals on foot, trying not to frighten them. She had already learned her lesson about how protective a cow could be when she'd ventured too close to a small calf and had been charged by the enraged mother. If Sam hadn't been there to drive the cow away, she might have been seriously injured or even killed. Cole had called her every kind of fool and had threatened to make her stay in the house if she ever did anything so stupid again.

Stephanie wasn't taking any chances. Though these cows didn't seem to care, she had no idea how old a calf had to be before the mother stopped charging anything she saw as a threat. Timidly, she worked her prized herd out of the brush. After what seemed like an eternity, she emerged from the thicket, a smile of smug satisfaction on her face.

"Now what have we here?" a deep voice asked.

Stephanie jerked her head toward the sound and almost fainted in fright. Sitting on a bay mare not ten feet from her was the most terrifying man she had ever seen. With a slouch hat pulled low over his eyes, a bushy beard, and long, lank hair reaching clear to the collar of his heavy buffalo coat, he looked extremely dangerous. By far the most frightening aspect of the man, however, was the rifle he had trained on the middle of her chest.

CHAPTER 16

Stephanie glanced nervously toward Sunrise.

"Forget it, lady. You'd never make it."

"Why are you pointing that rifle at me?" Stephanie tried to sound imperious, but it came out more like a croak.

"Cattle rustling makes a man nervous."

A cattle rustler! The story of Charlie's wife popped into Stephanie's mind. Her throat closed in panic, and she fought the black terror that threatened to engulf her.

"Where are your friends?" the stranger asked with a menacing frown.

Stephanie's thoughts flew to Josh. "I'm alone," she whispered. Immediately, she could have bitten her tongue off. Why hadn't she told him there were half a dozen men likely to show up at any minute?

Some of her inner thoughts must have shown in her face, for he gave a humorless laugh. "I'd have known you were lying, sister." He gestured toward Sunrise with his rifle. "Get on your horse. We're going to take a ride to the ranch house."

The ranch house! Stephanie's heart began to pound in panic. What if he was part of a gang of outlaws who were planning to take over the Cantrell Ranch as their headquarters? It sounded like something out of a bad novel, but what did she know about rustlers? Maybe they really did things like that. Slowly, she walked to where Sunrise was tied.

"Don't try anything," the man growled. "I'd hate to shoot such a beautiful horse."

Stephanie tried to ignore the threat, her mind desperately searching for a plan as she mounted her horse.

If she could lead him off in the wrong direction... Turning Sunrise toward the south, she froze at the sound of the rifle being cocked behind her.

"I said the ranch house, lady. It's the other way."

Without a word, she changed direction and headed home. She knew it would be worse than useless to make a run for it. With the stranger right behind her, there seemed no way for her to get the upper hand.

When they reached the house, he made her dismount first. Stephanie's mind screamed for her to run before he got down, but she felt the hard metal of the gun pressed into her lower back almost before the thought even had a chance to form in her mind.

Cole was seated at the table, focused on the bridle he was fixing when they entered. "Oh good, just the person I needed. Could you give me a hand with—" He stopped mid-sentence when he glanced up and saw the man behind her. His chair clattered to the floor as he sprang to his feet, his face ashen.

Suddenly, the paralysis in Stephanie's mind lifted. If she could get the gun, Cole might be able to overpower the man behind her. With lightning speed, she whirled around and jerked the rifle from the man's strangely lax hold. She was aware of Cole grappling with the stranger as she fell backward, the rifle clutched in her hands. There was a loud explosion as the gun went off and the sound of breaking crockery when the bullet hit the cupboard.

The mortal combat between the two men halted abruptly. Both watched in stunned amazement as Stephanie scrambled to her feet and pointed the rifle at the stranger. "One move, mister, and you're a dead man!"

To her utter astonishment, a grin slowly crossed the rustler's face. "I think you'd better tell her who I am before she puts a bullet in me, little brother."

Suddenly, both men were laughing uproariously and clapping each other on the back. "By God, Levi, I ought to let her shoot you just for giving her the gun," Cole said when he finally caught his breath.

"I didn't give it to her. She jerked it out of my hands," the stranger said. "Anyway, it was your fault. I walk in holding a vicious rustler held at gunpoint, and you welcome her with open arms."

Stephanie looked back and forth between the two men in dawning comprehension. The stranger wasn't a desperate rustler, he was the long-lost Levi Cantrell. Cole's attack had been nothing more than a huge bear hug for his brother.

Cole threw back his head and laughed even louder. "Steph, a vicious rustler? Even with that rifle she's not my idea of a dangerous criminal."

Levi shrugged, his eyes twinkling merrily. "The way she was sneaking around in the brush after those cows looked mighty suspicious to me. When I accused her of being a rustler, she didn't deny it."

"You said *you* were a rustler!" Stephanie said indignantly. "And I wasn't sneaking. I was only being quiet so that none of the cows would charge me if I got too close to their calves."

That set the men off again. Stephanie had finally had enough. She'd been frightened badly, and now they were laughing at an act of bravery that had cost her dearly.

Their hilarity ringing in her ears, she wrapped her wounded dignity around her, marched over to Cole, thrust the rifle into his hands, and stomped out the door with her chin in the air.

Kate nearly collided with her. "Stephanie, what happened? I thought I heard a gunshot!"

"I believe Cole's brother has returned, though they haven't stopped laughing long enough to introduce us."

"LEVI?" Kate screeched in delight and rushed into the house.

Stephanie was just about to ride Sunrise out to find the cows again when she caught sight of Josh. It took about two seconds to realize he was bringing in her tiny herd, and she gritted her teeth in vexation. She didn't really begrudge Josh his small victory, but it was the last straw. There was only one thing left for her to do. She went to Kate's cabin for a good long sulk.

"Kate!" Levi shouted as his step-mother rushed into the kitchen. Gathering her in a bone-crushing hug, he lifted her off the floor. "God, I've missed you!"

"You're a sight for sore eyes yourself," she cried, hugging him back, "though I hardly recognize you with all that hair." When he set her down, she stepped back and put her hands on her hips. "And just where have you been the last four years?"

Levi grinned at Cole. "I told you she'd be giving me the sharp side of her tongue before long."

Kate ignored his sally. "Well?"

"I got shanghaied. The last I remember, I was drowning my sorrows with a couple of sailors in San Francisco. The next thing I knew, I was waking up on a ship headed for the Orient. It took me four years to get back to California again. I caught a train back as soon as I could." He rubbed his chin ruefully. "One of the first things I plan to do is get a shave and a haircut."

"That can wait," Kate said emphatically. "Right now you're going to have a good home-cooked meal."

Levi grinned down at her. "I was hoping you'd say that."

When Charlie and Josh came in a few minutes later, the exclamations of surprise and welcome echoed around the kitchen once more, and the story of Levi's abduction was told again.

Levi was right in the middle of describing how he'd felt when he found himself bound for the Orient, when an exclamation of horror from Kate stopped him in mid-sentence.

They all looked up to find her staring in dismay at the bullet hole in the cupboard. "I knew I heard a gunshot." She turned an accusing eye on the brothers seated at the table. "Which one of you is responsible for this?"

The brothers exchanged a glance. "It wasn't either of us." Cole grinned. "Steph did it."

"Horsefeathers! As if Stephanie didn't know any better than to shoot a hole in the wall!" Kate crossed her arms and tapped her foot.

"It was all a mistake," Levi explained. "She thought I was some kind of outlaw and grabbed my rifle. It went off when she fell over backwards with it."

"Of all the stupid..." Kate eyed Levi. "You're as bad as your brother. I don't suppose it ever occurred to you to tell her who you were?"

Levi shifted in his chair. "Well, no. When I first saw her in the willows, I thought it was Maggie, so I figured I'd just sit there quiet-like and surprise her. By the time I realized it was someone else, the way she was acting made me suspicious." He glanced around the room. "Where are Pa and Maggie anyway?"

"Pa and Uncle Daniel are in England settling Great Uncle Hedley's estate," Cole said.

"And Maggie?"

An uncomfortable silence fell. "She's gone, Levi," Cole said at last.

"Gone? What do you mean 'gone?'"

"She died last year," Kate murmured.

Levi stared at them all blankly. "Maggie's dead? I can't believe—" He swallowed hard, the upsurge of grief clearly visible in his face. After a long moment, he blinked and looked up. "Well, if this...Stephanie isn't a friend of Maggie's, who is she?"

"To tell the truth, we don't really know for sure." Gratefully turning his mind away from Maggie's death, Cole told the story of Stephanie's mysterious appearance in the middle of the prairie and her amnesia. Soon Josh, Kate, and even Charlie were anxiously adding their own tales. When Charlie described Stephanie's 'Midnight ride,' Levi raised his brows.

"Good Lord! If she can stand up to you and your temper, little brother, I'm lucky she didn't shoot me!"

Kate laughed. "I think she wanted to. She didn't look too happy when I met her outside. Josh, why don't you run and tell

Stephanie it's time to eat?"

Josh found Stephanie sitting on her bed staring out the window. "Grandma Kate says to come eat."

"I'm not hungry."

"Ah, come on, Stephanie. It just isn't the same without you."

Josh's expression was so earnest that Stephanie felt some of her feelings of ill-usage dissolve. "Well, when you put it like that..." She rose from the bed and walked to the door. "But don't you dare brag about how you won our bet. If it hadn't been for your uncle, I'd have brought those cows in instead of you." She glanced down at him. "And if I hadn't worked them out of the brush, you'd never have found them."

"I guess maybe I could help you with the dishes before I beat you at checkers, at least tonight anyway."

Stephanie smiled ruefully and ruffled his hair. "You're impossible!"

"Did you really try to shoot my Uncle Levi?" Josh ventured.

"I didn't know he was your uncle. He never introduced himself," Stephanie said over her shoulder as she opened the kitchen door.

"I beg your pardon for the oversight," Levi said, extending his hand. "My friends call me Levi. I hope you'll forget our first meeting and do the same."

Stephanie shook his hand, smiling in spite of herself.

"I can hardly refuse, can I?"

"I certainly hope not."

During lunch, Levi entertained them with a humorous account of his life as a reluctant sailor, and Stephanie found herself liking the man. Without his hat and buffalo coat, he wasn't nearly so intimidating. His booming laughter was infectious, and the blue-gray eyes twinkled merrily. By the time the meal was over, Stephanie was willing to admit their first encounter had been an unfortunate misunderstanding and thought she might even enjoy this new addition to the household.

Cole spent the afternoon bringing Levi up to date on the ranch. When the conversation came around to Stephanie, Cole told his brother everything he knew or had surmised.

"Seems strange no one came looking for her," Levi said, rubbing his beard pensively.

Cole nodded. "I know. I figure whoever she left behind doesn't know where to start looking. I thought about advertising, but it occurred to me she might be in danger from someone. Her dreams are always of being chased."

"She could be running from the law."

"She's not the type," Cole said with certainty. "At first I didn't trust her at all and watched her pretty close. After a while I started feeling foolish, especially after the way Charlie and Kate took to her."

Levi gave his brother a devilish look. "She's a pretty little thing, and I've been out of circulation a longtime. Maybe I'll take my chances."

Cole's features darkened in a forbidding frown. "Leave her alone." When Levi's eyebrows rose in surprise, Cole finished in a milder tone. "You're forgetting she's probably married."

Levi swallowed a smile.

CHAPTER 17

"**I** don't see why we have to eat breakfast so early," Josh grumbled as he polished off his second helping of flapjacks.

"Because Prudence Simpson wants me to visit her today, and I'm leaving as soon as breakfast is over, that's why." Kate slipped her apron off and hung it on a nearby peg. "Levi, if you're finished, would you mind hitching up the team?"

"You see how it is, Josh?" Levi said, pushing back his chair. "I've been home less than two days, and she's already telling me what to do. You'd better give me a hand before she sets you to washing the dishes." He winked at Stephanie as Josh dashed out the door ahead of him.

"Has anyone seen my good boots?" Cole asked from the door of his bedroom.

Kate paused in the middle of clearing the table. "What do you need those for?"

"Because these have seen better days." He looked down at the hole in the bottom of the boot he held in his hand.

Kate gave him a disgusted look. "They're probably right where you took them off."

A thorough search of the house turned up nothing, however, and Cole finally put on his old boots and left with a dark scowl on his face.

It wasn't until Stephanie walked Kate to the barn that she realized she'd seen the missing boots. "Kate, I think I know where Cole's boots are." Excitedly, she climbed up the ladder into the hay loft and appeared moments later with a pair of mud-encrusted boots in her hand. "How do you suppose they got up there?" she asked as she climbed down.

"For heaven's sake," Kate said. "I can't imagine—" All at once, her eyes began to sparkle. "Oh my, I remember now. Sally Langton got her buggy stuck in a mud-hole last spring after a dance. Cole pulled her out, but he was madder than hops because he figured she did it on purpose. He came into the house in stocking feet grumbling about ruining a good pair of boots over a damn-fool woman. You know his temper."

Stephanie nodded. "He probably took them off and threw them up there in a rage."

"You know," Kate said, surveying the boots critically, "they really don't look too bad. With a little saddle soap and some elbow grease, I expect they'll be good as new."

"You think so? Hmm, maybe I'll give it a try." Stephanie said. "Where would I find the saddle soap?"

"It should be on a shelf in the tack room, though with Josh using it the last few days, it's hard to say where you'll find it. He's not one to make sure things are put away where they belong."

Stephanie shook her head. "Like father, like son."

"If that isn't the truth," Kate said with a laugh. "You should have seen Cole and Levi when I first came to the ranch. What one of them didn't think of, the other one did. Lordy, but I had my hands full with those two."

As soon as she saw Kate off, Stephanie went in search of the saddle soap. Luckily, it was easy to find, and she was soon headed back to the house, determined to salvage the boots. Perhaps she'd be able to make a positive impression on Cole for a change.

Humming softly to herself, Stephanie poured hot water into the washtub and opened the can of saddle soap. She dipped a wet rag into the greasy contents and tried to work up a lather with her hand, but no suds appeared. Frowning in surprise, she stared at the rag for a few seconds, then shrugged and began to scrub the boot.

After several applications, Stephanie threw the rag down in disgust. The stains were still there. Wondering if more water would help, she gingerly dipped the side of the boot into the washtub. Gently rubbing it with the rag, she gave a crow of delight as the leather took on a darker hue. Relieved, Stephanie immersed the boots and attacked the dirt with renewed vigor. It took a good bit of soaking before all the stains disappeared, but at last the leather was a uniform color. Satisfied, she set them near the door to dry while she fixed the noon meal.

With a pot of beef stew simmering on the stove, Stephanie took a leisurely half an hour to change into her new green wool dress. By the time she returned, the men had come in for lunch and the boots slipped to the back of her mind.

Josh spent most of the meal describing his dog's newest accomplishment. "I've trained him to hunt mice," he told them proudly. "All I have to do is say 'Find a mouse' and he—" At the words, Sam jumped to his feet, ears alert.

Stephanie laughed when the dog began to search the immaculate kitchen for the promised prey. "Poor Sam. You got him all excited for nothing."

"Yeah, but he caught hundreds of them at the line shack this morning didn't he, Charlie?"

"I didn't count, but it was a whole passel of 'em," Charlie said, then pushed back his chair. "You know, Cole, it looks like we might get a storm. I think I'll ride on over to Simpson's and see Kate home."

"That might not be a bad idea," Cole said, glancing out the window with a frown.

Charlie shrugged into his coat. "You want to go with me, Levi? Prudy and John'd be right glad to see you."

"Actually, I'd planned on going into town to get that haircut and shave I promised myself." He gave his brother a bland look. "If the storm breaks, I'll just stay in town."

Cole snorted. "Or even if it doesn't."

"I'll ride part way with you, then," Charlie said. settling his hat on his head. "Come on, Josh, you got work waitin' for you in the barn."

As the three trooped outside, Cole took a last quick swallow of coffee and jumped to his feet. Glancing down as he neared the door, he stopped mid-stride. "My boots!"

"That's right, I forgot to tell you!" Stephanie said with a big smile. "I found them in the haymow covered with mud, so I washed them for you."

Cole whirled on her. "You *what?*"

Startled by his unexpected reaction, Stephanie stammered, "I—I got some saddle soap from the barn, and I washed them for you."

"You *washed* my boots? In *water?*" Stephanie nodded wordlessly, and Cole's frustration turned into anger. "Damn it, woman, do you have maggots in your brain? You ruined the only decent pair of boots I own."

Unsure what had gone wrong, Stephanie tried to explain. "Kate said to use the saddle soap, but it didn't work very well in the water until I submerged the boots."

"That's because you use it alone... *without* water!" he yelled. "What kind of fool doesn't know any better than to get leather wet?"

"Well, how was I supposed to know how saddle soap works? It's not like there are directions on the can!" She frowned. *At least I don't think there are. I probably should have looked.* "I'm sorry," she said. "Maybe they'll be all right when they're dry."

Cole closed his eyes and pinched the bridge of his nose. "Oh, hell," he muttered. Then, with a deep sigh, he jammed his hat on his head and stomped out the door.

Torn between embarrassment at her own ignorance and anger at Cole's unreasonable attitude, Stephanie cleaned the kitchen with her thoughts in a turmoil. When the work was done, she threw on her cloak and walked to the barn, hoping a long ride would bring her solace. Sunrise was abnormally skittish, but Stephanie barely noticed as she saddled the mare, mounted, and headed down a road she'd never taken before, one that led to the open prairie. Preoccupied with her thoughts, Stephanie paid no attention to where she was going as she galloped farther and farther from home.

Why did they call it soap if it wasn't supposed to be used with water, for heaven's sake? It wasn't like people were born knowing how to— Suddenly, an odd inconsistency occurred to her. The fact that she didn't know how to use saddle soap probably meant she'd never used it. She'd obviously spent a lot of time on horseback before her accident, so why didn't she know how to clean tack?

It didn't make a lot of sense. Just one more thing to add to the growing list of incomprehensible details. Stephanie sighed. It shouldn't have come as a surprise that she'd failed so miserably. She was like a fish out of water here. No matter how hard she tried to please Cole, she always wound up doing something wrong. If only her memory would return. She could go back where she belonged and never see Cole Cantrell again.

A sudden lump in her throat and a swooping pain in her chest caught her by surprise. Never see Cole again? She might as well wish to stop breathing. When had she fallen in love with him? The wonder of it filled her with an indescribable feeling, part joy, part trepidation.

All at once, Sunrise began fighting her head, and Stephanie patted the mare's neck reassuringly. "What is it, love?" She looked around and saw with some surprise that sometime during her ride, fluffy snowflakes had begun to drift lazily down from the heavy gray clouds overhead. Cole and Charlie had been right about the storm. She'd better head home before it got any worse.

When she turned Sunrise and started back the way they had come, she realized she had no idea where they were. Enough snow had accumulated that the land was totally unfamiliar. The snow was so thick, there were no landmarks. Even the mountains and hills were completely invisible in the gray-white gloom surrounding her. The road she had been following had turned into little more than a track; one that was rapidly filling with snow. The snowfall became heavier, and a slight breeze started to blow as Sunrise trudged on. When the snow began to swirl around them, Stephanie fought rising panic. *It's all right*, she told herself. *All I have to do is let Sunrise have her head, and she'll head straight for the barn.*

Slackening her hold, she whispered encouragingly, "Come on, sweetheart, take us home." The wind increased until it was impossible to see more than a few feet in any direction. Sunrise kept moving, but Stephanie began to fear the mare was as lost as she was.

Without warning, a jackrabbit exploded out of the sagebrush at Sunrise's feet, and the horse reared in fright. Equally startled, Stephanie lost her hold and was thrown from the saddle. Stunned by her fall, she lay on the ground as the mare disappeared into the gathering gloom.

Knowing her only hope was to follow Sunrise's tracks, Stephanie struggled to stand. There was an ominous rip as she stepped on the hem of her cloak, and she pitched forward into the snow again. By the time she regained her feet, the wind was shrieking all around her, and the hoof prints in front of her were filling rapidly.

On and on she trudged until the tracks disappeared, and fear gripped her. The entire world was a gray and white maelstrom filled with snow and wind. Unsure of her directions, Stephanie kept pushing forward, hoping she wasn't wandering in circles. As the snow piled deeper, she tripped and fell again and again. Each time, she dragged herself to her feet, though the effort cost her dearly.

As she plodded on and on through the ever-deepening snow, an exhaustion such as she had never before imagined dogged her steps, and she realized she couldn't continue much farther. Repeatedly, she fell and battled her way back to her feet. At last, incapable of rising, she wavered on hands and knees for a moment before collapsing in the snow.

Stephanie lay still, unable to move, her energy gone. She'd really done it this time. Cole would never forgive her for this. Would he even mourn her?

"Annie! Don't give up, he's coming for you. Hang on just a little longer." The dearly familiar voice inside her head was soft but insistent.

Lizzie? Stephanie tried to get the name out, but her voice wouldn't work. A strangely different image of Josh floated through her mind. Stephanie knew she should understand, but it was too difficult to grasp. She was warm and cozy and so very tired. Perhaps she'd sleep for a little while...

CHAPTER 18

Cole glanced at the leaden sky. It looked like they were in for a bad one. Pitching great forkfuls of hay into the corral, he mentally reviewed his stock. Most of the animals were in fairly sheltered areas; he hoped they'd have the sense to stay there.

At least he didn't have to worry about his family. Charlie and Kate had ridden in ten minutes earlier, just as Josh was finishing his chores. Levi was probably safely settled in the saloon. His worst threat was a ferocious hangover.

Cole was the only one in danger of freezing, and that from a pair of icy green eyes. He deserved it, and he knew it. Maybe that was the best solution anyway. If Stephanie was mad at him, it wouldn't be so difficult to keep his distance. It had been a very near thing this afternoon when he'd yelled at her for his boots. She'd looked so hurt and confused it was all he could do not to pull her into his arms and kiss that expression away. He'd somehow managed to leave before he gave in to the temptation, but it had been a very near thing.

"Cole, *Cole!*"

He looked up in surprise as Kate came running toward him. "I can't find Stephanie anywhere. Charlie says Sunrise and the sidesaddle are gone."

Cole cursed under his breath as huge flakes began to fall. "Why doesn't that damn fool woman stay put?" He grabbed his saddle from the barn, threw it on Midnight, and whistled for Sam. "I'll go find her. If she's still out there when this storm hits..." He looked at the sky again.

"Stephanie doesn't understand, Cole," Kate said, handing him an extra bed roll. "She won't realize this could turn into a blizzard."

"I know." He tied the blankets onto the back of his saddle. "We may wind up closer to Sally's or the line shack, so don't worry if we don't make it back tonight. *Just pray I can find her,* he added to himself.

Sam came trotting up, his tongue lolling from his mouth. Cole hunkered down, his hands on either side of the dog's head. "Sam, find Stephanie." As the dog bounded off, Cole swung into the saddle and set off after him, hoping Josh's training had stuck.

The snowfall thickened rapidly. Cole had to call Sam back several times because the dog disappeared into the gloom. The wind began to blow, and the storm became a full-scale blizzard. Cole prayed Stephanie had sense enough to let Sunrise have her head.

As if on cue, the mare appeared out of the swirling snow, her reins dragging. Cole saw the wide, frightened eyes and knew it would probably be futile to try to catch her.

He couldn't take the time anyway. Stephanie was out there somewhere. *What if Sunrise bucked her off, and she's lying hurt somewhere?* Cole's stomach tightened into a knot. *She doesn't stand a chance if I don't find her.*

Fighting despair, Cole tried not to think of her wandering aimlessly until the cold overcame her. Time was short; even Midnight would soon reach his limits in this.

After what seemed like hours of only wind and snow, Sam came out of the storm barking frantically. When he saw Cole and Midnight, the dog turned and ran back the way he'd come.

Following his excited yips, Cole found him next to a lump in the snow. Stephanie? In a heartbeat he was off his horse, brushing the snow away. "Thank God," he murmured as the familiar russet wool of her cloak emerged. He'd found her! But she lay so still. Almost afraid to hope, he stripped off his glove and pressed his fingers against the side of her neck. Relief surged through him. Her skin was cold to the touch, but her pulse fluttered under his fingers. She was still alive.

Stephanie groaned as he picked her up in his arms but didn't waken, a sure sign she was freezing to death. He had to get her out of the cold and warmed up fast. With all landmarks swallowed up in the blizzard, Cole wasn't exactly sure where they were, but the line shack shouldn't be too far. Praying he hadn't miscalculated, Cole draped Stephanie over his shoulder and tried to calm Midnight.

He dropped his burden twice as the horse shied away but somehow managed to keep hold of the reins. If he lost Midnight, he and Stephanie were both doomed. Finally, with grueling effort, Cole pulled himself into the saddle and shrugged Stephanie off his shoulder into his arms. As he settled her in front of him, he contemplated his next insurmountable problem: he had no idea how to get to the line shack.

Sam could probably find the way if Cole could somehow make him understand. Suddenly, Cole remembered his son telling about Sam catching mice there at noon. Even as a long shot it was crazy, but he was desperate.

"Sam, find a mouse."

The dog cocked his head as though trying to understand.

"Sam, find a mouse," Cole repeated, feeling foolish. It was ludicrous to expect the dog to comprehend their need, but there was no other way.

Watching Sam with hopeful eyes, Cole had the distinct impression that the dog gave a canine shrug before he turned and headed back into the storm once more. *The cold is affecting my mind,* Cole thought.

The bitter wind and driving snow were beginning to take a toll on all of them. No longer running ahead, Sam stayed in front of the horse, and Midnight followed as if he knew the dog would lead them to safety. Several times the stallion stumbled, his hooves slipping on snow-covered rocks, but he kept plodding on.

Cole's arms were starting to go numb. He knew it wouldn't be long before they all dropped from exhaustion. Just as he was beginning to fear Sam hadn't understood, the outline of a building appeared in front of them. He didn't think he'd ever been happier to see anything in his life as he guided Midnight into a shed built next to the cabin. Sam collapsed onto the fresh straw. A mouse scampered by almost under his nose, but he ignored it.

Cole knew he'd never be able to dismount with Stephanie in his arms. Bending over as far as he could, he lowered her to the floor, holding her limp hands until she was almost sitting. Then, using all his strength, he threw her forward so she wouldn't fall under Midnight's feet. He winced as she fell with a thud. Well, it couldn't be helped. He dismounted and removed the blankets from the back of the saddle. Wrapping them loosely around Stephanie, he made her as comfortable as possible before turning his attention to Midnight. The horse was near the end of his strength, and Cole knew their survival might well depend on the stallion's ability to take them home again.

Cole pulled the saddle off and wiped the stallion down with a handful of straw before leading him to the hay that was always kept there for emergencies. Sam was already curled up and sound asleep. Cole shook his head over the two faithful animals. It wasn't much, but it was the best he could do.

With grim determination, Cole took the lariat from his saddle and slung it over his shoulder. If the storm got any worse, they'd need it. He picked Stephanie up and staggered back outside to the front of the cabin.

The latch was stiff with cold, and he fumbled with it for several minutes before it gave beneath his fingers. Stumbling inside, he deposited Stephanie on the single bunk, then stripped the gloves from his hands and laid kindling for a fire. It was a good thing Charlie insisted this cabin be well stocked.

The dry wood began to blaze almost immediately, and Cole turned back to Stephanie. He was relieved to see none of the dead white patches that meant frostbite. While the room gradually warmed, he removed her shoes and gently rubbed her hands, face, and feet, determined to get blood back into the near-frozen limbs.

She lay still as death for so long Cole was close to desperation when she finally began to moan. "James, it hurts.

Help me!"

Cole knew the pain she must be feeling. His own hands and feet were beginning to ache almost unbearably as the circulation slowly returned.

"Please, James, it's so cold!"

Cole blinked. James again. He pulled off his boots and draped his coat over a chair before carefully unwrapping the blankets from around Stephanie. Though the heavy cloak was soaked through, it had probably saved her life. He had a difficult time removing her wet clothing with his fingers still chilled and clumsy, but it had to be done. It was the only way to get her warmed up.

Cole rolled her against him, pulled the blankets of the bunk free, and lay her gently back on the bed. Then he stretched out beside her and rearranged the blankets to cover them both. Stephanie kept moaning and thrashing around, trying to escape the pain that twisted through her body.

He wrapped his arms around her. "Shh, it's all right now. You're safe, shh..." He kept repeating the soothing phrase over and over until finally she settled against him. The moaning stopped, and she fell into a deep sleep. As the warmth stole over him, Cole relaxed, and soon he, too, was asleep.

Hours later, Cole awoke to a darkened room, with the wind howling and shrieking outside. He disentangled himself from Stephanie and padded over to the window. Looking outside, he swore softly. Instead of blowing itself out, the storm had intensified. Even the shed was no longer visible.

Frowning, he walked to the fireplace. The fire had died down. It was the chill that had awakened him. He stirred the embers then added more wood and watched the flames rekindle.

He unearthed the lantern, lit it with a splint from the jar on the mantle, and took stock of their situation. A well-used ax leaned against a box of kindling, and one entire wall was covered with stacked wood. At least they'd stay warm. There wasn't as much in the wooden provision box as he'd have liked.

They had enough food for several days, but he could remember blizzards that raged on for a week or more.

"Have to go. Must escape," Stephanie said quite distinctly.

Two strides took Cole to the bunk, but she was sound asleep. "Love you, James," she murmured. "No time to say goodbye. I have to leave now, or he'll catch me." Her voice trailed off. It was impossible to say if her moan was part of her dream or pain she was feeling from her thawing limbs.

Cole sat on the edge of the bed and touched her shoulder gently. "Stephanie?"

Her eyes popped open, wide and fearful, then she relaxed. "Oh, it's you." She closed her eyes and murmured drowsily, "Don't leave me, Cole."

He brushed a strand of hair away from her cheek. "I won't, Steph."

"Safe with you," she murmured as she turned her head, rubbing her face along his calloused palm.

Cole's mouth twisted at the irony. She was far from safe with him, whatever she thought.

Rising to his feet, Cole put more wood on the fire then blew out the lantern and lay down on the bunk once again. With a soft sigh, Stephanie snuggled against him, and his arms automatically went around her. Settling her more comfortably against his chest, he glanced down at her. The dark circles under her eyes reminded him how close she'd come to death.

The firelight glinted off the gold ring where her hand lay against his chest. It was strange that she had automatically put it on her right hand. Did that mean it wasn't a wedding ring at all, or was it a subconscious urge to deny an unhappy marriage? Could James be a lover and Stephanie fleeing an abusive husband? Whatever kind of trouble she was in, she loved James. Unconsciously, he tightened his arms around her, and his breath caught in his throat as something painful constricted in his chest.

CHAPTER 19

The wind was howling, but Stephanie felt warm and cozy. In her dream, an iron band circled her body and held her safe against a hard, warm wall. How very odd. Gradually, the wisps of sleep cleared from her mind, but neither the warmth nor the wall altered. Opening her eyes, she found herself staring at a button. *A button?* A body then, not a wall. Her gaze traveled upward to a firm jaw covered with a growth of stubble. "Cole?"

Lazily, he opened his eyes. "You're finally awake. I was beginning to wonder if you were hibernating rather than sleeping."

Stephanie peeked over his shoulder and stared at the unfamiliar room in surprise. "Where are we?"

Cole stretched then rolled out of bed. "It's a line shack we use during round-up. We're here because it was considerably closer than the house."

"But how did we get here?"

"We arrived on Midnight, led by the ever-faithful Sam." Cole yawned and scratched his stubble. "It's a good thing Sam is always ready for a game no matter what the circumstance."

"What do you mean?"

"Do you remember the new game Josh taught him?"

Stephanie nodded. "To hunt mice."

"Right, and Josh taught him that game right here at the line shack." Cole bent over to stoke the fire. "By the time I found you, the storm had turned into a blizzard, and I was completely disoriented, so I told Sam to find a mouse."

She blinked. "And he brought us here?"

"Hard to believe, I know. It was a long shot, but I couldn't think of any other way."

"And it worked." Stephanie smiled slightly. "You do realize Josh will never allow us to forget this?"

"Probably not. I'm just glad I had Sam along. I wouldn't even have been able to find you without him."

"He's a smart dog, but then, all the Cantrell animals seem —" Suddenly, her eyes filled with panic. "Oh my gosh, Sunrise! She —"

"Is safe at home. I met her about fifteen minutes after I left, headed for the barn. I didn't even try to stop her. Don't worry, she made it."

"I don't understand." Sitting up, Stephanie watched Cole add wood to the fire. "I'd only been riding about forty-five minutes, and I was part way back when Sunrise bolted."

He turned to look at her with raised eyebrows. "So?"

"So how is it we couldn't make it home?"

"It took me nearly an hour to find you," Cole said, rummaging through the grub box. "By then we couldn't have made it even halfway. It's a miracle we made it this far. Midnight couldn't have kept going much longer." He pulled a can of beans out with a flourish. "Your lunch, madam."

"Lunch?" Stephanie blinked. "Don't you mean supper?"

"You slept close to twenty hours. I'm not precisely sure it's noon, but since I got up to feed the fire twice since dawn, I figure it's about that."

"Twenty hours! That's impossible. I never sleep over —"

"Steph, you almost froze to death out there yesterday."

Her eyes widened. "I what?"

"You were already unconscious, which is the first sign of freezing. If I hadn't found you when I did..." He shrugged. "It takes your body a long time to recover after something like that."

Stephanie was silent for a time, mulling things over in her mind. "I'm sorry about your boots," she said at last. "I wanted it to be a surprise." Her lip quivered slightly as she attempted to smile. "It was a surprise, all right."

"Look, Steph, I overreacted. The whole thing is best forgotten. The boots can probably be fixed. Anyway, they sure as hell weren't worth risking your life over." He turned back to his cooking. "I suggest you get dressed. It's not very warm in here, even with the fire going."

"Cole," she said, "I'm covered with bruises."

A sudden image of how he'd gotten her off Midnight flashed through his mind. Cole became very busy with the fire. "I...ah...dropped you a couple of times getting back on Midnight after I found you."

"Oh." Stephanie sighed as she slipped the limp green wool over her head. "My favorite dress, and now it's ruined."

Cole snorted. "Be glad it was only your dress."

As soon as they finished their meal, Cole rose from the table and put on his coat. "Would you mind getting me a can of beans from the box?"

"Where are you going?" she asked fearfully.

"I have to check on Sam and Midnight and take them some water. The beans are for Sam." He picked up the ax and his coiled rope.

"What do you need those for?"

"I plan on coming back." He gestured toward the storm howling outside the window. "It's dangerous to go out in something like that. I've known grown men who died because they got lost on the way to the outhouse in a blizzard."

Stephanie watched nervously as he wrapped one end of the lariat firmly around his waist and tied a knot.

"Hand me that bucket of water, will you?"

"It isn't very much."

"I know, but it'll have to do for now. It took all day just to melt that much." Cole opened the door and Stephanie gasped in shock as the force of the wind seemed to fill the tiny room. Cole sank the ax into the outside wall of the cabin, then put the loop of the lariat around the handle and pulled it tight. He turned back to Stephanie as he put on his gloves.

"Once I get there, I'll tie this end to the shed. That way I'll have a line I can follow back." He had to shout to make himself heard over the shrieking wind. "It may take a while. Whatever you do, don't try to come after me, especially if I don't come back." He picked up the bucket of water and was gone.

The next quarter of an hour was sheer torture for Stephanie. She paced back and forth, trying not to panic. She opened the door several times to check the rope and found some measure of relief when it remained taut. Closing the door took every ounce of strength she possessed, but she had to keep checking.

Finally Cole staggered in, wet and covered with snow. Stephanie threw her arms around his waist and hugged him tightly. "I was so scared."

He pulled her close. "So was I, Steph, so was I."

She thought she felt his lips brush her hair before he set her away from him and went to the fire.

"It could have been worse, I guess. I only hit the end of the rope three times before I found the shed."

"How are Midnight and Sam?"

"Just fine. Sam loved the beans." Cole took his coat, hat, and gloves off and warmed himself in front of the fire. "There's plenty of hay, so Midnight's content. I don't think he's done anything but eat since we got here."

Cole lay down on the bunk and closed his eyes.

It wasn't long before Stephanie was thoroughly bored and began searching the cabin for some sort of diversion. All she unearthed besides dust, mouse nests, and cobwebs was a packet of needles and a spool of thread.

At her sound of disgust, Cole opened his eyes. "What are you doing?"

"Looking for something to occupy my time." Stephanie wrinkled her nose. "But all I found was this." He laughed when she held up the sewing materials. She got down on her knees and looked under the bed. "I guess I could mend my cloak, but surely—Oh, look," she cried with delight. "A checkerboard!" The ancient board was dilapidated and covered with dust, but she carefully wiped it off with the edge of her skirt and set it on the table. "Now if I can just find the pieces," she said, delving under the bunk again. "Aha, pay dirt!" She blew the dust off the top of a wooden box then opened it. She frowned as she reached inside and pulled out an oddly shaped piece of wood. "Not checkers. I wonder what..." She studied it for a moment, then set it on the floor, took out another and ran her fingers over it. "Oh, for heaven's sake," she said, lifting a third lump of wood from the box. "I think they're chess pieces!"

Cole sat up, and she handed him one of the chunks of wood. "I remember this. It's a set Josh started to whittle for me a couple of years ago. He must have left it out here during a round-up." He gave her a cocky grin. "Madam, would you care to be beaten at a game of chess?"

She raised her brows in astonishment. "Surely you don't expect me to *let* you win."

The afternoon passed quickly as they played with a degree of hilarity that would have set the chess masters frowning. The pieces were so incompletely carved it was next to impossible to tell what was what. The confusion thus created caused a great deal of good-natured banter back and forth between the two opponents.

"Check and mate!" Cole sat back with a satisfied look on his face.

"That's my Queen, and you just put yourself into check. Look, right there."

"What? That's my bishop."

"Then what's this?"

"My knight, of course."

"It moved like a bishop two turns ago. Are you trying to take advantage of a poor, defenseless woman?"

Cole snorted. "Defenseless, my eye! Where is your king, anyway?" He looked at her suspiciously. "Is it still on the board?"

And so it went until the light began to fade. The feeling of revelry lasted through the supper preparations. Though Stephanie obviously had little or no experience cooking over an open fire, she managed to turn out some acceptable biscuits to go with the beans. Afterwards, Cole went out to check Midnight and Sam again and to take them more water.

When he returned, Stephanie was wrapped in a blanket, her dress and corset neatly draped over the back of a chair. He looked from the clothes to her face with raised eyebrows.

She blushed. "I didn't want to get undressed with you in the same room."

"I can't sleep on the floor; it's too cold," he said. When she gave him a blank stare, he tried again. "We have to share the bunk."

"So?"

Cole sighed. "Look, I think you'd be more comfortable in your dress."

"If you'd ever tried to sleep in a corset or a heavy wool dress, you wouldn't say that. Besides, we slept together last night with no problem."

Cole didn't bother pointing out that she'd been comatose. He built up the fire again, blew out the lamp, stripped down to his long underwear, then crawled into bed and turned his back to her.

The bunk was so narrow, they both had to turn on their sides to fit. Stephanie eyed his back for a moment, then snuggled up to it. It was too cold to worry about propriety. With a sigh of contentment, she closed her eyes and drifted off to sleep.

Several hours later, she awoke with a start. Still in his underwear, Cole stood at the window, staring out. Quietly, she slipped out of bed, wrapping the blanket around her as she joined him. "What is it?"

He looked down at her. "Listen."

Stephanie cocked her head. "The wind stopped!"

Cole nodded. "The storm blew itself out."

She clapped her hands. "We're saved!"

Cole couldn't help grinning at her exuberance. "Not quite, but we'll be able to hold out until we are. Come look outside."

Pulling her to the window, he cleared a place in the frost-covered pane low enough for her to see out.

Stephanie caught her breath in wonder. As far as the eye could see, a pristine blanket of snow sparkled in the moonlight like a field of diamonds. The sky was black velvet filled with a million twinkling stars. "It's beautiful!"

"Very." Gazing down at the woman beside him, Cole felt an odd little twist in his stomach. In the mellow light from the fire, her hair glowed with soft highlights as it tumbled about her shoulders in disarray. Like a man in a dream, he reached out and removed the few remaining hairpins, watching in fascination as the glowing mass fell to her hips in a shining cloud. She looked up at him.

"You have such beautiful hair," he whispered, sinking his hands into the soft silkiness on either side of her face. Green eyes stared into blue for a timeless second before their lips met in a kiss filled with magical promise. Seduction had not been Cole's intention, but he'd been drawn to her like a moth to a flame. Now he was unable to quell the tides of passion that enveloped them both. He didn't even want to.

With a sigh, she melted against him and willingly opened her mouth to the tender invasion of his. The blanket fell to the floor, forgotten, as Cole's fingers untied the drawstrings at her waist. One by one, the petticoats pooled at her feet until only her shift and drawers remained.

As he pulled her closer into his embrace, Stephanie's body molded to his in beautiful symmetry. The heat burned through the thin fabric of her underwear as though it wasn't there, kindling an unfamiliar need deep within her.

Cole's mouth traced tantalizing patterns down her neck while he untied the ribbon that held her shift together. He pushed the delicate fabric down her arms and slid his hands across the soft warmth of her ribs, his thumbs gently tracing the curve of her breasts as he kissed the soft skin revealed in the glowing firelight. With a groan, he lifted her in his arms and carried her to the bunk.

Stephanie was so lost in sensation she hardly noticed when he removed her shift and drawers. She was only aware of his hands gently stroking and lips that touched her with fire. Tingling skin marked the path of his kisses as he caressed her body from her shoulders clear to her toes.

Emboldened by the excitement pounding through her, Stephanie undid the buttons that hid his glorious body and reached inside to stroke the curly hair and hard muscles of his chest. Kissing the hollow of his throat, she slid her hands up and pushed the material off wide shoulders, only to sigh in frustration when it caught on the thickness of his arms.

Cole sucked in his breath, then pulled away and rose from the bunk. She closed her eyes in disappointment, but he returned almost immediately, minus the long underwear that had hindered her explorations. Pulling the blankets over them both, he kissed the delicate skin below her ear. "So sweet," he whispered huskily. "So beautiful."

Unrestrained, her hands caressed his back and shoulders, the smooth skin warm and vibrant under her fingers. She reveled in the difference between his rock-hard body and her own soft curves. Shivering with delight, she rubbed her toes along the rough hair of his leg, lips and hands tracing the contours of his beautiful masculine body. The fire in her blood began to gather somewhere near the center of her being, and she felt an urgent need for something she couldn't name.

Sensing her readiness, Cole rolled her gently onto her back, kissing her deeply. Her legs parted instinctively to accept him, and he entered smoothly. For a passion glazed second, the thin membrane he encountered had no meaning for him, and he pushed through it before he realized its significance. Surprise and confusion washed over him almost instantly as the full import of that obstruction burst upon his consciousness.

With something akin to horror, he opened his eyes and

stared down into the twin emerald pools that reflected shocked pain. "Oh Lord," he murmured, burying his face against the side of her neck. It was much too late to stop now; the damage had already been done.

Reclaiming her mouth, he kissed her softly, stroking her body with gentle hands, willing her to respond to him again. With patience and care, he rekindled her desire, waiting until he knew she was ready. He began to move, keeping a maddeningly slow pace until her breathing changed. When tiny sighs greeted every thrust, he increased his tempo until they exploded in a harmony of joyous fulfillment as old as mankind itself.

He lay for a moment, exhausted. Then he rolled onto his side, wrapping his arms around her and pulling her still quivering body close. They lay silent for a few minutes while their breathing slowed. He smoothed the hair back from her face. "Are you all right?"

She gazed at him in mild surprise. "I've never been so all right in my life. I'm sure of it." Her voice held such a strong note of conviction; Cole knew the significance of what had just happened hadn't occurred to her yet.

He sighed and kissed her forehead. "Well, we know James isn't your husband."

She raised her eyebrows. "We do?"

"Remember the pain?"

She nodded. "Pretty hard to forget."

"That only happens once, the very first time."

She continued to stare at him, puzzled, then her expression changed. "Oh, you mean I was a —"

"A virgin," he finished for her. "Yes, yes you were."

"Is that all?" She sighed in relief. "I was afraid I'd done something wrong." Her brow wrinkled in sudden alarm. "I didn't, did I? I mean, you seemed to like — that is, I thought..." Her voice trailed off in confusion.

He smiled softly and traced the line of her jaw with his fingertip. "You were wonderful, perfect in fact." He gently pushed her head down onto his shoulder. "Relax now and go to sleep."

Sighing happily, Stephanie snuggled against him and fell asleep almost immediately.

Cole lay a long time staring at the moonlit window. It had never occurred to him she might be a virgin, though he wasn't sure what difference it would have made if he'd known. He didn't think he could have stopped even if he'd wanted to.

What now? James wasn't her husband, but Stephanie loved him. An unsuitable beau perhaps? It was possible. She might even have a husband; some marriages were like that. Or maybe it was an abusive father she was running from, one who didn't approve of James. Whatever the situation, she was bound to return to her lover's arms sooner or later; a lover who had obviously resisted the temptation Cole had given into.

Cole sighed. He couldn't replace her virginity, but he could damn well keep his hands off her in the future. It wouldn't repair the damage, but it would keep the situation from getting any worse. She'd be free to leave when the time came, and he'd be able to watch her go with his heart whole.

The noble decision made, Cole tried to go to sleep. He knew it was the right thing to do, so why did he feel like the little boy whose peppermint stick was snatched away just as he got his first taste?

CHAPTER 20

At daybreak, Cole gave up trying to sleep and slipped from the bed. Stephanie made a small noise of protest but didn't waken as he adjusted the blankets over her. He stared down at her for a long moment, gazing at the thick eyelashes fanning the translucent skin of her cheeks and tousled hair lying around her in glorious abandon. *So sweet,* he thought to himself. *So beautiful!* He remembered whispering those words against her soft skin and swallowed a groan.

It only took a few minutes to dress and stoke the fire. Then, with one last look at Stephanie, he put on his coat, hat, and gloves and went outside, hoping the frigid temperatures would cool his blood.

The sun was well up in the sky when he returned. He stomped the snow from his boots and set two buckets of water on the table.

A soft smile played around Stephanie's mouth as she stretched luxuriously and opened her eyes. She propped her head on one hand and gave him a glowing smile. "Good morning!"

Bathed in the glory of that smile, Cole's good intentions took a severe beating. Stephanie lay on the bunk, the blanket draped enticingly across her still-naked body. The temptation to slide into bed and spend the entire day making love to her was nearly irresistible.

"Good morning," he said, smiling back as he tried to ignore the memory of her hair caressing his naked skin. "I dug out the well, so we won't have to melt snow anymore."

"Oh."

She continued to smile, and he could feel himself getting very warm. He knew he couldn't stay in the same room with her, or he'd be giving into his baser self. Searching his mind frantically for an excuse, he walked to the fireplace. "You know, we may be able to leave today."

He heard a rustle of blankets and a noncommittal, "Mmmm," behind him.

"Midnight's strong, but it may be too drifted out there for him to carry us both all the way back to the house." Stripping off his gloves, Cole turned and almost dropped them on the floor. Draped only in the blanket and her thick mane of hair, Stephanie sat cross-legged on the bed, her chin on her hands, elbows resting on her knees as she watched him.

Sweat began to pop out on his forehead, and he knew he'd have to make his escape soon or he wouldn't be leaving at all. "I'm going to scout around and see if the snow is this deep everywhere. Sometimes a blizzard will pile a drift fifteen feet high in one place and strip the ground almost bare somewhere else." He turned back to the fireplace and added more wood. "You stay here and keep the fire going. I should be back about noon, but don't panic if I'm not."

"What if—"

"Whatever you do, don't leave the cabin," he interrupted. "It's bitterly cold out there, and you have no idea how to survive in it. Do you understand me?"

"Yes," she said irritably. "I understand. I'm not stupid."

Cole gave her enigmatic stare. "You call going out for a ride when there's a storm coming intelligent?"

"How was I supposed to know? You and Charlie only said it *might* storm."

"Of course we said might. Those same clouds could have just passed right over us, but nobody takes a chance on being caught in a storm."

"Levi wasn't worried."

"He was going to town, not heading out on the prairie. He knew he had time to make it."

She watched Cole wrap his scarf around his neck and pull his bandanna over his nose and mouth. "What am I suppose to do while you're gone for maybe several days?"

He grinned at her even though he knew she couldn't see it under the bandanna. "You did find that needle and thread yesterday. Why don't you take the flour sack and sew something?"

He opened the door and ducked just as the pillow came sailing over his head to land in the snow outside.

Chuckling, he picked it up and tossed it back to her, snow still clinging to the sides. Stephanie squealed when the snow hit her naked flesh. He knew she could hear his laughter as he quickly stepped outside and shut the door behind him.

Time hung heavy on Stephanie's hands. She heated water and scrubbed every dish in the place, then set a can of beans on the hearth as she mixed up a batch of cornbread. While it was baking over the hot coals, she gave the cabin a thorough cleaning, probably its first in years. When she started to make the bed, she discovered blood on one of the blankets. Touching the tell-tale stain, she grimaced. It would have to be washed out.

Washing the heavy wool blanket in unheated water was a cold, difficult job. By the time Stephanie had hung it up to dry, her hands and arms felt frozen. She removed the golden cornbread and set it aside to cool, then threw several pieces of wood into the fireplace. Even with the fire burning, the cold seemed to creep in through the walls, and she began to shiver.

Finally, she set one of the chairs in front of the fireplace then wrapped herself in her cloak and snuggled into it. How she wished Cole were here to warm her. If only he hadn't been in such a rush this morning. Oh well, maybe he'd find the snow so bad they'd have to stay another night. She smiled in anticipation.

Realizing she had suddenly become very warm in her cloak, Stephanie took it off and started to lay it over the back of her chair. Then she remembered the tearing sound she'd heard when she'd stepped on it during the blizzard. She sighed heavily. At least the mending would use up some time.

It only took a few seconds to retrieve the sewing materials. Threading the needle, her thoughts returned to Cole. Could he have made love to her with such delightful sweetness if he had no feelings for her? Then there was the smile he'd given her this morning. Her stomach had done a couple of flipflops over that.

Stephanie picked up the cape and searched for the tear. "Well, no wonder," she muttered in disgust when she located a six-inch rip where the hem had torn out. It was obvious from the ragged stitches that still held that she'd sewn it before. *That's probably why it tore,* she thought as she stuck the needled through the fabric. *Further proof that I didn't make my living as a seamstress; as if I needed any.*

She had barely taken the first stitch when a piece of paper stuck in the hem of her cloak caught her eye. "What in the world?" Curiously, she reached inside the hem, tugged the paper free, and brought it out into the light. "For heaven's sake." She stared at the one-hundred-dollar bill she held in her hand.

How on earth had it found its way into the hem of her cloak? Could there be a hidden pocket or a hole she wasn't aware of? Maybe something else had fallen through, something that could give her a clue to her former life.

With mounting excitement, she reached inside, her hand closing on another piece of paper wedged in the hem. Praying it wasn't just a random scrap, she tugged it free and found herself holding another one-hundred-dollar bill. Frowning, Stephanie once again reached into the hem and came out with a third bill identical to the first two. A closer look at the hem revealed the entire seam had been sewn with the same ragged stitches. With a feeling of doom hanging over her, Stephanie began methodically ripping them out.

By the time Cole returned forty-five minutes later, Stephanie was putting the last few stitches back in her cape. Her tear-streaked face was the first thing he saw when he opened the door, and his stomach twisted at her anguished expression. He took an involuntary step toward her. "Steph?"

Stephanie raised tear-filled eyes to his. "Oh, Cole, when the note said dishonest, I had no idea it was something like this." She gestured to the table.

Cole's eyes widened in shock when he saw the pile of one-hundred-dollar bills. "Where in God's name...?"

"They were in the bottom of my cloak, each one tacked in by a single stitch. That's why the hem of my cape was so stiff."

Stunned, Cole removed his hat and sat down in the other chair. "Why are you so sure they have anything to do with the note?" he asked, unbuttoning his coat.

"Cole, there are fifty of these. That's five thousand dollars! Now, tell me where you get that kind of money honestly?"

What she said was true. It was more money than they made off the ranch in two years. "But how do you know you had anything to do with it being sewn in the hem of your cloak? You've said yourself it's probably a hand-me-down from someone else."

"Who'd give away a cloak with five thousand dollars in it?"

"All right, but maybe somebody else put it in there. Maybe the money and the note were to frame you for something. After all, your dreams are always of someone pursuing you."

"Yes, and he's probably a Pinkerton detective! The whole thing was sewn with my wonderful stitches. Nobody else in the world sews like that. I hid that money there; I'm certain of it." She put her head down on her arms. "Oh, Cole, what have I done?"

Kneeling to take her in his arms, Cole tried to soothe her. "Shh, it's all right. Nobody knows where you are, or they'd have found you by now. You're safe with us."

His mind was working fast. Could it be some sort of ransom? Was James being held somewhere? Or perhaps she'd been forced to steal it to protect him. Kidnapping, blackmail…either one was an ugly business.

"Look Steph, if somebody's missing this kind of money, they'll be looking for it. They probably won't want you as badly as they want the money back. All we have to do is lay low and keep an ear to the ground. Sooner or later we'll find out who it belongs to. Then we'll return it without anyone knowing where it came from, and you'll be in the clear."

He raised her head from his shoulder and handed her his handkerchief. "Don't cry, everything's going to be fine."

"I wish I could believe that."

"I won't let anybody hurt you. Are you all right now?"

She nodded as she wiped her eyes and blew her nose.

"Good. Now listen, while I was outside, I saw a rider headed this way leading an extra horse, and I'm pretty sure it's Charlie. He'll be here in about fifteen minutes. We'll hide the money, and he won't know a thing about it. It's to stay between the two of us—there's less chance of it leaking out that way. Don't even tell Kate."

She nodded again and gave him a shaky smile.

"That's better. Just remember…"

There was a sudden loud explosion, and they were hit with tiny bits of something hot.

"What the…" Cole wiped the side of his face.

Stephanie glanced toward the source of the explosion and clapped her hands over her mouth. "Oh no, I forgot the beans. I set a can of them on the hearth, they must have gotten too
hot!" She giggled. "You should see your face."

"You're not exactly tidy yourself." Wiping a dollop of beans from her nose, he stuck it in his mouth. "Hmm, not bad, but I think they could use a little salt."

It wasn't long before Stephanie had the happy notion of letting Sam in to help clean up the mess, and his canine joy at the unexpected feast was unbounded.

Charlie was relieved to find them at the line shack, neither one apparently the worse for wear. Though he didn't know about the argument that had caused Stephanie to run away, he remembered Cole's earlier coolness toward her and had half expected to find two people ready to tear each other's throats out. Instead, he found them scraping beans off the walls and giggling like a couple of giddy children.

'Kind of amazin' what cabin fever'll do to a person,' he thought with satisfaction.

CHAPTER 21

"Pa! Stephanie! You're alive!" Hastily scrubbing his eyes so they wouldn't know he'd been crying, Josh rushed out to meet them.

Kate wasn't ashamed of her tears; they streamed down her face in torrents. "I don't know when I've been so happy to see anybody," she said, giving them each a hug. "I was afraid we'd lost you both."

Over steaming bowls of nourishing stew, Cole entertained his audience with the tale of their adventures. He carefully avoided any mention of Stephanie's discovery, but he didn't hesitate to tell how delighted they'd been to find the chess set, or of Stephanie sewing her cloak out of sheer boredom. Even the exploding beans figured prominently.

After lunch, Kate sent Stephanie to bed and started the dishes. The minute Charlie and Josh left for the barn, she turned to Cole with a militant light in her eye. "Are you planning to marry her?"

The question was not unexpected, and Cole sighed. "No, I'm not."

"And why not?"

"It wouldn't be fair—not to Stephanie, anyway."

"You ruin her reputation, and it wouldn't be fair to make an honest woman of her?" She crossed her arms and glared at him. "How do you figure that?"

"Her reputation is fine. Nobody knows we were gone but the family." He frowned. "She's in love with somebody else, Kate."

Kate was startled. "Who?"

"James. She was talking to him in her sleep again, and she said she loved him." He sighed. "Someday she'll remember, or someone will come looking for her. How would she feel married to me when the man she really loves walks back into her life? Besides, you're forgetting she may already have a husband."

"There is that, of course." Kate was silent for a moment while she digested this unexpected information. "What if she's with child?"

"Kate Cantrell, what do you think I am?"

"Huh! I think you're a red-blooded man, and she's a beautiful woman. That combination has caused early babies more than once."

"You're overly suspicious."

"Maybe I am at that." She turned back to the dishes. "But it wouldn't be the first time two people got carried away in a blizzard."

Actually, the possibility of a child was one he hadn't considered. Would Stephanie even realize she was pregnant? Unbidden, the vision of a little girl with red pigtails, green eyes, and freckles rose in his mind, accompanied by a feeling very like longing. He stubbornly pushed both the image and the feeling away. Mentally, he counted off the days. It would be nearly Christmas before he could be sure one way or the other. There was no sense of mentioning it to her until then.

He glanced at Kate, who had apparently forgotten her dishes as she stood at the sink with a half-smile on her lips, fingering the cameo at her throat the way she often did when she was thinking of his father. Suddenly, Cole found himself wondering what had gone on between Kate and Jonathan before their marriage. Could they have... No, not with Kate's strict morals. He dismissed the idea with a shake of his head.

Stephanie slept deeply for several hours and awoke refreshed. Her muscles were stiff and sore—remnants, she was sure, of last night's activities—but there was a poignant sweetness connected with the pain. The discovery of the money had taken her mind away from her joy temporarily, but she still felt as though she held a wonderful secret hidden away.

When she entered the kitchen, Kate welcomed her with the usual comfortable chatter. It wasn't long, though, before her friend casually brought up the subject Stephanie had been dreading. "Did Cole do anything...unseemly at the line shack?"

"He threw snow on me this morning," Stephanie said indignantly. "Then he suggested I make something out of the flour sack to occupy my time!" She told herself she wasn't lying to her friend. Cole hadn't done anything. Nothing she hadn't wanted him to, anyway.

Kate chuckled. "Cole's Pa is one for teasing a body, too." Then she glanced at Stephanie, choosing her words carefully. "Some people get strange ideas about a man and woman spending the night alone together. It might be best if we just forget it happened."

Stephanie nodded. The most beautiful experience of her life, and she was supposed to forget it happened? Not likely.

The door opened, spilling a draft of frigid air into the kitchen. Stephanie looked up into a vaguely familiar face. "Levi?" She could hardly believe the change a shave and a haircut had wrought.

"In the flesh." He rubbed his cold-reddened face. "Now I remember why I wear a beard during the winter." He looked expectantly toward the stove. "Do you suppose I could talk you ladies out of some of that coffee? It's mighty cold out there."

Stephanie poured a cup of coffee and watched him struggle out of the heavy buffalo coat. Without the long hair and the beard, it wasn't difficult to tell he and Cole were brothers. They both had the same chiseled features and powerful builds. Two inches shorter than his younger brother,

Levi was still well over six feet tall and was the more muscular of the two. Though Levi didn't share Cole's coloring, the chestnut hair and blue-gray eyes were striking, and his lively sense of humor showed in his face. He was fully as attractive as Cole, though in a more understated way.

"Will I do?"

Stephanie blushed when she realized she'd been staring. "I was just thinking how much you look like Cole."

"No, he looks like me. I had the face first. So, what do you think?"

Setting his coffee down on the table, she walked around him, pretending to view him critically on all sides. "You'll certainly never make it as an outlaw," she announced at last. "I'm afraid your days of cattle rustling are over."

He sighed dramatically. "Ah well, I was thinking of giving it up anyway. It's hard on a man being held at gunpoint and all that. What about you?"

She looked at her nails consideringly. "Actually, I was looking for a new partner, but if you aren't interested..."

"If you two will stop your tomfoolery," Kate said, "you can try these new cookies Prudy gave me the recipe for."

By the time Cole walked in several minutes later, Levi and Stephanie were on their third cookie and teasing Kate unmercifully. Telling himself he was pleased to find Stephanie getting along so well with his brother, Cole tried to ignore the surge of jealous anger that knifed through him.

Stephanie had expected Cole to find a way to rekindle the intimacy they'd shared in the line shack, but she was doomed to disappointment. In fact, over the next few weeks, Cole became increasingly distant. Even the nightly chess games ceased. It didn't take long for her to decide his change of attitude stemmed from the discovery of the money. Stephanie didn't blame Cole for not wanting to get too close. Her mind shied away from even considering how she'd come by such a huge sum. There were so many horrible possibilities.

In her hurt, Stephanie turned to Levi for comfort. Levi had an entertaining sense of humor and, unlike his brother, always seemed to be in a good mood. A deep friendship rapidly developed between them.

Levi wasn't fooled by her determined cheerfulness. "Why the long face?" he asked one day when he found her leaning against the corral watching the brood mares.

She looked up and smiled. "Oh, I was just thinking."

"Then you've been thinking an awful lot lately. I haven't seen you look happy for a long time now." He raised an eyebrow questioningly. "Do you want to talk about it?"

"There's nothing to talk about."

"It's my brother, isn't it?"

"Cole? Heavens, no! I just..." she trailed off in embarrassment at the disbelieving look on his face. "Is it so obvious?"

"Females have been falling in love with Cole since he was a kid. I've learned to recognize the signs."

Stephanie sighed unhappily. "It's foolish of me, isn't it?"

"Not necessarily. He's a good man." Levi's eyes twinkled. "Kind of slow sometimes, though. Here's a beautiful woman ready to melt in his arms, and he doesn't realize it. I'm far more observant. In fact, if you'd care to melt in this direction..."

Stephanie gave a gurgle of laughter. "You are so absurd sometimes."

"Absurd!" Levi put a hand to his heart. "And you, madam, are unkind. How is a man to recover from such a wound?"

"Oh, stop it." She gave his hand a playful slap.

Levi smiled at the new lightness in her tone. "That's more like it. Now, let's talk this thing out, and you'll feel better."

"I don't think talking will help." She sighed. "I've fallen in love with a man who detests me."

Levi looked at her in surprise. "Cole doesn't detest you."

"How do you know that?"

"From something he said when I first came home."

Stephanie leaned her folded arms back on the fence dejectedly. "That was before. He's changed his mind since then."

"Why, what happened?"

Stephanie had an urge to unburden her soul to him, but what if he turned away from her when he found out about the money? It wasn't worth the risk. "Cole found out something about me that...well, he's been avoiding me ever since."

"If Cole's avoiding you, it's probably because he's more upset with himself than you. He judges people by what they are, not for what they've done." Suddenly his eyes twinkled. "We could try to make him jealous, if you like." Levi pulled her into his arms and gave her an exaggerated hug.

She laughed and hugged him back. "Oh, Levi, you always make me feel better. Why couldn't I have fallen in love with you?"

Levi sighed dramatically. "Your heart must have already been taken before you ever clapped eyes on me. Otherwise Cole wouldn't have stood a chance!"

CHAPTER 22

"All right, but next time we'll beat you," Josh said as he closed the gate to Black's stall.

Stephanie smiled. "Don't be too sure. Sunrise is pretty fast."

"Josh, your grandmother just took a batch of molasses cookies out of the oven. If you hurry, you might be able to talk her out of some." At the unexpected sound of Cole's voice, Stephanie's heart gave a little jerk.

"Molasses cookies." Josh's eyes brightened. "Come on, Stephanie, I'll race you to the house!"

"You go ahead, Josh, I want to talk to Stephanie. And save some of those cookies for us!" Cole called as his son hit the barn door at a run.

Stephanie picked up the brush and started on Sunrise's neck. After practically ignoring her for six weeks, he suddenly wanted to talk? "What did you want, Cole?"

He rubbed his moustache as though unsure how to begin. "We need to talk about what happened in the line shack."

She closed her eyes as her throat constricted painfully. She'd held onto the memory like a precious jewel. Discussing it in the cold light of day could only tarnish its brilliance.

Hesitantly, he cleared his throat. "There might be certain results of that night that we —"

"Don't worry," Stephanie cut in. "No one has the faintest idea anything happened. Your reputation and mine are spotlessly clean!"

"That's not what I meant," he said in surprise.

"Then what are we talking about?"

He sighed in frustration, then tried again. "How have you been feeling?"

"Fine."

"What we did...I mean, you could be...Oh, hell, are you

with child?" His face darkened as the blunt question hung in the air between them.

Stephanie made a small noise. "No."

"You're sure?"

"Positive. Two days after we got back...well, I'm certain I didn't conceive."

Cole was aware of a small flash of disappointment even as a wave of relief washed over him. "Thank God. We won't have to get married." Her look of shocked pain pierced his heart like an arrow. "I didn't mean that the way it sounded, Steph. It's just that we don't have any idea who or what you left behind." He knew he should tell her about James, but the words stuck in his throat. "It wouldn't be fair," he finished lamely.

"I know what you meant. Too bad you didn't ask me sooner. You've spent all this time worrying for nothing." Stephanie walked to the door, her back stiff and unyielding. She glanced down at the brush in her hand as though she'd forgotten she held it. "I'll come back and finish Sunrise later." She lay the brush on the shelf then walked out the door.

"Stephanie, wait." But she only pulled her cloak tighter around her body and kept walking. "Damn it," Cole said, kicking a sack of grain. Suddenly he whirled around and peered into the shadows as Levi stepped away from the wall where he'd been leaning.

"When did you sneak in?" Cole snapped.

"I've been here longer than you have," Levi said, calmly rolling a cigarette. "You just didn't notice."

"Then you heard?"

"I heard. Sounds like you and Stephanie did more than play chess at the line shack."

Cole's face darkened. "It wasn't intentional. It just happened."

Levi licked the paper to seal the cigarette and reached into his pocket for a match. "What about the husband?"

"I'm beginning to think there may not be one, at least not in the true sense of the word."

"Oh?"

"She was a virgin." Cole's hand knotted into a fist. "You don't have to say it; I know I'm the worst kind of sidewinder around."

Levi leaned on the gate of one of the horse pens and nonchalantly watched the smoke from his cigarette drift toward the ceiling. "You forced her, then?"

There was a moment of stunned silence. "Hell no, I didn't force her. You think I'd do that?"

"No, but you seem to have forgotten she was a willing partner. As I remember, she was pretty happy when you came back. Not exactly mourning her lost virginity, was she?"

"I guess not."

"Stephanie probably has fond memories of that night, and you just told her it was all a bad mistake."

"I did not."

"Sounded like it to me. Right now, she's probably hiding somewhere crying her eyes out." He flicked the ash off his cigarette and looked at Cole. "One of us is going after her. It really should be you, but if you don't, I will."

Cole glared at his brother for a moment, then turned on his heel and stalked out the door. Levi smiled. Whatever Cole's problem was, it certainly wasn't because he didn't like Stephanie. Stubbing out his cigarette, he headed for the house in search of molasses cookies.

Stephanie threw herself on her bed, her misery complete. Nobody knew better than she that it would be unfair to drag Cole down with her when her crime became known. If only she'd never discovered that accursed money. Once the tears started, she couldn't stop them. She was sobbing into her pillow when Cole burst unceremoniously through the door.

"Ah, Steph," he said, pulling her into his arms. "Please don't cry. I didn't mean that the way it sounded. I only meant I was glad you wouldn't have to suffer any more for what I did to you."

"I didn't suffer." Her answer was muffled against his chest.

"Not yet maybe, but the time may come when you'll hate me for it." He hugged her tighter. "I know I should apologize, but I could never bring myself to do it."

She pulled away and glared up at him. "That was the most beautiful night of my life. If you ever try to apologize, I swear I'll punch you so hard it will send you tail over teakettle!" she threatened, delving into Josh's vocabulary.

He smiled. "It was memorable for me, too." He wiped a tear from her cheek, his smile fading. "If that's not what's bothering you, what is?"

She looked at him silently for a moment, then glanced down. "I hate not being your friend."

"What?" Cole sounded honestly shocked. "Whatever gave you that idea?"

"You n-never talk to me anymore." She stared at the third button on his shirt. "You won't even play chess with me."

He lifted her chin. "Steph, I can't be around you without wanting to kiss you, only I'm afraid I wouldn't stop there. We can't have that kind of relationship."

"I just want you to like me again."

"That's something you don't have to worry about, Steph." He pulled her back into the shelter of his arms and buried his face in her hair. "I like you more than is good for either of us."

That Thursday, Kate and Stephanie went to town. It was the first time Stephanie had ever been to the general store, and she was fascinated. The store was filled with everything from plows to hair ribbons.

In her browsing, she came across a lovely china mustache cup, just the sort of thing one friend would give another. She carried it to the counter where Kate was ordering her supplies.

"Do you think Cole would like this, Kate?"

"Probably. Why?"

"I thought it would make a nice Christmas present."

Kate nodded. "It would at that."

Waiting for the storekeeper to finish Kate's order, Stephanie casually glanced at the bolts of cloth behind the counter. A beautiful sapphire blue the same shade as Cole's eyes caught her attention. With his black hair and deeply tanned skinned, Cole would be devastating in a shirt made of it. With a regretful sigh, she turned away. A shirt was far too intimate a gift for her to give him.

Just then, the door opened behind them. "Well, well," came a sugary sweet voice. "If it isn't dear little Stephanie."

"Good morning, Sally." Stephanie turned and smiled pleasantly. "Nice to see you again."

Sally's eyes narrowed maliciously. "Apparently your memory hasn't returned since you're still here. How very convenient for you."

"Not really, but the Cantrells have all been so kind, I feel like part of the family." Stephanie's brows drew together in concern. "Have you been ill, Sally?"

"No, why?"

"Oh, you just look a bit haggard. It's probably the light."

Unable to think of a suitable reply, Sally glowered at the storekeeper instead. "Tom is coming by with the wagon later. Has that shipment we've been waiting for come in yet?"

"Yes, ma'am. I'll have it ready for him when he gets here, Mrs. Langton."

"See that you do!" Sally's tone was imperious. She turned back to Stephanie with a haughty look. "Actually, I'm surprised to see you here. I thought you'd left."

"Oh? Why is that?"

"Cole didn't even mention you when he stopped by the other night. Of course, I didn't ask."

"Good heavens, I should hope not! How boring it is to talk about other people when they aren't there. I hope Cole hasn't been so incredibly rude as to discuss me when he's with you."

"Cole and I have far better things to do than talk about you," Sally snapped.

"Did you manage to sell him that cow?"

"Cow, what cow?"

"I don't really know," Stephanie said, looking confused. "I thought I overheard Charlie and Levi discussing you the other day. Charlie said not to worry, Cole had no reason to buy the cow when the milk was free." She looked apologetic. "I guess they were talking about somebody else."

Sally gasped in shock. Then, speechless with anger, she flounced out, two bright spots of color burning high on her cheeks. Though Stephanie had remained calm throughout the exchange, angry sparks glowed deep in her eyes as she turned back to the counter.

"Mr. Collins, I find that I've changed my mind. I need enough of that blue material to make a shirt for a very large man." She looked down at Kate. "Do you suppose, with your help, I could turn out something wearable?"

"I'll have you sewing like a dream inside of a week."

Frank chortled as he cut the fabric. "That was the best dern show I've seen in a long time. It did my old heart good to see the Widow Langton get her comeuppance."

Stephanie blushed. "I can't seem to help myself. That woman brings out the worst in me."

"It seems to me she started it just like she always does. Reckon it's 'bout time someone gave it back to her."

CHAPTER 23

With Christmas almost upon them, secrets abounded, and Stephanie was nearly as excited as Josh. Even sewing Cole's shirt hadn't dampened her enthusiasm. When the day finally arrived, Josh crept in at the crack of dawn.

"Are you awake, Stephanie?" he whispered.

"Huh, of course we're awake," Kate remarked acidly from her bedroom. "Who could sleep with you stomping around like a buffalo?"

Before long, they were all sitting down to a festive breakfast. "What's Christmas like in China, Uncle Levi?" Josh asked.

"Actually—" The words froze on his lips as the door suddenly burst open, and all eyes turned toward it.

"Merry Christmas!"

There was a moment of stunned silence, then pandemonium broke loose as Kate jumped to her feet and rushed into the newcomer's arms. "Jonathan!"

Watching everyone crowd around Jonathan Cantrell, welcoming him home with undisguised delight, Stephanie knew she'd have recognized him anywhere. Both of his sons resembled him a great deal, though he was shorter and his features more refined. Even with silver-gray hair and creases in his skin from years of facing the elements, he was an extremely handsome man.

His reunion with Levi brought tears to Stephanie's eyes, but hers were not the only ones. As they watched the two men hug, Kate sniffled, and Charlie blew his nose. When she saw a glimmer of wetness in Jonathan's eyes, she suddenly realized what a toll Levi's disappearance had taken on his father.

"And you must be Stephanie," he said, turning to her at last. "I can't tell you how happy I am to finally meet the legend."

Stephanie blushed. "Oh, hardly that."

"Yes, indeed. Every letter I got was filled with your name." He smiled, and Stephanie saw unexpected dimples in his cheeks. She understood why Sally had pursued him. The hearts he must have broken when he was young!

"Grandpa, Grandpa, did you bring me anything?" Josh said, dancing around Jonathan gleefully.

"I don't know, sprout. Were you good while I was gone?"

"I was perfect." Josh glanced at his grandmother. "Well, almost."

Jonathan chuckled. "I have a whole wagon full of things from your Aunt Belle. She might have sent something for you."

"Can I unload it?" Josh asked.

"After breakfast," Jonathan promised. "Maybe you can talk your father and uncle into giving you a hand."

Kate gave Jonathan another hug. "How was your trip?"

"Fine. Daniel and I got back to Chicago at the end of last week." He dropped a kiss on her forehead. "All I could think of was getting home for Christmas and surprising everyone."

"You certainly did that." Kate wiped her eyes and moved back to the stove. "Sit down now, and eat some breakfast."

Cole and Stephanie's close call during the blizzard had to be repeated in detail. Jonathan's trip to England was discussed, then Levi's to the Orient. As the lighthearted conversation flowed around her, Stephanie felt a deeply satisfying sense of belonging. Her heart swelled with love for the people who had taken her in and made her feel one of them. Even Jonathan, a virtual stranger, treated her as though she was part of the family.

After breakfast, the wagon was unloaded, and it was time to open the gifts. Stephanie waited in breathless anticipation as Cole unwrapped his shirt. It was, indeed, the same color as his eyes, and she sighed in satisfaction at his obvious pleasure.

"Stephanie made that for you," Kate said with a pleased smile.

Stephanie giggled at Cole's shocked expression. "You don't need to look like that. Kate did most everything that shows, like the pocket and the cuffs. All I did were the long seams."

"But I haven't heard a single scream of rage in weeks."

Stephanie tossed her head. "My sewing has improved. I only curse under my breath now."

"Open mine, Stephanie," Josh said, handing her a small package. "I made it for you."

She tore open the brown paper and pulled out a tiny hand-carved whistle hanging from a leather thong. "It's beautiful, Josh."

"Blow it!"

As the whistle emitted its high, sweet note, Sam jumped up from his place by the fire and ran to her side.

Josh beamed. "If you ever get lost, just blow on that whistle. I trained Sam to find you and bring you home." His face sobered. "I don't want you to ever get lost from us again."

"Oh, Josh." There was a lump in her throat as she hugged him.

Swept up in the excitement of the day, Stephanie reveled in the love and laughter surrounding her. It was an unfamiliar feeling, but one that she found utterly wonderful. Surely life could be no sweeter than to belong to such a family.

Amidst a great many exclamations of surprise and pleasure, the rest of the gifts were opened one by one. There was a pair of chaps for Josh, a new set of leather-working tools for Charlie, saddle bags for Levi, a beautifully embroidered wool shawl for Kate, a new hat for Cole, and a musty old book of Greek mythology for Jonathan. Only Stephanie was surprised at the older man's obvious delight in the tattered volume.

"I found it in San Francisco," Levi told him. "I figured it would probably take you a couple of months to read."

Jonathan's eyes gleamed as he rubbed his hand over the book. "It's been so long since I translated any Greek, it might take a year."

Stephanie was still wondering about that when Jonathan glanced at his wife. "I suppose it's time for that box you and Belle had me cart half-way across the country."

"It is indeed. I hadn't expected it so soon, but Christmas is the perfect occasion." Kate retrieved a large, flat box from the pile of supplies by the door and set it on Stephanie's lap with an expectant smile.

Stephanie looked up in surprise. "For me?"

Kate shrugged. "You'll be needing something for parties this spring. I asked my sister-in-law to see what she could find in Chicago."

Opening the lid curiously, Stephanie gasped. Inside was a lovely dress of emerald green silk. "Oh, it's beautiful!"

"We got you something else, too," Cole said a bit gruffly as he handed her a small package. Nervously, she tore away the paper and string. When she saw the beautiful set of gold inlaid mother-of-pearl hair combs, her eyes involuntarily flew to his. Encountering an intent look, she knew he, too, was remembering strong hands unpinning her hair in a snowbound cabin.

That evening, after the supper dishes had been washed and put away, Stephanie took a bowl of apples out to the barn for the saddle horses. It was a happy notion she'd come up with while trying to think of an unobtrusive way to give Jonathan and Kate some time alone before she went to bed. Feeding the last apple to Midnight half an hour later, she jumped when a deep voice sounded in her ear.

"Spoiling my horse again, I see." The look Cole gave her sent a shiver of delight down her spine.

"No, I've given them to all the horses in the barn. I saved Midnight for last because I was afraid he'd take them all if I didn't."

"The last thing I expected when I came in here was to see

all our future apple pies disappearing down my best horses." He sighed. "Oh well..." He reached into his pocket and pulled out a small velvet case. "I didn't want to explain this to the others."

Not quite knowing what to expect, Stephanie opened it gingerly. Nestled inside was a finely wrought golden snowflake suspended from a delicate chain. There was a note tucked under the necklace.

Instead of the apology neither of us wants me to make, I give you this to remember, as I shall.

Cole

Tears came to her eyes.

"Steph, what is it?" Cole's voice was hurt and confused. "I thought you'd like it."

"I do, oh, I do. It's been such a wonderful day and now this! Oh, Cole, you've made me so happy I just..."

Gently, he gathered her in his arms. "I know, Steph, I know. I feel the same way." He rested his chin on the top of her head. "I still can't believe you made me a shirt. I seem to remember being pelted with a pillow for merely suggesting you take a needle in hand."

Stephanie gave him a tearful smile. "It matches your eyes. From the moment I saw that cloth, I could see you wearing it, and I couldn't resist."

"Neither can I," He whispered, lifting her chin and kissing her softly. It was gentle and incredibly sweet. When at last he broke it off, he tenderly smoothed the hair back from her face. "I only wish—"

Stephanie was not to find out what he wished, for Levi came whistling into the barn. If he noticed them jump apart, he gave no indication of it, and after calling hello, disappeared into the tack room.

"Thank you for the necklace," she murmured. "I'll treasure it."

He traced the line of her cheek with the backs of his fingers.

"I'm glad." With one last tender smile, he turned and was gone.

Later, as Stephanie lay in bed, a feeling of peace stole over her. Even Kate and Jonathan in the next room didn't make her uncomfortable. Though she could occasionally hear the vague murmuring of their voices, no other sound came through the wall, and she didn't feel like an intruder.

Maybe it wouldn't be so bad if she never regained her memory. This was surely far better than anything she could have left behind. Her hand lovingly touched the gold snowflake from Cole where it lay against her breast. Thinking of Josh's whistle and the dress from Kate, Stephanie smiled and closed her eyes. These Cantrells surely had a way of winding themselves around a girl's heart.

CHAPTER 24

Jonathan gave his wife a regretful look as he folded the letter. "I have to go, Kate."

"Oh, Jonathan, you just got home."

"I know, but this is something I can't turn my back on. If Governor Moonlight had his way, the whole territory would be turned over to the farmers. If he takes away our rights to the open range, we could lose everything we've worked for."

"The Cattleman's Association will never let that happen, and you know it."

Jonathan raised his eyebrows. "Do my ears deceive me? Could this be my wife, erstwhile defender of the homesteader and small stockman, singing the praises of the hateful Cattleman's Association?"

"Hardly, but you're not the only member they could send."

"No, but I may be the only one who can understand both points of view. On one side, the Governor is looking out for the interest of the small businessman, on the other, the Cattleman's Association is trying to protect those who've built this territory. Without some pretty level-headed decisions being made on both sides, it could become an all-out war."

"He's right, Kate," Cole put in. "Pa's about the only member of the Association who doesn't think of homesteaders as vermin to be stomped out like so many coyotes."

Levi nodded. "And he may be the only one who can keep everyone calm enough to discuss the question rationally."

Kate threw up her hands in defeat. "All right, you win. Go to Cheyenne. Be on the governor's committee. I don't know why I even try with you three. Now, get out from under our feet so Stephanie and I can get some work done."

As the two women cleaned up after lunch, Stephanie thought she detected a sheen of tears in the older woman's eyes.

"Kate?" she asked gently.

Kate shook her head. "Oh, it's just this January weather. I'm so tired of the cold I could scream." She glanced at Stephanie and sighed. "All right, it's more than the weather. I was feeling sorry for myself. I understand why Jonathan needs to go, but I hate it when he's gone."

"Why don't you go with him?"

"To Cheyenne?" Kate shook her head. "I wish I could, but it isn't possible."

"Because you need to stay here and be my chaperone?" Stephanie asked quietly.

"Good heavens, no. Charlie can keep those boys of mine in line. It might look a little odd, but with Prudy Simpson's help, we could pull it off." She smiled ruefully. "It has to do with Jonathan and me. The one bone of contention in our marriage has been politics. We almost never agree. Seventeen years ago we decided that no matter how much we argued, politics would never follow us into the bedroom. If I went to Cheyenne with him, it would."

Stephanie could think of nothing to say.

As the day of Jonathan's departure approached, Stephanie was surprised to see Kate acting normally. She would have thought her friend reconciled to her husband's leaving if she hadn't awakened one night to the sound of quiet crying in the other bedroom. A deep voice spoke soothingly, and soon the sobs ceased, but Stephanie felt a wrench of unhappiness for her.

Levi seemed inordinately restless as well. He went out for long rides or went to town and didn't come back until the next morning. Doubting it was because of his father's sojourn in the capital, Stephanie decided to find out what was bothering her friend. She found him in the barn pitching hay to the stock in the corral.

He smiled when he saw her. "Well, well, what brings you out braving the cold?"

"You."

"I'm flattered."

"Something's bothering you."

"You're right." Levi sighed dramatically. "I've fallen in love, but I don't stand a chance."

"Are you sure?"

He gave her a mournful look, but she could tell he was teasing. "She's in love with my brother. Thinks of me as a friend and nothing more."

"Don't waste your time on her," Stephanie said flippantly. "She's obviously an idiot." Then she sobered. "Seriously, Levi, what's wrong?"

"Seriously?" Levi leaned on the handle of the pitchfork and sighed. "I'm thinking of leaving."

"Leaving! But why?"

Smiling a little sadly, he shook his head. "I don't really know. For the last four years, all I wanted to do was come home. When I finally got here, I swore I'd never leave again. But the last few weeks I've been edgy. When Pa said he was going to Cheyenne, I realized that's what I needed to do."

"Join the Cattleman's Association?"

"No, leave for a while."

"And go where?"

"I don't know, maybe to Cheyenne with Pa and then on down to Colorado to visit my cousin Cassie and her husband."

Stephanie felt a knot rise in her throat. "I don't understand."

"A very wise woman once told me you can't ever go back. The horse operation is Cole's now. He's more than willing to let me back in, but I'm not sure I want that anymore. All I know for sure is that I can't find the answers here."

"I'll miss you."

He smiled. "Don't worry, I'll be back."

"I could be gone." Tears started in her eyes. "I might never see you again."

"Oh, I have a feeling you'll be here when I come back." He gave her shoulder a squeeze. "I don't think my brother's going to let you go."

It was too much for Stephanie. Her lip quivered, and the tears spilled over. "You don't understand, Levi, he may not have a choice. I'm not sure he wants me anyway."

Levi gave her a hug. "Don't worry, Stephanie, he wants you."

"Oh, Levi." Impulsively, she stood on her tiptoes and kissed his cheek. "I hope you find whatever it is you're looking for."

"Oh, I will. It's probably just—"

Suddenly they were torn apart, and Levi went crashing to the floor. Cole stood over him, fists clenched in anger.

Stephanie screamed as Levi surged back to his feet and dove at Cole. The two brothers fell to the floor, and she watched in horror as they started throwing punches. Knowing it was futile to try to separate them herself, she ran outside to find help.

Jonathan and Charlie were just riding up as she burst out of the door. "Thank goodness you're here," she gasped. "Cole and Levi—in the barn. Come quickly!"

The two men exchanged a look then dismounted and hurried into the barn. They came to an abrupt halt just inside the door.

"Well, I'll be damned," Jonathan said, leaning up against the wall to watch. "I haven't seen those two go at it in years."

"Aren't you going to stop them?" Stephanie asked in disbelief.

"Can't," Charlie said matter-of-factly. "When them two get goin', there ain't no stoppin' them."

"But they're bleeding!"

Charlie glanced at her white face. "I think you'd best go to the house, Miss Stephanie. It ain't gonna do no good for you to stand here watchin'."

Jonathan gave her a cheerful smile. "Don't worry. They'll stop before either of them gets hurt."

Just then, Levi's fist hit Cole's face with a sickening thud, and Stephanie felt the bile rising in her throat. She left without a backward glance.

Charlie and Jonathan remained an appreciative audience through the entire fight, and it was a long one. Cole and Levi were big men and evenly matched. Finally, Levi delivered a telling blow. Cole fell to the floor and lay there unable to rise.

Levi stood over him gasping. "It wasn't what you thought, you damn fool." Then his knees buckled, and he collapsed on the floor next to his brother.

Ten minutes later, Stephanie jumped to her feet as Charlie and Jonathan walked through the door. Cole and Levi staggered in right behind them, holding each other up.

When Stephanie had told Kate what was going on in the barn, the older woman had gotten bowls of warm water, clean rags, and iodine ready with the ease of long practice. No one but Stephanie seemed the least disturbed by the fact the two brothers had just tried to beat each other insensible.

The two were still arguing, but not about their fight. "What do think you're going to find that you don't have right here?" Cole asked.

Levi shrugged. "I'm not sure. I just know I have to try."

Kate looked back and forth between the two men. "What's going on?"

"Levi says he's leaving."

Kate's hand froze in the process of washing the dirt and blood off his face. "What?"

"Now, Kate—" Jonathan began.

Fixing a stern eye on her eldest son, Kate ignored Jonathan's interruption. "Where are you going?"

"I think I'll go on down to Cassies's. From there, who knows?"

"Who's supposed to help Cole and Charlie with the ranch with both you and your father gone? We're just coming into the busiest time of year."

Levi gritted his teeth as Kate dabbed iodine on his scraped knuckles. "You got along well enough without me for the last four years. Anyway, Billy Ray Simpson and Jake Summerfield are both old enough to make good ranch hands."

"But you can't be seriously thinking of leaving in the middle of January!" Cole said, trying another tack. "You'll be lucky if you don't freeze."

Levi shrugged. "It's as good as any other time. Besides, I'm going clear to Cheyenne on the train with Pa."

"What about the Injuns?" Charlie put in.

Stephanie, who was gently cleaning a wound on Cole's face, jerked in alarm. She didn't even notice Cole wince or suck in his breath as the iodine oozed into the cut on his cheek. "What Indians?" she asked, wide-eyed.

"There's a reservation about a hundred miles south of here. Some of the young bucks jump the rez now'n then and go lookin' for trouble. Could be mighty dangerous for a lone white man runnin' into them."

Levi laughed. "They're hardly likely to go down into Colorado."

"Well, I don't think—" Kate began.

"It doesn't matter what any of us think," Jonathan said, putting his hand on her shoulder. "This is Levi's decision, and he's already made it."

Levi glanced at the forlorn faces around him. "Look, I'll be back by early summer, and I'll probably be more than ready to settle down."

"I certainly hope so," Kate said.

It was an unhappy group that stood watching Levi and Jonathan prepare to leave two days later. Stephanie and Kate were tearful. Cole and Charlie wore long faces. Even Josh was abnormally subdued as Levi tied his bedroll to the back of his saddle and Jonathan loaded his bags into the wagon. In a flurry of handshakes and kisses, goodbyes were said.

When Levi came to Stephanie, she hugged him, completely ignoring Cole and his disapproving glare. "Take care of yourself, Levi."

"I will." He gave her a friendly kiss on the cheek, then turned to Cole and encountered a murderous expression. Levi grasped his brother's hand and shook it warmly. "I hope you aren't planning on another round, little brother. It wasn't near as much fun as when we were kids. I don't heal as fast now."

"I noticed that myself," Cole said, fingering a bruise on his jaw. "To tell the truth, I don't know what came over me."

Levi gave him a wry look. "Give it some thought. You might be surprised by what you discover."

CHAPTER 25

February dawned dismally cold and bleak, the days a perfect reflection of everyone's mood following Levi's and Jonathan's departure. Cole hired Billy Ray Simpson and Jake Summerfield when the mares started foaling and the cows calving. Having the two young men around helped some, but even with their good-humored banter, spring seemed impossibly far away.

One chilly morning, Stephanie could stand the gloom no longer and decided to take Sunrise out for a ride. The snow crackled under the mare's hooves, and Stephanie breathed the sharp air appreciatively as the cold, invigorating air lifted her spirits.

When she first saw the riders cresting the hill to the west, she paid little attention. But as they turned and headed in her direction, she realized they were riding without saddles. Stephanie stared at them in horror. There was only one group of people who rode without saddles summer or winter: Indians!

In a panic, she turned Sunrise toward home and kicked the mare into a gallop. The Indians fanned out in front of her, making escape impossible. Wheeling Sunrise around, Stephanie headed for a grove of trees. She didn't know what she'd do once she got there other than find a stout branch to defend herself with, but at least it was something.

Sunrise ran like the wind, but they were less than halfway to the trees when Stephanie saw two braves out of the corner of her eye. As they closed in, she suddenly jerked back on the reins with all her strength. Sunrise reared, and Stephanie pulled her around and headed back the way they'd come. There was a surprised shout from behind as Stephanie leaned forward and urged Sunrise to even greater speed.

With her heart in her throat, she saw two men right in front of her. Trying to ignore the terror that threatened to strangle her, Stephanie smacked Sunrise on the rump with the reins and headed straight at them. She knew it was hopeless, but there was a slight possibility she could surprise them enough to break through. It was her only chance, and she couldn't give up without a fight.

Hope flared in her breast as the other horses seemed to jump out of the way. But it died a moment later when one of the braves grabbed Sunrise's bridle, and his horse kept pace as he slowed the running mare. Stephanie tried to jerk the bridle from his grasp, but it was impossible to dislodge his hand.

They came to a stop, and Stephanie bit back a scream as the others caught up. She stared straight ahead as they jumped from their horses and gathered around the prancing Sunrise.

Stephanie's lips curled with satisfaction when the mare tried to bite the man that held her. The smile turned to a gasp a few seconds later when she felt herself being pulled from the saddle. She clung with all her might to the saddle horn, but strong hands plucked her fingers loose as an arm around her waist jerked her away.

Stephanie bit the inside of her cheeks to keep from screaming as six leering faces surrounded her. The hood of her cloak had blown back during the wild ride, and she gasped with pain when one of them pulled the braid loose from the tight coil on her head. She closed her eyes in horror as she felt the fingers unplait her hair.

Did Indians still scalp people? Frantically, her mind searched for a way to save herself, but she had no weapons or anything remotely resembling one. She thought of Josh's whistle and almost laughed hysterically. Josh hadn't trained Sam to save her from Indians. An image of Cole rose in her mind, but what could he do against six warriors? Still, the thought of him bolstered her courage, and she held on to it with grim determination.

"Brave Eagle!" Half convinced she was imagining it, Stephanie's eyes popped open in surprise when she heard

Cole's voice. But there he was, speaking gibberish to the tallest Indian as though they were old friends.

Without warning, the Indian reached out and grabbed a handful of her hair. "Belong to Sky Eyes?" he said in heavily accented English.

Cole nodded, tapped his chest and said a few unintelligible words. Then he spoke to her in a quiet voice, "Steph, come here."

Fighting the impulse to run screaming to his side, she walked over to him. The brave touched her hair, then pointed to Sunrise. Cole shook his head and spoke again.

For several minutes, the two men talked with the Indian repeatedly pointing first to Stephanie and then to Sunrise. Cole would listen and shake his head. Finally, Brave Eagle held up both hands and looked at Cole expectantly.

Cole stood there pondering the Indian's words for several moments as Stephanie watched nervously. "Cole?"

"He just offered me twenty horses for you and Sunrise."

"And?"

"And I'm thinking about it. He has damn fine horses."

"Cole!" Stephanie was aghast. "What are you...?"

To her shock, Cole reached up and cuffed her with the back of his hand. While she stared at him in hurt surprise, he shook his head and spoke, rolling his eyes heavenward. All six Indians laughed. Regretfully, the tall brave touched Stephanie's hair once more and then ignored her.

He and Cole spoke at length and finally appeared to reach an agreement. Brave Eagle looked at Stephanie again, then said something else. When Cole replied, the Indian closed his eyes and began an unearthly chant. It was a hauntingly sad sound and Stephanie glanced at Cole uncertainly. "What's going on?"

"He wanted to know why Maggie would let me keep another wife when white men can only have one. I told him she died. He's mourning her."

As suddenly as it began, the eerie wailing stopped, and the Indians all mounted their horses, each with a seemingly effortless leap.

"I think you'd better come with us so I can keep an eye on you," Cole whispered in her ear as he lifted her onto her saddle. "Brave Eagle isn't above stealing what he wants. And stay to the back. They'll be insulted if you ride ahead of them."

Swinging up into his own saddle, Cole turned Midnight to the south, and the Indians all followed. Stephanie was more than happy to bring up the rear. She didn't want any of them behind her where she couldn't see what they were doing.

At last they rode into a narrow draw. Pointing to a small herd of cattle, Cole spoke to Brave Eagle. The Indian nodded to his men, who cut five steers from the herd and headed off over the hill with them.

Brave Eagle turned to Cole. "Brave Eagle sad Morning Star walks with Great Spirit but is good Sky Eyes has new wife. This one brave." He looked at Stephanie consideringly. "Should call her Wind Rider." Then he added something in his own language.

Cole's delighted laughter floated on the cold air as the brave rode away. "I might have known he'd come up with an Indian name for you. It offends him that our names don't mean anything. You should feel complimented that he spoke in English. He considers it a barbaric language."

Turning their horses toward home, Stephanie asked curiously. "What else did he say?"

Cole laughed again. "He just reminded me if you warm rattlesnake slowly over hot coals it's quite enjoyable."

"What a strange thing to say." Stephanie didn't find the statement humorous at all. "Did he really want to buy me?"

"Oh, definitely. It seems he thought you and Sunrise had been touched by the Great Spirit. I'm afraid you wouldn't have been worth half that by yourself."

Stephanie looked bewildered, and Cole grinned. "It's because your hair is the same color as Sunrise's mane and tail. Brave Eagle had never seen a matched set before and figured there must be a lot of magic in such a pair, especially after he'd seen you ride."

"What made him change his mind?"

"You did when you talked back to me." He looked slightly embarrassed. "I'm sorry I hit you, but no Indian wife would ever talk to her man like that. I wasn't quite sure how I was going to get you out of it until then."

"What did you say?"

"I just told him you were as warm as a good buffalo robe at night but had the tongue of a rattlesnake during the day. He said he already had a wife like that and didn't need another." Cole chuckled again. "His parting remark was a bit of fatherly advice."

"I don't understand."

"Brave Eagle was referring to making love. He meant if I took my time getting you warmed up, I'd find it worth the effort."

"Oh!" Stephanie blushed. After several minutes of silence, she suddenly remembered the eerie keening cry. "What about Maggie? Surely they don't mourn all whites that way."

Cole sighed. "Maggie saved the life of Brave Eagle's son. Lame Deer was just a boy when she found him sick with a fever. Being Maggie, she brought him home, nursed him back to health, and then helped him get back to his people. Brave Eagle never got over a white woman doing such a thing. He's considered us almost family ever since. I've never lost a single animal to the Shoshone, though some of my neighbors have from time to time."

"Is that why they came, because you're friendly to them?"

"Sort of. Brave Eagle says the government is late with a herd of cattle they promised, and his people are starving. They came north to hunt or raid or whatever it takes to find food." Cole took off his hat and ran his fingers through his hair. "Damn, I'd have given him the steers if I could have done it without hurting his pride. He'll be sending me a horse in a few days."

"If Brave Eagle is your friend, why did you let him think I

was your wife?"

"Indians are either married or they're not. There's no way I could have made him understand our relationship."

Stephanie was tempted to say she really didn't understand their relationship herself. Instead she changed the subject. "Does he really have good horses?"

Cole smiled. "Some of the finest I've ever seen. You can bet the horse he sends will be worth more to me than those five steers."

"I'm surprised you didn't take him up on his offer for me, then," Stephanie said sarcastically.

"I told you I was thinking about it, didn't I?" Cole's lips twitched. "If he hadn't wanted Sunrise, too, I might have considered it."

"Thanks a lot." She stuck her tongue out at him, wishing she could get down long enough to pelt him with a snowball.

Three days later, a young brave arrived with a beautiful coal-black mare. The minute Cole saw the horse, he said he had not paid enough for such a magnificent animal and insisted on sending five more steers. The young man nodded, then handed Cole a leather pouch with a rather long explanation. Then he rode away.

Cole joined Charlie and Stephanie, who were standing by the corral watching. "He said Brave Eagle had a vision telling him to send this mare because I'd give him more cattle." Cole gave Stephanie a puzzled look. "Lame Deer also said the Great Spirit told Brave Eagle to send this gift to the sister of Morning Star, for it would bring strong medicine to his people. Someday it would help clear the fog from her eyes so the Great Spirit could show her the path she should take. I guess he means you, Steph," he said, handing her the pouch. "But I don't know why he thinks you're Maggie's sister."

"I expect it's got somethin' to do with one of their customs," Charlie said. "When a man's wife dies, an unmarried sister can take her place. I reckon since you told him Maggie was gone and Miss Stephanie was your wife, he figured she must be

Maggie's sister."

"I guess so, but that part about the fog clearing from her eyes sounded like he was talking about her amnesia." Cole shook his head. It was just such a strange coincidence. How could an Indian in a peyote trance know anything about Stephanie?

"Oh, how pretty!" Stephanie cried, holding up a set of beautifully beaded hair thongs, the kind worn by Shoshone women. There was even a matching conch to put on Sunrise's bridle.

Cole showed her how the women used the thongs to hold their hair in braid-like tails worn over the shoulder, and Stephanie was delighted.

"I only wish there was something I could do for Brave Eagle's tribe to thank them for this wonderful gift."

"I reckon you've given 'em hope," Charlie told her. "If they really believe you and Sunrise are strong magic, just knowin' you've got somethin' from them will make 'em happy."

"I wish I really did have magical powers," she said with a sigh. "I'd be able to do something for them."

"You never know," Charlie said philosophically. "Maybe you will someday. Could be a mite more magic in you than you realize."

CHAPTER 26

"**Y**ou'll do just fine, Stephanie," Kate said as she finished her packing. "Anybody who can be attacked by ferocious Indians and come out of it in one piece can handle Cole and Josh Cantrell for two weeks. Charlie will help you keep them in line."

Stephanie laughed and gave the older woman a hug. "That's right, so go to Cheyenne, and don't give us another thought. Your husband deserves your full attention while his committee isn't in session, and I'm sure he'll be delighted to have it."

Kate blushed and muttered something about being too old for such foolishness, but Stephanie noticed she couldn't quite hide her smile of anticipation.

When Kate was ready to leave at last, Cole, Stephanie, and Josh waved goodbye amid a flurry of last-minute instructions. Charlie was grinning broadly as he drove away with Kate still reminding Josh to behave.

Stephanie missed Kate's chatter and soon found herself looking forward to the older woman's return with longing. It seemed strange to be alone in the house so much of the time, though she was far from bored. Cooking became a full-time occupation. With appetites to match their growing bodies, Billy Ray Simpson and Jake Summerfield kept her busy just trying to fill them up. Stephanie enjoyed having the two sixteen-year-olds around and encouraged them to come in for an afternoon snack on the days when they had time.

One afternoon, they were late getting in. Since Billy Ray was going to take Josh home with him to spend two days with the two youngest Simpson brothers, Josh hung around the kitchen like a vulture. Two minutes after Billy Ray had taken the last bite of his fifth cookie, Josh had him pushed out the door and halfway to the barn.

Instead of leaving with Billy Ray as he usually did, Jake stood by the door nervously twisting his hat in his hands. Stephanie was surprised, for she had never seen him at a loss for words before.

"What is it, Jake?"

"I, uh...Miss Stephanie." He took a deep breath. "Would you mind if I was to court you?"

Stephanie blinked in astonishment. "Why, Jake, I never even considered—"

"I knew you'd say no." He looked so crestfallen, Stephanie felt a pang of sympathy.

"It's only because I'm much too old for you." She gave him a maternal smile. "You need a girl closer to your own age. Think how embarrassing it would be to have someone ask if I was your mother."

He shook his head. "Nobody in his right mind would think you was my mother." He sighed. "It's Cole, ain't it? You're in love with him." Stephanie's face turned bright red, and he nodded. "I suspected as much. Well," he said philosophically, "if I have to lose out to another man, I'd rather have it be Cole Cantrell than anybody else. You ain't sore cause I asked, are you?"

"Oh, Jake, no woman would be insulted by such a sweet offer. Someday, when you really fall in love, you'll look back and laugh about wanting to court me."

"No, I don't think that'll ever happen. Can we stay friends?"

"Of course, and I'll expect you for cookies tomorrow afternoon as usual."

"I'll be here," he said with a grin.

She watched him walk down the path, whistling. *So much for breaking his tender young heart*, she thought with a wry smile as she closed the door.

With Josh gone and Charlie planning one of his infrequent Saturday nights in town, Stephanie was looking forward to an evening alone with Cole. She had planned a special meal and was just beginning to fix it when he stormed in the door, anger radiating from him like heat from a fire.

"Just what the hell do you think you're doing?"

"I'm fixing supper," was Stephanie's startled answer. *Good Lord, what have I done now?*

"I'm not talking about that, and you damn well know it!"

"Maybe if you'd tell me what you *are* talking about, I could give you an answer. I can't read your mind."

"Jake Summerfield just apologized to me for trying to court my woman!" Cole shouted at her.

Stephanie felt her own temper snap at the unjust attack, and her ire rose to meet his. "You're mad because he apologized, or because he called me your woman?"

"Neither one, dammit. I want to know why you didn't stop it before it got this far."

"This far? All he did was ask if he could court me."

"What if he'd tried something?"

"Oh, for goodness sake, Cole. He's sixteen years old."

"He's damned near a man. You've been encouraging him every chance you got."

"Encouraging him?" Stephanie's eyes flashed. "By feeding him cookies and milk?"

"You just don't understand the kind of abuse you're setting yourself up for."

She put her hands on her hips and glared at him. "*Jake* has never been the least bit abusive to me. Today was the first time I realized he had any feelings for me other than friendship."

Cole grabbed her upper arms in a painful grip. "You *should* have realized it. Don't you have any idea what you do to a man?"

"If you're an example, I'd say I infuriate them for no reason," she said, twisting free of his grip. "Even if I did it on purpose, which I didn't, it doesn't give you the right to man-handle me." She turned away from him and stalked over to the hoosier. "This conversation is *over!*"

"Stephanie!"

Stephanie added a cup of cornmeal to the flour in her bowl and stabbed at it with a wooden spoon. "If you want any supper, I suggest you get out of my kitchen *now,* and don't come back until you've changed your attitude!"

There was silence behind her for several long moments, but she refused to look over her shoulder at him. If he thought he could bully her, he had another think coming. At long last, she heard the sound of his boots on the wood plank floor. Good, he was leaving.

"Stephanie." His voice was calmer now, and she jumped as his breath brushed her ear in a warm caress. Gently but inexorably, he turned her to face him.

"I'm not in the mood to talk to you right now," she said, trying to hide the shivers of excitement that raced up and down her spine.

But it appeared talking wasn't what he had in mind. He took the spoon from her hand and laid it on the hoosier. Then he pulled her close and claimed her with a burning kiss that threatened to consume them both.

Stephanie tried to hang on to her anger. She raised her hands to push him away, but the intensity of his kiss turned her muscles to jelly, and her arms circled his neck instead.

There was an almost desperate quality to their kiss, as though fate would intrude to pull them apart. Cole's tongue explored the sweet warmth of her mouth as he removed the ever-present hairpins, and the heavy curtain of hair cascaded around them with irresistible sensuality.

"Damn it, woman, why do you always do this to me?" he whispered against her temple.

"Do what? Make you angry?"

"No." He nibbled on her earlobe. "Make me lose my better sense." Lifting her in his arms, he carried her, unresisting, to his bedroom and set her gently on her feet. Once there, he removed her clothing slowly, erotically, until she stood naked in a pool of skirts and petticoats.

With her breath catching in her throat, Stephanie undid the buttons of his shirt and slipped her hands inside, glorying in the feel of his naked chest as she slid her hands up to his shoulders. She pushed his shirt off their broad expanse and gazed up at him.

His eyes smoldered with blue fire as his shirt slithered to the floor, and she leaned forward to kiss the pulse beating in the hollow of his throat. With a sigh of pure pleasure, she rubbed her cheek against the curly black hair of his chest.

Cole drew his breath in sharply when she pressed her soft breasts against him. Stephanie never knew how he shed the rest of his clothing; she only knew it happened very fast. Without opening her eyes, she felt herself swept up into strong arms and carried the short distance to the bed.

With infinite tenderness, Cole caressed every part of her body with hands and lips until Stephanie felt like a leaf tossed upon a sea of desire, every nerve screaming with pleasure. When he finally took her, she responded with all the pent-up longing she'd held inside for so long.

This time there was no pain, only beautiful sensation washing over her in rolling waves. Each time she thought she would surely die from the ecstasy building inside her, Cole would take her even higher. At last they reached the pinnacle for which they had been searching, and in shuddering fulfillment, began the descent back to earth.

They lay quietly for a long time, wrapped in each other's arms as their hearts slowed. Stephanie finally broke the stillness with a happy sigh. "I had no idea it could be like that."

Cole smiled and kissed her forehead. "It isn't always."

"Does it get better every time?"

"I hope not. Much better and I don't think I'd live through it."

She smiled at him dreamily. "Oh, what a way to die!"

Tenderly, he touched the golden snowflake resting against her throat. "I think we found something else we have to avoid besides secluded cabins and blizzards."

"Oh? What's that?"

"Anger. You get carried away when you're mad."

"I seem to remember it was you who started it." She batted her eyes at him. "Besides, it's a perfectly lovely way to end an argument."

"That's a good point," he agreed.

"I don't see why you were so mad in the first place. All Jake did was pay me a compliment. I don't think he expected anything but a polite refusal anyway."

"I guess I was just afraid you'd trust the wrong person." He raised his hand and traced the curve of her face with the back of his fingers. "I don't want anyone taking advantage of you except me."

Stephanie rolled herself onto his chest and stared down into his face, her hair fanning over him. "Why Cole, I do believe you're jealous! And of a sixteen-year-old boy, at that."

"A very good-looking sixteen-year-old boy."

Stephanie smiled. "I never really noticed."

"You expect me to believe that?"

"My tastes run to more mature men." She picked up a lock of her hair and traced intricate patterns along his arm and chest. "You, on the other hand, are truly beautiful. I could spend hours just looking at you."

He smiled lazily up at her. "I'm supposed to say that."

She looked surprised. "Don't you think it might sound a bit conceited? I don't think I'd like a man to tell me he was beautiful."

Cole laughed. "You think you're pretty clever, don't you?" He lifted one hand to push the hair back from her face. Smiling up at her, he caressed her cheek lightly with the back of his hand and stroked her naked back under the silky mass of hair with his other. "Steph?"

"Mmmm?"

"We can't let this become a habit. The reasons haven't changed."

"I know."

"Then you'll understand when I say you have to leave now."

"Why?" she whispered as she nibbled his neck.

"Because," he growled, "I don't know how much longer I can take what you're doing without making love to you again."

"Good."

"What do you mean good?"

"I *want* you to make love to me again!"

"Steph, this isn't a game we're playing. You could get pregnant if we continue with this madness."

"I know, but it seems to me that if we're going to beget a child, we've probably already done it." She propped herself up on an elbow and smiled down at him. "We're going to spend the next month worrying anyway. Making love again tonight won't make it any worse, and we have a whole night ahead of us. No sense in wasting it."

"If we're going to pay the price, we might as well enjoy ourselves first, right?" His eyes gleamed wickedly in the last rays of sunlight. "I like the way you think, woman." And he pulled her down for a kiss.

CHAPTER 27

Stephanie awoke and smiled softly at the early morning light streaming in through her window. *Light! Oh no, it's morning already.* It seemed like only a few minutes since Cole had carried her to Kate's cabin and put her to bed. Of course, maybe it hadn't been that long. They'd made love once more before he left, and they certainly hadn't rushed it.

A glance at the clock showed that it was only a little after six. She jumped out of bed, dressed, threw on her cloak, and hurried to the chicken coop to gather enough eggs for breakfast. She laughed happily as the birds sent up a sleepy squawk at her intrusion. The sun was just beginning to peek over the horizon, painting the sky with brilliant pinks and yellows. It matched her mood perfectly as she walked back to the house.

What a night! As a decent woman, Stephanie knew she should have never allowed such a thing to happen. But it was impossible to feel remorse for spending the night in the arms of the man she loved. She'd be repentant later, she promised herself, but right now she intended to enjoy the exhilaration she was feeling. Stephanie gave a delighted skip. The eggs clicked together ominously.

"I'm glad to see you're so happy this morning," Cole said from behind her.

"It's a gorgeous morning."

"It is, isn't it?" He gave her a heart-stopping smile that threatened to melt her bones. "I'm afraid Charlie doesn't share your good spirits." Cole indicated the bucket of milk he was carrying steaming in the chilly morning air. "He wasn't even up to milking."

"Oh no." Stephanie was instantly concerned. "Is he sick?"

Cole laughed. "I'm afraid he had a little too much good cheer at the Snap last night."

"The Snap?"

"It's the local saloon. He's got one hell of a hangover. Whatever you do, don't offer him eggs for breakfast. He'll want good hot coffee and plenty of it."

Twenty minutes later, Charlie sat in the kitchen staring morosely into his cup of coffee. He started when Stephanie laid a cold rag over the back of his neck and then gave her a grateful glance as the throbbing in his head receded a bit. Even through his misery, he could tell something had happened during his absence. Cole and Stephanie kept smiling at each other like a couple of fools. He winced when Stephanie dropped her fork.

"Sorry," she murmured.

Charlie resumed the contemplation of his cup. It was a good thing Kate was gone. Those two would have given themselves away immediately, and the fat would be in the fire for sure. Cole had never liked to have his hand forced. If he decided to marry Stephanie, it would have to be entirely his own idea. Personally, Charlie couldn't figure out what the hold-up was. Stephanie was about as close to perfect as Cole was ever going to find.

"Here, Charlie, try to drink some of this." Stephanie held a steaming cup in her hand. "It doesn't taste very good, but it'll make you feel better."

He looked at her suspiciously but saw only gentle concern. "I don't reckon it can make me feel any worse." He swallowed the bitter draught and set the cup down with a sigh. With Stephanie gently massaging his neck and shoulders, some of his discomfort eased.

"Feel any better?" she asked.

"I ain't ready to run a race, but I reckon I'll live now. I wasn't so sure for a while, though."

"Good, then I'll fix some dry toast."

Charlie watched as Stephanie toasted the thick slab of

bread over the hot stove. No, Cole could do a whole lot worse than to marry Stephanie.

Stephanie tucked the sweet memory of that long, wonderful night away in her heart. If she spent a bit too much time daydreaming about it, she had herself well in hand by the time Kate returned from Cheyenne.

It seemed as though Kate had brought spring with her from the South. The snow melted, and the buds began to swell on the trees. To facilitate the calving operation, the herds had been brought closer to the house, and Stephanie spent a great deal of time helping. Charlie and Cole both remarked on how unusually early the nice weather had come, but Stephanie only reveled in its glory.

Suddenly, Stephanie found her thoughts dwelling on tiny babies with black hair and bright blue eyes. Perhaps it was all the new life around her, or maybe the feel of spring in the air that gave her such strange notions. Whatever the reason, she was almost disappointed when she discovered she wasn't pregnant after all.

Oddly enough, the news didn't seem to give Cole any great joy either. For several seconds he stared silently down at her. Gently touching her cheek, he started to say something. Then, shaking his head, he dropped his hand and turned away. During the next few days, they quietly slipped back into their old relationship, both feeling as if they had lost something very precious.

Late spring was traditionally the time set for Horse Creek's most festive event of the year, the Box Social. After the frantic months of late winter and spring, there was a slight lull in the work, and all the neighbors took advantage of their free time to relax and celebrate.

The day before the big event, Cole announced he was going to town to buy a new pair of boots. Kate immediately gave him a list of commissions to carry out, and he left shaking his head, grumbling good-naturedly about women in general and mothers in particular.

Frank Collins looked up as Cole entered the store. "What can I do for you today, Cole?" he asked cheerfully.

"I need some new boots, and as usual, Kate sent a list." Cole handed Frank the slip of paper and glanced casually around the store. Suddenly, his look intensified as his eyes focused on a poster hanging on the wall.

REWARD OFFERED
WANTED FOR QUESTIONING
YOUNG WOMAN IN MIDDLE TWENTIES
5 FOOT, 7 INCHES TALL,
AUBURN HAIR, GREEN EYES
LAST SEEN CHEYENNE, WYOMING TERRITORY
Anyone with information
concerning whereabouts
should contact Orson Pickett,
Scott Manufacturing Co.,
St. Louis, Missouri.

Cole was conscious of a sinking feeling in the pit of his stomach. This was what he'd been waiting for, but he'd begun to hope it would never appear.

"Kind of amazing how much that sounds like Miss Stephanie, ain't it?" Frank removed his spectacles and casually cleaned them with a rag from under the counter. "Folks have sure been surprised when they read that thing. 'Course we all knew it wasn't Miss Stephanie right off. Her hair isn't red, and she's shorter than that. Besides, she ain't no desperate criminal, and that's for dang sure."

"Strange coincidence," Cole said. He wondered how many people Frank had actually managed to convince. "I need to run a few more errands," Cole said. "I'll be back in a few minutes to look at your boots and pick up Kate's supplies."

Deep in thought, Cole didn't even see Sally Langton wave to get his attention. She watched in chagrin as he walked down the street, completely ignoring her. Cole hadn't been to see her since before Christmas. She was losing him.

When Sally entered the store, she was dwelling on the horrible things she'd like to do to that red-haired witch who'd pushed her out of Cole's affections. While Frank was measuring and cutting the ribbon she'd chosen, she happened to glance up, and the wanted poster fairly leaped off the wall at her. As she read the words, a dozen plans began to form in her mind. There was a good chance the missing woman wasn't Stephanie at all, but there must be a way to make use of the startling likeness.

Her first thought was simply to show the poster to Cole, but she soon decided that would be worse than useless. Cole simply wouldn't pay any attention, and she'd probably find herself the target of one of his horrible tempers, to boot. Perhaps if she were to contact this Mr. Pickett and tell him she'd found the woman he wanted, he'd take it from there. It was worth a try anyway, and with the usurper gone, Cole would surely come back begging forgiveness for straying from the path of true love.

Sally was so intent on her thoughts of revenge she didn't notice the look of dismay on Frank Collin's face as he watched her reaction to the poster. In fact, she didn't pay attention to much of anything until she met Cole on the sidewalk just outside the store.

"Why, Cole, how nice to see you!" She fluttered her eyelashes.

"Hello, Sally," Cole answered, unimpressed with her blandishments.

"Are you going to the Box Social tomorrow?"

"We're planning on it. I suppose we'll see you there?"

"Why, of course!" She gave him a coy look. "You know, I just bought the most beautiful pink ribbon, but I can't decide if I should use it on my box for the social tomorrow night." She held it out for his inspection. "What do you think?"

It was such an obvious ploy that Cole almost laughed. Sally wanted to make sure he'd recognize her box at the social, hoping he'd buy it. "Looks just fine to me. If you'll excuse me, I have some things to pick up. Good-bye." He tipped his hat and walked away without a backward glance.

Sally's eyes narrowed into angry slits. It was that Stephanie's fault that Cole had turned so cool, and it was time she paid. Marching straight to the telegraph office, Sally sent a carefully worded telegram to Mr. Orson Pickett in St. Louis.

It didn't take long for Cole to pick out his new boots; the selection in his large size was quite limited. While Frank was wrapping them, Cole noticed the tray of ribbon still sitting on the counter. On an impulse, he bought a length of emerald green ribbon to match Stephanie's dress.

"You know, that poster bothers me," Frank said, giving him a troubled look. "Being as how this is a Federal Post Office, I can't rightly take it down, but if it was to disappear, well there wouldn't be a dang thing I could do about it."

Cole didn't comment, but when he left the store, there was an empty place on the wall where the incriminating piece of paper had hung.

Orson Pickett sat behind his desk in a large St. Louis office building. He was a handsome man of medium height, with sandy hair and bushy sideburns. Frowning, he looked at the pretty young blonde sitting across the desk from him.

"I don't know, Nance, it's all so strange. Both telegrams were sent from the same town within minutes of each other."

Leaning forward, he picked them up. "This one from a..." he studied the name at the bottom, "Mr. Cantrell, says he has my money which he'll gladly return if I'll let him know where to send it."

He looked at the other telegram. "The second one talks about a young woman fitting the description claiming to have a memory loss. This Mrs. Langton offers to buy a train ticket for the woman and send her here if I'll let her know when it would be convenient."

Nance leaned forward eagerly. "Do you think it's Stephanie?"

Orson dropped the telegrams back onto the desk and rubbed his forehead. "Who knows? If you knew someone who had lost their memory, would you stick her on a train whose destination was hundreds of miles away if you weren't sure who was waiting for her at the other end?"

Nance looked horrified. "Heavens, no!"

"The other one is just as bad." He sighed. "This Horse Creek is close to where I lost her. It sounds like a town full of lunatics, but if she's there and lost her memory, she couldn't very well leave."

"Oh, Orson, if she doesn't remember, how will we ever know if it's Stephanie or not?"

"I think I'd better check it out myself. God knows we've had enough responses to that poster, but all the detectives I've sent out have come back empty-handed. In every case, it was only the reward they were after. These two don't even mention it." He pinched the bridge of his nose tiredly. "Another thing that bothers me: Mr. Cantrell knew exactly how much money she took: five thousand dollars. That's too much of a coincidence to ignore."

Nance was shocked. "Did she take so much?"

"She was desperate, or thought she was." He rose and came around his desk. Taking one of Nance's hands, he patted it comfortingly. "I need to get some things taken care of here first, but I'll leave for Wyoming Territory as soon as I can manage it."

Nance stared up at him with worshipful eyes. "You always know just what to do, Orson."

CHAPTER 28

The day of the Box Social had finally arrived, and Stephanie could hardly wait. She laid out the green dress on her bed and lovingly touched the green hair ribbon Cole had surprised her with the day before. If her heart hadn't already been his, he'd surely have won it then. Hugging herself in delight, Stephanie glanced at the clock and hurried back to the house to put the finishing touches on her dinner box. Though it hadn't turned out quite the way she envisioned, she hoped the food she planned on filling it with would make up for it.

Since Stephanie and Kate were using the kitchen, the hip bath was set up in Kate's cabin. Kate had a rigid schedule for its use and fully intended to make sure everyone followed it. At precisely three o'clock, she glanced at the clock and frowned. "Stephanie, you'd best go make sure Josh is finished. And see if he's put the water on to heat for Charlie," she called as Stephanie walked out the door.

She knocked on the door and waited for the muffled, "Come in," before entering. "Kate wanted to know if you..." Her voice trailed off, and her eyes widened in shock. Sitting in the tub, his face mirroring her surprise, was not Josh, but his father.

"Cole, I...I...Kate said to come check Josh—" Abruptly she stopped and put her hands on her hips. "What's the big idea of yelling come in when you're still in the tub?"

"I thought you were Charlie. He's next, isn't he?"

"Yes, but you aren't supposed to be here. It's Josh's turn!"

Cole's expression reminded her strongly of his son. "We traded. He had something he needed to do. Say, Steph, would you mind scrubbing my back?" He gave her a pleading look. "I can't reach it."

"Oh...I suppose."

It was a pleasant task and Stephanie soaped the broad expanse well. As she lovingly ran the rag over his wide shoulders, she suddenly noticed the bath brush lying within easy reach of the tub, and her eyes narrowed. "Is that good enough?" she asked sweetly.

"Actually, I think you missed a spot just under my left shoulder blade." Cole's voice was lazy and relaxed.

Stephanie obligingly scrubbed the spot for the third time, then stood up and handed him the rag. "I think you're ready to rinse off." She picked up the pitcher of cold water from the nightstand and dumped the entire contents over his head.

Before the gasp had even cleared his lips, she was at the door. "That was for conveniently forgetting the bath brush, which was right there all the time!" She giggled at the look on his face.

"Steph..." He drew her name out in a threatening manner as he started to stand up.

"Ah, ah, ah," she said, shaking a finger at him, "remember how easily shocked Kate is," and whisked herself out the door.

She avoided being alone with Cole for the rest of the day and was very careful to take her bath last, when Kate was in the cabin with her.

Stephanie's excitement mounted as she dressed for the party. The green dress was stunning, the low neckline showing her slender throat and white shoulders to perfection. Her only jewelry, the delicate snowflake Cole had given her, emphasized the simplicity of the design. Using the green ribbon with two of her mother-of-pearl combs, she piled her hair high on her head, leaving long curls to fall enticingly over one shoulder. The end result was simple yet elegant, and Stephanie smiled at herself in the mirror, pleased with the effect. She whirled around to face Kate and struck a pose. "Well, what do you think?"

"Lord have mercy on the men tonight!" Kate said with a smile. "Why, you'll have all the ladies hating you the minute you step through the door."

Stephanie smiled. "Heavens, I hope not! That would make

for a very uncomfortable evening."

There was a knock at the door, and Cole stepped inside. "Josh and Charlie got tired of waiting so they—" The words died on his lips as he stared at Stephanie.

Her eyes widened in appreciation, no less stunned by the picture he presented. If Cole Cantrell was handsome in his everyday work clothes, he was spectacular when he dressed up. His black suit appeared to have been tailored for his tall, muscular frame, and it fit flawlessly. The jacket and brocade vest set off the blue shirt perfectly; the color reflected in his eyes made them more startlingly blue than ever.

"You're beautiful!" she breathed.

"I'm supposed to say that." They both smiled softly at the memory the words evoked. The two stood gazing at each other for a long moment, unable to pull their eyes away. Finally, Cole collected himself and made an exaggerated bow.

"Ladies, your carriage awaits." He picked up Kate's shawl and placed it around her shoulders. "Mrs. Cantrell, you'll have the other ladies eating their hats with envy."

She gave him a playful slap on the hand. "Don't try your flattery on me."

He did his best to look wounded. "I only speak the truth. I have no doubt Maude will be searching for the salt to do just that as soon as we arrive."

Since the lady in question was an old rival of hers, Kate greeted this new sally with a flip of her skirt as she headed for the door. "Now *that* I'd like to see."

As Cole helped Stephanie with her wrap, his breath brushed her ear. "I haven't forgotten the water, my little she-devil. You will pay."

"Not if I stay close to Kate," she said, batting her eyes at him over her shoulder. Then she scooted out the door.

Charlie and Josh had already left with blankets, coats, and all the food stowed in the back of the buckboard, leaving Cole the task of transporting the two women to town in the buggy. The Box Social was held at the only public building Horse

Creek had — the school. It made a fine community hall with all the benches up against the wall and tables scattered about.

Prudy Simpson greeted Stephanie with a hug almost as soon as she walked in the door. "If you don't look scrumptious! I see Sally's turning green as grass over there," she added in a satisfied tone. "You're taking the shine right out of her, and that's not setting too well."

Stephanie glanced toward Sally and was rewarded with a glare. "I won't let her ruin my evening," she said, and resolutely turned her back, hoping the blonde would ignore her.

A table at the front was covered with the beautifully decorated dinner boxes that would soon be auctioned off to the men. When a gentleman purchased a box, he was entitled to share the meal inside with the lady who had prepared it. Soon an expectant hush fell over the crowd as the auctioneer picked up his gavel. Amid much joking and squeals of delight, the auction began.

Cole watched Stephanie from a distance, pleased to see she was enjoying herself. One look at Sally had been enough to make him realize he needed to do something to keep her from ruining Stephanie's fun. He sighed. Spending the evening with Sally certainly hadn't been in his plans, but he didn't see any other way out. When the gaudy box with the pink ribbon came up, he reluctantly raised his hand. As usual, there was some pretty stiff competition, for Sally was the uncrowned beauty of the small community.

What am I doing? Cole suddenly thought to himself. *Why should I spend my evening eating Sally's mediocre food when I could just as easily have Stephanie's?* With that, he crossed his arms and let the bidding go on without him.

In the end, he wound up paying far more than he'd expected to for the privilege of being Stephanie's dinner partner. Word had gotten out, probably through Josh, which box belonged to her, and more than one man was willing to pay for the opportunity to become better acquainted.

After the auctioneer brought his gavel down on the final bid, Cole approached Stephanie with the rather plain box in his hand. "Madam, I believe this is yours."

Stephanie fluttered her eyelashes. "Oh, sir, how kind of you to buy it."

"I happen to know what you put in here, and I'll be damned if I'll let some other man eat it. Now, quit batting your eyes at me in that ridiculous way, and we'll find a place to sit."

They found two chairs at one of the long tables and sat down to watch the last few boxes sell. The honors for the highest priced box went to a pretty young woman of sixteen.

"I wonder if this raised enough money for the new church," Stephanie said as they watched the young lady walk away with her beau.

"I don't know, but the fund must be getting close."

"May we join you?" Sally's sugary voice broke over them like ice water. Since she was already starting to sit down, it was impossible to refuse her request. Cole prayed the widow would behave herself for once.

"Cole, I believe you already know John McGruder?" The men nodded to each other, and Sally turned a malevolent eye to Stephanie. "And this is dear little Stephanie. I'm sorry I can't tell you her last name, but she seems to have forgotten it."

Stephanie smiled pleasantly at Sally. "You really must stop calling me little, Sally. You're surely not that much older than I am."

Sally's friendly facade slipped a trifle. "I wasn't referring to your age."

"Oh, Sally, you're so sweet. It's nice of you to try, of course, but the minute I stand up, Mr. McGruder will see what a giantess I am, especially next to you." She turned her smile on Sally's escort. "Sally has tried so hard to help me overcome my unfortunate height, but alas, I fear it's quite useless. Nothing will make me anything but tall."

Sally's eyes narrowed as Mr. McGruder hastened to assure Stephanie she was statuesque rather than tall.

"What a charming little necklace," Sally said, touching her own diamond and sapphire choker. It had been in her late husband's family for generations, and she flaunted it at every opportunity.

"Why, thank you. It was a very special gift." Stephanie's eyes met Cole's in the warm look of two lovers sharing a secret. Only a blind man could have missed it, and Sally wasn't blind. Her eyes glittered angrily.

"Have you discovered anything more about your past?" Sally asked at last.

Sally waited for Stephanie's response with such a malicious expression on her face, Cole couldn't help wondering if she knew about the wanted poster.

Stephanie looked surprised by the question "No, I really haven't given it much thought."

Cole watched in amazement as Stephanie turned every vicious innuendo back to the fuming Sally. Not once was she anything but a perfect lady making polite conversation. Had he been protecting the wrong person all this time? Sally certainly looked as though she could use some help.

Finally, Stephanie apparently decided that she and Sally had traded enough insults for one night. "Shall we eat?"

It was the perfect opportunity to end the hostilities, but Sally was in too much of a rage to let go so easily. Untying the ribbon to her own box, she smiled condescendingly as Cole opened Stephanie's. "My goodness, Kate certainly outdid herself this time."

Stephanie looked at Kate, who was sitting directly behind Sally at the next table. "You're right. Mr. Collins looks like he's enjoying himself immensely." It was true; both he and Kate were listening to the exchange with pleased expressions on their faces.

"I meant the food she fixed for you." Sally's voice had

become distinctly acid, and Mr. McGruder shifted uncomfortably.

"Steph made all this herself." Cole sighed and patted his flat stomach. "I'll bet I've gained ten pounds since she started cooking for us."

Giving Stephanie a vicious look, Sally removed the lid from her meal and uttered a piercing scream. There, sitting in the middle of the fried chicken, was a very large toad.

CHAPTER 29

It took both Cole and Mr. McGruder several minutes to calm the hysterical Sally and remove the toad. Stephanie was the only one of the four who noticed Josh and the two youngest Simpson boys laughing themselves silly clear across the room. It wasn't difficult to figure out who was responsible for the prank. Deciding the information was best kept to herself, Stephanie held back a smile and calmly unpacked her supper.

As soon as everyone finished eating, the tables were cleared away except for one set against the far wall. Stephanie helped the other women load it down with all the pies, cakes, and cookies they had brought for refreshments during the dancing. Charlie sauntered by just as a large bowl of punch was set in the middle of the heaping table.

"Reckon that punch is spiked, Miss Stephanie," he told her in an undertone. "I'd go real easy on it if I was you."

Stephanie stared after him, perplexed by his cryptic words. Peering curiously into the dark liquid, she searched the bowl, but there didn't seem to be anything that even remotely resembled a spike. Probably just another of Charlie's little jokes.

The punch was delicious, and Stephanie sipped a glass as she watched the dancing. The square dances and reels were completely unfamiliar to her, though they looked like great fun.

"Do you want to try it?" Cole asked.

She smiled up at him. "I think I'll wait a while. The steps look difficult."

"It really isn't that hard. You just have to understand the language." He sat down next to her and spent the next several dances explaining what the caller's instructions meant. Then the musicians struck up another sort of tune.

"Oh, Cole, a waltz."

"It sure is." He gave her a quizzical look. "More familiar

than the others?"

"Definitely. I think I may even know how to dance this one."

"Well then, madam, would you do me the honor?"

"I'd be delighted, sir."

Cole took her hand and led her onto the floor. With his arm encircling her waist, he swept her away into the dance. They both danced superbly, and it wasn't long before they forgot everything but the music and each other. When their gazes locked, it was as though everyone else disappeared. It wasn't far from the truth. The other couples stopped one by one to watch the tall, graceful pair whirling around the room with such expertise.

When at last the music died away, Cole bowed, and Stephanie sank into a graceful curtsy. They were abruptly brought back to earth by the sound of applause. Startled, they looked around at the circle of smiling faces. Cole led a blushing Stephanie from the floor, murmuring in her ear, "I think we can safely say you've waltzed before."

Prudy was awe-struck. "My goodness, I didn't know the waltz could be so beautiful. It was a pleasure just to watch you." Everyone seemed to agree, except Sally, who suddenly developed a splitting headache. Stephanie barely noticed when she left, escorted by a very solicitous Mr. McGruder.

Thinking they had already given the gossips enough fuel for one night, Cole decided he'd better dance with a few others. Sipping her punch, Stephanie watched the dancers from the sidelines, swaying in time to the music, and was soon wrapped in a warm glow of contentment.

"Miss Stephanie, would you mind...uh, would you dance with me?" Billy Ray Simpson stood blushing before her. It had obviously taken him a long time to screw up his courage enough to ask, and she suspected he'd come to her because he was afraid of rejection from a girl his own age.

She wasn't any more sure she could perform the intricate steps of the dances than she had been before, but the music had wrapped her in a warm glow of contentment and she felt more courageous. "I'd be delighted to, Billy Ray, but you'll have to teach me how."

Despite his shyness, the young man was a good teacher, and it wasn't long before Stephanie was following the calls reasonably well. Nobody minded when she missed a step or made a mistake, and soon she was dancing every dance, dizzy with pleasure. She never lacked for partners, and the evening passed in a pleasant blur with an occasional trip to the punch bowl to quench her thirst.

When Cole figured he'd socialized enough to keep the old tabbies happy, he made his way back to Stephanie.

"Oh, Cole, it's nice to see you again," she swayed dizzily as she tried to focus on his face.

Cole was astonished. "You're drunk!"

"Is that why you have three eyes?" She squinted up at him, trying to see him better. "Can't be drunk, though. I didn't have a thing 'cept this punch. It's very good." She held up her glass. "Try it."

"Good Lord, woman, didn't Charlie tell you it was spiked?"

"Course he did." She wrinkled her nose. "Silly thing to say. I didn't see any spikes at all. Not a single nail in the whole bowl."

"Oh, it was spiked all right—with straight whiskey."

"Oh." She stared into her glass and hiccupped. "'Scuse me."

Cole shook his head. "I think it's time to go home."

"Can't leave. Kate."

"She left hours ago with Josh and Charlie."

"She did?" Stephanie was surprised. "Didn't see her go."

"How many glasses of that stuff did you drink?" Cole asked.

Stephanie shrugged. "Don't know, lost count." She sighed and set her glass carefully on the table. "Is it really time to go?"

Cole draped her shawl around her shoulders. "Yes, most

definitely."

By the time Cole finally got her into the buggy and they'd started for home, Stephanie's head had cleared a little. She leaned against him and sighed. "I love you, Cole. You saved me from a blizzard, and wild Indians, and now a punch bowl." She giggled. "You're very brave!"

"I certainly am. It's dangerous to have a drunk next to you in an open buggy." He looked down at her head resting against his shoulder. "Besides, you saved me from a cattle rustler."

"It was only Levi."

"True, but you didn't know that."

"You both laughed at me."

Cole chuckled. "If you could have seen yourself holding that gun and threatening a man the size of Levi, you'd have laughed, too."

He enjoyed the feel of Stephanie resting against his side. She was quiet for so long Cole began to think she'd fallen asleep.

"Cole?" Her voice was very clear, as though the fumes were clearing from her brain. "I'm sorry I was rude to Sally. I try to be nice, but she—well anyway, I shouldn't have treated your mistress that way after you've been so good to me."

"What?" Cole was startled. "Who told you Sally was my mistress?"

"Nobody. It wasn't too difficult to figure out. When I made you mad, you went running to her." Her voice was hesitant. "Do you love her?"

Cole stopped the horse and looked at her. "Steph, she's not my mistress anymore, and I never loved her. I haven't shared her bed for months."

She sighed. "I'm glad, Cole. She's not a very nice person. I don't want you to marry her."

"Good lord, I'd as soon marry a rattlesnake."

"You told Brave Eagle *I* was a rattlesnake," she reminded him.

"You are. You'd make a devil of a wife, stealing my horse

and yelling at me. And there's a certain pitcher of very cold water I still owe you for. Which reminds me..." He shook the reins and made as though to turn off the road.

Stephanie sat up. "What are you doing?"

"There's a little creek right over there. It will be nice and cold this time of year."

"Don't you dare, Cole Cantrell. Kate gave me this dress, and I won't let you destroy it!"

He leered at her in the darkness. "We could always take it off."

She looked consideringly in the direction of the creek. "Hmmm, now that has possibilities."

He laughed and started the horse toward home again. "It certainly does. The possibility of pneumonia."

"Maybe you should just forget your revenge," she said, snuggling up to him again.

"Never."

Before long, they arrived at the ranch. Peering at the dark houses, Stephanie cuddled closer to Cole. "I'll go to the barn with you. Josh will be at Kate's, and I don't want to wake them up. Besides, I don't think I can walk in by myself. Maybe I'll just sleep in Josh's bedroom."

Cole smiled and shook his head as he drove the horses to the barn.

Perched on a pile of hay, Stephanie watched as he unhitched the horse. When he turned the animal out into the corral, she rose unsteadily to her feet, humming under her breath. Grinning, Cole took her arm and steered her toward the house.

Suddenly she stopped. "Cole, dance with me again. I've always wanted to dance the waltz by moonlight." She paused. "At least, I think I have."

Having himself been a fairly frequent visitor to the punch bowl, as well as taking a few friendly nips from a bottle hidden outside, Cole appeared to find her request quite reasonable. They waltzed all the way to the house, amid Stephanie's giggles and Cole's off-key rendition of the Blue Danube.

The dance ended in a kiss just outside the front door. That kiss was their undoing. Almost before either of them realized what was happening, Cole was kicking the door to his bedroom shut behind them. The sharp sound brought him to his senses.

"Sorry," he said apologetically as he set her on her feet and straightened her dress. "I got a little carried away."

She smiled as she ran her hands up his arms. "Maybe we should get a *lot* carried away."

"I won't take advantage of a drunk."

"I'm not drunk anymore, and I *want* you to take advantage of me."

"If you aren't drunk, why couldn't you walk in by yourself?"

"I lied." Reaching back, she pulled the combs from her hair and shook it free. "Please, Cole, don't make me beg."

He stared at her for a moment, then with a groan, pulled her close, his hands molding her body to his. "I'd never make a lady beg," he whispered against her mouth.

Piece by piece, their clothes drifted to the floor as they undressed each other in the soft moonlight. When both were naked, Cole lifted her in his arms and carried her to the bed, her hair swirling around him in erotic splendor. With soft words and touches, each worshipped the other's body, their senses humming with tender ecstasy. They came together at last in an explosion of passion that seared their senses and rocked them down to their toes. The world ceased to exist as they completely lost their individuality and became one.

Later, they lay holding each other, stunned by what they had just shared. Stephanie reached up and touched his cheek. "You lied to me. It does get better every time."

"We may have to test that theory." He kissed her forehead. "With a little practice, you might get pretty good at this."

"Oh, you." Stephanie playfully hit his chest. Then her smile faded. "Cole, what I said before? It's true. I do love you, with all my heart."

"Steph, I—"

She placed her fingers on his lips. "No, you don't have to say it. I know you don't feel the same way. I'm not asking you to. It wouldn't be fair to involve you in whatever I did, and I won't let it harm you or your family. When I find out where that damn money came from, I'll take it back myself. That's why I wanted you to love me tonight—in case I never get another chance."

He pulled away in consternation. "You thought it was the money that kept me away?"

"Wasn't it?"

"Lord, no!" He exhaled sharply and pulled her close again. "I knew I should have told you. During the blizzard you talked in your sleep. You mentioned James again, and you were very upset you'd had to leave without saying goodbye."

"So?"

He was silent for a long moment. "You said you loved him."

"And that's why you've tried to keep me at arm's length all this time? Oh, Cole, it doesn't matter if I did love him." She ran her fingers along the curve of his face. "I know what I feel for you is a thousand times stronger. I couldn't forget feelings like these no matter how many horses hit me in the head. As soon as I knew James wasn't my husband, I stopped caring who he was. It's you I love—deeply, passionately, and irrevocably— not some mythical person I may never see again!" She paused. "Doesn't it bother you at all that you may have just made love to a thief—or worse?"

He pulled her to him. "I made love to a very wonderful woman. One who is kind and loving, and who can put a conniving bitch in her place without turning a hair, the woman I—" She silenced him with her lips.

Cole lay staring at the ceiling. He was in love with

Stephanie. He hadn't realized it until he'd almost said the words. Now he knew it wasn't James that stood between them; it never had been. The possibility of another man had only been a convenient excuse. The true reason had suddenly become crystal clear, and he was consumed with guilt. *Oh, Maggie, what have I done? I swore I'd never love anyone but you. How could I have let this happen?* But there was no answer.

CHAPTER 30

Stephanie dragged herself out of bed the next morning wishing she would just die and get it over with. Charlie gave her a knowing look as she sat down at the table and put her aching head in her hands.

"I wondered if you wasn't hittin' the punch a little hard. I tried to warn you."

"I didn't know what you meant," she told him morosely. "I do now."

"You're not the first to make that mistake," Kate told her. "You'll feel better directly."

"I certainly hope so." She glanced around the kitchen. "Where's Cole?"

Kate poured her a cup of coffee. "He's out getting the herds separated to go to the mountain."

"But I thought that wouldn't start for another couple of weeks."

"I reckon he decided to do it early this year," Charlie said, studying the bottom of his coffee cup.

Stephanie looked from Kate to Charlie, noting how they carefully avoided each other's eyes, and a chill ran down her spine. Something was wrong. Her memory of the night before was very clear. She and Cole finally had everything worked out, so why was he gone?

Charlie hunkered down next to the campfire a few days later. "You gonna tell me what's eatin' you?" he asked as Cole poured him a cup of coffee.

"Nothing. I'm just getting the herds ready to trail up the mountain."

"Sure, that's why you're stayin' away from the house. Hell,

boy, you ain't even usin' the line shack. Something is drivin' you near crazy to sleep on the cold ground this time of year."

Cole stared stubbornly into the fire. Charlie let his breath out in exasperation. "I tell you it ain't hardly livable at home no more, with you sulkin' out here on the prairie and Miss Stephanie the way she is."

"What's wrong with Steph?"

"Don't rightly know unless a hangover can last three days. I just can't understand you two. When I was young, a man hung around when he was in love, whisperin' sweet words and such. Reckon things have changed."

Cole stood up and walked away from the fire. "I don't need any of your cowboy philosophy right now."

"What you need is a good kick in the pants!" He studied the back of Cole's head. "It's Maggie, ain't it?"

"Go away, Charlie. I'm in no mood to listen to your ramblings."

"Well, you're gonna listen. What you and Maggie had was real special, but she's gone, Cole, and you can't bring her back by shuttin' yourself away from the world. Did you ever stop to think what would've happened if Maggie had been here when Miss Stephanie came? They'd have loved each other on sight. Then you would've really had your hands full." He snorted. "Hell, when you think on it, them two are as alike as two peas in a pod. They would've been careenin' all over the prairie, lookin' for trouble."

Cole gave a ghost of a laugh. "And probably riding double on Midnight while they did it."

"I reckon if Maggie could've picked another woman for you, it would've been somebody like Stephanie."

"Damn you, Charlie Hobbs, you can make me feel like a crazy fool faster than anybody I know," Cole said with feeling.

Charlie stood up and clapped the younger man on the shoulder. "Somebody needs to when you get on your high horse like you do."

He threw the rest of his coffee in the fire and handed his

cup to Cole. "I'm goin' back to the house. Them two ladies was plannin' on baking one of Miss Stephanie's special cakes for lunch. I reckon Josh'll eat it all by himself if I ain't there to help him out." He walked to his horse and swung into the saddle with the ease of a man half his age. "You want me to tell 'em you'll be in for supper?"

"Yeah, I'll be there." Suddenly Cole smiled. "Thanks, Charlie. I don't know what we'd ever do without you."

"Don't reckon any of you Cantrells would get around to gettin' married. Your pa needed a nudge with Kate, too." Turning his horse toward home, Charlie shook his head. "Never could figure out how men so smart could be so dumb when it comes to women."

Stephanie spent the afternoon nervously waiting for Cole to come home. When he finally did, his smile made her go all warm inside. It seemed as if his eyes never left her face during supper.

"I'm going up to check the range on the mountain tomorrow. Want to go along?" he asked her.

Stephanie's heart lurched. "I'd love to!"

"Likely to be cold," Charlie warned.

"I'll borrow a pair of Cole's winter woolies."

"Cole Cantrell, what are you thinking of? It's too early for —" Kate got a look from Charlie and stopped mid-sentence.

Josh jumped up from his chair in excitement. "Can I go, too?"

Cole ruffled his son's hair. "Not this time. Charlie needs your help around here tomorrow. Don't worry, there will be plenty of trips later."

They left at daybreak. The Mesa trail wasn't nearly so intimidating this time. If Stephanie didn't precisely enjoy the ride, at least she wasn't frightened. At the top she gasped in surprise. The entire grassy mesa was covered with wild blue iris as high as the horses' knees. The sea of flowers stretched clear to the horizon, and Stephanie felt as though they were riding into heaven as they crossed the grassy meadow.

The new green grass, budding aspens, a tiny fawn, all brought exclamations of delight. At last they came to the meadow near Rat Springs. Now wild flowers of every imaginable color and shape dotted the landscape.

"It's so beautiful up here," Stephanie said as she dismounted.

"That's why we came. I know how much you like this place." Hobbling the horses, Cole watched her with an indulgent smile as she ran around happily picking wildflowers. At last she came back, her arms full and her eyes sparkling.

"Come here," he said.

"I don't think so."

He raised an eyebrow. "Oh?"

"You think I've forgotten you owe me for that pitcher of water, but I haven't."

His eyes gleamed, and he gave her a wolfish grin. "All the more reason for you to come here."

The flowers cascaded to the ground as she let them drop. "If you want me, you'll have to catch me." With a saucy toss of her head, Stephanie lifted her skirts and ran.

It wasn't long before he caught her, but he didn't pull her into his arms and kiss her as she expected him to. He just stood there holding her upper arms and staring down into her face. In apprehension, she watched his smile fade and his eyes become deadly serious.

"I'm not sure how to say this," he said uncertainly.

Her heart sank. Was he going to send her away after all?

"I've been a jackass, Steph."

"Cole—"

He shook his head. "No, let me finish. I love you, Steph. I think I have almost from the beginning, but I wouldn't let myself admit it. I've had a dozen different excuses, but the reality is I was scared."

Stephanie blinked in surprise. "Scared of me?"

"No, scared of losing you the way I lost Maggie. I guess I thought if I didn't fall for you, it wouldn't hurt when you left."

"I see," she said uncertainly.

"Do you?" He pulled her into his arms. "Do you see that I love you and want you to stay here with me?"

"What if we find out I'm married?"

Cole shrugged. "It really doesn't matter if your married or not. In fact, I don't care if you have several husbands hidden away somewhere." He kissed her. "All that matters is that I love you. If a husband shows up...well, we'll cross that bridge when we come to it."

"Oh, Cole." Closing her eyes, Stephanie briefly savored the moment. Then she sighed. "What if somebody comes looking for the money?"

"Don't worry, it's already well on the way to being taken care of."

"Then you've learned something about my past?"

"No, just about the money. I found out where to return it, and I've already set the wheels in motion. After the dust settles a bit, I'll see if I can discover anything else without leaving a trail that leads back here. We ought to at least find out your name and where you're from without rousing too much suspicion. After that, it's a fairly simple matter to locate marriage records if they exist."

"But we still don't know if I'm a thief. Doesn't that bother you?"

"No." He crooked his finger under her chin and tilted her face up to his. "The past doesn't matter, only the present and the future, our future."

"Oh, Cole, I love you so much!"

"And I love you," he whispered against her lips.

She didn't offer a single murmur of protest when he undressed her in the chilly mountain air, or even when he wrapped the scratchy wool blanket around her. It was only when he picked her up and carried her over to the small creek formed by the spring that she had any premonition of danger.

There was a devilish gleam in his eye as he squatted on the bank next to the stream. "Now then, about that pitcher of water I owe you."

"Cole Cantrell, don't you dare—" her voice turned into a squeal when he pretended to drop her into the frigid water. Instead of letting her fall, he caught her to his chest and kissed her until she was breathless with longing. He lay her back across his lap, and she closed her eyes as his fingers gently parted the blanket, exposing her breasts to the cool air. Her smile turned to a gasp of shock when he scooped up the freezing water and dribbled it down her chest.

With effortless ease, he intercepted the slap she aimed at his face. "Ah, ah, ah, ah," he admonished in a near perfect imitation of her voice. "I wouldn't do that if I were you." Lowering his head, he began to lick the drops of water from her skin.

When he was finished, he looked down into smoldering green eyes, but the fire he saw there was born of passion, not anger, and he laughed deep in his throat. "Now we're even," he said huskily as he ran his finger down the valley between her breasts. "I always finish what I begin."

"Oh, I do hope so," she murmured as his mouth closed over hers and they sank to the ground together. In a bed of fragrant wildflowers, they came together in joyous abandon, their bodies melding together in glorious fulfillment.

They spent the rest of the afternoon talking and loving. Stephanie asked Cole about his life with Maggie, and he poured his heart out. Stephanie was struck with a wave of regret that she'd never known the other woman.

"I don't understand it," Cole said at last. "My heart is full of love for you, and yet I love her as much as I always did."

Stephanie smiled and caressed his cheek with her hand. "A part of you will always belong to Maggie, and that's as it should be." She flicked his mustache impishly. "I'll share you with Maggie's memory, but not with Sally."

"That's something you'll never have to worry about."

"Good, because I'd certainly hate to have to put her in her place," Stephanie said.

It was almost dark when they rode into the ranch, tired but extremely happy. If there had been any doubts in the minds of Charlie or Kate about the real reason for the trip, they disappeared as soon as Charlie asked Cole how the range looked. Cole stared at him blankly for a minute and then exchanged a look of loving chagrin with Stephanie. That neither had paid any attention to the range was patently obvious, but Charlie pretended to accept Cole's noncommittal answer.

Cole and Stephanie had decided to keep their changed relationship quiet, but it proved to be more difficult than they had anticipated. They both wanted nothing more than to spend every night in each other's arms but knew it was impossible, at least for the present.

The very next night Stephanie was unable to sleep and wandered down to the corral. She was leaning on the fence, watching the horses, when Cole suddenly materialized out of the shadows by the barn.

"I certainly didn't expect to find you here."

She smiled up at him. "I couldn't sleep."

"Neither could I." He sighed and leaned on the fence next to her. "All I could think of was you."

"What a coincidence. The same thing happened to me." Stephanie's laughter was low and melodious. "It appears we have a problem, my love."

"But one that's easily solved." He pulled her into his arms. "I think all that's needed is a little physical exertion, and we'll both sleep like babies."

"Just what did you have in mind?" she asked, nuzzling his neck.

"Can't you guess?"

"Perhaps if you were to show me..."

His lips found hers, and neither of them spoke again until long after they entered his bedroom.

It was a scenario that was to be repeated frequently over the next few nights. Stephanie spent her days living in a blissful haze of joy. She was sure nothing could happen to mar her happiness.

She was wrong.

CHAPTER 31

Sally couldn't believe her plans were falling apart. Her gift for plotting and planning had always gotten her what she wanted. This ranch, a comfortable inheritance, even Cole Cantrell as a lover were all the results of her carefully laid plans. When she'd sent her telegram to Orson Pickett, her scheme had involved a nebulous idea of putting Stephanie on a train to St. Louis. She hadn't really worked out the particulars of how she was going to make that happen, but she'd been sure something would come to her, as it always did. Once Stephanie had arrived in St. Louis, Orson Pickett wouldn't have paid for a return ticket even if she wasn't the woman he was looking for, and Cole would never know where she'd gone. It had seemed so easily orchestrated. All she'd have had to do was come up with a way to get Stephanie on that train. Claiming Pickett was a close relative probably would have done it.

It had never occurred to Sally that Orson Pickett might come to Horse Creek himself, yet that was exactly what he was doing. If Stephanie wasn't the woman he was looking for, all Sally's careful planning would be for nothing. There might still be a way to use him to rid herself of Stephanie, but Sally didn't like the uncertainty of it. She was in a less than buoyant mood when she went to meet the train.

Sally searched the handful of passengers that disembarked and saw Orson Pickett immediately. He was impossible to miss. At least six feet tall and dressed in unrelieved black, he'd have stood out in a crowd even without the rattlesnake hatband and deadly pair of six guns. *A bounty hunter? Perfect!* He was deliciously dangerous looking, and Sally couldn't help a little shiver of delight when his glacial eyes turned her way. "Hello," she said in the low, husky voice she knew drove men wild. "I'm Sally Langton."

"Well, hello!" His voice was deep and rough, and Sally wondered if she was going to swoon right there. The stranger was in the process of giving her an appreciative once over when another voice broke into the conversation.

"Ah, Mrs. Langton. It's a pleasure to meet you." Another passenger, one previously unnoticed by Sally, stepped forward with a smile on his face.

Sally raised her perfect eyebrows in a manner calculated to squash pretensions. "I don't believe we've been introduced."

"No, of course not. My manners are sadly lacking today, I'm afraid. The long trip from St. Louis seems to have befuddled my brain. I'm Orson Pickett, of course."

"Orson Pickett? Then who—"

But mister tall, dark and dangerous was already moving away with nothing more than a touch to the brim of his hat and a knowing smile.

"Where is Stephanie?" Orson asked, scanning the train platform.

"What?" Sally jerked her gaze back to the real Orson Pickett. He looked more like a businessman than any kind of law enforcement official.

"Isn't Stephanie with you?"

"Uh...no, she isn't. I thought it would be better if I met you alone first."

"Why?"

Sally brightened suddenly. "Say, are you a Pinkerton Detective by any chance?"

Orson was taken aback. "Certainly not. Whatever gave you an idea like that?"

"I just thought maybe..." She paused. "What did she do, anyway?"

"Do?"

"Why are you looking for her?"

"I'm sorry, Mrs. Langton, I'm afraid that's between Stephanie and me."

Stung by his abruptness, Sally stiffened. "But we haven't

exactly proven she is your Stephanie, have we?"

"That's true," Orson said, "but I'll know as soon as I see her."

"Perhaps, but I'll only have your word for that, won't I? You'll be a stranger to her either way."

"I see your point." He looked thoughtful. "All right. The woman I'm looking for was headed to Wyoming last August. As far as I can tell, she never arrived."

"Yes, that's when she showed up!" Sally felt a flicker of hope. "An accident caused her to forget everything, so she didn't know where she was going. What does she look like?"

"Tall, slender, with reddish brown hair and green eyes. She's one of the most beautiful women I know." He gave a wry smile. "And one of the most difficult to deal with."

Irritated by hearing yet another man extolling Stephanie's virtues, Sally's lips tightened. "Everyone thinks she's perfect, but she uses words as weapons and fools everyone with her sweet smiles while she does it," Sally snapped.

Orson surprised her with a chuckle. "That's Stephanie for sure. I'd like to see her as soon as possible, and I'm sure she's anxious too. It can't be easy not knowing who you are or where you belong."

"Actually, she doesn't know you're coming. I thought it best not to get her hopes up."

Orson frowned. "But now that I'm here and we know she's the one I've been searching for, surely that changes things. Seeing me might even jog her memory."

Out of the corner of her eye, Sally saw the man in black climb back on board the train and felt like screaming in vexation. His destination was obviously farther down the line. Things were not going her way at all.

"When can I see Stephanie?" Orson demanded.

"It may take a while to set up a meeting."

Orson's eyebrows raised a fraction. "Why?"

Sally gestured toward her buggy. "My ranch isn't far from town, Mr. Pickett. I can explain the situation on the ride out."

"Is Stephanie there?"

"Uh...no."

"Then where is she?"

"She's at the Triple C Bar ranch."

"Perhaps that's where we should go, then," Orson suggested.

Sally's face blanched. "No, I don't think that's a good idea. The man she's living with is—"

"Stephanie's living with a man?" Pickett was clearly horrified.

"It's not like that," Sally said quickly. A forced marriage between Cole and Stephanie was the last thing she wanted. "But Cole is a very difficult man and—"

"Cole Cantrell?" Orson looked more confused than ever. "He never even mentioned Stephanie in his telegram."

Sally was startled. "You know him?"

Orson took Sally's elbow in a firm grip and headed toward the buggy. "Perhaps we'd better do as you suggested. There seems to be a great deal of this story I haven't heard yet."

By the time they reached Sally's ranch, she'd told him what she knew and convinced him it would be futile to approach Stephanie without first talking to Cole. In the end, it was decided Orson would wait at Sally's ranch while she went to get Cole. Orson wasn't at all satisfied with the arrangement, but Sally convinced him there wasn't any alternative.

Sally found Cole mucking out the barn. Barely able to restrain herself from holding her hand over her nose, she forced a smile. "Can't you take a minute to talk to an old friend, Cole?"

"I don't have time for your games, Sally," Cole said unencouragingly. "Why don't you just come to the point?"

Angrily, Sally twitched her skirt away from the pile of manure that landed at her feet. "If you must know, there is a Mr. Orson Pickett sitting in my parlor this very minute. He's come looking for your precious Stephanie."

Cole stopped and stared at her. "Orson Pickett? How in the hell did he wind up at your place?"

"I contacted him when I saw the reward poster in the store."

"Damn. I might have known," Cole muttered, sticking the pitchfork in the ground. He strode from the barn, walked into the empty bunkhouse, and pulled a leather bag from its hiding place in the mouth of the chimney. Without a word he returned to the barn, saddled Midnight, and headed out.

Sally was hard pressed to keep up with him. It wasn't until she rode into her yard that Cole spoke to her at all.

"I want to see this Pickett alone. If you interrupt or I catch you listening at the door, I'll wring your neck. Is that clear?"

Sally nodded nervously.

"Where is he?" Cole asked.

Silently, Sally led him to the parlor and closed the door behind him. She'd never seen him this way. He wasn't angry precisely, more like coldly determined. She shivered. It wouldn't be at all wise to tempt him when he was in this uncertain mood. She went to the front hall to wait.

Orson Pickett looked up from the book he was reading, his eyes widening in surprise when he took in Cole's size. Orson schooled his features as he stood and extended his hand. "Good afternoon, Mr. Cantrell. I'm Orson Pickett."

Cole ignored the proffered hand. "Why didn't you let me know you were coming?"

Orson self-consciously dropped his hand. "To be honest, I didn't think of it. I figured it would be an easy matter to arrange a meeting once I was here."

Cole gave him an unreadable look. "You certainly made an unusual choice for a go-between. Sally is hardly my idea of a liaison."

"Mrs. Langton volunteered."

"I suppose you can prove you're who you say you are?" Cole really didn't care, but he was afraid it would look suspicious if he was too anxious to get rid of the money.

"Of course. I have identification and the wires sent by yourself and Mrs. Langton."

Cole glanced briefly over the papers. His face darkened slightly when he read Sally's telegram. "Everything seems to be in order." He handed the packet back and threw the leather bag onto a low table. "There's your money. I suggest you take it and go back to St. Louis."

Orson blinked in surprise. "But what about Stephanie?"

"You've got your money back. If you care to count it, you'll find it's all there."

"Mr. Cantrell, you don't seem to understand. I have no intention of leaving without Miss Scott."

"As Sally already told you, Stephanie has lost her memory. What good would it do to punish her for something she can't even remember doing?"

"I want to take her back where she belongs."

Cole eyes narrowed in thought. Suddenly he nodded in understanding. "It's the interest, isn't it? I hadn't thought of that." He was silent for a moment then nodded toward the window. "If you care to take a look outside, you'll see one of the finest studs in the country. His foals have already proven to be outstanding animals. If you'll take the money and forget about Steph, I'll have papers drawn up giving you half interest in Midnight and fifteen percent of the proceeds from his offspring."

"I haven't the slightest desire to go into the horse breeding business, Mr. Cantrell."

Was the man's desire for revenge that strong, or didn't he understand how much Midnight's foals would bring in over the years? Cole sighed. There was a way he could raise a great deal of cash quickly. When an eastern buyer had offered him two thousand dollars for Midnight and Black, he'd turned down the ridiculously high offer without a qualm. Now it seemed the only solution. It would set him back at least ten years, but he and Stephanie could rebuild together.

"Would two thousand dollars change your mind? It may take several weeks because it entails selling some of my stock, but it should more than compensate you for Stephanie having taken your money."

Orson walked to the window and stared out at the beautiful black stallion tied to the hitching rack. "It isn't my money," he said quietly. "It's hers."

There was a moment of silence. "What do you mean it's her money?" Cole's face darkened ominously.

Orson turned to face his adversary and swallowed nervously at the black look he encountered. "Stephanie's father built a prosperous company and invested the profits well. When he died almost a year ago, she inherited his entire fortune."

"How much of a fortune?"

Orson gave a short laugh. "Five thousand dollars doesn't even scratch the surface."

"Then why is she here?" Cole's voice dropped ominously.

Orson's mind was working rapidly. Considering Cantrell's reaction, perhaps an embellishment of the truth would suffice. He smiled. "Stephanie has been the darling of polite society since her debut, but I suppose you've noticed she's a very active young lady?"

Cole's only reaction was a deep scowl.

Orson cleared his throat. "Yes, well, occasionally she gets bored and leaves for a few days. She finds it quite adventurous to mingle with the dregs of society. That's why we weren't concerned at first. When she didn't return, I began searching for her." It wasn't true, but Orson had no desire to tell this volatile man the real reason for her hasty departure.

"Are you saying my Steph is nothing more than a rich little society brat out looking for a good time?"

Orson shrugged. "I wouldn't put it in quite those terms, but essentially, yes."

Cole's eyes narrowed in suspiciously. "You say Steph's father died a year ago, but she's been here almost that long."

"He died shortly before she left."

"How long before?"

"A week."

"I see," Cole said noncommittally. The man was obviously lying through his teeth. Stephanie would never leave on a lark so soon after her father's death. "Tell me, where do you fit into all this?"

"Stephanie's father was my business partner. His health had been poor for several years before his final collapse, and he had gradually shifted the management of the company over to me. When he died, Stephanie was left without any family, so I assumed responsibility for her, too. That's why I'm here, to take her back where she belongs."

"Who owns her father's company now?"

"Basically, Stephanie and I. Between us, we own almost all the stocks, though she has the controlling shares."

"And were you compatible business partners?"

Orson's face darkened. "No, she fought me at every turn."

"Then I fail to understand why you've gone to such lengths to find her," Cole observed. "I'd think you'd be glad to be rid of her."

"Stephanie and I are more than mere business partners, Mr. Cantrell."

"How so?"

"She's my fiancée."

"Your what?" Cole exploded.

"The wedding was postponed, of course, but as soon as I get her home, I fully intend to marry her."

"Like hell! She has no memory of you or anything else." A speculative gleam suddenly appeared in Cole's eyes. "Does Stephanie have a nickname for you?"

Orson was startled. "Why, no."

"Are you well acquainted with her friends?"

"Certainly, we mingle with all the same people, but I fail to see —"

"Is there a James among them?"

Orson thought for a moment. "Not unless you mean Jim Hazen, but he's a mere child."

"How old is this child?"

"Why, I believe about eighteen, but he only came to town a few months before Stephanie left. She doesn't know him very well."

Cole wondered briefly if Stephanie knew Jim Hazen better than Orson realized. "Your story seems to have a great many things that don't add up, Pickett. I find it hard to believe that a girl of Steph's tender years was left in control of a large fortune without anyone to oversee the management of it."

Orson gave a ghost of a laugh. "Stephanie has run her father's house for years. She was even in charge of their personal finances. She has a solicitor for everything else. Believe me, she doesn't need anyone to manage her affairs for her."

"Still, I find myself unwilling to trust you. Steph left home within a week of her father's death, dressed in rags with a small fortune sewn into the hem of her cloak. I think someone, or something, frightened her badly. Since she didn't go to you, I can't help wondering if it was you she was running from."

"That's ridiculous," Orson blustered. "Stephanie has nothing to fear from me!"

"Maybe not, but there's no way for me to know for sure, and I'm not willing to take that chance." Cole scowled forbiddingly. "While she's under my protection, I know she's safe, and that's where she'll stay. If her memory returns, she will be able to decide her future without fear of you or anyone else."

Orson was incredulous. "You mean after I've come all the way to this God-forsaken country, you aren't even going to let me see her?"

"You're very perceptive, Pickett. That's exactly what I mean." Cole's eyes glittered dangerously. "And we shoot trespassers on sight in this God-forsaken country, so forget trying to see her. You may as well take the money and go back to St. Louis."

"But the money's hers!"

"So you say, but if she doesn't have it, she can't be arrested for stealing it, can she?"

Orson stared at Cole. "You don't believe a word I've said, do you?"

"Let's just say I've heard better stories in my life. While Stephanie is here, she poses no threat to you or anyone else. If her memory returns, that may be a different matter, but you'd know that better than I. Either way, I'm more than capable of protecting her." He paused, his face darkening ominously. "Crossing me might very well be the last mistake you ever make."

"Are you threatening me?" Orson asked.

Cole shrugged. "Not unless you're stupid enough to try anything."

"Stephanie has nothing to fear from me. We've had our disagreements, but I'd never hurt her." Orson sighed. "You may not believe it, but I care about her as much as you do."

Cole eyed Orson sardonically. "If you really do have Steph's best interests at heart, you'll just have to be content with the knowledge that she's with people who love her and is happy." He turned on his heel and strode to the door, slamming it behind him.

Sally jumped to her feet. Cole took one look at her hopeful face and snorted. "You should be more careful when you choose your friends. I think your Mr. Pickett is an unfortunate man with a vivid imagination."

"He isn't my Mr. Pickett." Sally looked sympathetic. "Do you mean he doesn't know Stephanie? I had hoped he'd be able to help her."

"You can cut the false solicitude. We both know you're mad as hell!" Cole glared at her look of wounded innocence. "I'd like to beat you for trying to cause trouble, but I'll resist the temptation because we've had some good times together. I'm sorry if I hurt you, but it's over, and I'll tolerate no further interference in my life."

"But, Cole, after all we've meant to each other, you can't just expect me to — "

His expression hardened. "If you're smart, you'll stay away from me. I'm not sure I'll be able to control myself if I see you in the near future. Send your foreman if you need to discuss business." He put his hat on his head. "Goodbye, Sally."

Sally stared after him for several minutes while tears gathered in her brown eyes. The door to the parlor opened behind her.

"Mrs. Langton," Orson began, "if you don't mind, I'd like to have a few words — " He broke off when he saw her tears. "Why, what's the matter?"

Without a word she ran past him and fled to her bedroom, where she had a good long cry.

During the long ride home, Cole pondered what he'd heard. Could any of Pickett's story be true? Stephanie was nothing like the rich debutantes he'd known during his years at Princeton. It wasn't possible unless her memory loss had completely changed her personality. He wouldn't believe it until he heard Stephanie admit it, and there was little likelihood of that.

Even if Stephanie was the heir to the company Orson Pickett ran in her absence, he was probably trying to get possession of her shares. Once that was accomplished, he could easily have her killed.

The certainty grew in Cole's mind that Orson was the man Stephanie had been fleeing from. No woman of unlimited funds would dress the way she had unless she had a very good reason. Her very life might be at stake. The idea that Pickett might be telling the truth, he dismissed out of hand. Cole knew the kind of woman Pickett had described; he'd been surrounded by them at Princeton. Penelope Van Horn and her friends were as different from Stephanie as night was from day. He refused to even consider the possibility that Pickett might be telling the truth.

CHAPTER 32

For almost a week, Cole waited for Orson Pickett to make a move. When nothing happened, he decided the man must have returned to St. Louis. Though Pickett would probably be back with reinforcements, Cole would be ready for him.

As he finished smoothing the bottom of Midnight's hoof with a file, Cole paused to watch Stephanie. She was giving cheerful advice to Charlie and Josh while they worked a two-year-old filly. Cole wished he could sneak away with her and spend the afternoon making love.

Smiling, he remembered how his father and Kate used to disappear sometimes when they were first married. He'd been a full-grown man before he figured out what was going on.

Suddenly he straightened. That was it! As Stephanie's husband, he'd be in a far better position to protect her. If she had been married already, Pickett would surely have mentioned it.

They could go to Horse Creek this afternoon, buy a wedding ring, and find out how soon the circuit preacher would be in town.

"You know, I don't think these shoes are going to fit right. I'd better take Midnight and Sunrise to the blacksmith. How would you like to go with me, Steph?"

"That sounds like a wonderful idea. These two don't listen to me anyway."

Cole snorted. "Maybe they would if you knew what you were talking about."

"Well, I like that!" she said, throwing a handful of straw at him.

Cole ducked out of the way. "Just for that, I'm not going to tell you about the surprise I have for you."

All the way to town she teased and cajoled, but he refused

to tell her what he was planning. They were still laughing together when they left the horses at the blacksmith shop and headed down the street. Stephanie didn't even see the stranger until she heard Cole's muttered, "Damn!"

Following his gaze to the other side of the street, Stephanie sucked in her breath in horrified recognition. Tugging on Cole's arm, she pulled him into an alley. "It's the man from my nightmares," she whispered. "And he's coming this way. Do you think he's seen us?"

"Oh, he's seen us all right, though why he's still in town —"

"What?"

Just then, the stranger entered the alleyway with a determined look on his face.

"Good afternoon, Mr. Cantrell." Orson stepped forward and took hold of Stephanie's arm. "Come, Stephanie, we need to talk."

Stephanie backed away in fear. "Leave me alone." Jerking her arm free, she fell backward. Pain exploded in her head as it hit the wall. Fighting the blackness that threatened to engulf her, she forced herself back to reality. The alley swam before her, and the wall in her mind crumbled.

She saw Cole shaking the stranger like a rag doll. No, not a stranger…Orson. "Cole, stop. It's Orson. He'd never hurt me. Let him go."

Cole immediately dropped Orson to the ground and grabbed her shoulders in a crushing grip. "Steph, you've remembered?"

It was as though a dam had broken in her brain. Memories poured through her mind like the roiling waters of a flood. "Y-yeah, sort of…"

"Are you a St. Louis rich girl like he says?"

"I—"

He gave her an impatient shake. "Did you inherit a fortune when your father died?"

She nodded.

"And left less than a week later in disguise?"

"Yes, but—"

Cole's eyes burned into hers. "Are you betrothed to this man?"

"I—"

"The truth, Stephanie, did you promise to marry him?"

"Well, yes, but—"

The look on Cole's face was frighteningly intense. "Did you come here because you were afraid of him?"

"Afraid of Orson?" She looked surprised. "No, of course not, he's—"

"Then everything he said about you was true?" A look of pure disgust crossed his face. "Jesus, what a fool I've been." Thrusting her away, he strode angrily out of the alley.

"*Cole!*" Her agonized cry went unheeded as he disappeared from sight.

As she started after him, Orson finally gained his feet and grabbed her hand.

"Let him go, Stephanie. He's not worth it. Let's go home where people are civilized."

She whirled on him, her eyes blazing. "Mind your own business, Orson Pickett."

"But Stephanie—"

"I don't have time to argue with you right now, Orson, and I really don't give a damn what you think. If you're smart, you'll go back to the hotel and stay out of my sight!" With that, she lifted her skirts and ran down the street after Cole. She was out of breath by the time she caught up with him. He didn't even slow down.

"Cole, please—"

"Go away. You don't belong here."

"But Cole, I'm not—"

"No, you're not what we thought, are you?" He snorted. "Lord, how you must be laughing at me, laying all my worldly possessions at your feet. Ha! You could buy and sell everything I own and never even feel the pinch."

"No, Cole, it's not like that."

"Yes, it is. You're no different than all the rest of them." He turned away, and she grabbed his sleeve.

"Damn you, Cole Cantrell, listen to me. I came to find my sister, Lizzie."

"Your sister?"

"Yes, she lives around here somewhere."

"And where has she been all this time?"

"I—I don't know, unless she's moved."

"What's her name?"

"Elizabeth Scott, at least it was Scott. I don't know what her married name is." Watching his features harden to granite, her mouth went dry with fear.

"So, I can add lying to your list of charms, too?" He pulled his arm from her grasp and started walking again. "You should have thought of a better story. There's never been an Elizabeth anything around here. Besides, Pickett told me you don't have any family left."

"But Cole, it's the truth!"

He kept on walking.

"Cole, I love you!"

They had reached the blacksmith's shop. Through the open door they could see the smith putting shoes on Sunrise, and Cole yelled in the door. "Keep her overnight, Joe. I'll send Charlie after her in the morning."

As he turned, Stephanie stepped in front of him. "I said I love you. Doesn't that matter anymore?"

He stared at her coldly for a second and then lifted her out of his way. Untying the reins, he led Midnight away from the hitching rack.

"Cole!" Stephanie called after him. "You were the one who said the past didn't matter, only the future, our future."

"We don't have a future; not anymore. The last thing I want is to be tied to someone like you." Reaching into his pocket, he pulled out a roll of bills and stuffed them into her hand. "Here, this will get you a room at the hotel and a ticket back to St.

Louis. I gave all your money to Pickett, and I won't leave even you at his mercy."

"I don't want your money, Cole."

"Consider it payment for the work you did at the ranch." He swung up into the saddle. "It was to buy your wedding ring, and I don't want to be reminded I almost made the mistake of my life."

She grabbed his leg and looked up at him, her eyes pleading. "Cole…"

He stared at her, his eyes like twin glaciers. "Don't you understand?" he said flatly. "I despise your kind. I hate everything you are and everything you stand for. I never want to see you again."

Stephanie's whole body slumped in defeat as he wheeled Midnight away and rode out of her life. Her heart pleaded for him to turn back, but she never made a sound. Once he slowed and looked back, but then he spurred his horse on faster.

Her heart numb, she turned and walked slowly up the street to the hotel. When she entered, Orson jumped up from a chair where he'd been sitting with a piece of steak over his eye.

"Stephanie."

She glowered at him. "Don't even speak to me, Orson Pickett. Believe me, you don't want to hear what I'd like to say to you right now."

Ignoring him, Stephanie registered and went to her room. As she sat down on the bed, a flash of gold caught her eye and she glanced at her hand. She remembered taking Orson's engagement ring off and angrily tossing it into her jewel chest. She'd realized the engagement ring might give her a modicum of protection from the advances of strangers, but she'd chosen to wear her mother's wedding ring instead. It had protected her, all right—too well.

Stephanie looked out the window and sighed. Even if she hadn't had amnesia, she would have hit a dead end when she'd reached Horse Creek. Her father had been so sure Lizzie was here. On his death bed, he'd pleaded with Stephanie to find her half sister and share the inheritance with her. It was the first time Ashton Scott had mentioned his step-daughter in over a decade. But it had turned out to be a wild goose chase. If Elizabeth Scott had ever been in Horse Creek, she was gone now.

The disappointment was nearly unbearable on top of Cole's inexplicable behavior. When he'd brought her to town, he'd loved her enough to buy a wedding ring, and now he never wanted to see her again? Surely he'd change his mind. He was mad now, but when he cooled off, he'd feel differently. What if he didn't relent, though? She'd never see him again.

Stephanie hadn't even taken time to say goodbye to Kate or Josh when she left. Too miserable to sit still, she tucked Cole's money into the sleeve of her riding habit and left the hotel. She walked down the street to the blacksmith's shop, oblivious of the gorgeous sunset that painted the sky.

The smith had gone home to supper, but the door to his stable was open. It didn't take long to find Maggie's sidesaddle. She slipped the money into the saddlebag before making her way to where Sunrise was penned. Unwilling to leave her last link with Cole, she stayed with the mare until the light began to fade.

On her way back to the hotel, she stopped at the general store, but Frank Collins only confirmed what Cole had told her. There hadn't been a woman named Elizabeth living around Horse Creek for as long as he could remember. Dejectedly, she returned to her room and sat on the bed without even bothering to light the lamp. She didn't need to see to know how miserable she was.

Even a lifetime of memories brought her no comfort. In fact, they made it worse. Technically, she was still betrothed to Orson Pickett. It had been her father's fondest wish that they marry, but she had decided long before she ever met Cole Cantrell that Orson was not the man for her. If she had any doubts, the week following her father's death would have convinced her to end the engagement.

In her grief, Stephanie had clung to her father's last wish as a lifeline. Thinking all would be well if she could find her beloved Lizzie, she'd asked Orson to escort her to Wyoming. Orson refused. They had fought about it for days. He'd even recruited Stephanie's best friend Nance to try and talk her out of going to Wyoming. Between the two of them, they never left her alone.

At last, Stephanie could stand no more. Pretending she was ill, she had rid herself of her self-appointed watchdogs and withdrawn all the household money. Since it was the beginning of the quarter, she found herself with a small fortune in cash. She knew she'd need a disguise for protection and to throw Orson off track.

A quick survey of her wardrobe convinced her none of her clothes were appropriate, so she'd borrowed a dress from her housekeeper. The dress fit like a sack, and with her hair braided the way she wore it when she rode or worked in the garden, she looked downright plain. Gazing at her reflection in the mirror with delight, Stephanie couldn't have imagined how much she'd come to hate the gray dress before she was finished with it.

She'd decided to take her old riding cloak too. Not only was it appropriately dilapidated, it was heavy enough to hide the money by sewing it into the hem. When she'd caught the train for Wyoming, she thought herself very clever and safe from pursuit and had traveled slowly to regain her strength after weeks of nursing her father.

Unfortunately, Orson had figured out where she'd gone and came after her. They'd wound up on the same train out of Cheyenne and ran into each other within miles of her destination. The argument that ensued was a repeat of those that had gone before.

So when Orson had insisted she return to St. Louis with him, Stephanie said she needed time alone to think about it and sent him away. When the locomotive made an unexpected stop to take on water, she'd jumped off the train—right into the arms of Cole Cantrell. Nothing else had mattered from that moment on.

After he'd known her all those months, how could he think she was like the wealthy women he'd so despised in his years at Princeton? She fell back on the bed, fully dressed, and lay staring into the darkness in dry-eyed misery until she finally fell into exhausted slumber just as the eastern horizon turned pink.

Stephanie was awakened several hours later by a knock at the door. "Miss Scott? There's a man downstairs says he wants to see you."

"Tell Mr. Pickett I don't want to talk to him."

"It ain't Mr. Pickett."

Stephanie was out of bed like a shot. "I'll be right there!" Straightening her hair and clothes, she hurried downstairs.

Charlie was standing by the window, nervously twisting his hat in his hands. Hiding her disappointment, Stephanie took a deep breath to dissolve the lump in her throat.

"Good morning, Charlie. What brings you to town so early?"

"Cole sent me."

Hope flared in her breast but was dashed at once by the way he refused to meet her eyes.

"I've got your things in the wagon." He cleared his throat. "Where do you want me to put 'em?"

Stephanie felt as though Cole had just plunged a knife into her heart. He was thinking rationally by now, and he still didn't want her. With Lizzie gone, there was no reason for her to stay in Horse Creek.

"Would you mind taking them to the depot? I'll be leaving for St. Louis later today."

He gave her a sympathetic look. "You want to write Kate a note?"

"Yes, I would. Thanks." Obtaining paper and ink from the desk clerk, she hurriedly dashed off a note begging Kate to write to her in St. Louis.

Charlie shook his head sadly. "I don't rightly know what happened, Miss Stephanie, but I'm real sorry."

She tried to smile. "Yes, so am I." Standing on her tiptoes, she kissed the leathery old cheek. "Goodbye, Charlie. I'll never forget you."

Charlie looked as though he wanted to say something, but he nodded instead. Jamming his hat on his head, he walked away before he choked on the lump in his throat.

Several minutes later, Orson Pickett heard a knock and opened his door. His eyes widened in disbelief when he saw Stephanie standing there.

"How soon will you be ready to leave, Orson?"

He gaped at her. "What? You mean back to St. Louis? Why? What changed your mind?"

A dangerous light entered her eyes. "Don't ask questions, Orson. If you ever mention this again, I swear I'll black your other eye!" With that, she stalked off down the hall to her own room.

When Charlie walked into the kitchen at home, he didn't even have to see the expression on Kate's face to feel the tension filling the room. Josh stood angrily facing his father across the table.

"You promised you wouldn't make Stephanie go away, Pa."

"I told you, son, she remembered who she was and decided to go back where she belongs."

"That's not true. She'd never leave without saying goodbye."

"She told me to tell you for her."

Josh's eyes filled with tears. "Stephanie will come back if you ask her to, Pa. I know she will."

"Possibly, but I'm not going to ask her."

"Why not?"

"You're not old enough to understand."

"I'm old enough to understand you ran her off, and I'll never forgive you for it. Never!" The last word came out in a sob, and Josh ran from the house.

Cole sat drinking his coffee in stony silence, until Charlie cleared his throat. Without looking at him, Cole growled. "Well?"

"She's leavin' today."

"Good!"

"I reckon you best think about this pretty hard, son. Could be you'll regret it down the road."

"What I regret is not sending her away in the first place," Cole said.

Charlie shook his head in defeat. "She sent you a note, Kate."

"I'll take that," Cole said, grabbing it out of his hand.

"Cole Cantrell, you give me that note this instant or I'll..." Her voice trailed off at the look on his face.

"I want nothing of that woman left in this house." Cole grabbed his hat and stomped out the door, the note wadded into a ball in his hand.

Kate spoke first. "Lord have mercy, he hasn't been like that since—"

"I know, since Maggie died." Charlie shook his head sadly. "You should'a seen Miss Stephanie. The look on her face like to broke my heart."

Kate shook her head. "I can't imagine what happened."

Charlie walked to the door. "I ain't real sure I want to know."

CHAPTER 33

The trip to St. Louis was long and unpleasant. Stephanie only spoke to Orson when it was absolutely necessary. His attempts at conversation were met with a blank wall of silence. Slowly, he began to realize it wasn't just anger; Stephanie had shut herself completely away from him.

Nance met them at the station, and her delight was impossible to ignore. "Oh, Stephanie," she said, giving her friend a hug. "I missed you terribly."

A brief smile crossed Stephanie's lips as she returned the hug. "It's good to see you too, Nance."

In spite of Stephanie's assurances that she was perfectly capable of getting home by herself, Orson and Nance insisted on accompanying her. As Orson told Nance about the trip, they both tried to pull Stephanie into the conversation, but she answered in monosyllables, if at all.

When they reached Stephanie's home, the door was opened by a ramrod-straight, gray-haired butler. "Welcome home, Miss Stephanie."

"Thank you, James."

"Will you be requiring refreshments for your guests?"

"No, Mr. Pickett has had a long journey. I'm sure he wishes to go home as soon as possible."

Without even glancing toward the astonished couple on the doorstep, James firmly shut the door and followed Stephanie to the library. As a young man, he had watched a succession of governesses fail woefully with Elizabeth and Stephanie Scott. Finally, when they'd dispatched the third one in a month, James had taken over. With an innate understanding of the mischievous sisters and a firm hand, he'd taught them control. To the world, he was Ashton Scott's very proper British butler, but to Stephanie and Elizabeth, he was their beloved James.

Stephanie tossed her hat into a chair then hugged him fiercely. "Oh, James, I'm so glad to see you. I was afraid you wouldn't be here."

James smiled. "I thought perhaps you'd wish to find your home the way you left it when you returned."

"But I told you I'd only be gone a short time. Surely by now you must have wondered if I was ever coming back."

"It seemed reasonable to wait and see what developed."

"How on earth did you manage to run this house for nearly a year when I took every cent?"

"Mr. Pickett was aware of the situation. I merely applied to him for funds. I believe he used money set aside for you by your father."

"Ah, yes, the ever-resourceful Orson." As soon as the words left her mouth, Stephanie was ashamed of them. In this case, Orson's meddling had averted disaster. "I thought I would only be gone a short time, but I shouldn't have left you in such a position."

"I think, perhaps, you had other things on your mind at the time," he said gently. Then, pulling himself up to his full height, he looked down his nose in his haughtiest manner. "Now, would you be so good as to inform me where you've been these last ten months and why you didn't bother to write?"

"Actually, I've been to Wyoming Territory."

"Hobnobbing with cowboys and Indian chiefs, no doubt."

She gave him a saucy grin. "Of course." Then she sobered. "I went there looking for my sister."

"I thought as much. Did you find Miss Elizabeth?"

"No, not a trace," Stephanie sighed. "Did my father ever tell you why he thought Lizzie was in the West?"

"I was his confidant for many things, but not that. In fact, he never mentioned her to me after she left, though I do think he regretted their argument."

"I agree. It weighed heavily on his mind there at the end. But I can't figure out why he sent me to Horse Creek, or how he even knew it existed. As far as I could tell, she'd never been there."

"If she wasn't there, why did you stay?"

"There was an accident, and I lost my memory." Unexpectedly, her lower lip began to quiver. "Oh James," she said, burying her face against his coat, "I've made such a muddle of things."

Stephanie never shed a tear, but the anguish in her heart was obvious as she told him her story. Though she said very little about her relationship with Cole, James drew his own conclusions from the carefully worded story.

The next two weeks were sheer torture for Stephanie. She refused to leave the house and told James to turn away all visitors. Everything she did reminded her of Cole. The sapphire blue of her bedroom drapes made her think of eyes the same color. The chess board in the library held poignant memories of countless games played on a kitchen table. Even working in the garden and going riding were beyond her, the misery was just too intense.

Stephanie knew she couldn't wallow in self-pity forever, but she couldn't seem to shake the pain eating away at her soul. Finally, hoping to banish her private demons, she decided to unpack the trunk Charlie had left at the station for her.

The sight of the contents filled her with bittersweet memories of the only time in her adult life she had ever been truly happy. The hair thongs from Brave Eagle and his people, all the clothes Kate had made her, and even the hated gray dress were there. Her heart lurched painfully when her fingers touched the mother of pearl hair combs. Rubbing the glowing surfaces sadly, she suddenly remembered the green hair ribbon Cole had given her before the box social. Stephanie dug clear to the bottom looking for the length of ribbon, her only memento of an unforgettable night of love. It was nowhere to be found.

Still searching for the elusive ribbon, she shook out the green dress. A small wooden whistle fell to the floor with a clatter. As she bent to pick it up, Stephanie wondered wistfully what would happen if she were to blow it. Would Sam find her and take her home? Never in her life had she felt so lost.

Tears gathered in her eyes, and a sob rose in her throat. Kneeling among her treasures, Stephanie put her forehead on the trunk and cried.

At long last, the hard knot of pain dissolved, and with it came release. The tears she had not been able to shed now cleansed her soul. Cole no longer loved her, but she couldn't spend the rest of her life dwelling on what might have been. It was time to put her hurt away and start living again.

By the time she had stored her things away, a plan had formed in her head. Pleased with her idea, she hastily sat down and wrote a quick note to Nance inviting her to go shopping the next morning. She handed it to James and asked him to order her carriage. Twenty minutes later, she set out on a mysterious mission with a smile on her face.

Nance arrived an hour early the next morning. Stephanie was still eating breakfast when James ushered the beaming woman into the room.

Stephanie raised her eyebrows. "Good heavens, Nance, are you that anxious to go shopping?"

She shook her head. "I was anxious to see you."

"I'm flattered. Would you like some tea and toast?"

"No, I already — oh, Stephanie, what a pretty necklace."

Stephanie smiled a little sadly as she touched the golden snowflake at her throat. "It was a gift. Perhaps I'll tell you about it sometime."

Nance tipped her head. "A rather special one, I'd guess, from the look on your face."

"It was." Stephanie patted her mouth with her napkin. "Speaking of gifts, I've forgotten to wish you a happy birthday. I have a very special present in mind for you," she said, scooting her chair back. "I'll give it to you later at lunch."

"Your note yesterday was gift enough. I'm so pleased you've given up, uh..." Her voice trailed off in embarrassment.

"Moping? Yes, well, there's no sense in destroying myself

over something that can't be changed. That's why we're going shopping, so I can start afresh with new clothes."

The two women spent a pleasant morning visiting their favorite stores. By eleven o'clock the carriage was loaded with packages.

Nance sighed contentedly. "What a delightful morning this has been. I can't tell you how much I've missed doing things like this with you. Where did you have in mind for lunch?"

Stephanie smiled. "Lunch is part of your birthday surprise. It's early yet, and I have some business with Orson. Would you mind terribly if we stop there first?"

"Of course I don't mind." Nance colored slightly and looked down at her hands. "Maybe he'll decide to join us."

Stephanie smiled to herself but said nothing as the carriage stopped in front of the building that housed Scott Manufacturing Company. The two ladies alighted. "We'll be finished here in about forty-five minutes, John. Please take the packages home and come back for us then."

The young driver touched his hat and winked. "Yes, ma'am."

"Stephanie, he winked at you!"

"Did he? I didn't notice."

Nance was aghast at her friend's nonchalance. "But Stephanie, don't you think that's rather forward for a servant?"

"I suppose, but I doubt he meant any disrespect." Stephanie was already walking toward the door. "Come, we mustn't keep Orson waiting. I'm sure he has a very busy schedule."

With one last look at the carriage disappearing down the street, Nance shrugged and followed her inside.

Stephanie entered Orson's outer office with the air of someone who belonged there. "Good morning, Mr. Jones. Is Mr. Pickett ready to see us?"

"Yes, Miss Scott. He's waiting for you." The middle-aged clerk started to rise.

"Don't bother, Mr. Jones. We'll show ourselves in." She

swept into Orson's office with Nance in tow.

Orson came out from behind his desk and kissed their hands. "Good morning, ladies. You're both looking lovely."

Stephanie nodded. "Thank you, Orson. Yes, it's a beautiful morning, and we've had a very enjoyable outing. Now that we've exchanged pleasantries, may we get down to business?"

Orson raised his eyebrows while Stephanie seated herself and smiled benignly at her two companions. "Well?" she said.

"You're in a very strange humor this morning." Orson observed, holding a chair out for Nance.

"Not really. If you ask Nance, she'll tell you I've been acting quite like my old self."

Orson looked at her with resignation as he seated himself behind his desk. "So, it's to be like that, is it?" He sighed. "Very well, then. What can I do for you?"

Stephanie gave Orson a direct look. "You're not going to like this, but please do me the courtesy of hearing me out. You're the head of Scott Manufacturing, but with my father's shares, I can control it if I choose. Father poured his life's blood into this company, and I don't want it destroyed because you and I don't agree on the course it should take. The only solution is for one of us to buy the other out."

Nance started to rise. "This is a private matter between the two of you. I'll just wait in the outer office."

"No, Nance," Stephanie said. "I'm not finished, and I want you to hear the rest." She smiled, and Nance sat back down uncertainly.

Stephanie turned her attention to Orson once again. "You were like a son to my father and helped him make this company what it is today. He wanted you to run it, and so do I."

She produced two bulky documents. "I've been to see my lawyer and had two different sets of papers drawn up. One transfers my stocks to you. I think you'll find the price is more than fair. I realize you may not have the capital on hand right now, and I have no immediate need of the money. I've set up a schedule of payments over the next three years that should cause you no hardship."

Orson leaned back in his chair, steepling his fingers. "Our marriage will also unite the company. Have you forgotten how pleased your father was when we announced our engagement?"

"I have no desire to be your partner, in business or in life, Orson, and Father wanted us both to be happy, which brings me to my next point." She laid a beautiful diamond ring on the desk. "I think if my father were aware of the situation, he'd understand why I'm calling off our betrothal. Besides," she added, smiling softly in memory, "I've been told I'd make a devil of a wife, and I suspect it's true."

"And if I refuse your offer?" Orson sat back complacently, ignoring the ring. "You think you have the upper hand, my dear, but you know very little about the running of a business. I own a great deal of the company, too—enough to thwart anything you try."

"I realize that, Orson, which brings me to the second set of papers. I've received a very attractive offer from John Whitmeir. He has wanted to consolidate this company with his for years, and these papers turn my shares over to him. He knows a great deal about business and has quite a reputation for ruthlessness. He offered me twice what I've asked you to pay, I might add. I can easily invest the money elsewhere and preserve Father's inheritance. The extra money should more than compensate me for seeing my father's company go down."

The smile was wiped from Orson's face in an instant. "The only reason John Whitmeir wants this company is to drive it into the ground! He'd destroy everything your father and I have built."

"I know that. It's a step I don't want to take, but you've meddled in my life long enough. I want out from under your thumb, and I'll do anything to accomplish it. That's why I brought Nance along. It's important for you both to realize I'll brook no more interference from either of you."

"Interference!" Orson exploded. "I've never done a thing

that wasn't in your best interest."

"That's your opinion, Orson. I know you both meant well, but neither of you would listen to me when I tried to tell you how important it was for me to find Elizabeth. It wasn't just a whim, it was my father's death bed request. I felt he wouldn't rest until I had accomplished it."

Stephanie felt a guilty pang at the flush on Nance's face, but then, she hadn't meant it to be easy for them. "When I decided to go by myself, you made me a virtual prisoner in my own home. I had to sneak away, and when I did, you came after me, forcing me to jump off the train in the middle of nowhere. The reward poster was the frosting on the cake."

Stephanie smiled sardonically at Orson's startled expression. "Oh yes, I know about it. James asked if that was how you were able to locate me. What did you accuse me of? Embezzlement? Murder?"

"I didn't accuse you of anything," Orson said defensively. "It only said you were wanted for questioning."

"Oh, so you only implied I'd done something wrong. Do you realize if a bounty hunter had found me first, I might have been killed? Did it ever occur to you or Nance you might be putting me in danger? Did you even care?"

Orson slammed his fist down on the desk. "Now wait a minute. Nance only tried to steer you down the right path. She was against the reward poster right from the beginning," he admitted, "but without it you might never have remembered who you are. You'd probably still be in the middle of nowhere with that uncivilized barbarian!"

Stephanie gave him a level look. "Exactly!"

There was a moment of silence, the only sound the ticking of the clock. Then Stephanie stood and placed her hand over Orson's. "You're a good man, Orson, and you have many wonderful qualities. You're just not the man for me. It's this company you love, not me. You'd have known it long ago if your love and admiration for my father hadn't blinded you. I think once you have control of the company, you'll know I'm right."

"We could be comfortable together," he said.

"I'm not willing to settle for comfortable, and I don't think you should either. You have a much better candidate for a wife right here. Nance has been secretly in love with you for years." There was a gasp behind her, which Stephanie chose to ignore. "She appreciates you far more than I ever could, and if you search your heart, I'm certain you'll find your feelings for her are deeper than you realize."

Stephanie pointedly looked at the clock. "I'm afraid I have another appointment. Would you mind taking Nance to lunch, Orson? My driver will be back with the carriage in about half an hour. John thinks we've set up a little birthday surprise for Nance. I suggest you go along with it; you know how servants will gossip."

When they didn't reply, she continued. "It will give the two of you plenty of time to discuss how much I've changed. I'll leave the papers with you and will expect an answer no later than noon tomorrow. If not, I have an appointment with Mr. Whitmeir at two."

Stephanie turned and walked to the door, where she turned. "You've been very good friends, and I love you both. I would be devastated if that friendship were destroyed, but you have to let me be myself."

Ignoring the stunned look on her friends' faces, Stephanie walked out, calmly shutting the door behind her. Smiling to herself, she made her way down to the street. "Check and mate, Orson, my friend!"

CHAPTER 34

At precisely ten o'clock the next morning, a messenger delivered the papers with Orson's signature scrawled across the bottom. In an attached envelope, she found the first payment for the stocks and a note containing a single word: *'Touche.'*

Stephanie sighed in relief. She didn't know what she'd have done if Orson had called her bluff. Though she had taken the precaution of having the papers drawn up in case Orson decided to check, she'd never have sold her father's company to John Whitmeir.

A week later, Orson and Nance came to apologize for their interference, and Stephanie welcomed them with open arms. Before long, the three of them were going to the many social events as a trio, much as they had in the past.

Stephanie watched the growing romance between Nance and Orson with a benevolent eye. Each day, Nance grew more beautiful as her love bloomed, and Orson looked happier than he had since before Ashton Scott's health had begun to fail.

Stephanie was pleased to see how well her plan was working, but their obvious happiness filled her with an aching loneliness. Finally she understood why Levi had left. If she'd had anywhere to go, she'd have done the same thing.

To escape her heartache, Stephanie threw herself into the social scene with all her energy. For the first time in her life, she made an all-out effort to enjoy the things her contemporaries found so engrossing.

Clothing became her passion, and she was careful to always appear in the latest fashion, whether it be a social occasion or just a ride in the park. She accepted every invitation she possibly could and flirted outrageously with all the single men. She even allowed a few to steal kisses, though she found the experience disappointingly tame.

Nor was anyone willing to discuss anything but their own pleasure. Stephanie grew very tired of exchanging banalities all evening, every evening. For the first time, she saw her world through Cole's eyes and began to understand why he hated it so much. It was depressing.

She tried to attribute her growing despondency to the heat of summer, but she knew it was the blue, blue eyes that haunted her day and night. Her dreams were of strong arms holding her and a deep voice whispering words of love in her ear.

Night after night she'd awaken to stare at the ceiling and mourn what she'd lost. Daily she felt her need to escape grow, but there was no escape. Everywhere she went, her memories went with her. She even found herself wishing her amnesia would return to block the pain from her mind.

When the family lawyer asked her to come to his office to clear up the final details of her father's estate, she went willingly, eager for anything to give her thoughts a new direction.

Benjamin Harris had known her all her life and greeted her with genuine pleasure. "Come in, come in. It's good to see you again, Miss Scott."

She raised an eyebrow. "Miss Scott? Am I in disgrace, Ben? I thought we had agreed selling the company to Orson was the proper thing to do."

"And so it was, but you're now a very wealthy young woman. It isn't seemly for me to call you by your first name."

"It was my father's money, and you called him Ashton."

He chuckled. "And I can see your resemblance to him more and more."

"Why thank you, Ben. Now then, what was it you wanted to see me about?"

"As you know, your father's will was read several weeks after his death, but I still need to go over it with you."

Stephanie nodded. "Of course. I'm sorry I wasn't up to it when I was here before."

"Understandable, and there is, as I said at the time, no urgency."

There were no surprises in her father's will. He had left rather large bequeaths for Orson, James, and several other long-time servants. The bulk of her father's fortune, his investments, and the house were hers.

As Harris's voice droned on about the various business enterprises that she now had a part of, Stephanie felt a lump forming in her throat. She would gladly trade it all for the love of one bullheaded cowboy. She pushed his image from her mind and signed all the necessary documents.

"That takes care of it," Benjamin said with a smile. He picked up a thick packet and slid it across the table to her. "These are some of your father's personal papers that he gave me for safekeeping. The deed to the house, that sort of thing."

Stephanie returned his smile. "Then they probably should stay with you."

"If that's your choice, but perhaps you should look through them first."

"All right." She picked up the packet and stood. "Thank you for all you've done, Ben."

"I've only done what you asked." He shook her hand warmly. "Your father would have been proud of the way you handled things. He would have approved of young Pickett owning the company. You're a very generous woman."

Stephanie gave a self-satisfied smirk. "I'm not so sure Orson would agree with you."

It was several days before Stephanie got around to going through her father's papers. Finally, out of sheer boredom, she opened the packet. It contained pretty much what she had expected: various deeds, her parent's marriage contract, her grandfather's business journal. Suddenly, an envelope addressed to her caught her attention.

"Now, what's this?" she said aloud as she pulled the letter from its place among the others. When she slit the envelope and pulled out the letter inside, her heart began to pound with excitement. It was from Lizzie! From the date she realized with a shock it was almost nine years old. Why had her father never given it to her? She carried her treasure over to her favorite chair, curled up, and began to read.

My Dearest Annie,

Stephanie's eyes misted at Elizabeth's use of her pet name. It brought back poignant memories of her sister. To the world they were Stephanie and Elizabeth Scott, wealthy young heiresses. But to each other they had been Annie and Lizzie, sisters and best friends despite the difference in their ages.

Please forgive me. I should have written long ago, but my anger at your father kept me silent. When I discovered our mother divorced my father to marry yours, I hated her. It seemed as though she'd forsaken her marriage vows for your father's fortune. I could think of nothing but finding my real father and somehow making up to him for my mother's defection. Your father tried to stop me out of what I was sure was spite. I realize now his only sin was loving me too much. Ashton had never met my father, and only knew what our mother told him. I'm sure he was afraid of what would happen to me if I came west.

Our mother's first marriage was not, I think, a happy one. You don't remember her, but she was a gentle person and very social. She loved parties and beautiful clothes. Your father was perfect for her, and I think they loved each other very much. I do know they were very happy during the short time they had together.

My father, Conner O'Reilly, is very different from Ashton Scott.

Stephanie looked up, her brow furrowed. Where had she heard the name Conner O'Reilly before? She shrugged and went back to her letter.

He carved an empire out of the wilderness and loved his land and cattle almost to the exclusion of everything else. He had no patience with what he termed our mother's frivolities and was as disappointed in her as she was in him. I think he was happy to see her go.

Annie, you'd never believe how much I changed after I found my father. At first he was not at all pleased to see me; I was her daughter, you see. It didn't take me long to break through his gruffness, however, and we soon found ourselves quite pleased with each other. Father is a hard man, but I love him dearly, and I am truly his daughter, for I love this untamed land as much as he does.

Soon after I arrived, I discovered that I had been christened Margaret Elizabeth after his mother. I suppose it was an act of defiance that led Mother to call me Elizabeth rather than Margaret, but it wasn't difficult to change. Everything else was so new it seemed fitting somehow.

Elizabeth Scott died the day I left St. Louis, and I became Margaret O'Reilly with hardly a qualm. The two years I had with my father were wonderful.

I only left him because I married a man I love more than life itself. We have a son, who is my greatest joy. He reminds me very much of you. Unlike our mother, I find I am perfectly suited to this life. It's hard, but good, and I truly don't miss any of the things I left behind except you.

You must wonder why I have not written to you sooner. Though I wanted to, I feared it would cause strife between you and your father. You're old enough now to come for a visit. Hardly a day goes by that I don't think of you and wish you were here with me. I long to share my family and friends with you. Who knows, maybe you'll find you like it here as much as I.

I've written a letter to your father telling him that I am safe and happily married. He knows where to find me but not that I changed my name. It may seem silly to you, but Ashton Scott is a very powerful man, and while I don't think he'd stoop to petty revenge, I hurt him deeply when I left.

You have always been a sensitive person, and I leave it to your judgment how much to tell your father. If he has forgiven me, please convince him to come with you. In spite of all that has passed between us, I still think of him as the tender, caring father of my childhood.

Perhaps I should warn you, I have told my husband very little of my former life. He knows the important details, but I neglected to tell him of the way we were raised. He has a severe prejudice against wealth, and I felt there was no need to tell him until you arrive. If you choose not to come, nothing would be gained other than to confirm his belief that all rich people are self-centered and focused only on their own pleasures. He isn't unreasonable, only hard-headed and stubborn, and I wouldn't change him for the world. Cole Cantrell is unlike any other man I've ever known, and I love him with all my heart.

Stephanie gave a cry, and the letter dropped to the floor from her shaking fingers. Her head was whirling in confusion. Elizabeth married to Cole? How could that be? What about Maggie? Then it hit her, Elizabeth *was* Maggie! Cole had shortened Margaret to Maggie the same way he'd shortened Stephanie to Steph. He'd never known his wife as Elizabeth; that's why he'd never heard of her. All at once, Stephanie knew why she'd always been so attracted to Josh. He resembled his mother.

After traveling halfway across the country, unsure of her destination, she had stumbled upon the very place she was looking for by freak accident. The whole thing was just too bizarre a coincidence to be real. If Stephanie had come out of her self-imposed misery long enough to remember the music box, she'd have known the truth sooner. It had belonged to their mother, the only memento Elizabeth had taken with her.

Suddenly Stephanie gave a cry of pain. Elizabeth was dead! Grief tore through her in agonizing waves. Even in her loneliness, Stephanie had been comforted by the certainty that, somehow, she'd find her beloved sister, and they'd be together again. Now she'd lost Cole and Lizzie both.

Cole! Oh Lord, she was in love with her sister's husband! It put their whole relationship in a different light, a very unpleasant one. She'd had so little hope, and now even that was gone. She was staring blindly out the window, still trying to absorb the enormity of it all when the door opened, and James announced Nance.

"I wanted you to be the first to know," she said, breezing into the room. "Orson and I are engaged!"

"Well," Stephanie's smile was distracted. "I must say, it's about time. Have you set a date yet?"

Nance lowered her eyes and blushed. "No, but Orson says it will have to be soon, or he'll have to marry me just to make an honest woman of me."

Stephanie turned back to the window and stood gazing at the street.

Nance was puzzled as she watched her friend's face. "You aren't sorry you pushed Orson and me together, are you?" she asked uncertainly.

"What? Heavens no! The first time I saw you together after I got back, I knew the two of you had fallen in love. He was just too stubborn to admit it, even to himself."

"You don't seem particularly overjoyed at the news."

"Oh, no, Nance, it's not that." Stephanie gave her friend a hug. "I can't say I'm particularly surprised, but I couldn't be more pleased."

"Then what's wrong?"

Fingering her snowflake charm, Stephanie regarded her friend silently for a moment. "Perhaps it's time I told you what happened to me during the ten months I was gone."

"There's no need if it's painful for you." Nance shuddered delicately. "Orson told me all about the primitive conditions and the terrible man you were living with."

Stephanie gave her a wry smile. "Did he also tell you it was the happiest ten months of my life?" If she hadn't been so miserable, she'd have laughed at Nance's look of stunned surprise. "Have a seat, Nance. This is probably one of the strangest stories you'll ever hear." She shook her head. "I've only just now found out how truly bizarre it is. I can hardly believe it myself."

For the next hour, Stephanie talked. Nance blushed more than once, but Stephanie spared her friend nothing. Nance was shocked when she read Elizbeth's letter but didn't see the situation quite the same as her friend.

"It sounds as though you love this Cole very much," Nance said when the tale was told.

Stephanie gave a short laugh. "When I'm not ready to strangle him. He's the most stubborn, hot-headed, wonderful man I ever met in my life. When he looks at me with those eyes,

I feel like a giddy school girl, and when he touches me, my bones melt and...Well, I've already made you blush too many times today."

"And his son?"

"Josh? He's as wonderful as his father. Everywhere I go I think how Josh would love to see this or that. Oh, Nance, I don't know if I can live without them."

"Why do you have to? What's stopping you from hopping on a train and going back?"

Stephanie whirled around. "Haven't you been listening? The only reason I came back with Orson was that Cole wouldn't let me stay. When he found out what I was, he turned against me. He hates me!"

"Are you sure? I mean, he said he loved you."

"No, he loved who he thought I was. When he found out the truth, he changed his mind."

"Just like that?" Nance was incredulous. "How could finding out you were rich make that much difference?"

"He judges people with money by the arrogance and condescension he encountered at Princeton. It's unreasonable, but he believes we're all like that. Even Lizzie—I mean, Maggie—said so." She rubbed her forehead. "I don't even know what to call my own sister anymore." Suddenly it was all too much. With a sob, she burst into tears.

Putting her arms around her friend, Nance thought of how she'd feel if Orson suddenly decided he didn't want her anymore and sent her away. She closed her eyes against the pain, and tears for her friend's horrible anguish slipped from beneath her lashes.

CHAPTER 35

"There's a gentleman waiting to see you in the library," James informed Stephanie as she walked in the front door.

"Oh, drat. Who is it?" She and Nance had spent the morning shopping and were ready to kick their shoes off. If she had her way, this person, whoever he was, wouldn't be staying long.

"He said he was an old friend from your cattle rustling days."

"From my..." Stephanie's eyes widened, and a delighted smile split her face as she hurried down the hall to the library, vaguely aware of Nance following behind.

Her heart leapt when she saw the tall, broad-shouldered figure by the window. "Levi!" she cried as she ran into his outstretched arms and hugged him for all she was worth. "It's so good to see you."

"It's good to see you, too," he said, hugging her back. "I think your friend is leaving."

Stephanie whirled around just as Nance was about to slip out the door. "Oh, Nance, don't go. This is Levi Cantrell. Levi, I'd like you to meet my good friend, Nance Carstairs."

"Oh," Nance said in sudden comprehension, "the brother."

Levi gave Stephanie a wounded look. "The brother? A beautiful woman who has never laid eyes on Cole calls me *the brother*? I thought you were my friend."

"I am your friend. Nance is getting married in three weeks."

Levi gave a dramatic sigh. "The story of my life."

Stephanie laughed in genuine pleasure. "I can't believe you're actually here. What brings you to St. Louis?"

"You."

"Me!"

"Yes, you. I came home early in the summer just like I promised, but when I got there, I wished I hadn't come. Kate and Charlie were walking around on tiptoes, Josh acted like he'd lost his last friend, and my brother was about as much fun as a mountain lion with his tail in a trap. Cole said you'd regained your memory and decided to come home. It didn't make sense, so I figured I'd better find out for myself what was going on. It's not the easiest task I ever set for myself."

Stephanie raised an eyebrow. "Why is that?"

"All we knew was your full name from the hotel register and that you were going to St. Louis. You're not the only Stephanie Scott in St. Louis, by the way. I started introducing myself as an old friend from your cattle rustling days. I had three doors slammed in my face before I got here. Your butler didn't even bat an eye."

"James wouldn't."

"James?" Levi's brows rose a fraction. "The one Cole thought you were married to?"

"It's a long story. Why didn't you just get my address from Kate? Surely Charlie gave her my note."

"Ah, so that's what it was about," Levi said. "Kate said Cole took it before she got a chance to read it. He was so mad she didn't dare push the matter right then. When she asked about it later, he said he'd torn it up. What happened between you two, anyway?"

Stephanie sighed. "I don't know. When he found out I had money, he couldn't get away fast enough. It just doesn't make sense. He had to know I wasn't like the wealthy women he knew in Princeton. I'd been there for ten months."

"That is peculiar," Levi agreed. "Cole has a hot temper, but he's not generally stupid. There must be something else."

"But what?"

"Perhaps it had something to do with what Orson told him," Nance said in a small voice.

"Oh? Just what did my good friend Orson say?" Stephanie asked ominously.

"He said you'd always been society's darling, but occasionally you got bored and went looking for diversion."

Levi was puzzled. "That should have pleased him. Cole hates society."

"What sort of diversion?" Stephanie's expression was distinctly dangerous, and Nance almost wished she'd kept silent.

"Orson told him you liked to dress in old clothes and live among the...the common people. H-he said you found it quite amusing."

Stephanie groaned and buried her face in her hands. "Leave it to Orson to say exactly the wrong thing. No wonder Cole rejected me."

Levi shook his head. "No, he might not approve of it, but that wouldn't make him send you away."

"He didn't believe it, especially when he found out you left a week after your father's death. He thought Orson was lying and that you were in great danger," Nance explained. "When you regained your memory, you were angry with Orson but not afraid. You admitted to being his fiancée and even that you'd left right after your father died."

Stephanie paled. "He must have thought everything Orson said was true. It must have sounded like my father's death was unimportant to me, that my pleasures came first. It's just the sort of thing he'd expect from a wealthy woman. He probably thinks I'm the most heartless woman alive."

"I don't understand," Levi said. "Why *did* you leave so soon after your father's death?"

"I was looking for my sister. My father's final request was that I find her and make amends for the years they had been estranged. The last time he'd heard from her, she was in Horse Creek."

"Why didn't you tell Cole that?"

"I did, but he thought I was lying because he'd never heard of Elizabeth Scott."

"Elizabeth Scott?" Levi frowned. "I don't remember

anyone by that name."

"No, you wouldn't." Stephanie picked up Elizabeth's letter from the desk and handed it to Levi. "I found this after I got home. It puts a different light on things."

The two women watched as Levi began to read. After only a few seconds his eyes widened. "Conner O'Reilly!" He looked up. "Good God, *Maggie?*"

Stephanie nodded. "My sister. We had the same mother but different fathers. Think how that little piece of information would please Cole."

"You're Maggie's 'little Annie?' She talked about you all the time." Levi shook his head in stunned disbelief. He stared pensively at the floor for a moment. "You know," he said slowly, "there's really nothing wrong with a man marrying his dead wife's sister. The Indians do it all the time."

Stephanie's eyes widened. "Brave Eagle, he *knew!* He called me Morning Star's sister and he sent a gift to help clear the fog from my eyes so the Great Spirit could show me the road I was to follow! Cole thought he was talking about my amnesia."

"Oh, Stephanie." Nance's voice was filled with awe. "He was telling you to marry Cole."

"It does sound that way," Levi said. "I guarantee the family all think you and Cole belong together."

"Cole certainly doesn't. He hates me."

"No," Nance said. "I think he hates your money."

"What?" Stephanie asked.

"Well, I don't know the man, of course, but it seems to me he loved you when he thought you were a thief. When he gave the money back, he offered to pay the interest by giving Orson half ownership in a beautiful black stallion. He didn't even ask what it was you'd supposedly done. Orson said he was tempted. It was a truly magnificent animal."

"Midnight?" Stephanie and Levi said in unison. Then exchanged an incredulous look.

"Not only that," Nance continued. "When Orson refused, your Cole offered to sell some of his horses and pay Orson two thousand dollars to forget he'd ever found out where you were."

"Holy hell." Levi ran his fingers through his hair. "He was talking about Black and Midnight. Some rich horse breeder from New York wanted them."

Stephanie gasped. "But those are his two best stallions. They mean more to him than anything in the world!"

"Apparently not as much as you do," Nance said softly.

"But that was before he found out who I am. He doesn't feel that way anymore."

Levi shook his head. "When Cole falls in love, it's forever. From the way he's acting, I don't think he's any happier than you are. He's just too darn bull-headed to do anything about it."

Nance bit her lip thoughtfully. "It's not you he doesn't want, it's your money. That's what you have to change."

"You mean get rid of it?" Stephanie was aghast. "Nance, I can't do that."

"Did you miss any of this when you were in Wyoming?" Nance asked, her gesture encompassing the well-appointed room.

"No, of course not, but there's more to it than that," Stephanie said, trying to explain. "My father worked his whole life for that money—not just for me, for all his descendants, his grandchildren."

Nance shrugged. "If you don't do something, he won't have any grandchildren except Josh, and Cole will never let you give any of your father's money to him."

All at once, Stephanie straightened. "His grandchildren— that's it! I'll put the money in a trust for his grandchildren, and great-grandchildren, and however many generations it takes to use it all up." Stephanie bounded to her feet. "Oh Nance, it's the perfect solution."

"I don't think that's necessary," Levi broke in. "If I know my brother, he'll welcome you with open arms with or without your money."

"No, Levi, I'm not taking any chances. When I get to Wyoming, I'll be so poor Cole will have to take me in just to keep me from starving."

"But to give up everything..." Levi shook his head.

"I'm not giving up anything," Stephanie said. "I was happier in Wyoming with nothing but an ugly gray dress and a worn-out cloak than I am with all my father's millions."

"Well then," Nance said, "what's our first step in transforming the rich but terribly unhappy Stephanie Scott into Stephanie Cantrell?"

"The first thing I'm going to do is buy a herd of cattle."

"A herd of cattle! I thought you wanted to be poor," Nance said.

Levi grinned. "Are you by chance planning to send them to a certain tribe of Indians on the Wind River Reservation?"

"As a matter of fact, I am. Brave Eagle's vision was that I'd bring them luck. According to what Cole said, food is the kind of luck they need most."

It was almost dark by the time Stephanie and Levi returned to the library.

"Won't Brave Eagle be surprised when those drovers deliver the cattle," Stephanie said with obvious pleasure as they settled themselves in the library.

Levi laughed. "I'm not so sure. From what I've heard of the man and his visions, he's probably expecting them. At any rate, you seem happy again."

"Happy isn't even close to how wonderful I feel. My life is back on course. I don't know how to thank you."

"Make my brother happy so I can go home to visit. That will be thanks enough."

All at once her smile faded. "Oh, Levi, I haven't even asked about you. Have you found what you're looking for yet?"

"Actually, I think maybe I have, though I'm probably in big trouble for being gone so long."

"It's a woman, isn't it?" Stephanie asked, searching his face eagerly. When he just smiled enigmatically, she crossed her arms in disgust. "And you're not going to tell me a thing, are you?"

"Not yet. One day, maybe. Anyway, I have to leave first thing in the morning, so if you're serious about doing away with all your property, we better sit down and make some plans."

"Oh, all right, but I won't pretend I'm not dying of curiosity."

They worked for an hour compiling a list of her assets. Suddenly, Stephanie sat up with a cry of delight.

"Oh, Levi, I've just thought of the most marvelous wedding present for Nance and Orson. I'll give them this house! Nance has always loved it, and it will take care of the servants, too. I was worried about them having to find new situations."

Levi gave her a wry look. "And that way you won't have to wait until it sells."

In the end, it was several weeks before Stephanie could leave, and she chaffed at every second she was delayed. Orson and Nance both protested when she first told them of the wedding gift she planned, but when she said her feelings would be permanently hurt if they refused, they finally capitulated.

The day of Nance and Orson's wedding, Stephanie turned over the keys to the house with a kiss and a hug for each of them. They insisted on taking her to the station before they left on their honeymoon. There was a tearful goodbye at the station, and she was gone.

Nance wiped her eyes and looked up at her new husband. "What if he sends her back?"

Orson frowned. "Worse yet, what if he doesn't?"

CHAPTER 36

Cole stared at the imposing mansion, glanced at the note in his hand, and sighed. If this was Stephanie's house, Pickett had been telling the truth. Well, that's why he'd come, to see Stephanie as the high-society lady she was, to put her firmly in the ranks of Penelope Van Horn and the others. Only then, when she'd filled him with disgust, could he walk away with his heart whole again.

Reluctantly, he approached the front door and lifted the brass knocker. Somehow he wasn't surprised by the very correct British butler who answered the door.

"I'm here to see your mistress," Cole said.

"I'm sorry, sir. Mrs. Pickett is not in at the moment. If you wish to leave your card..."

Cole felt his heart lurch. *So she married Pickett after all. The wisest thing to do now is turn around and walk away.* "I'll wait."

The butler raised a haughty eyebrow. "I'm not certain when she will return."

"It doesn't matter."

"Perhaps if you told me your business..."

"We're old friends."

"I see. Well, perhaps...Ah, I believe this is Mrs. Pickett now," the butler said, indicating a carriage rolling down the street toward them.

When the coach reached the front of the house, Cole was there waiting for it. The tight control he'd kept on his temper dissolved instantly. "Mrs. Pickett, is it!" With a growl, he jerked open the door and found himself staring into the face of a total stranger.

"Y-yes, I-I'm Mrs. Pickett," Nance said nervously.

"Where the hell is Steph?"

"Y-you mean Stephanie?"

"Damn right I mean Stephanie. What have you and Pickett done with her?"

Nance looked into blazing blue eyes and had a sudden intuition. "You're Cole Cantrell, aren't you?"

He frowned. "How did you know that?"

"Stephanie described you in great detail."

"Where is she?"

"Stephanie is just fine, Mr. Cantrell. If we could go into the house, there are some things we need to discuss."

"The only thing we need to talk about is what you've done to Stephanie."

"Mr. Cantrell, if Stephanie were in any danger from me, would she have told me about you?"

"No, but Pickett might have."

"I recognized you because you have beautiful blue eyes," she said dryly. "Orson would have hardly told me that."

Cole regarded her silently for several long moments then sighed. Nothing would be gained by scaring the timid little creature any further. "All right, I'll listen to what you have to say." He held out his palm to help her down, noting how the delicate hand shook when she placed it in his. "There's no need to be afraid. I won't bite you."

"Of course not," Nance said, hoping he couldn't tell how hard her heart was pounding. She gave James a shaky smile as they entered the house. "Would you wait about an hour and then send a message to Mr. Pickett that Mr. Cantrell has arrived? Tell him to bring the papers for the trust home with him. He'll know the ones I mean."

"Certainly, madam." James glanced at the Stetson in Cole's hand. "May I take your hat, sir?"

"No, thanks. I'll hang on to it."

Nance turned to Cole. "If you'd care to wait in the library, I'll be with you presently."

Her hands were still trembling as she removed her bonnet a few moments later in front of her bedroom mirror. What was she to do now? They had promised not to meddle in

Stephanie's life, but none of them had considered the possibility of Cole coming to St. Louis.

She'd have to tell him the truth, of course, and preferably before Orson arrived. With all the antagonism between the two men, she'd have to move quickly to circumvent disaster. Nance squared her shoulders and pinched some color into her cheeks. No matter how terrifying the man was, he couldn't be all bad. Stephanie loved him, and she was never wrong about people.

When she entered the library, she found Cole studying the chessboard. "This is Stephanie's favorite room," she said.

"I'm not surprised," he said with a smile.

Nance was amazed at the difference in his face when he smiled. For the first time she began to see why Stephanie was so attracted to him. "Please, sit down," Nance said, seating herself on the sofa. "I think I should begin by telling you what took Stephanie to Wyoming in the first place."

"I'm more concerned about where she is now."

"I'll get to that, but you should hear the whole story first. It may be somewhat difficult, but I hope you'll bear with me."

"It would appear I have no choice," he said ungraciously. Then, apparently realizing how curt his words sounded, he sat down. "All right. I'll listen."

"Thank you." Nance gave him a somewhat tremulous smile as she folded her hands in her lap. "Stephanie was only two when her mother died. Shortly after that, Scott Manufacturing filled a large order for the Union army in exchange for a shipment of gold bullion, which never arrived. Ashton was a loving father, but the battle to save his company made it impossible for him to spend much time with his two daughters."

"So she really does have a sister, then?" Cole asked.

"Oh, yes. A half sister, actually. They had the same mother but different fathers. Neither that nor the fact that there were six years differences in their ages mattered. Stephanie and Elizabeth were inseparable. I'm sure you know what a warm, loving person Stephanie can be?"

A ghost of a smile crossed Cole's face. "I realized it when she had everyone in my house wrapped around her little finger in less than a week. She even made friends with my horse."

Nance returned his smile. "Her sister was much the same, and the bond between them was very strong. Anyway, because she had lived with Ashton Scott since infancy, Elizabeth always thought her own father had died. One day, the girls discovered, through some documents hidden in the attic, that her parents had been separated by divorce rather than death."

"Divorce!" Cole said in surprise. "That can't have been easy to live with!"

"No, I'm sure it wasn't, and I suspect that's why Mrs. Scott preferred to keep it quiet. Elizabeth didn't see it that way, of course, and went to Ashton Scott with the proof of his deceit. He tried to explain the decision to keep the divorce a secret had been her mother's, but Elizabeth wouldn't listen. She was outraged, and they quarreled bitterly. In the end, she ran away from home, and Ashton Scott disinherited her. Stephanie was only twelve years old at the time and was devastated. She never stopped hoping Elizabeth would come home again."

"And Elizabeth never contacted her?" Cole asked. "If they were so close, she must have realized how hurt Stephanie would have been."

"Stephanie never got any of the letters. I don't think she ever doubted her sister's love for her, though. We were about fifteen when Stephanie told me the story. She said she was sure Elizabeth was happy somewhere, but I'll never forget the anguish in her eyes."

"Poor Stephanie," Cole said.

"Yes, that's what I've always thought too. Anyway, about eight years ago, Stephanie's father began training a young man to take over his business. Orson Pickett had been a friend of the family for years and in many ways was like a son to Ashton Scott."

Cole snorted, then had the grace to look abashed. "I'm sorry. I forgot that he's your husband."

"I think, perhaps, the two of you met under less-than-ideal circumstances," Nance said with a slight smile.

"You're probably right."

"At any rate, as time went on, Orson and Stephanie drifted into an understanding that they would someday marry. It was her father's dearest wish, and I don't think Stephanie ever gave it much thought. It wasn't until Ashton's health began to fail, and he insisted Stephanie choose a wedding date, that she began to have doubts. She came to realize she didn't love Orson and tried to end the betrothal. Both her father and Orson just thought she was having prewedding jitters."

Nance sighed. "It's hard to say what she'd have done to convince them otherwise. It would have been something dramatic, I'm sure, but she never got the chance. Her father collapsed and went into a coma. For nearly two weeks, Stephanie didn't leave his side for more than a few hours at a time."

"Did he ever wake up?" Cole's voice was deep and compassionate. "Was she able to say good-bye?"

Nance nodded. "Ashton woke up once near the end. It almost seemed as though he forced himself to consciousness. He told Stephanie he loved her, then he said he'd been wrong about Elizabeth and told her where to find her."

"He knew where she was?"

"Apparently. It was remorse, I suppose, that gave him the energy to try and make amends before he died. With almost his last breath, he begged Stephanie to find Elizabeth and share the Scott fortune with her."

"And he thought Elizabeth was in Wyoming?"

"That's what Ashton said. Stephanie wanted to leave immediately after he died, but Orson and I thought she was just over-wrought." Nance looked down at her hands. "I'm afraid we were a bit presumptuous in assuming we knew what was good for her."

Listening as Nance described the events after Ashton's Scott's death, Cole felt a stab of guilt. He'd been so quick to believe the worst of Stephanie. He could imagine how difficult it had been for her. So anxious to carry out her father's last wishes but thwarted on every turn by her well-meaning friends. No wonder she'd been haunted by nightmares. The feelings of frustration had stayed with her even though her memory of the cause was gone.

"In spite of how awful we'd been to her," Nance was saying, "Stephanie didn't want me to worry, so she sent a note saying she was leaving to find Elizabeth on her own." Nance sighed. "I panicked. To me, she was acting irresponsibly, and I wrote her back asking her to reconsider. I felt she was being..."

"Dishonest," Cole said with sudden understanding. "So, you're Nance. We found your note among her things when we brought her to the ranch. I've often wondered why you used that particular phrase."

"I'm afraid it was an unfortunate choice of words as well as a waste of time. She was leaving for the depot when my note reached her and didn't even read it until she was on the train." Nance sighed. "Anyway, Orson left on the next morning and finally caught up with her outside of Cheyenne. He insisted she return with him, but Stephanie said she needed some time to think about it. She had no intention of going back, of course, and took the first opportunity to get off the train. You know the rest better than I do, though she told me all about it."

"All about it?"

When Nance blushed and dropped her eyes, Cole snorted. "Yes, I can see she did." His eyes narrowed. "Didn't Orson try to find her?"

"Of course he did, but he had no way of knowing where she'd gotten off, and he'd forgotten the unscheduled stop for water. He searched as long as he could and then sent detectives to every town within two hundred miles of where he'd last seen her. Nobody anywhere had ever heard of her or Elizabeth."

"That's why I didn't believe her story myself. There's never been an Elizabeth anything in Horse Creek as long as I can remember."

"Yes, I know, that's because Stephanie told you the wrong name."

Cole frowned. "She didn't know her own sister's name?"

"Actually, no. You see, when Elizabeth found her father, she discovered her mother had changed her first name. To please him, Elizabeth started going by what was actually her real name." Nance paused as though to gather her courage. "It was Margaret O'Reilly."

Cole looked as if he'd been sucker punched. "*Maggie?* Stephanie is Maggie's little sister, Annie?" He nearly choked on the words.

Nance nodded. "Annie was Elizabeth's pet name for her baby sister."

"Maggie never gave up hoping she'd come." Cole put his head in his hands. "It never occurred to me she finally had."

Nance reached for the bell pull. "How could you possibly have known?" James entered the room so quickly Nance suspected he'd been waiting right outside in case she needed help with her volatile visitor. "James, please pour Mr. Cantrell a good, stiff brandy."

James took one look at the distraught man and poured him a glass of scotch instead. He handed the drink to Cole, who accepted it without even looking up.

"Thanks," he mumbled, his mind whirling with Nance's revelation.

"Will that be all, madam?"

"No. We'll need another place set for dinner, and please have the blue room made ready."

"I'll see to it."

Cole sat back, blindly sipping the drink, his face pale under the dark tan. Nance watched silently. At last, he looked up. "How is it that I find you married to the man I thought was her fiancé and living in her house?"

Nance sighed. "Yes, that must seem very strange to you."

"It's a damn sight more than strange! And you still haven't told me where she is."

Nance cleared her throat uncomfortably. "I'm not sure I can tell you the rest."

"Why not?" he asked sardonically. "What could be worse than telling me I slept with my own sister-in-law?"

Nance turned a fiery red. "That isn't what I meant. Stephanie was very adamant about Orson and me not meddling in her life anymore. I'm not sure I have the right to tell you."

"Maybe you don't," Cole said with a deep sigh. "I was brutal to her that last day. She was like an animal caught in a trap, all fight and fury, throwing all my reasons right back in my face. It wasn't until I told her I didn't want her anymore that she finally gave up. She looked up at me with the most sorrowful, liquid eyes I've ever seen." He ran his fingers through his hair roughly. "The last time I saw her, she was just standing there in the street watching me ride away. That picture has haunted me day and night for the last three months."

Nance studied him. He looked so broken that her heart went out to him. Whatever suffering he had caused Stephanie, he'd gone through as much himself. In that moment, she made her decision. Only the truth, and all of it, would suffice.

"Would you like another drink, Mr. Cantrell?"

Cole sighed dejectedly. "I tried that, and it doesn't work. I spent a great deal of time in a bottle this summer, but the dreams still came no matter how drunk I was." He shook his head. "I thought she was a heartless bitch, but I couldn't stop loving her."

"I think Stephanie felt much the same. It was two full weeks before she would even talk to anyone. I can't tell you how pleased I was when she invited me to go shopping with her, saying she wanted to put the past behind her and start afresh. Stephanie was so much like her old self that when she said she had business with Orson, I didn't think anything about it. But when we entered his office, she changed. I've never seen her like that. She was...ruthless."

Cole's eyes gleamed in appreciation as Nance told him of the way Stephanie had forced Orson to buy her out. "I wish I'd been there to see that."

"It was quite a show, though I didn't enjoy it in the least. When Orson pointed out that, without his intervention, she'd still be stuck in the wilderness with no memory of who she was, Stephanie looked him right in the eye and said, 'Exactly!'"

Cole's eyes widened in surprise. "But her loss of memory was distressing to her."

"Perhaps so, Mr. Cantrell, but she told me later those were the happiest ten months of her life. I know it changed her. She'd have never stood up to Orson like that before."

"I almost feel sorry for Pickett," Cole said.

"He was quite upset; we both were. Orson, though, kept thinking about what she'd said and began to wonder if maybe she wasn't right after all. He even began to agree with whoever told her she'd make a devil of a wife, though I can't imagine who would say such a thing."

"I did, as a matter of fact."

Nance looked disconcerted. "Oh. Well, perhaps you had a reason?"

"Several."

"I see." When it became obvious he wasn't going to elaborate, she cleared her throat and continued. "At any rate, when she finally went through her father's papers, she found a letter that Elizabeth had written years before. That's when she realized Elizabeth was your wife. I have often wondered if Elizabeth was somehow watching out for Stephanie when she stepped off the train that day. It seems a rather incredible coincidence, don't you think?"

Cole was taken aback. "Are you suggesting that my wife's ghost directed the whole thing?"

"I don't claim to know anything about ghosts or spirits, but I do know love is the strongest of emotions, and the bond between them was very strong. When Stephanie told me her story, it sounded as though you felt a certain responsibility for her right from the beginning."

Remembering the strong protective urges that had assailed him, Cole felt a prickle on the back of his neck. "Yes, but to say Maggie was behind it —"

"As I said, it's the merest whimsy on my part. At any rate, Stephanie's knowledge only made things worse. She felt she'd done something wrong and that you'd hate her even more if you found out she and Maggie were sisters. It wasn't until Levi showed up that she began to realize there was another way of looking at it."

Cole's eyebrows shot up. "My brother was here?"

"Yes, and it was the first time I'd seen her happy since she came back." Nance smiled. "I don't think it's possible to remain despondent with your brother around. It certainly didn't take him very long to make her see the light. Well, that's the whole story."

"Not quite. You still haven't told me why you're living in her house or where she is."

"She gave Orson and me the house as a wedding present." Nance smiled. "I'm surprised you haven't figured out where she is by now."

"Levi told me he was thinking of settling down, but I never considered..." The look he gave Nance was painful to see. "She went with my brother, didn't she?"

"Heavens, no. Levi left long before Stephanie, and she was quite put out that he wouldn't tell her where he was going." Nance paused. "Mr. Cantrell, Stephanie is on her way to Wyoming."

CHAPTER 37

"**W**yoming!" Cole's voice thundered across the room, and Nance winced.

"Mr. Cantrell, please. You'll upset the servants."

As if on cue, James entered the room. "Do you require my assistance, madam?"

"Oh, no, James. Everything is fine. Mr. Cantrell just discovered he'd passed Stephanie on his way here." Nance glanced at Cole, but he was staring at James as though he'd never seen the man before.

The name James had finally registered in Cole's mind, and he was astonished. Could this be Stephanie's James? Though not an unattractive man, the silver-gray hair and crows-feet around the hazel eyes indicated a man in his sixties. Surely not her lover.

Hastily reviewing what he knew about James, Cole realized with a shock that Stephanie could have been talking about a much-loved servant, one she depended on heavily. "Were you Stephanie's butler, James?"

"Yes, sir," he answered stiffly.

Cole laughed joyously. "The butler, for God's sake!"

"I was with the Scotts for many years," James said as though challenging Cole to dispute the fact. But Cole surprised him by rising from the chair and shaking his hand enthusiastically. "You have no idea how glad I am to meet you at last."

James blinked in surprise. "Sir?"

"Stephanie often called out to 'James' in her sleep. It sounded as though he were someone she loved a great deal. I can't tell you how pleased I am to have that little mystery cleared up."

"She called for me? How very gratifying."

"But not at all surprising," Nance commented. "James has seen Stephanie through more scrapes than either of them will admit to." She smiled. "Mr. Cantrell, we'd be delighted if you'd stay with us while you're in St. Louis."

Cole shook his head. "No, thank you. I have to be heading back."

"You won't be able to get another train until tomorrow morning, and Stephanie made certain arrangements before she left that I think you should be aware of. You can easily discuss it with Orson after dinner. Besides, we'd love to have you."

Cole gave her a disbelieving look. "I doubt your husband will feel the same."

"Please, Mr. Cantrell, I feel we owe it to Stephanie. Perhaps, in some small way, it will atone for some of the unhappiness we have unwittingly caused both of you. James will show you to your room and send someone after your bags. Dinner will be at seven." She swept from the room before Cole could protest.

He blinked in surprise as the door closed behind her. "Well, James, I think I've just been out-maneuvered," he said after a moment. "You may as well show me to my room."

James's expression was wooden. "Right this way, sir."

James showed him to a spacious bedroom. "If you'll give me the name of your hotel I'll send for your bags," he said, opening the drapes. "In the meantime, if you need anything, just ring."

"I'm sure I'll be fine. Thanks." Cole gave him the address of his hotel, and James quietly closed the door. Cole tossed his hat onto the end of the bed and sat down. If he had to stay here for three hours, he might as well be comfortable. He pulled off his boots and lay back with his hands behind his head.

That Maggie and Stephanie were sisters boggled his mind. Maggie had talked about Annie so much, Cole felt as if he knew her. But the image he carried in his head was far different than the reality. If Stephanie had showed up as a skinny kid with red hair and freckles, he'd have recognized

her instantly. Still, it was best she'd come as a total stranger.

If she had tried to give him the money she'd brought for Maggie, he'd have sent her away with a few curt words.

Unlike Orson's story of Stephanie going to seek pleasure days after her father's death, Cole had no trouble picturing her deathbed vigil and her determination to fulfill her father's last request. That was the Stephanie he knew, and he hurt for the pain she must have suffered watching her father slip away just as he had Maggie.

Pulling a crumpled green ribbon from his pocket as he had so many times over the last few months, Cole smiled. What a reunion they'd have.

He was awakened sometime later by a knock at the door. He stretched and sat up. "Come in."

James set Cole's bag on the floor. "Mrs. Pickett thought you might be wanting a bath after your long journey."

"A bath would be nice. Thank you."

Within a very short time, Cole sighed with pleasure as he relaxed in the steaming tub. When the water finally became too cool for comfort, he dried off and donned the dressing gown that had been laid out for him. He was just collecting his shaving things when James knocked at the door again.

"Would you like me to assist you with your dressing, sir?"

"My coat could use some help," he said, eying the rumpled suit he used for business trips. "I packed in a hurry, and it suffered the consequences."

"I'll be glad to see what I can do, sir."

"And one more thing. Could you call me Cole when there's just the two of us? I can't abide 'sir.'"

"Of course, s—I mean, certainly." There was near silence in the room as James shook out the coat. "If you'll permit me to say so, I'm pleased you came to St. Louis," James said at last. "I was most anxious to meet you."

Cole glanced at him in surprise. "Why is that?"

"I watched Miss Stephanie and Miss Elizabeth grow from babies into young women, and I was quite curious about the man they both fell in love with." He gave Cole a direct look.

"You're not exactly what I expected."

Cole gave him a wry smile. "Neither are you."

James regarded him silently for a moment. "It isn't really my place, but since Miss Stephanie's father is no longer with us, I feel obligated to ask what your intentions are."

"Strictly honorable," Cole said. "I plan to marry her as soon as I possibly can."

"Excellent." James nodded with satisfaction and went back to work on the suit. "I think Mr. Scott would approve."

Cole lathered his face. "What were Stephanie and Elizabeth like, James? When they were young, I mean?"

James smiled fondly. "They had the entire household wrapped around their little fingers."

"Somehow that doesn't surprise me."

"They managed to get Cook to teach them the culinary arts, and they teased the head groom until he'd turned them into expert riders. They were even able to soften up Mr. Adams, the gardener, enough to show them all he knew about plants. There's a vegetable and herb plot right in the middle of the formal gardens."

"I take it no one was willing to teach Stephanie how to sew?" Cole asked with a smile.

"Miss Stephanie said she had no aptitude for it."

"No aptitude!" Cole laughed. "That's rich." The good humor still showed in his face as he began to trim his mustache. "Had Elizabeth made her come-out before she left?"

"Why, yes, she'd been out for nearly two years."

"I don't suppose she liked it much."

"As a matter of fact, she enjoyed it a great deal. She was quite popular with the young men, though she didn't favor any particular one. Miss Stephanie was the one who didn't care for the social whirl."

Cole digested the unexpected bit of information in silence.

Dinner was a pleasant affair. Though Cole and Orson showed a great deal of constraint with each other at first, Nance soon had them involved in a spirited discussion of national politics. Both men were surprised to discover they shared many of the same views.

After dinner, they adjourned to the library, where Cole once again studied the chess board. He glanced at Orson. "Do you play?"

"Why, yes. It's a game I rather enjoy."

"Did you teach Stephanie?"

"Lord, no. Her father taught her when she was quite young. I only played her a few times."

"Why is that?"

"Orson doesn't like to lose," Nance said dryly. "There's something more you should know about Stephanie. When she told me of your life together and your parting, it sounded to me as though the only thing coming between you was her money. Stephanie came up with the notion of putting it in a trust. Since she left the papers with Orson, I'll let him explain it to you in detail. I'll leave you gentlemen to your wine and your talk. Good night."

As the door closed behind her, Cole smiled. "Your wife would make a good general."

Orson nodded. "I know, and she used to be the most biddable girl imaginable."

For the next hour the two men talked. Orson explained the details of the trust and gained a new respect for Cole's business sense in the process. The questions the rancher asked were pertinent and intelligent.

"Your and Stephanie's lawyer have done a good job on this," Cole said finally. "How long will it take you to write up something that will give Stephanie back her money?"

Orson stared at him in stunned surprise for several seconds. Then, slowly, he began to smile. "About as long as it will take Stephanie to tell you she'll do as she damn well pleases."

"You already tried to talk her out of it?"

"I did."

"Maybe I'll have better luck."

Orson chuckled as he pulled a fresh sheet of paper out of his desk drawer and picked up his pen. "If I were a gambling man, I'd make a wager with you on that."

"I'm not so sure I'd take it," Cole said.

The next morning, Cole awoke at first light, as he always did. When the servants began to stir, he sought James out in the nether regions of the house. The two men discussed a great many things as James went about his early morning chores. It was then that the last piece of the puzzle fell into place for Cole.

When he'd discovered Stephanie came from a wealthy family, his prejudice had caused him to reject what he knew of her and replace it with what he would have expected her to be like if he'd met her with full knowledge of her social standing. Only when he realized his beloved Maggie not only came from the same environment but had been quite happy in it that his perception began to change. It wasn't wealth and power he hated, but conceit and total disregard of other people. Maggie and Stephanie had grown up judging people for themselves, not by their possessions. Stephanie was no different now than she was before her memory returned.

Soon after breakfast, Orson and Nance went to the depot with Cole. As his train pulled out of the station, Orson shook his head. "I'll admit it. I was dead wrong about him."

"He's a little overwhelming, but I like him," Nance said with a smile. "I doubt he and Stephanie will have a calm marriage, though."

Orson laughed. "That may be the understatement of the century.

CHAPTER 38

The late afternoon sunshine was pleasantly warm on her shoulders as Stephanie worked in the garden. A deep sense of loneliness settled over her and she wished for a moment that she had gone to Simpson's barn dance with Kate and Josh. But no, it was better that no one outside the family know she was here until she saw Cole again.

Her nervous anticipation had reached monstrous proportions by the time she'd ridden up to the ranch house on a rented horse, only to find he'd left two days before. No one knew where he'd gone.

After getting things in order, he'd hired Jake Summerfield to help Charlie and ridden away with no explanation other than he'd be back in time for the round up. Stephanie had spent the last week waiting, and the suspense was becoming unbearable.

Kate had been quite surprised to learn Stephanie and Maggie were sisters. "She talked about you all the time," she'd said with a pleased smile. "Now that I think about it, there's even a slight resemblance, though it's more in the way you move than how you look."

If only Cole would take it as well. The chance of that was very slight, and Stephanie knew it. If only he would come home. The uncertainty of it all was driving her crazy.

The sound of a horse in front of the house pulled her thoughts back to the present. That would be Charlie returning from town. Strange, she usually heard the wagon long before it reached the house. Stephanie stood and stretched. It was time to start supper; Charlie would be hungry. Picking up her bundle of basil, she turned and gave a startled cry. There stood Cole, leaning against the corner of the house.

"Cole!"

"I saw Charlie in town. He said you were back."

"Yes, I—"

"I thought you'd be married to Pickett by now."

"No, I—"

"Best not keep a rich man like that waiting for long."

The idea of remaining calm and making Cole understand was rapidly receding from Stephanie's mind. "For your information, he's married to somebody else."

"That must have been a terrible disappointment for you."

"You fool," she snapped. "I didn't want Orson; I never did. When I went back, I found I only wanted..." She stopped. It was impossible to reason with him now. He wasn't in the mood to listen, and she certainly wasn't going to feed his high opinion of himself.

"You only wanted...?" he prodded.

She turned away. "Oh, never mind."

"The same thing I've been wanting, perhaps?" Without waiting for an answer, he took three steps, pulled her into his arms, and kissed her with all the love he'd denied for four long months.

Stephanie's legs suddenly lost the ability to support her weight, and she sagged against him. The basil fell to the ground, forgotten, as he picked her up and carried her unprotestingly into the house.

Once in the bedroom, he set her gently on her feet, his fingers deftly releasing her hair. Running his hands reverently through the shining mass, he groaned deep in his throat. "How I've missed you."

"No more than I've missed you," she whispered. "Cole, I have to tell you why I came back."

"I know why you came back. We'll talk about it later. Right now we have some very important business to take care of." He stopped her half-hearted protest with a soul-searing

kiss. There was no leisurely erotic disrobing this time; they removed each other's clothing quickly, almost desperately.

"Oh, Cole, it's been so long," she murmured against his naked shoulder as he settled them both on the bed.

"Too damned long."

They were almost frantic in their need to touch each other, both afraid they'd awaken to find it had only been another dream. When they came together, it was with an explosion of long denied passion that left them both shaking with pleasant exhaustion.

Nestled against his chest, Stephanie lay listening to his heart as it slowed. Lovingly, she gazed up into his face. His eyes were closed, and a soft smile played about his mouth as he caressed her naked back beneath the silky hair.

"Cole, we have to talk."

He sighed and kissed the top of her head. "Yes, I suppose so." Regretfully, he released her and rolled onto his back.

"Cole," she began nervously. "I have something very shocking to tell you."

"You know," he interrupted, "I had a very productive business trip."

"That's nice, but—"

"I met some nice people."

"Cole! I'm trying to—"

"One was a man named James."

"What?" Suddenly he had her full attention.

"He was a very proper English gentleman."

"You went to St. Louis?"

"I had to get you out of my system. I thought if I saw you as a society belle, it would be like a dose of cold water."

"You didn't go to bring me home?"

"I didn't think you'd want to come." He sighed. "I truly thought once we saw each other again, we'd realize how great the difference between us was. It wasn't until I thought you'd married Pickett that I understood how much you still meant to me. I knew then I couldn't just walk away."

"What did you do?"

"I lost my temper. I'm afraid I gave Mrs. Pickett quite a shock when I almost tore the door off her carriage."

"Oh, how could you? Poor Nance. You must have

frightened her half to death!"

Cole snorted. "Well, your timid friend recovered quickly enough. Within the hour, she was ordering me around just like Kate."

"Nance? Impossible." Stephanie couldn't picture shy little Nance finding enough courage to even talk to someone as intimidating as Cole.

"I think marriage has done something to her. Pickett got more than he bargained for with that one. She's well on the way to ruling the roost."

"How would you know?"

"You'd be surprised how much you can learn about people in eighteen hours."

"Eighteen hours?"

"Nance insisted I stay with them."

"You stayed there—under the same roof with Orson?"

"Yes, and we were perfect gentlemen. We even played a game of chess, though he's about the worst player I've ever seen. Nance told me a very interesting story, by the way."

"St-story?"

He stroked her cheek with his thumb. "I know about Maggie."

"Oh." Stephanie bit her lip, not sure she wanted to hear what he had to say next.

"You're a great deal like her, you know."

"I am?"

"Yes, though she was a bit more eager to please me."

"She was probably just intimidated," she said, poking him in the ribs.

"Maggie?" Cole chuckled. "Nothing intimidated Maggie, especially me." He smiled tenderly. "She thought the world of her sister, Annie. I heard so much about you I felt like I knew you. If you had showed up with freckles and pig tails, I'd probably have recognized you."

"Then you don't mind."

"No—though I'll admit it was quite a shock at first." He

traced her lips with the tip of his finger. "The trust isn't necessary, you know."

"So, Orson and Nance told you about that, too, did they?"

"They were right to. It's ridiculous for you to throw your money away just because I acted like an idiot." He rolled over, picked his shirt up off the floor and pulled a paper from the pocket. "I had Orson draw this up before I left. It dissolves the trust. All you have to do is sign it, and the money is yours again, just as it should be."

Propping herself up on one elbow, she smiled at him. "Foolish man. As far as I'm concerned, the trust can stay just the way it is. Everything I want is right here."

"When I think of how much you gave up for me —"

"I didn't give up anything that mattered."

"I won't let you do it."

"Ah, but you don't have a choice in the matter. This is Wyoming Territory, and I can do as I please." She ran her fingers playfully down his chest. "If you insist on being noble, remember your son is now the sole heir to his Grandfather Scott's estate. That makes the money more your problem than mine."

"Good Lord, I hadn't even thought of that."

"Meanwhile, I'm free to do whatever I want, completely unencumbered by all the responsibilities that go along with being an heiress."

"Just what is it you're planning to do with all this freedom?"

"Actually, I'm thinking of marrying for money."

"Is that right?"

"Uh-huh. I have my eye on a Western horse breeder. He has some of the best horses in the country. In a few years, he'll be as rich as Midas."

"Anyone I know?" Cole asked, smiling lazily up at her.

"Possibly, though I doubt it. He's from Montana. Have you ever heard of Richard Kincade?"

"What?" Cole's smile disappeared in a heartbeat, the

307

muscle in his jaw bunching ominously as he glowered up at her. "Who the hell—"

"You deserved that, my love," Stephanie said as she kissed the end of his nose. "That's what you get for acting the way you did when you came home today."

Cole gave her a sheepish look. "Maybe I shouldn't have baited you like that, but I didn't want to take time for explanations right then. I had other things on my mind." His eyes gleamed wickedly. "I knew if I made you mad, you'd lose control."

"Does that mean you're going to make love to me every time I get mad?"

"Yes, and even when you aren't. It's a matter of necessity."

"Oh?"

"I'm very concerned about Josh inheriting all that money. It's up to us to keep it from corrupting him."

Stephanie grinned. "And just how are we going to do that?"

"By making sure he isn't the only heir, of course. First, we'll get married, then we'll give him plenty of brothers and sisters."

"We'll have to devote a great deal of effort to it." Stephanie warned. "These things take time."

"I know, but no sacrifice is too great for my son," he said huskily as he kissed the hollow of her throat. "In fact, we probably should get started right away."

"It's our duty," Stephanie agreed.

"This is one responsibility I intend to take seriously," he whispered against her lips. "Very seriously, indeed."

And somewhere, on another plane of reality, Maggie smiled.

Reviews are pure gold to authors. If you enjoyed Cole and Stephanie's story, please leave a review on Amazon.

ABOUT THE AUTHOR

Carolyn Lampman is a fourth generation Wyomingite who grew up on the ranch homesteaded by her great-grandparents in 1887. She still lives in Wyoming with her husband, a Welsh Corgi, and a herd of her own grandchildren who come and go.

Turn the page for a sneak peek at *Willow Creek*, Book 3 of the Cheyenne Trilogy

Willow Creek

Chapter 1

Wyoming Territory, March 1886

"**W**atch it, sodbuster!" The drunk cowboy glowered down at Nicki, or what he could see of her. Only faded dungarees and small booted feet were visible beneath the heavy winter coat and wide-brimmed hat. "Don't you know enough to get out of the way when your betters come along?"

Nicki swallowed a retort and stepped away. The man had blundered right into her as she came out of the mercantile, but the last thing she needed was trouble with three cowpokes from the Bar X.

"Hey, boy," said the man's tall, rangy companion. "You owe Shorty an apology."

Nicki gritted her teeth. She'd rather spit in his face. "Sorry," she mumbled.

"We'd best teach this squatter some manners, Buck," the third man said with a sinister smile. "I say we throw him in the horse trough."

Nicki backed up against the wall and watched the three men warily. She wasn't afraid of a dunking, but such things had a tendency to snowball when whiskey was involved, and these men had clearly been drinking a long time. At least they were too drunk to realize they were dealing with a grown woman instead of an adolescent boy. Barely five feet tall, Nicki was used to people making that mistake. Even without her heavy coat, the bulky long johns effectively hid her slender figure.

Suddenly one of the cowhands lunged, and Nicki struck out with a small fist. As her assailant clutched his midsection in pain, the third man grabbed her from behind, pinning her arms to her sides. Struggling wildly, she soon realized it was impossible to escape that way.

She slumped in apparent defeat and waited while the other cowboy approached. When he was a mere two feet away, Nicki leaned back and swung her foot up in a vicious kick. Taken unaware, the man holding her stumbled backward as his friend howled in agony when the boot connected with his knee. But it wasn't enough, and Nicki knew it.

Her heart thumped frantically in her chest as the two she'd injured picked themselves up and headed for her. Desperately, she fought the hands that held her but to no avail. It would take a miracle could save her now.

"All right, gentlemen, I think you've had enough fun for one day." The four combatants froze at the sound of a rifle being cocked. "Let the boy go."

Nicki twisted around in surprise. The voice belonged to a complete stranger. Standing well over six feet tall, his bulk seemed to fill the doorway of the mercantile. A full beard hid his expression, but the blue-gray eyes glinted dangerously as he stepped forward onto the boardwalk. His appearance was nearly as menacing as the rifle he held pointed at the man restraining Nicki.

"Now, mister," said one of the cowboys lifting his hands. "You don't understand what's going on. This here is my little brother. He snuck off to town, and Pa sent my friends and me to fetch him home."

"He doesn't seem to want to go with you."

"That's because he was planning on going to the saloon and gettin' himself a woman," Nicki's captor replied.

All at once Nicki found her voice. "That's not true. I—" A hand was clamped over her mouth before she could finish.

The cowboy holding her smiled nervously. "He's a lyin' little brat, too." He yelped as Nicki sank her teeth into his hand. "Why you little—" He raised the injured hand to cuff his captive, then froze as the rifle barrel jabbed into the underside of his jaw.

"Somehow I find it hard to believe he's your brother," Levi

said. "Now, are you going to let him go, or am I going to have to get nasty?"

Nicki was released, and all three men backed away. "What business is it of yours whether he's my brother or not?"

"Let's just say I don't like the odds." Her savior patted his rifle. "My Winchester and I even them up." He glanced down at Nicki. "Can you shoot this?"

Nicki took the rifle from his hands, fired it once, making a clean hole through one of the cowboy's hats and sending it flying into the street. She ejected the shell and looked up at him.

He grinned. "That answers my question. Is that your wagon in front of the store?" Nicki nodded again, and he squeezed her shoulder. "Good. Keep these sidewinders covered while I go get it."

In a matter of minutes, the wagon rattled to a stop beside Nicki, and she felt the large, comforting presence next to her once more.

"Well, son, I've had enough excitement for one day. What do you say we leave these gentlemen to find other entertainment and be on our way?"

With a nod, Nicki handed him the gun. Barely glancing at the big bay mare tied to the back, she climbed into the wagon, picked up the reins, and waited for him to join her. Then, with a sharp snap of the reins across the rumps of the horses, they headed out of town.

"Friends of yours?" he asked.

Nicki snorted. "Not hardly. They're two-bit cowpokes from the Bar X Ranch." She glanced at her companion. Without the steely glint in his eyes, he wasn't nearly as intimidating. "I'm sorry you had to get involved in that."

He shrugged. "Looked to me like you were doing all right. If there'd been one less of them, I'd have probably had to save the other two from you."

She was vaguely embarrassed by the compliment. "Well...thanks anyway."

"Glad I could help out. By the way, the name's Levi

Cantrell."

"Nicki Chandler."

"Pleased to meet you, Nicki." With a friendly smile, Levi extended his hand to her. The large, callused palm was pleasantly warm as it closed over Nicki's smaller one. In spite of his size, there was something reassuring about his ready smile and twinkling eyes.

"It'll be late when we get home. Would you like to stay for supper?" Nicki asked impulsively.

"Maybe you should ask your mother first."

"Don't have one, and I do the cooking," Nicki said sharply, her gaze fixed on the road ahead. "It's the least I can do. Besides, Papa will want to meet you."

"In that case, I accept," he said with a smile.